The Halley Traveler

Book One: The Children of Mars

Mike Mollman

First Edition

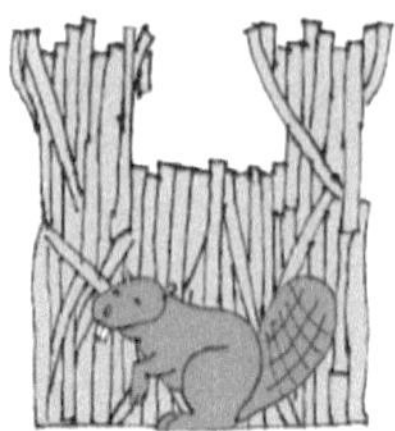

Beaver Castle Media

Cover by Matt Slay

The Halley Traveler

The Martian Traders Saga, Book One

ISBN   978-1-958265-04-8   Hardback
978-1-958265-05-5   Paperback
978-1-958265-06-2   Ebook
978-1-958265-17-8   Audiobook

DEDICATION

*I could never produce such a polished
product without the insight from my beta
readers, editor and proofreader.
I can't thank you enough for the jobs you do.*

For free, downloadable maps and ship schematics,
use the qr code above or go to:

https://drive.google.com/drive/folders/1puazAKBqWPgnbEt0_qU
Ux_eJB7bp89Kx?usp=drive_link

The Halley Traveler

The Martian Traders Saga, Book One

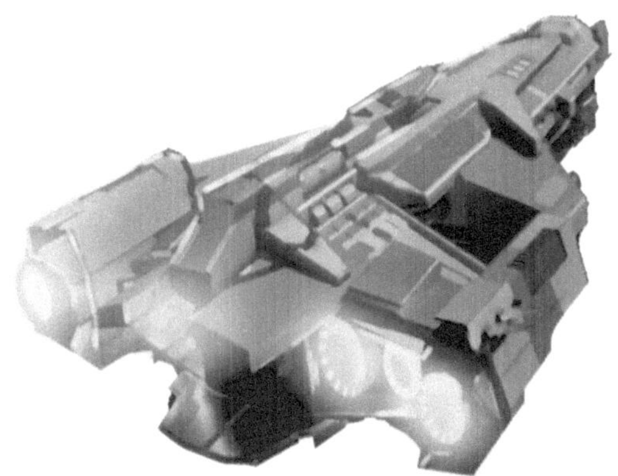

Table of Contents

It is likely that the plethora of ill-equipped and ill-designed private ventures on Mars will deplete the existing Earth provided resources. The lack of a centralized oversight body will delay the bi-planetary efforts for Martian self-sufficiency by well over a century. Without further regulations, the Martian colonies will be reliant upon Earth into the twenty-fourth century.

Requirements for the Self-Sustainability of the Martian Colonies Report, 2168
United Nations Commission Office of Extra-Planetary Management

CHAPTER 1   CHRIS

Phobos

The night side of Mars is rotating into view as the fourteen addle-minded New Martians jump around like the fools they are. The landing zones for several cities are illuminated below. Not one of them notices, nor do they take in the setting sun over our glorious red planet. I'm the one stuck making sure their experience is *magical.*

This is my personal version of hell.

I may have to let them do this, but if one more of them makes fun of our ship, or the flying rubble pile, as Harold called it, I'll end this excursion immediately. They have no clue about maintaining a space-worthy ship. The *Halley Traveler* may not be the prettiest ship, but it will get where it needs to go.

Will this never end? The interface with my spacesuit is a thousand times lamer than my PCD, the personal computing device embedded into my left arm. If I could at least use that, I'd have something to do other than watch these fools.

The gravity on Phobos is about four hundred times less than Mars, so a true athlete could jump up over seven hundred meters, overcoming the escape velocity and achieving a temporary orbit around Mars. Of course, the descent to the Martian surface would end badly for them. On Earth, they'd light up the sky as they plunged into the atmosphere. Not so much on Mars. They would make a new crater, though.

Would it be named after the human missile?

My back still hurts from stowing all the luggage, but when I try to stretch, my spacesuit's crotch digs into me. Why can't we have one spacesuit that fits me? And why so much luggage for a one-day trip? They do this every time. They see the planetary sights; they change clothes and party. They jump around here on Phobos; they change clothes and party. They go to the Stickney Crater Botanical Garden; they change clothes again. Don't they have anything better to do?

We're fully behind Mars now, so only the ship's high intensity flood lights and the much more feeble spacesuit locators are visible. Since they've kicked up so much dust, the area around the ship is a bright gray. It makes my job that much harder. I count the tourists again, but only come up with eleven in the main pack. Three have broken off and are heading towards the front of the ship. I start run-hopping toward them.

Why do they never listen to the safety protocols?

Two are crouched over and the third is ten meters away. The lone one hops from one leg to another. Are they going to hurl him up on to the loading platform? The fool is likely to break something expensive.

"You don't want to do that." I call over the comm. "The landing could be dangerous."

His buddies ignore me and toss him upward. His ascent isn't fast, but high velocity isn't needed to break free of gravity's grip. The channel fills with their laughter as the tourist-turned-projectile disappears into the bright gray cloud.

"Where did you guys go?" the man calls.

"Uh, I think we may have an issue here," one of them shouts. The incessant chatter instantly gives way to silence.

Dad responds from the cockpit. "This is the captain. What's happening?"

"He's disappeared. Harold, can you swim back down?"

Of course it's Harold.

That's typical of a New Martian. Only one of them would be so dumb to think that swimming in a vacuum is a solution.

"Chris, I need an update," Dad says.

"A guest has been thrown upwards and I've lost visual. I'm heading to the top of the ship now."

The other guests collect around me, as if my vantage point is somehow charmed. Their calls of "where is he?" and "I want to see," are not helpful. If I could get a straight line to the ship, I could reach it in a couple of super hops, but now the tourists get clingy.

I take a couple of steps to the side, only to have them follow me.

"Can you see him from over there?" one of them asks.

Why do they follow me around now?

"Please, just give me some room," I say as I spread my arms wide. "No need to worry. I'll retrieve Harold in no time."

They bunch up around me even tighter.

"Please, make way; I have to get to the ship," I call over the comm.

"You can't leave us alone," a woman says. They crowd even closer.

Oops, that wasn't smart.

They'll be fine as long as they don't do anymore stupid stuff, but how to tell them that without being insulting?

"Dad, please direct the tourists while I retrieve our lost guest." He can deal with these people better than I can. Dad regurgitates our safety spiel. It's the perfect diversion. After an inconspicuous slide sideways, I'm clear of the scrum.

I take three huge hops and launch myself toward the ship. Too short! I'm not even close to making it topside. I click on my mag boots. If I can absorb enough shock with my knees, the electromagnets will catch and I won't bounce off the ship. I yank my shoulders back and try not to think about the suit pinching my nether region.

My knees buckle under the impact as my boot magnets click against the metal of the hull. My butt collides with the ship and I'm tossed backward, except for my feet. They remain attached to the ship. My back flexes even further and my crotch is full on assaulting me. I hold back my scream, but only just. When I open my eyes, the passengers are standing upside down on the moon.

My boots are sticking to the top edge of the ship, but my back is against the side. I throw my head forward and back to build up momentum before performing a super-fast crunch. I slide my feet so the momentum doesn't send me headfirst into the hull.

I take a breath; getting myself killed won't help anyone. If I lose contact with the ship, waiting for gravity to pull me back down will take forever. It's impossible to run with mag boots, so a fast waddle is the best I can do.

"Need a status update," Dad calls.

"I'm topside and I can't see anything through this dust cloud. I'll go to the high-gain antenna." It's the ship's most fragile component. "Switching to thermal view."

"Harold went up and didn't come back down," an anxious voice blurts.

"When was he last seen?" Dad asks. I know he's trying to determine Harold's trajectory.

"I don't know, twenty, thirty seconds ago? We were right in front of the ship when we tossed him over."

In my mind's eye, I can see Dad leaning forward in the cockpit and craning his neck to catch a glance of this Harold guy. For structural reasons, the triple paned windows are fairly small and trying to see in any direction other than straight ahead is nearly impossible.

"Chris, can you see him?" Dad barks.

"No, nothing. Have you pulled up his telemetrics?"

"Give me a second. The holomap is still booting. You'll have to use the mag launch system. Head forward and attach the bow cable to yourself. Then go aft to the launcher."

I speed waddle to the cable in the front of the ship. We have two emergency cables with electromagnets attached, but the aft cable is frayed badly. It means that once I'm launched from the middle of the ship, the bow tether will pull me forward during my ascent.

Dad always insists I wear an iron ring around my waist so he can corral me if I lose contact with the ship while on extravehicular maneuvers. The last time that happened was when I was seven. I guess every once in a great while his precautions pay off.

"Where is he?" I call. The silence is unnerving. I need an answer.

"Got him!" Dad exclaims. "His rise is slowing, and he's coming over the ship. Can you spot his emergency beacons?"

This is worse than being in a planet-wide dust storm. Visibility is zero, but we have trackers and emergency lighting on all our suits.

"No," I reply. "I can barely see my hands." I attach the cable and head to the launcher. On the way, I activate the holomap view against my visor.

"He's never coming back, is he?" someone wails, stirring their anxiety to new heights.

I roll my eyes. During a rescue attempt, starting a general panic is always appreciated.

"Chris, go to channel two. I'm setting up the coordinates for the launcher now," Dad commands.

The passengers' incessant caterwauling stops. Thank the stars for that.

My visor is fogging. The suit has a very good air system, so I must be hyperventilating.

Relax. Acting impulsively in space is a good way to kill yourself.

"He's six hundred and fifty meters up and just above escape velocity."

"How high will he be when he's overhead?" I ask.

"He'll be just clear of seven hundred meters."

"I'm almost there." The distance to the launcher is only thirty meters, but when you can only slide one foot at a time, it seems like forever.

The mag launch is a disk on the outer hull of the front of the ship. With Dad's flip of a switch, the battery will unleash a huge amount of current, repelling my boots and hurling me upward.

"It's now or never, Chris."

"I'm going as fast as I can."

"Hurry."

Thanks Dad, any faster and I'm likely to break contact with the ship. But by all means, keep adding to my stress level.

I make it to the launcher. "Go!"

My spine compresses and everything in the perimeter goes black. When I look down to orient myself, all I see is a wobbling tether disappearing into the dust cloud. My eyes are stinging from sweat. I can't remember ever sweating in a spacesuit before. The air handling system is supposed to prevent that.

Is it malfunctioning or am I really, really nervous?

"There he is!" His green lights are obvious once I'm through the dust.

Dad pounds the panel. "It's no good Chris; the computer says he will be out of range by one point three meters."

I'm so close. The tether isn't taut yet, so I still have a little time. Getting as good a grip on the tether as my right glove will allow, I grope with my left hand to deactivate the electromagnet.

"Chris, the electromagnet is dead!" Dad shouts.

"I know, I did it." I can get Harold, but there's no time to explain.

"Chris, at that speed, you have no chance of manually holding onto the cable."

"He's wobbling," I say. "Can you give me his axis of rotation?"

I pull my knees up and press the cable to my mag boots. I hit the button and my feet lock onto the magnet. This should be enough to make up the one point three meters. Standing upright is trickier than I thought, but I don't have time, so I reach upward and wait for Harold to arrive.

He's flailing his arms and legs like a crazy person. If he doesn't stop, this rescue attempt will get very dicey.

His internal helmet cam allows me to see his bulging eyes. They're like, freakishly big.

Is he losing air from his suit?

That would explain the giant bug eyes. If so, he'll be unconscious soon. That would make my job much easier.

Is it bad of me to hope for a leaky suit?

The line goes taut as I grab Harold's left ankle. He kicks my hand and I almost lose my grip.

I switch to channel one. "Harold, stop kicking me. I've got you."

Harold finally reaches down and grabs my arms as we lazily soar over the ship.

"I got him," I call over channel one. The tourists cheer at the news. I change back to channel two.

"Dad, he's a squirmy bastard. Can you get us down before he wiggles free and we have to do this all over again?"

The tether jerks my feet as it recoils at high speed. The acceleration toward the ship makes my lunch climb up my throat. I can't puke in my spacesuit. That's about as dangerous as my rescue attempt and a lot grosser. Swallowing hard, the acid burns as it camps out in my esophagus. I pull Harold even with me and he grabs me in a bear hug. The suits have some structural support, but his adrenaline is more than equal to the task. Any harder and I'll have trouble breathing.

We're still in Mars' shadow, so I get a great view of the Milky Way stretching across the blackness of space. I bask in the realization that my crazy plan worked. Then the dust cloud obscures my perfect view.

Thwack!

My back slams into the ship's hull and Harold crashes into me an instant later. I see stars again, but they're all inside my eyes.

The crunching sound from my chest can only mean that Harold has broken one or more of my ribs. I try to scream, but taking a deep breath sets fire to my rib cage. It comes out as a whimper as my lunch squeezes back into my mouth. I fight down the overwhelming urge to spit the puke out and swallow it instead.

Harold scrambles over me in a blind panic and knees my chest. I reflexively give Harold a quick push away and he loses contact with me. His hand is only a few inches from me, but that's all you need to be floating helplessly. He's not in any real danger, but his eyes are bugging out again as he reaches in vain for anything solid.

I take perverse pleasure at Harold's predicament, though I resist the urge to tell him to swim down. I guard my chest with my left arm and take my time getting up, not that I have much choice in the matter.

"Harold, you're in no danger. I'll get you in one second."

He continues to reach desperately for me.

If I wait much longer, I'll hear about it from Dad.

Why can't Harold just once listen to me?

I reach out and pull his visor into contact with mine. He grabs my helmet with both hands. The contact between visors allows him to hear my muffled voice. Between that and the comm, maybe something will get through to him.

"Harold, you need to engage your mag boots," I say loud and slow. "Kick your feet together to turn the magnets on." I repeat myself two more times before Harold does as I say. His feet gently drift downward and make contact with the ship. He grabs my arm in a death grip. Now he stops taking any more chances.

We slowly waddle toward the quarterdeck airlock, leaving clean streaks as we push aside the dust. I can't trust him to use the suit pods, so we'll have to bring all the fine particles in with us. It's going to be a pain to clean up. The comm two channel beeps, and I flip over to talk to Dad.

"Chris, get him inside. I've been monitoring the other passengers and they want in *now*. I'd like to get Harold in first and make sure he's okay before the rest of them return."

That's typical for Dad. No need to congratulate my fast thinking, just move on to whatever is next. Without waiting for a reply, he switches back to channel one.

"Attention everyone," Dad says. "Harold has been safely retrieved and is in the process of boarding the ship. Please form up into five lines in front of the suit pods and we'll get everyone back onboard as soon as our daredevil is safely inside."

I know Dad has to be unnerved by this ordeal, but his voice is so smooth, the tourists will never guess it. Once we are in the airlock and waiting for it to cycle, I have nothing to think about except the excruciating pain in my chest. Breathing is sheer agony. My body is demanding deep breaths and my chest is screaming every time I attempt it.

Dad stands at the inner airlock doors with a concerned look. I check his right hand; yep, it's in his pocket rubbing that old Earth coin of his. He says it brings him luck, but he only rubs it when things are bad. Over the ship's internal comm he says, "You've had quite the ordeal Harold." The light goes yellow and the air jets stop. The filtration system starts up in its clunky fashion, and most of the dust from our suits is siphoned away. Harold tries to remove his helmet while there's a vacuum. Fortunately, he has no idea how to accomplish this life-threatening act. The pumps kick back on and refills the airlock with air. The light goes green and the inner doors open.

"Let me help you out of that suit, and then I'll escort you to our med-bay for a quick checkup," Dad tells Harold. The visor is removed and in one deft movement, the pants drop to the floor.

"Raise your hands." Harold complies and Dad tosses the top of the suit into the corner. Gray dust billows from the discarded suit.

I swallow my comment for now.

"We can't be too cautious now, can we?" Dad escorts the fool away.

I hit the cycle button. The door closes and the pumps begin evacuating the air. "Thanks for asking if I'm all right," I grumble on channel two, not that Dad can hear me in the gangway. Now I have to face the rest of our tourists, which means I'm not getting any pain relief for at least an hour.

"Hello everyone, this is Cornelius Halley, your captain speaking. Harold is back on board the *Halley Traveler* without so much as a scratch. He has a whopper of a story to share, no doubt. Once the airlock cycles, Chris will join you and bring everyone back on board. Please line up in front of the suit extractors. You'll be safely back inside in no time."

The outer doors open and I'm facing a horde of idiots. Thirteen of the rudest, most self-entitled people in our entire red world are converging on me and the open airlock door. The amount of dust . . . I tap in the code to close the door before any of them can rush inside.

"Well, that was more excitement than we expected," I say with fake enthusiasm. "I hope you enjoyed your Phobos experience, and remember, we still have the Stickney Greenhouse to tour." I point as I move toward the suit extractors. "Watch your step. Easy now, we can only accommodate one person per pod." Smiling, I hide my physical pain from our customers. "There's a gorgeous sunrise coming in just a few minutes, so if you wait patiently, you'll get to see it. Please, no pushing. I can only help one at a time."

Phobos dust is particularly nasty. It has never been weathered, so it resembles microscopic needles. To avoid bringing it into our ship, we use suit capsules. From the interior, our customers enter through the back of the spacesuit. Then the capsule seals the back of the suit and attaches the breathing apparatus and visor. After a quick check by us, the capsule closes, and the air is evacuated. As long as they don't freak out in that minute and break something, the outer door will open and the person is free to move about planetside. Now we're doing the reverse. Once they are secured, the capsule closes and re-pressurizes. Once that's complete, the visor and breathing gear are removed and the back of the suit opens, allowing the person to step backwards into the ship without bringing in all the toxic dust.

I can only use one arm as I load the passengers individually. Of course, they're all impatient. It takes all of my dexterity to keep from being hit in the ribs. I was wrong before.

This is my personal version of hell.

CHAPTER 2   CHRIS

Phobos

I save a person's life by my quick thinking and I end up with a broken rib for my effort. It would be nice if someone, *anyone,* would acknowledge that fact. Harold only wants to talk about how many times he nearly died. He never mentions that he and his nimrod friends are the ones to blame.

We'll take off for Stickney Crater any minute. It's the big finish to our tour, and it never fails to delight the tourists. Years ago, the New Martians forked over scads of money to build a dome over the whole crater. Then they paid for an obscene amount of air to be hauled up to fill it. After spending all this untold amount of money, they planted a garden. A garden! Not something that would produce food or be particularly good at purifying the air, just useless flowers and leaves and stupid stuff like that.

The trip should take less than a minute, but we always spend half an hour floating in space so they can play in zero g in the comfort of their own cabins. The hard part of the trip is over, and it's just a few hours before we return to port. With luck, I won't have to speak to any of them ever again.

The whole left side of my chest is a swollen purple mass that radiates pain with even the lightest touch. The med-bot has proposed a regiment of pain blockers for the next couple of weeks. I hate them. They make me sluggish and irritable. The pills don't alleviate the pain; the Earthers learned long ago that removing the pain can lead to addiction. Modern meds allow the sensation of pain to remain; but they stop me from caring about it. I smack my chest. Yep, the pain still registers, but I don't even flinch because some chemical switch in my brain has been turned off.

What really bothers me is that Dad is acting so distant. Okay, I'm beyond the age where he would hug me and say how happy he is that I'm alright. I am almost eighteen, but he didn't even blink when he found out about my ribs. He didn't let me out of my responsibilities, either. He still had me settle all the passengers in their cabins before getting fixed up.

I have a few moments of peace in my own quarters before the tour starts. The passenger voices are all masked by the reassuring hum of the ship. Dozens of instruments are happily working to keep us safe and warm in space. Whenever I get down, I remember that in the history of humanity, only a few humans have spent as much time in space as I have.

I open the cover and peer out of my ocular window at the dark void of space. It bothers me that there's so much space and nothing in it.

If I have nothing better to do than ponder nothingness, then I need to stop stalling.

I walk up the gangway with my mag boots activated. Normally I would float up, but moving my arms to grab and release the toe rails doesn't seem like a great idea. I won't care about the pain, but it will take longer for my side to heal.

At last I reach the cockpit and inhale deeply. I shouldn't have let the idiots throw Harold. Even though I had to keep track of all fourteen tourists, that won't matter in Dad's eyes. I might as well get the debrief over with.

"You've been to med-bay?" Dad asks.

I nod.

"Good, close the door behind you." He takes a long glance at my PCD. He thinks I get distracted if I leave it on during one of our chats.

I punch in the code to put it in standby mode. If Dad's going to act like my injuries aren't a big deal, I won't either. I step around the "captain's chair" and crouch down to turn off my boots. Pushing off against the floor, I grab the headrest of the copilot's chair and make a graceful arc over the seat. Years of practice allow me to make a feathery soft landing. Thanks to the meds, I don't even grimace as I stick the landing.

"They're all in their quarters, changing clothes and playing in zero g," I say coolly.

"Good." He's rubbing that stupid coin of his like crazy.

"Are you alright Dad?"

"I'm trying to keep my voice down so our passengers don't know how upset I am with you," he says tightly.

"I can't be everywhere."

"No, you can't. But you can try not to kill yourself," Dad says slowly.

"If they would have followed the safety guidelines—"

"What the hell were you thinking back there?" He explodes with a hushed fury. "You disconnected yourself from the ship while being shot upwards at a tremendous velocity. Dammit, Chris!" He slams his fist into the armrest. His coin goes floating away. "You know better than that!" He doesn't even try to retrieve his coin.

I'd thought I'd get a scolding, but this is . . . intense.

"Do you know what the odds were of your little stunt working? You gained what, another meter? Were you aware that your mag boots, and the tether were opposite polarities, or did you just do it? What if they had repelled each other instead of attracting? There's no possible way you could hold on when the line goes taut. You'd have gone flying off into space in who knows what direction."

I can see each pulse of blood racing through the vein in Dad's right temple.

"You never worry about the consequences." His anger makes him over-annunciate each word.

To avoid his gaze, I stare at the floor.

"You went with the first crazy-ass idea that popped into your head." Spit flies into the windows as he speaks. We're in microgravity, so it doesn't arc downward, I note silently.

"Why do I always tell you that space doesn't care? Because one simple mistake can kill you!"

My idea worked! Why couldn't he at least be fair and congratulate me on that?

"I had to do something!" I retort. "Was I supposed to watch him float away? How will we ever get more paying customers if we can't protect them?"

"Did you consider loading up the tourists on the ship and going after him instead? Harold and the rest of the passengers had seventy-five minutes of oxygen left. We had more than enough time to get him. More importantly, how much oxygen did you have remaining?"

"I don't know."

Who takes time to check in an emergency?

"You had barely ten minutes left when you made it inside today. That means you didn't top off your tank. That means if Harold hadn't been thrown upward, you would have had to come in and change suits, leaving our tourists unsupervised. You heard how panicked they were when left alone out there. What if one of them fell and cracked their visor? What if one of them tore their suit? What would you have done to help them?"

Each question feels like a slap in the face.

Dad lowers his voice. "If your stunt hadn't worked, you most likely would have died in space."

"But I had twenty-five minutes of oxygen left and, and I had to do something! Was I supposed to let him float away?"

Dad is being totally unfair.

"And how long would it take me to get the tourists away from the engines, liftoff this rock, locate you, suit up, cycle through the airlock—which would leave the ship unmanned I might add—attach the cable and get the mag launcher? Then I would have to remotely plot a trajectory while you and the ship are going at different speeds and engage the launcher flawlessly. Assuming I could have got you inside in time, I would have to do it all over again for Harold, who would no doubt be flying off in a different vector."

Once Dad gets started, he's relentless in listing every possible awful outcome.

"Assuming that I could save both of you in under an hour, then I would have to fly back to Phobos, land the ship without killing anyone with the thrusters, and get them inside before their air was gone. What's the likelihood that I get all of that done before their seventy-five minutes of oxygen is consumed?"

"I didn't think about that."

"And what happens in space if you don't think?"

"Bad things happen." I respond automatically. Okay, I had been a little reckless, but my plan worked. Why doesn't he acknowledge that? "If those New Martians had followed directions, none of this would have ever happened!"

"Two bad decisions do not cancel each other out." Dad strokes what little hair he has backward. "I *need* to depend on you, Chris. Have you been taking your pills?"

"Yes! I just told you I've been to med-bay."

"Not the pain pills, your anxiety pills. You haven't acted out this way in quite a while."

"Yes Cornelius, I've been taking those pills too."

He gives me a long look, but he says nothing about me calling him Cornelius. His anger spent, Dad goes silent and stares out the front windows. "Go on to bed. I'll take the tourists to the greenhouse and handle the disembarkment."

I stare at his stupid coin flipping over and over just above the cockpit floor, ashamed and angry at the unfairness of it all. "Stupid newbies."

The Martian economic system was based on the barter/share principle prior to the arrival of the New Martians. Their vast infusion of currency led to the emergence of a market economy. It is an unfortunate truth that governments can't govern without regulations and taxes. Thanks to a monetized economy, a strong central government has become a possibility.

The Emergence of Mars
Kulap Bunnag

CHAPTER 3   CHRIS

En route to Newton Crater

"How are you feeling?" Dad asks after a stony ten minutes of silence from me. We're traveling to Newton Crater to transport zinc and aluminum ingots to Maunder Crater this morning, so I don't have any responsibilities.

"I'm in excruciating pain, but thanks to the meds, I don't really care. See, I can even wiggle my rib a little and it really hurts, but—"

"Stop!" Dad turns away as he keeps from gagging. "Don't do that. It will only delay the healing."

He won't even look at me when I move my rib.

"It's kinda cool, don't you think?" In truth, the meds are not a hundred percent effective, but this is his punishment for not even noting that I saved the day.

"Chris, since you are feeling so good, why don't you go to engineering and run diagnostics?"

"Really? Are you that desperate to avoid seeing my new magic rib trick?"

"You can also clean up all the dust you and Harold left in the airlock while you're back there."

"That's just mean Cornelius." I call him by his first name whenever he gets on my nerves. It's becoming more frequent, but I'm trying to work with him.

"Are you going to stick around and let me find more jobs for you? I have never yet run out of cleaning jobs."

"Bye."

If Dad found out about my pain, he would probably freak out and not let me leave my quarters. I wouldn't mind the rest, but Dad would futz around in engineering. I've seen him ignore the readouts he doesn't like and continue flying the ship like there's nothing wrong. I'm too young to die in a fiery explosion.

I grab hold of a toe rail and fly down the gangway until I'm opposite the quarterdeck airlock. I can see footprints left in the dust. Dad really did just leave it all for me.

Seriously? He couldn't even take care of this?

I pound on the open button and it sticks inside the recessed space. Great! Now I'm going to have to pry this stupid thing out before Cornelius sees it and yells at me some more. After I fix this, I have to sneak into med-bay and get rid of a handful of stress pills. If he finds out that I stopped taking them a month ago, his head might explode.

The quarterdeck airlock is directly opposite the galley and the cargo bay, the farthest back in the ship the passengers can go. We keep the galley clean and empty, or else our piggish guests will take whatever isn't locked away. Beyond the galley are the reinforced doors of engineering. The doors sense my PCD, the personal computing device that's embedded into my left arm.

A soothing whoosh beckons me to enter and the soundproof doors close behind me, granting me uninterrupted solitude. The din of machines wraps me in a comforting embrace. I find listening to the ambient noise soothing, but I can't stay and destress yet. I grab my de-wedger tool, otherwise known as a retractable knife, and give the room one last look. If I wanted to, I could fly the ship from back here. But Cornelius needs something to keep him busy, otherwise he dreams up more work for me.

The super-fast trick to getting rid of the dust is to depressurize the cabin and then re-pressurize it again so fast that all the dust is airborne. Then hit the emergency eject button, and the dust is carried out into space. Of course, we lose some air and the filters need to be cleaned soon after, but it sure beats trying to suck up the dust from every single crevice. If Dad paid attention to the sensors, he'd know that I've been doing this for the last couple years. The man misses so much of what happens on board this ship.

And just like that, I'm way ahead on my chores. As an added benefit, the airlock has the nice clean smell of ozone after being opened to space. When we drop off the ore, they'll be sure to complement us on the ship's cleanliness.

* * *

At a glance, I see that the helium-3 and deuterium tanks are fine. I check the engines and notice engine two has some irregularities in the temperature profile. I might as well check it out while we're still in microgravity. Maneuvering with a cracked rib will only be worse with full g.

"Dad, engine two has some high temp readings. I'm going to crawl into the wing shaft and take some manual readings."

"The temperature is still within acceptable limits."

"This is why I have been in charge of engineering since I was fourteen. You would get us killed by ignoring problems until the control panel says we're all going to die. I'm going to check it out now before it becomes a problem." I grab my diagnostics bag. Now, as long as he doesn't rotate the engines while I'm inside it, no one dies today. Stopping, I look toward the fore of the ship where my father sits in the command section, and I program a lock on the engine orientation. Dad means well, but his memory is nonexistent.

The shafts were designed for short Earthers, another reason to hate them. Of course, if Dad would get rid of all the old broken-down equipment, there would be more space for a two meter tall Martian to maneuver. Most of this junk is older than me, but Dad thinks that in a pinch, we'll be able to salvage parts to fix up our old, iffy systems. So we keep pushing them into any open space. I have no idea what eighty percent of this crap is supposed to do.

I do my best to wiggle around the equipment boneyard without hitting my ribs, but I'm not very successful. I kick a metal disk and it clangs loudly as it ricochets around. I grab it, bend it over my knee and wedge it between two pieces of junk.

"Hope we don't end up needing that." My elbow hits something else that tumbles behind the big boxy thing in front of me. "Why don't we throw all this out?" Nothing in the boneyard answers me.

Finally, I make it to engine two. The shaft temperature is now below optimal and falling. These things don't magically fix themselves, so Dad must be overcompensating by throttling down the engine.

"Dad, did you turn off engine two?" I call. "It's hard to get a temperature reading when the engine is off."

"Of course. I can fly the ship without it. We'll have it checked out once we're back at Asimov."

"I'm already here, Dad," I say slowly. "I'll find out where the problem is."

"I don't like you going into the wings while we're underway."

"And I don't like exploding into a fireball because the engines aren't properly maintained."

Dad lets loose with one of his rumbling grunts. "Fine, I'll give you twenty-five percent power."

Finding the problem is easy, once the crazy man in the cockpit actually gives the engine some helium-3 to fuse.

"The fourth magnetic coil is sub-optimal. It's distorting the field and allowing the plasma to get too close to the engine wall. You'll have to shut it down for the rest of the trip."

"What a great idea, Chris. I wish I'd thought of that."

This is the one time his 'cover your eyes and don't look' approach is the right answer. The problem will require someone with proper training. I groan. I will be hearing about his mystical oneness with the ship for the next month.

How did he accumulate so much junk? I swear it multiplies!

The space I'm in is so tight I can't even turn around. Trying to maneuver blindly backwards with broken ribs is not something I want to try. I look above me. If I push myself up, I'll rise above the engine and be able to rotate in the free space. Thank you, microgravity for making my job bearable.

I nudge myself towards the bulkhead and feel my left-hand sink into a viscous, greasy ooze. Dad must have got in here while I went into Noctis Labrynthus last week, and now there's space goo everywhere. It's super tacky and won't let go of my hand. Only my thumb is free.

"For the love of Mars, stop throwing space goo everywhere!"

"Hey Chris, we will be landing at Newton in about ten minutes, so you probably don't want to be in those shafts much longer."

I check my PCD. Phew, I wasn't broadcasting my rant.

Of course, he never mentions the mess he makes during his repairs. If he inadvertently got space goo on the Sabatier reactor, it would slowly smolder and possibly crack the ceramic housing. That's all we need is a methane leak on board. We'd both be rendered unconscious and fly off into the black.

With my left hand stuck, I use my right elbow to push off the bulkhead. In the blink of an eye, I'm thrown back into the Sabatier reactor housing. Since my seventh rib is broken, it kindly moves out of the way and lets my eighth rib absorb this collision. I release a muffled scream as my ribs remind me once again that big breaths are a mistake. The pain blockers definitely need to be upped.

I catch a whiff of burned meat. My elbow is blackened and my thumb . . . where is my thumb? Only a smoking, charred bone extends from my last knuckle. I feel the sharp pain now screaming up my arm. It's as if my brain has to decide which to focus on.

My left hand is red and burned from where the space goo used to be. Blood and a clear fluid are pooling on the end of my hand. Right, only microgravity, so the fluids don't drip.

"The Sabatier reactor is giving off an error message again. Watch what you're doing, will you," Cornelius sounds aggrieved over the ship wide comm. "I'll shut it down for now."

There's a loose wire where my elbow made contact while I was touching the wall. Cornelius must have gooed the live wire then forgot about it when he was here. When I hit it, my elbow and thumb completed a circuit and sent who knows how much current through my arm to the bulkhead before it shorted out. "I'm on my way back up to the cockpit," I whimper.

Dad doesn't respond. "Dad?"

I can't see my thumb bone anymore. The fluids have covered my fingers entirely. As I move, small waves appear in the liquid. I grab a filter of some sort and insert my hand into it. Closing my eyes, I decide to not pass out. I better leave the wing now before we land.

* * *

Maintaining my methodical pace takes all my willpower. I have to make a special effort to protect the now blood-filled filter as I back out of the wing.

"Chris, answer me," Dad's voice says over the comm while he pounds on the engineering door. "Now is not the time."

Right, I changed the passcode yesterday. I keep my right hand on the console to steady myself as I stagger toward the door. The door whooshes open and I fall into Dad's arms.

He grabs my shoulders and steadies me. He's back to his all-business tone. "Tell me what happened." He puts my right arm over his shoulder and gingerly steers me toward the med-bay.

"There was a live wire and my hand touched it." I ignore my pair of broken ribs for now. I'll have to take a larger dose of the limbic system blocker. My hand, well, that's a much bigger problem.

He rubs my back softly. "It's okay. We'll get you fixed up right away." Dad's taking charge. I can relax. "With the money we're making on this haul, fixing you up won't be a problem."

"But we need to have engine two overhauled and the Sabatier reactor . . ."

"Let me worry about the bills. You focus on healing."

"Focus on healing." It's a struggle to remain conscious, but now I have something to do.

We keep a culture of our stem cells on board ship for such emergencies. Dad injects several shots of mine, starting at my elbow and moving down to the hand. It's hard to inject directly into bone, and that's pretty much all that's left once my thumb is scrubbed. Dad crudely slaps some syn-skin from my elbow to my blackened thumb bone, or distal phalanx as Dad likes to call it, when he's playing health engineer.

"That's the best I can do for now. We'll get it fixed up proper when we get back."

"That's great. I just want to sleep."

"I'm surprised you're not more upset over your PCD."

My PCD, my link to everything interesting, is now a melted film on my left arm. That explains why Dad never responded to any of my calls. My shoulders sag in defeat, sending a cascading pain from my ribs. I slump even further into the medchair.

* * *

The next thing I know, I wake to silence. It's been ages since this has happened, so I doze for a while. By the time I make an appearance in the galley, the cargo bay is empty of metal ingots.

"It's good to know you're alive," Dad says, trying to keep the worry out of his voice.

"Pajamas, Dad?" I look down at my too small sleepwear. "I stopped wearing these when I was fourteen."

"I didn't have a lot of choices. Why didn't you tell me you need clothes?"

I attack my breakfast. Dad made pancakes, the greatest breakfast food ever.

"And another thing, why didn't you tell me that the limbic blockers weren't working? You tossed and turned all night and every time you rolled onto your side, you screamed out in pain."

"I don't remember that," I say between bites of sweet synthetic buttery goodness.

"That's probably for the best. You had some choice words for me each time I ran in to check on you."

"Really? I don't remember any of this." I can't help but smile at the thought of cussing Dad out multiple times in one night.

"I ended up taking us into orbit so you'd sleep undisturbed in zero g."

"How long was I out?" I try to mentally do the math, but my mind is still too foggy.

"A day and a half."

"Did you take on more tourists?"

"Nope, there were only three people, so I pushed them to next month."

"I can't remember ever sleeping so long," I say with a smile. Pancakes always make me happy. "What's our upcoming schedule like?"

"I'm afraid we'll have to go see Keev again," Dad says. "I had to refuse a transport job, so we don't have the credits to pay for the repairs on the Sabatier, engine two, your collection of injuries, and supplies. We also have a bad solar cell assembly." Dad tries to sound nonchalant, but I know better.

"I'm assuming the Sabatier is back up and working?"

"I fixed it."

"The engine two mag coils have to be pulled and re-calibrated. That should be our top priority, then." I don't have the energy to discuss his use of space goo just now.

"We needed that to happen like we needed a hole in the hull."

"What's wrong with the solar cell assembly?"

"While you were out, I made a quick check of the ship. The assembly was loose, so I had to use space goo to hold it in place."

"Again with the space goo? Really?" I slam my fork down.

"Well, solar assemblies aren't cheap and we can't very well have it fall off, now can we?"

"Nice, Cornelius. I bet you used that ridiculous aluminum suit for your spacewalk."

"Of course. It's so much more maneuverable than the bulky suits."

"You mean the suits that keep dust out of the ship? What is that puny thing rated for, fifteen minutes before hypothermia sets in?" I point my fork at Dad. "You know I'm going to eject that into space one of these days."

"Perish the thought. Do you know how much more I can accomplish in fifteen minutes with that suit?"

If he would just listen to me.

I shake my head in disapproval. Sooner rather than later, I better take our portable CT scanner up and check for hairline cracks in the Sabatier reactor. I'm partial to having carbon dioxide converted back into breathable oxygen.

"Don't you have any other contacts besides Keev?"

I can't stand him. Keev is a slimy Earth goods importer, allegedly. Yet I rarely see him sell anything in the Ring, the central market of Asimov. He always has not quite legal jobs for us though. Usually it's transporting goods from one place to another without paying taxes, but occasionally it's larger, like trips to Luna. Dad always steers clear of drugs or any really serious stuff.

"I can't stand him. He's so full of himself."

"At least you didn't say stupid," Dad says. "And before you even think it, don't call him stupid this time."

"Dad! I was, what, twelve when I did that?"

"Which time?" Cornelius snorts. "You called him stupid just a couple of months ago."

"Well, yeah, but not to his face."

"You said it in the Ring loud enough for the people five floors below us to hear. All I'm saying is that we really need a job, so don't go irritating him."

"Me?" I say disingenuously. "I'm the very soul of courtesy."

"I knew I should have dropped you off with the homesteaders and flown away."

"It would be better than dealing with Keev every week," I say, not quite under my breath.

Dad lets that comment pass. He clumsily punches his PCD, changing the readouts projected onto the galley's viewing window. It's a list of transport requests pulled from all forty-three Martian cities.

He starts talking at the projection. "Keev is an acquired taste, but he keeps us flying." He flicks his finger as, line by line, he removes transport jobs from the list. "We're not likely to get tourists until we can get that engine fixed."

"Keev or New Martians, I don't know which is worse."

Cornelius frowns at me before deciding not to say whatever he's thinking.

"It does us little good to sit here moodily staring out the window."

"Well, I enjoy it, so I'm going to continue while I finish my next helping."

Dad grins at me as he shakes his head. "At this rate, I'm going to have to sell the ship just to feed you." He tries to tousle my hair, but I knock his wrist away before he can touch my scalp.

CHAPTER 4   CHRIS

Asimov City

Asimov City is built into the northwest wall of the crater. The only above-ground structures are the spaceport, which Dad calls the trident, the Ring, or the shopping complex, and the obdome over at the Kunselman substation.

The observation dome, as Cornelius insists on calling it, is where the down-and-out losers who can't afford vitamin D precursors go. Of course, they get plenty of cancers with their sunlight. Crickets and rickets, that's what Dad calls the people. If you hit rock bottom, the only thing the city will provide for you is cricket meal and water.

Crickets are super healthy, but they don't have any vitamin D, so people will eventually develop rickets without it. They go to the obdome to make it the old fashion way, but the dome doesn't block out UV rays, so they'll get skin cancer, but have healthy bones.

As for the spaceport, it costs way too much to land there. We don't use it unless we must, like when we're taking on tourists. We normally walk to the city transport tubes in our spacesuits from the space park. The locker fees for storing our suits are a tiny fraction of what the trident charges to land.

The Ring is the only place we frequent, and that's only to see Keev Khandapura. Keev is the acquaintance you never really wanted, but you're stuck with. His friendly face is a deep shade of brown with a bright white smile. His store front is located in the Ring, the central plaza for commerce in Asimov Crater.

Right in the center of the Ring is the Asimov Water Works. They have a gaggle of bamboo trees growing in the center, which they harvest to pour water into various containers. Steel pipes would last longer and be easier to clean, but for some reason people like bamboo better. I don't get it.

The outer circular wall is sixty meters away from the Water Works and it's filled with fun stores like *Body Coverings*, the extra drab apparel store, *Nutrient Additives*, the food paste store, and everyone's favorite, *Ceramics*, where useless pots can be purchased. That's why Keev's Earth luxuries store is so out of place. In the rich people's level below, it would make perfect sense. Here? There is no good reason to have it here.

The only store I frequent is the PCD store. I know we have to pay for repairs first, but I really want another unit. The smooth ceramic walls give the entire place a rosy hue. In the cavernous space between the Water Works and the outer circle, there are people with carts peddling their goods. As a rule, only the cart people sell actual food, not bio-derived extraction gels or vitamin packed fermented sludge. It's always fun to arrive in the Ring first thing in the morning and watch the cart peddlers fight for premium floor space, as if there's a good spot in a city where everyone's poor.

Most of the permanent shops are framed by shiny chrome columns, but not Keev's. His store has dark hardwood paneling straight from Earth. He calls it mahogany. If there was a more obvious way to advertise being in the Earth luxuries business, I don't know what it could be. The wood absorbs all the light, unlike the chrome, giving the place a sinister feel. Or maybe I just think that because I know Keev.

"Sorry Cornelius, I don't have any of the regular pickups scheduled for another couple of weeks. The only thing available is a human pickup from Tycho Crater on Luna."

Keev is a front man for the criminal Maitland Family. I mean, a legitimate Martian business, sure. Maitland Collectibles has incredible shops at Huygens, Noctis Labrynthus and Lowell, but then, those are the three largest cities on Mars. Like most things, Asimov Crater isn't big enough to have their own Maitland store, so it's long been assumed that all their illegal shipments come here, where there is no scrutiny.

Everyone knows there are fourteen "family businesses" that actually run the planet and *Maitland Collectibles* is one of them. The planetary government at Lowell is a sham. Their only function is to keep records and write reports that no one will read.

"What kind of person? Is it another addition to your brothel network?" Dad challenges.

"You injure me, Cornelius. I support nothing of the sort."

I snort at the blatant lie. Without acknowledging me, Keev continues.

"The person in question is an Earthling. I need you to pick him up from Tycho and bring him here."

"An Earther? How is he getting off of Earth?" I ask. Everyone knows that Earthers aren't allowed to leave their planet. Since the fall of their societies, no one can make spaceships anymore.

Apparently, I raise my voice too much. Keev's bionic eye darts to the nearby people. Dad joins in on the fun, but he's turning his head, since he doesn't have a fake eye. All this wide-eyed scanning is totally comical. They might as well hold up signs announcing their nefarious plotting.

Satisfied that no one cares, Keev sets his eye to scan back and forth while picking up right where he left off. I used to think it was his real eye, but ever since Cornelius told me it's artificial, it's just made it extra creepy.

"You know that Earther is a pejorative to them. They prefer Earthling. And there are over a billion people still living on Earth. You don't think a few of them can find ways off the planet?"

"When the Earthers can get here on their own, they can correct me. Is he a criminal? I don't want to keep all the doors locked for the whole trip." Dad sticks his hand in his pocket and rubs his old coin for good luck, his go-to move when he wants to seem nervous.

"Of course he's a criminal. The Martian blockade of Earth does not allow anyone to leave the planet without diplomatic credentials," Keev responds, while shaking out several woven green mats made of plant material.

"Come on, Keev, you know what I mean. Will my son and I be safe in his presence?"

"Of course you'll be safe. He's from Earth, so he wouldn't have much chance to learn how to fly a spacecraft, would he? The ship can't be piloted if you've been bled out, can it?"

"Thanks, that's very reassuring. Now, why do you want him here?"

"I don't really, but someone above wants him here to help me."

Keev is talking about Kenova Maitland. Everyone uses her name when they want to scare you. She's like the boogie . . . woman? I guess so. Kenova the boogiewoman. My attention strays to the cavern's ceiling.

And they wonder why no one wants to come here?

Most of the walking tunnels here in Asimov are still roughhewn. Even the 'showpiece' market has an unfinished roof. At least the powered walkways are shiny steel.

"Kenova doesn't trust you anymore?" Cornelius taunts.

"Funny." Keev's aggrieved face says otherwise. "Some people think I have gone soft and they can't understand why I refuse to visit her experimental lab in the north polar region." Keev tries to stand up tall and resume his jovial act. Since he's a native Earther and a full head shorter than Dad and me, he makes himself look more childlike than serious.

It's weird how he never mentions Lomonosov Crater by name. Everyone knows it's Kenova Maitland's private torture center. If the government wasn't corrupt, they'd have raided the place eons ago.

The whole negotiation is nothing more than an elaborate dance the two of them have devised. It would be so much easier to just come right out and say what the job is and what it pays.

"Besides Cornelius, the Newbies are losing interest in the local sites, and your last trip—"

"Was a disaster," Dad says.

"You will have to change up your strategy if you want to keep flying."

"I see. And if I do this job, will it cover the number two engine rebuild and the solar assembly's repair?"

"It will, and it will allow you to keep flying and eating for the next month!" Keev flashes the smile he saves for when he knows he's won.

We also need to have the Sabatier reactor inspected, but I know better than to mention it while Dad's negotiating.

"Everything has been quiet. Why is she sending people now?" Dad asks.

"I don't know. If you could take your time coming back, I might be able to find out and protect myself."

"And what do you expect us to do, keep flying around in space until you call us home?"

"Look for passengers to take to Luna. Surely someone wants to try their luck at Tycho Crater's gambling halls." Keev brightens.

Usually the conversation is filled with 'Keev facts'. These are statements that could be true but usually aren't. This is the first useful suggestion Keev has made in years.

"I see." Dad says. "So you want us to take on several miscreants, ferry them to Tycho Crater, wait for them to lose their money and morals, then take the drunken sots back to Mars along with this criminal?"

Keev flashes his perfect teeth. "Exactly. That's the type of service I appreciate from you, Cornelius. We have a deal?" He knows we have no choice. He knew it before we approached.

"Who is this person, and how do we find him?" Dad asks with a resigned air. He likes to let Keev preen after the negotiations. Dad says it's the secret to working with him.

"His name is Vikram and he will find you. I can assure you that he will be calculating, direct, and have little to recommend him as a human being."

"Sounds lovely."

"The whispers say that he is being sent to oversee the Chennai Botanicals rollout here on Mars, so I wouldn't cross him. It's the biggest new launch in years."

Keev turns to me, as if I just arrived. "Now, tell me what happened to this youngster's arm. No, better yet, you should go straight to the best health engineer in the city. I will let Adanna Adeyema, on level three, know you are coming." Keev gives us his fake smile again.

I'm legally an adult, yet Keev still insists upon treating me as if I'm a child. I hope this Vikram replaces him.

* * *

The Ring is fairly empty and so are the tunnels. The normal citizens are busy working, and the rich people are doing whatever the rich people do. Asimov only has like ten thousand residents and it's twelve levels deep. The only reasons to come up to the top level is to go to the Ring for supplies or to get on a spaceship.

"Why do we have to go to a body mechanic?" I ask.

"With any luck, you'll have another eighty years in you and I'm not going to allow a mangled limb to derail your future."

"You injected stem cells. It'll be fine. Besides, my PCD is ruined. We should spend the money on that instead."

There are three banks of elevators adjacent to the Ring. Two are for cargo and only one is for people. The woman leaving the elevator takes one look at my arm and gives us a wide berth. If she's not working, she must be one of the snooty rich. I eye her as she hurries away from us.

"You're dripping bodily fluid," Dad says as he points to my arm. He places his hand on my shoulder and guides me into the lift. The platform begins its slow descent.

"It's not like that's my fault." I hold my hand up at eye level to slow the oozing.

"You may find this hard to believe, but people can function without a personal computing device attached to their forearm."

"But who would want to?"

Dad chooses not to hear my question.

The elevator shafts were one of the first structures the robots dug for the city. The bare Martian rocks are polished smooth, but otherwise unmodified. That means the sulfur is still present at just high enough levels to make it smell like someone farted. Dad says that he's habituated to it and doesn't notice it any longer. More likely his nose has been fried, and he's no longer capable of smelling.

When I go off on my own, I'm going to live in a much cooler city than Asimov. Not as big as Huygens or Noctis Labrynthus, and not the tiny cities either. But it will be cool, even if I haven't found that city yet.

* * *

Adanna Adeyema, H.E. is emblazoned above the door in chrome letters on glass doors. That's not very smart. If there's a loss of air in the hallway, the glass won't hold against a vacuum. After Schiaparelli, every city retrofitted themselves with multiple modules capable of remaining airtight in the event that the next module over loses their air.

"How original, chrome," I mutter.

"Please register and come back to the examining room," a clipped tone announces over the speaker.

Dad raises an eyebrow. Why wouldn't they have a pleasant AI voice greet you instead of barking out orders from some back room?

A green light is activated over the only door after the registration is complete. Dad shrugs and leads the way. A severe-looking woman with a dark complexion waits for us in the exam room.

"I already scanned the arm while you were signing in," she says instead of a greeting. "When and how did the damage happen?"

"He had roughly a five hundred milliamp current run from his elbow to his thumb two days ago."

Sure Cornelius, don't mention your part in this debacle. Make it sound like I'm clumsy instead.

I look through the huge glass window separating us from her med-bay. She has two stations operational. If she can afford that, she has to be reasonably successful, or she's doing illegal work for Keev. The med-bots are three times the size as the one on Halley and they have eight arms each. Like spiders. I hate spiders.

"Is the PCD anchored to the bone?" She asks.

"Yes," Dad says.

"Treatment?"

"I gave him four shots of stem cells and applied syn-skin around his thumb and arm."

"That was a waste of stem cells, I'm afraid. Did you save some of his culture, or do I need to harvest more?"

"We still have a colony of his stem cells. I took them out of stasis last night and started multiplying them," Dad says.

Good. Biopsies are painful, even with pain meds.

"There are infections beginning here and here," she says as she jabs my wrist and arm. "Even though there are no signs now, the hand has to come off. No amount of stem cells is going to rejuvenate charred bone. Now the question becomes: do we replace the hand or the whole arm?"

"Why the whole arm? We still have more of my stem cells that we could use instead."

She ignores me and talks to Dad.

"Removing the melted PCD can be tricky, and expensive. Replacing the arm is actually an easier procedure with much less recovery time. The hand is very delicate work and it can be challenging to make all the proper connections."

"Replacing the arm is cheaper?" Dad asks.

"As long as he can use a standard printed model, yes." She glances at my arm. "I have an extensive catalog for my printers, but it shouldn't matter. His arm is within normal parameters, so I can print one while performing the amputation.

"Would that include synthetic nerves and skin?"

Dad's way too accepting of this idea.

"Of course. If you have the money, I can even regrow the whole arm in one of my tanks and attach it in about two months when it's mature."

"Let's just do the alloyed arm replacement for now. I'm assuming we can always have the biological arm regrown later?"

"Sure, but the longer you wait, the harder it will be to acclimate back to a natural arm." She shepherds us still further back in the building. She takes several blood samples and deposits them in her lab unit for processing.

My head is spinning as these two politely talk about hacking off one of my limbs.

"When will I have this procedure?" I ask.

"Now." She seems surprised by the question. "Were you hoping to let the infections linger a while longer?"

They both look at me as if I'm the crazy person.

* * *

The procedure takes three hours. New syn-skin is sprayed over a biodegradable mesh enriched with growth factors. Back at the ship, Dad seeds my fake arm with more stem cells. Over the next few weeks, my skin and nerves will regrow over the steel arm naturally.

I'll never admit it to Dad, but it's pretty cool. I practice rotating my arm and grasping objects. It's amazing how fast I'm learning to control it. I still lack fine motor control, but I'm getting better by the hour.

My door opens and Dad pops his head in.

"Good, you seem to have full control."

"I'm getting there. I don't know if I can move chess pieces accurately, so you might have a chance of beating me."

Dad smiles. "We'll have to save that for later. For now, you need to go round us up some customers while I fix that loose wire."

"No! You stay away from that!" I point at him with my metal finger. "We can't afford to buy me another arm."

Cornelius rolls his eyes. "Relax, Keev's men are fixing it, but thanks for your trust in me."

I concentrate really hard and I'm able to raise only my middle finger.

"That's good. Keep doing your exercises, though not that particular one while you're finding us some customers."

I look at my weapon, only one charge left. "I have Gerlach's gun with a full set of charges," I lie. "Get the men inside! I'll hold them back." Logan Hackney is a good man who does what he's told. I aim at the Earther leader as I slowly backtrack. I hear the airlock close behind me. I shoot the entry panel and for a brief instant, sparks fly. I illuminate my helmet interior and smile at the Earther scum. None of them will enter Huygens; they'll all die out here with Gerlach and me.

The Burrichter Repulse
Ares Pictures, 2242

CHAPTER 5   CHRIS

Asimov City Spaceport

Asimov's hangar lounge is, even by our low standards, pathetic. The benches are just one sheet of steel that has been loosely conformed to a person's butt. The air quality is always laced with particulates, and the people who show up here always have a story about how it's not their fault they find themselves in their position. Their money spends as well as anyone else's, as Dad likes to say.

In truth, I spend most of the time getting familiar with my new appendage. Whenever someone looks at me funny, I practice giving them the finger. The body mechanic stressed that I needed a lot of reps in order to master fine motor control.

48

I end up only securing one passenger for our trip to Luna. Ms. Rustie wouldn't give me her full name, so I have no idea who she is. By her size, she must be rich. No one can afford that much food without being loaded. She's probably a Newbie.

She insists on getting the largest cabin, even after I tell her they're all the same size. She only stops when I suddenly *remember* that the last cabin on the right is slightly larger than all the rest.

Oh, how I'm dreading this trip.

She grouses about the fare and the unassuming size of our ship and anything else that enters her mind. With the current orientation of Mars and Earth, it will take about a week each way to reach Luna. I wish she'd get dropped off somewhere in between - without a spacesuit.

It always feels weird when Dad parks the ship on the Trident, Asimov's landing pad that sticks out over the crater. It's like we're doing something extra special. With the docking fees being what they are, I guess it is kinda special. But when you want to pick up passengers, few, if any, are willing to walk across the surface of Mars to get to your ship.

"Sorry Dad, she's the best I could do on short notice."

"It'll have to do."

Dad makes no movement towards the console. Instead, he balances his lucky coin, so only the embedded central gemstone is touching his finger. He spins it like a top.

"Are we ever going to take off?" I ask.

"We're waiting until Phobos transits the sun."

"Dad, this happens at least once a day somewhere on Mars. Why do you need to see it again?"

"It's an auspicious symbol for the beginning of our trip."

"So superstition is your answer. Great."

"Quick, it's happening now."

Dad cranes his neck to see the silly rock fly past the sun, then behind Asimov city.

"Ooh. It's just as magical as the first hundred times."

"Okay, smart guy, we can leave now. But one day you'll see the value of admiring your surroundings. Dust storm season is almost upon us, so there's only a few more chances until late summer."

I roll my entire head from side to side just so Cornelius will know how ridiculous he's being.

"With what Keev told us, I don't want to have any misunderstandings with this Vikram, so I'll take any kind of luck we can get. Hopefully, he'll be the sick type and never leave his cabin."

"Maybe Ms. Rustie will eat him."

"She can't be that bad, but still, I think I'll be too busy to meet with her." Dad gives me his evil grin as he strokes the stubble on his chin. "Your grandfather took on undesirable clients like her all the time. He always made me deal with them and I always worried that it would be the death of us."

Thanks, old man, for more of your odd musings.

Dad stabs at the control panel automatically as he prepares for liftoff, but stops midway through. "Do you want to launch us this time?"

I've been begging for the last couple of months. Dad lets me pilot once the ship is up, but never for liftoffs or landings.

I eagerly punch in the remaining sequence. Beginning last month, I'd shout out the steps as Dad did them as a way to prove that I knew what to do.

"Is he the one who found and restored this ship? Your father, I mean," I blurt out before I realize what I'm saying. Dad never, ever talks about his father.

"He was. Your grandfather had little choice since he lost his father when he was fifteen years old."

"I never knew that. Why don't you ever talk about him?" I wait for the engines to work themselves up to standby power. Once they're ready, I'll divert power to the thrusters on the ship's bottom and take off.

"No one ever asks, and I have very few flattering tales to share."

The light on my panel is now green. I plot a slow sequence for engine power up. We need to make sure engine two is working properly. Once they're ready, I'll divert power to the thrusters for our vertical takeoff. We have a minute or so before liftoff.

"Tell me about Gramps while we're waiting."

Dad nods at his readout. "First, he would have slapped you for calling him that. He was a stickler for formality. You know that your great grandfather was Herman Burrichter, right?"

"Yep, and I've seen The Burrichter Repulse vid six times, so tell me about Gramps."

"As you might imagine, growing up as Herman Burrichter's son could be quite challenging."

"But his dad was a hero. Burrichter and his men saved Huygens Crater from being overrun by the Earthers."

Being a descendant of Herman Burrichter is the only thing I can point to that makes me special. Other guys may have money or a huge group of friends, but my family saved Huygen's Crater.

"Just because a holovid is made about you doesn't mean that everything is wonderful. Herman was torn up over the death he and his men inflicted. When Huygens held a lavish ceremony and gave him a medal, it must have pushed him over the edge. He was struggling to process all the carnage, but the leaders wanted a hero. After the ceremony, he ended up taking a walk outside without a spacesuit. Did you see that in the movie?"

"No, he died by staying behind and disabling the gate so the mob of Earthers couldn't get in."

There's no way Herman Burrichter committed suicide!

"So now you know you can't believe everything you see in the vids."

My head is trying to implode. "But why would he do that?"

"I don't know. Desperation, I guess. Everyone was so giddy to be spared Schiaparelli's fate that no one thought twice about what they were doing to the man."

Thanks Dad.

Herman Burrichter didn't lead a final stand against the Earthers? Maybe Dad will hit me in the ribs while he's at it.

"I've always felt sorry for him. Hearing his name universally cheered while it tore him up inside. Thankfully, I've never had to kill a man. I think death itself would be preferable." He pats my knee.

"Wow. Bitter much? You still have to tell me about Grampa. Was he part of the Repulse too?" I ask.

"Your grandfather wasn't much for compassion. He harbored a great deal of resentment towards his father and wouldn't even speak his father's name the last twenty years of his life. As for the Repulse, I have no idea. He never spoke about that either. My guess is that he wasn't and that may be part of the reason why he was so mad. When Herman committed suicide, Huygens decided that 'little Ernest' was not yet old enough to take care of himself. They were going to confiscate his property to pay for the communal creche."

"You mean the orphanage where criminals are taught their craft?"

"Yep. He had other ideas, so he sold off his possessions before the city could take them and found an abandoned Earther ship that was serviceable. He changed his name to Ernest Stecht, moved to Asimov and named his ship the *Happy Traveler*. I can assure you it was anything but."

"Is this ship the *Happy Traveler*?"

"Of course."

I Tycho Crater was built near the end of Earth's domination of the solar system. It was designed to entice their citizens to abandon the planet and move outward into space. Due to Luna's proximity to Earth, it was never designed to support its own citizens. Despite Earth's collapse at the start of the twenty-third century, Luna was never abandoned.

Loonies: The Moon People
Dr. Joshua Caudill

CHAPTER 6   VIKRAM

Tycho Station, Luna

Step, clank, step, clank. The walkway is dimly lit and has a total lack of smell. I've never *not* been surrounded by smells. It makes me uneasy, this nothingness that engulfs me. This must be what death feels like. Sound provides the only sensory trigger, and that's due to the metal pipe and flat plate extending from my left knee. I'm announcing my arrival with every other step. At least there's a bit of gravity now, though I still stumble around like a drunkard.

"Excuse me, sir, you can't be here." A spindly man scampers around the corner and ends up well within my personal space. His eye implant is slow to catch up with his quick movements. It's obviously a cheap model, worse even than what we have on

Earth. I'm told the latest replacements on Mars look just like a real eye, right down to the iris color matching.

I flash the Chennai Botanicals emblem at him.

"I don't care who you represent. There are no people on this manifest, so your being here is not sanctioned."

"Then I guess I'm nobody." I brush him to the side. Step. Clank. Step . . .

His bony fingers grab at me.

I drop my shoulder and spin, connecting on a roundhouse kick with my metallic left leg.

Damn, they're a lot taller than the people I'm used to.

The kick would have connected with the face of an Earthling, but here, I hit him square in the ribs. I send the guy sprawling backwards, impossibly far. I guess we really are exceedingly strong in the low gravity colonies.

Dammit, the hinge to my 'foot' is cockeyed now. I lean up against the wall to straighten it.

"I lost my eye!"

"Well, Polyphemus, tell your cohorts that you got beat up by nobody." I give up on the repairs for now. Step, squeak-clank, step, squeak-clank. Have they never heard of carpet?

Tycho Station's heavy airlock doors open, revealing an immense casino. The bright lights and a cacophony of sounds assaults the senses. A whiff of stale beer and broken dreams brings a smile to my face. Give me impaired people chasing their vices and I'll make a killing. Too bad I don't have more time here. I could own this place in less than a month.

"Patience," I tell myself. "Take over Mars first, then everything else will fall in line." I've made my plans, now it's only a matter of execution.

I have two hours before my transport arrives. My grumbling stomach makes food an iffy proposition. Thanks to the low gravity, I'm stumbling like I'm maxed out on happy pills, so alcohol is out too. I love alcohol, especially what it does to others. By the looks of it, there are plenty of drunken targets here. I have long since passed the days of pick-pocketing, but it's always best to keep your skills sharp, and it helps pass the time.

In under an hour, the more inebriated patrons kindly contribute to my upgraded wardrobe. Now I at least dress like an off-worlder and my chrome-plated leg is obscured. The padding on the plate will muffle my step, but my awkward, lurching gait will still draw attention to me.

I look at my reflection and think about how far I've come. I was fortunate to only lose my lower leg to the infection. It also meant that I was shipped off to Chennai, for Auntie Pari to raise me. I was bed bound for a month and I was never able to run like the other kids. Only after I stopped growing did I get this replacement leg - the best available to me.

Auntie Pari would read the Ramayana to me every night before I went to bed. It may be Rama's story, but it was the god Hanuman that I saw as the real hero. Hanuman jumped over the ocean to Sri Lanka and scouted the capital of the demon

Ravana. He brought secret messages to the captive Sita, Lord Rama's queen, and he saved his lord from a powerful sorcerer.

Hanuman is the true hero, but Rama received the acclaim. Well, I can relate to that. I grew up having to manipulate the other kids to get what I wanted. They celebrated each food heist as if they had done it on their own. But I was the Hanuman in my adventures, the one who did the work but let others crow about it. I scouted targets; I devised plans, and I signaled when to start. They merely followed my directions. It has worked for me all my life.

But that all changes now. Kenova wishes me to restore discipline to the Martian operations. Just like Hanuman, I will go into the hostile land and outsmart the locals. However, I will make sure to keep the spoils. In this story, I will write an ending befitting of me.

I glance at the thin film attached to a drunk lady's left arm. Is that what the Spaceys' communicators look like now? Noting the time, my meeting isn't for another hour. All the mindless lemmings playing the slot machines are slowly giving their money to the house. Tycho Crater is nothing like New Chennai, but people never change, no matter where they are found. That's a great comfort to those like me, because manipulation always travels well. In New Chennai, like most of Earth, credits don't mean much, because there's nothing worth buying.

Out here, on the moon, and even more so on Mars, credits are valuable because there are things worth coveting. My thoughts ebb away from my plans and toward the women here on Luna. They are all so tall, so pale and so lean. I can feel that most primal of hungers awakening within me.

"My appetite is coming back. I must be feeling better," I say aloud.

* * *

Everyone here carries a defeated air. Outside the gambling halls, the whole city is a series of grayish-white corridors. Only the truly destitute or those who have offended the wrong people end up here. I'm the only one in the spaceport who looks up at the beautiful blue Earth. A metaphor for their lives. Everyone is staring downward.

Tycho Crater has only four reasons for people to visit: gambling, cheap drugs, prostitution and smuggling. Directly or not, everyone supports one or more of these businesses. At one point seven meters, I'm shorter than most of the women. Add in my bum leg and I stand out in the extreme. What a pathetic place; just how I want it.

I watch my first two goons as they exit their ship. They're a father and son duo by the looks of them. Both of them must be close to two meters tall and together would barely be more than my hundred and twenty kilos.

"You must be Vikram," the middle-aged man says. "I'm Cornelius Halley and this is my son, Chris."

Quaint. They don't even try to hide their identities here. He sticks out his hand toward me.

"This is business, not a friendship." I stare at his hand until he drops it. Good, this goon catches on fast. "Now, I have two containers each in a standard cubic meter crate. You need to get your exoskeleton and come with me." I start off in the direction of the docks.

"Hold on one second," the man calls after me. I've already forgotten his name.

"Keev didn't tell us anything about transporting cargo. We were told to pick up one person and bring him back, and that's what we're prepared to do."

"Keev can't even do this right." I rub my temples. "Now you listen here," I wag my finger in his face. "I've been sent here because Keev is incompetent. You will bring the crates and you will do it now." I can feel the heat radiating from my face.

This guy, Kernel I think, looks only mildly disappointed.

"I don't know how you do things on Earth, but up here we go by a code. It's my ship and I have rules as to who and what I will transport. First, tell me what's in the containers, then we can see about addressing the other problems." He says all this in a reasonable tone; he doesn't fluster easily. That can be useful, or it can be a nuisance. For this one and only time, he has the advantage over me.

"Fine, the containers are filled with beans. They are only viable for a few more weeks. I have to get them to Mars and get them planted as soon as I can, so I need a little urgency on your part. That is, if you want me to continue using your services once we make it to Asimov Crater."

Enjoy this carrot now, because I'll be heavy on the stick soon enough.

"I don't mind carrying produce," the man says, "but it will take us seven days to get back to Mars, even with the fairly good alignment of the planets. We don't have a functional exoskeleton right now, so we'll have to go into the commercial district and rent one. That will probably take a day to sort out. Finally, we brought a passenger with us and she plans on staying for a week, so we can't leave until then. With all of that, getting to Mars in two weeks will be tight."

"Leave the passenger."

"Hold your engines friend, I run a business too. If I'm not reliable, then I won't retain my customers and you will lose a courier."

This guy is as ruthless as a kitten. "I'll pay her fare, but we are leaving this evening." It's the obvious play.

"That still leaves the problem of the exoskeleton," he reminds me. "Rentals are always in short supply."

"I'll buy a new exoskeleton. Leave the passenger and you can keep it once this trip is over." The suit won't even be a rounding error on my profits.

The two look at me in near shock. This little acquisition will cement their loyalty to me. It would be worth it at ten times the cost. They may not realize it, but they have just become the first members of my goon squad.

The kid speaks up. "What kind of beans are they? You should know that we have plenty of beans growing on Mars already."

"You don't need to know. You only need to obey orders."

"My son's right. I won't ship drugs. Until I know what exactly is in the crates, they aren't coming on board my ship; exoskeleton or not."

A freaking do-gooder. What the hell is Keev thinking, using this clown?

"Fine, since I won't be able to get it there any other way, I'll tell you; but this is the last time I will explain my business to you." I glare at both of them before explaining. "They are coffee beans. Coffee is a luxury item on Earth and barely available on Mars, if my intel is correct." My intel is always correct. "Instead of trying to run the blockade of Earth, I will go into the farming business and grow them locally."

"What are they even good for?" The kid whines. Why doesn't the father backhand him? It would do wonders for his disposition.

"Coffee beans are ground up on Earth and used to make a kind of drink," the father says questioningly to me, while simultaneously answering his son. I give a curt nod.

"Like Keev's tea?" The kid asks. He can put two and two together. He may be whiny, but he's not entirely stupid.

"Yes, like tea," I say. "But the good coffee beans only grow at high altitude. I figure it has to be either the lower temperature or atmospheric pressure that leads to the premium flavor. On

Mars I'll have both, and voilà, people can have their most magical mochas."

What the hell am I doing? Now I'm explaining my whole enterprise while playing word games? I'm disgusted with myself for losing focus.

"Are you coming with me to get the exoskeleton?" the captain asks. "Chris can inform our passenger of the change in plans and get the cargo bay ready. Right Chris?"

The kid rolls his eyes and huffs. I shake my head. One swift backhand to the chops would do wonders.

"Tell her there is a defect with the antimatter system and the fix is time sensitive. We don't trust them to do it here and we don't want to risk her life. Or something like that. Just sound sincere," the father says.

* * *

"The commercial district, such as it is, will be the next left," he says. "Let's get the exosuit, the loot and then let's scoot," the father adds with a smile.

I inhale deeply and slowly let my breath out. I've cast my lot with a couple of bumpkins. If my mission wasn't time sensitive, I would choke the very last breath out of the pair of them and find a new pilot.

The commercial center is depressingly small. Tycho is maintained by the Martians as a way to collect and ship helium-3. Because of that sole focus, smuggling couldn't be easier. Instead of bribing officials, we just avoid them. There are heavy tariffs on materials coming from Earth. If you are dumb enough to follow the rules, then you deserve to lose your money. The import-export office sports pink concrete and red bricks, declaring their allegiance to the Martians. Someone else must be smuggling today, because the officials are already drunk.

"You think coffee will be a big hit on Mars?" the man asks, pulling me from my thoughts.

"I know so. At least in the short run, it will be more valuable than anything else."

"Wow! How long will it take to grow?"

I take in the officials. They may not be as drunk as they seem.

"Three years or so, in the meantime I have stock lined up that can be delivered to the cis-lunar space station and then dropped off on Luna. I need to find a reliable transport to get the beans from here to Mars," I say, just to shut him up so I can concentrate.

"I think I can recommend someone."

Captain Coconut is grating on my nerves, but I can use this time to learn about my destination. "What's Asimov Crater like?"

"It's a small city, exports fine dust and ceramics to the other cities. There's not a lot to it, really."

My intel was right. "Your sleepy little home is going to become a new trading mecca on Mars."

"And you will be the richest, most powerful man on the planet." He whistles in admiration.

"Play your cards right, and you and your son will do well."

"So how do you get the beans off earth?"

"You don't need to know. However, you may have to make trips to Neng Yuan Weī Da Jia station in the future. You do know where that is?"

"It's the sole source for helium-3 in the solar system. Everyone knows where that is." He continues yammering, but I've stopped listening because we've found the exoskeleton shop.

This guy, Captain Coconut, or whatever his name is, so badly wants to impress me that he haggles to the last credit. I scarcely pay attention. In the commercial center, there are more than a few things to catch your eye. The women all sway sinuously back and forth, left, then right, and then left again. The effortless fluidity on display is mesmerizing.

"Here's the dock location where my cargo is stored," I cut him off in mid-sentence. "I'll meet you back at the ship. I have to meet with a contact before I leave." I send him the information without looking back.

I haven't met my contact yet, but she will sway just right with a body that is tall and pale and lean.

CHAPTER 7   VIKRAM

Tycho Station, Luna

If I was feeling charitable, I would say the ship with its dingy, sandblasted exterior exudes a faded glory. In truth, it looks wholly unremarkable. It will never attract attention and that's perfect.

Captain Coconut is waiting outside the front airlock. He's letting out exaggerated breaths and rubbing something in his pocket. I don't even want to know what it is, but it's plain somebody's nervous.

Our eyes meet, and he practically runs to me. If he played cards, he would be the easiest mark in history.

"Vikram, we have a small snag in the plan."

"What now?" I demand. I'm curious to see how he responds to a little tension.

"Chris was able to contact our passenger, but she decided to cut her trip short. She insists on flying back with us. Nothing will dissuade her." He raises his hand to forestall any objections from me. "Your containers are securely stowed in our locked cargo bay, but you will not be our only guest riding back." He manages to say all of this in one breath.

That's it? That's what has him falling to pieces?

"And what else went wrong?" There has to be something else.

"Nothing, your cargo is secure and we are doing the pre-launch check now."

I roll my eyes. This guy is as threatening as a rabbit. "When do we leave?"

He looks like he wants to say more, but I stop him with a scowl. I don't want him to yammer on about every minor thing that enters his head.

"We should be able to leave within the hour," he says.

I walk past him. He hurries to my side so he can slap the control and allow me entrance to the ship without breaking my stride.

As the outer door hisses open, a massive woman is gesticulating aggressively at the gangly teen on the other side of the airlock. The airlock lights up, highlighting her very plush features. She glances through the glass at the father before continuing her tirade unabated at the kid. All three of her chins are gyrating to a syncopated rhythm. The inner airlock door opens, and the woman begins caterwauling at Captain Coconut.

"You bring me back to this ship and then you make me wait with that scrawny, *alloyed* adolescent until your mystery guest arrives." She spares only a brief, affronted look at me. "You told me you had to get back to Mars at once for maintenance." In her cold fury, she spits out every word.

She faces us, points her finger savagely toward me, then the captain. "Who the hell is he, and why does he rank as important?" She sees my foot plate. "Another alloy?" Her voice goes up an octave. "You don't even try to hide your deformity!" This leaves her aghast.

I stare back at her for a second; I'm not getting ensnared in this little drama. The corners of her mouth draw upwards into a dangerous grin as she looks at me.

"Why is a crippled stooge like you going to Mars? Are you getting into the dust business? Did my daughter Kenova summon you? I will have you buried face-down if you get in my way."

Anyone paying attention could figure out I'm from Earth. I didn't really hope to keep that a secret. But how did Rustie Maitland, in all her copious flesh, make it on board this ship?

I keep my face neutral.

"Pardon me, ma'am, I also need to rush back to Mars and my good friend," I place my hand on Captain Coconut's shoulder, "extended me this courtesy. I have no luggage and I will not hold us up any longer."

I try to make it sound contrite, but that's never been easy for me. The last thing I need is the deposed head of the Maitland family business recognizing me. I will announce my presence at a more opportune time.

She eyes me suspiciously.

"Yes," she says, suddenly distracted, "let's get moving." She turns without a second thought and waddles toward the bowels of the ship, the boy chasing after her.

"Let me get you settled in, Ms. Rustie," he chirps.

She gives me one last calculated look before she disappears into her quarters.

"If you will come with me," a relieved Coconut says. He lightly grabs my elbow and leads me toward the cockpit. "She never left her quarters on the ride here, so she shouldn't be any trouble. She insists on eating alone and for Chris to bring all of her meals to her cabin. I had no idea who she was until just now."

Coconut can't stand to be in the presence of ruffled feathers, that's for sure. "I can understand her calling me an alloy, but why did she call your son one as well?"

"It's not generally accepted in polite society, but some people look down at those with prosthetics."

"I get that. She's a bitch and I have a shiny chrome plate instead of a left foot. What about your son?"

"It's still fairly easy to pick out the syn-skin on Chris's left arm," he says as if it's obvious.

"Damn, your technology is good."

"He just got it last week."

My brain is going into overdrive. Is he really a backwater bumpkin, or did he orchestrate this meeting? I glance his way as he dries a rivulet of sweat from the side of his face. No, he's too nervous. He clearly didn't want us to meet. But if he didn't plan it, and this ship was en route before I was even told about it, then Rustie couldn't have known either.

It is either a freakish coincidence or Keev did this. As a rule, I don't believe in coincidence. What is Rustie Maitland doing outside her Martian compound? Is Keev conspiring with Rustie against her daughter, or am I supposed to take her out?

I only left Earth five days ago. She has to know I'm connected to someone powerful on Mars, otherwise I'd never get off Earth. She even guessed that it was her daughter who summoned me.

Would she move against me on this ship? It couldn't be a physical attempt because I could easily overpower everyone on board.

Why exactly is she here?

It's common knowledge that her husband, Ceredo, and daughter pushed her out of the business. Everyone assumed she would live out her days exiled at her luxury estate at Hebes Chasma, wherever that is. If she is running free, what does that mean? Is she in control again? She mentioned the illicit drug, dust. Is she trying to create a new power base for herself? This trip just got a lot more interesting.

"Vikram. Hello, Vikram?" Coconut intrudes upon my thoughts. "Any questions?"

"Uh, yeah, so tell me how this ship works, will you?"

"I just did," he says with a chuckle. "But let's try it again."

"Great."

"This ship was designed to fly through the atmosphere of Earth, as well as deep space . . ."

What did she accomplish on Luna?

If she's no longer in exile, I need to know. She's a wild card and I don't play games unless I know what everyone is holding.

Even Coconut would recognize my fishing for information if I asked him about Rustie, and I don't want him to realize how little I know. The kid is the one to approach. He's also had the most contact with the old bat.

"Where is the kid?" I interrupt.

"He's probably in the galley. Why?"

"I'm going to sit with him." Step, squeak, step . . .

"We can't leave until you are strapped into your seat," he calls after me.

* * *

"Hey kid, did you get your passenger strapped in all nice and snug?" I ask as I stumble down the gangway. This damn reduced gravity is wreaking havoc on my balance.

"One of them," he replies curtly.

I like this kid. He has some fire in him.

"Yeah, maybe you should help me with the straps as well."

I take a seat and watch as the kid nimbly prepares my harness. "So, did good ole' Rustie say why she came on this trip?"

"She never *says* anything to me. She only yells."

"Look kid," I say kindly.

"I am not a kid. My name is Chris."

"Fine, whatever you say, Chris. Now I need to know why that old harpy is on this ship. If she's trying to rejoin the game, I need to know the details. Since your dad gets most of his business from my associates, it should be important to you as well."

"She's nothing but a vile old windbag," he says as he pulls the last strap extra tight. "She hasn't said anything concrete, but I get the feeling she's trying to meet someone on Luna."

"That's good kid."

"My name is Chris." He corrects me again.

"Yeah, that's right, sorry, Chris. When are we going to take off?"

"Shortly, so stay strapped into your seat." The kid pushes off from the galley wall and into the corridor. From there, he propels himself toward the cockpit and out of sight.

Damn. I can't even tell which arm is fake.

"Good afternoon, passengers," Coconut says cheerfully over the intercom. "We will be taking off in just a couple of minutes. Once we are past the lunar landing radius, we will briefly reorient the ship before accelerating home. The ceiling of our ship will be pointed toward Mars, and we will maintain the acceleration so that the force you experience on the ship is equal to the gravity on Mars. At the midpoint, we will flip the ship so that the floor is facing Mars and we will begin braking maneuvers. This will keep the floor under our feet and maintain Martian gravity. So please, sit tight until after the reorientation. It should be about twenty minutes before we're underway."

* * *

The ship starts to shutter as the engines start. The metal frame groans as we ease upward. At full throttle, my seat vibrates so hard I fear my vertebrae will shake loose. I unclench my death grips on the armrests and relax my fingers.

Concentrate on your breathing, that's what the yogi would tell you.

I have as little power as a new shoot of bamboo being whipped whichever way the monsoon winds demand. The raw power makes me realize just how feeble we humans are. Outside the window, there is nothing but white moon dust.

We clear the ground and the dust cloud fades to the blackness of space. The acceleration is crushing my head into my chest and I have to consciously push my chest out to take short, shallow breaths. I attempted deeper breaths when I left earth and I passed out. Now I know better.

Finally, the engines throttle down, and the noise and vibrations cease. Instantly I'm weightless and grinning like a child. To think I've gone from a handicapped kid in the slums of Tamil Nadu to being weightless in space. I release my restraints and glide around the room. I give it a minute, then I force this silliness from my mind.

No one else is moving around the ship. Using the toe rail like the kid did, I work my way to the cargo bay. I enter the code and slip inside. Once there, I confirm my containers are secure.

I unlock the lid of the nearest container and the earthy, slightly nutty aroma wafts upward. It smells like money to me. Two years of concerted effort has brought me to this point. I'm off Earth, I have these beans to start my credit reservoir and I have a plan. I exhale slowly and a calm contentment falls over me.

"What do you have there?"

I nearly jump out of my skin. I wrench my head backward to see Rustie Maitland holding on to the rail above her head with both hands as she floats behind me.

Dammit! I am not a silly schoolboy.

I inhale and slowly release my breath. I force my heart to slow down and nonchalantly close the lid on my container, making sure that my body screens her view.

"It's really not your business now, is it?" I reply with cold indifference. The old bat surprised me, but she damn well isn't going to intimidate me.

She smiles wickedly. "You think you can keep secrets from me?" She edges over to fully block the exit.

I push off the container, purposely aiming right at her. She unconsciously backs up and I grab the rail she had been claiming. I spin around and hit the control. The doors whoosh shut and a solid click lets us both know the door is locked. I reverse my spin to face her. After looking at her from head to toe, I ask, "why would I worry about the likes of you?"

Her face goes splotchy red. "Do you know who I am?! I'm Rustie Maitland! I changed my husband's pathetic group of do-nothings into the most powerful organization in the solar system." She begins spitting again as her rage builds.

So, it's that easy to get her flustered?

She was never more than a leader of a brutish gang. That's why she was deposed. Her tactics were too blunt for polite Martian society. She could be a formidable opponent if she's able to gather resources, and I can't let that happen. It would be best for me to deal with her now, before she can reestablish herself.

"Yes. I can tell by your entourage that you're someone important," I say, cutting through her blather. I look up and down the empty gangway to underscore my disdain. She sputters and makes awful noises partially resembling speech. My smile lets her know I'm claiming victory. I turn my back and make my way slowly toward the galley, one hand rail at a time. Her heavy breathing confirms that she's following me closely. This is going to be easy.

I reach the galley and I turn to face her once again.

Her finger nearly collides with my nose. "What are you doing here, Earther? And who summoned you?" Rustie explodes. "I don't know how you got those coffee beans through the quarantine, but if you're bringing them to Mars, I will get my cut," she informs me.

My eyes focus on the green coffee bean between her finger and thumb. How the hell did she get that? My mind races. The crates were locked and secure. I must have knocked one out. I check the floor, but we're at zero g. They could be floating anywhere. I had absently assumed any spills would hit the floor, and I'd hear it. Dammit. It's a no gravity environment. It was a stupid, stupid Earthling mistake. She must have stumbled upon one of them. My only option is to play dumb.

"Where the hell did that come from?" I sputter. I'm completely unconvincing. I'm not experienced at acting the fool.

"Nice try," she squeals. "I saw two containers, each a standard cubic meter in size. Once we leave, I will take one of them." She stares at me imperiously. "And you will thank me for my generosity." Her chins quiver as she laughs.

I want to give her one good kick and send her careening down the gangway. But that won't solve my problem, no matter how satisfying. Behind her, I see the big red button with the words 'Emergency Evacuation' above it. I can have the last laugh, if I steer this conversation properly.

"No, you don't understand. I only have a handful of coffee beans." I try to look earnest, and fail again horribly. I make my way to the galley, using the handrails. I allow myself to smile wickedly once my back is to her. My solution isn't going to be elegant, but it will be effective.

"How could they have spilled? I was so careful wrapping them." I try to sound like I'm deep in thought. She follows me as I float around the galley, looking to and fro for more beans.

"Whatever game you think you're playing isn't working," she says flatly.

"No game, I swear." I circle around her and start toward the airlock. She stalks me like a tigress, tight on my heels. I open the airlock doors and lead her halfway inside before pushing off the wall. I flail my arms as I float weightlessly toward the outer doors. Let her think I'm clumsy.

"You're just falling to pieces, aren't you?" She barks out. She still thinks she has the upper hand. How cute.

I launch myself off the doors, passing her as I glide back toward the galley. She lets out a pitiless laugh, thinking my speed is another mistake, but now I can smile.

"You've lost, you old harpy." I grab onto the toe rail and stop my momentum. My feet continue sailing past the doorway, but it doesn't matter. I smile as I hit the big red button. Klaxons blare and the doors create a slight breeze as they seal impossibly fast in front of my nose. The outer airlock doors open just a fraction later and Rustie barely has time to realize her fatal mistake. She starts to scream as she and the air around her are sucked out into space.

Because of the lower gravity, the average work required by a Martian's body (i.e. blood flow, locomotion) is about twenty-five percent less than an Earther. In addition, a restricted population has escalated the genetic differentiation. In this work, I will lay out my conjecture that we have become a separate species from our blue planet ancestors.

Homo Sapiens Marsus: Yes, We Really Are Different
Johnathan Lawrence H. E.

CHAPTER 8   CHRIS

Tycho Station, Luna

Cornelius is humming. I don't like it. I wait for him to lecture me about something, but he just keeps humming away. If he's so distracted, maybe I can get him to answer some questions.

"Why did you change your name to Halley?

"Well, it's a bit of an unusual story," Dad says. "It was sorta, well, it was kinda like . . ."

Uh oh, when Dad stops using proper English, he must be really uncomfortable. I bite my lip to hide my smile. Any excuse and he'll stop.

"Have you checked on engineering?"

"Of course I did. I hang out there every day for hours. You can't distract me Cornelius, tell me why you changed your name. Is it a family tradition now? Do I need to decide what I want my new name to be?"

"Is the quarterdeck airlock clean?"

"Yes, and quit trying to change the subject. Why did you change your last name?"

I'm going to be able to use this against him for the rest of his life.

"Your mother was, well, probably still is, a by-the-books sort of woman, and a little selfish too, I might add."

Dad is already mega defensive. This is going to be awesome!

"Anna Vennemann was her name, or Anna Venomous, as I prefer to think of her. She was adamant that she would keep the first child, and after you came, she had no use for me anymore. She didn't care if I got my own child or not. So, one evening, James Stecht went to visit Anna and Christian Vennemann. Later that night, Cornelius and Chris Halley boarded the *Halley Traveler* along with a full complement of guests and left Huygens Crater behind."

"So you kidnapped me?"

"I prefer 'rescued you', but essentially, yes. You are as much of me as you are of her. Every kid grows up with only one parent, so is it really a crime?"

I can't wait to remind him of this the next time he tells me I screwed up.

"You could have grown up as an organics engineer, dealing with Huygens's waste recycling system or you could travel the solar system and see all the wonders it contains. If you had been able to choose for yourself, which would you have gone with?"

My mind races. Somehow, Dad has managed to avoid this conversation with me for seventeen years. Also, I potentially have other family members. My brain explodes with the possibilities.

"Have I mentioned before that only twenty-one people have been to all eight planets?" Dad asks. "In just a couple more months, Jupiter will be in a good position to slingshot us to see both Uranus and Neptune. Saturn will be in a good position to slingshot us back home. This only happens about once every fourteen years. We'll be the twenty-second and twenty-third people to accomplish that feat."

I bet he thinks I'm unaware of him changing the conversation. I give him a disappointed look.

"Your mother could always have another child; assuming she could find another down on his luck, drunk and lonely pilot."

"I'm the result of a bad decision between a lonely drunkard and a hellcat? Real classy, Dad."

"Which would you rather have, the whole solar system to travel at your leisure or being knee high in a recycling tank?"

He starts punching buttons on the console. "Story time is over. If you will, finish up the sequence, then go tell Ms.

Maggie to secure herself in the gel chair, so she suffers no discomfort."

"Do you really think that this is over Cornelius? You have *so* much more explaining to do."

* * *

"Strap in," Dad says. Once he hears my restraints click, he announces we were good for takeoff. This is going to be a long trip. Neither Ms. Maggie nor Vikram are even tolerable to be around, and I just know Dad will keep himself up here, alone in the cockpit. This trip is going to be so boring.

Dad checks my launch sequence over before feeding it to the ship's computer. It was perfect! The ship rumbles beneath us as it slowly rises off the moon's dusty surface.

"Sorry about Ms. Rustie, but she wouldn't take no for an answer. She'd rather cut her holiday short than be left stranded." I might as well get my side of the story out before the recriminations start. I wait. Nothing.

What is going on?

Dad never fails to inform me of my mistakes. Is he still humming? And smiling?

"Cornelius, this humming of yours is unnerving. Why aren't you lecturing me?"

"Is there something you'd like to confess?"

"That's a hard no. Did you and Vikram bond on your trip or something?"

"We didn't make too much conversation," Dad says, still pleased. "I think he was expecting me to grovel and thank him, but we both know that will never happen. I played it cool and was able to get him to share some of his plans. His greed forced him to come to terms. He could be good for our finances, if he can be trusted."

My mind is wandering as usual until Cornelius turns to me and smiles conspiratorially.

"What?" His gleeful expression is all kinds of unnerving.

"I made sure each container was listed as one kilo lighter in the ship's logs than they actually are. I figure we should get a cut as well. I stored our two kilos in my quarters."

"What are you talking about?" I'm both confused and irked. He's humming, happy, and talking cryptically.

Who is this man?

"Sorry, I haven't been this excited in years. Vikram is smuggling in two cubic meters of coffee beans. He claims the beans are more valuable than helium-3, and he may be right. Once he and his cargo leave the ship, we'll have two kilos of our own coffee beans to sell."

I've never seen Dad this pleased with himself. He always acts like some honest rube without the slightest bit of drive. People will happily underestimate him even while he's pilfering from underneath their noses. He's so good at it that I didn't even see it coming this time.

"Cool! So I can get a new PCD?"

"We'll see."

Ugh, that means no. There's the Cornelius I'm used to. He flips his coin with the orange gemstone in the center in the air. He does this every time, right before he kills the thrusters. Once the thrusters stop, we're in microgravity, and there's no telling which way the coin will bounce off the ceiling.

"Da-aaad, what am I supposed to do without one?" It wasn't a whine. I'm too old to whine. It was a sincere expression of my exasperation.

The coin hits the ceiling and slowly drifts toward me. Dad snatches it before I can. I really hope he gets tired of this little game soon.

"Spend your time learning how to fly this ship."

"I was taking a vid class on intermediate flight on my PCD. How am I supposed to continue?"

"I can teach you more than any class, and we have several major purchases we need to make. So I can't guarantee—"

The ship lurches toward our left and starts to tip over as the decompression alarm blares. The ship disappoints me before Dad can.

Before Cornelius can say anything, I release my harness, grab hold of the headrest behind me, and push off the floor with my feet for my patented reverse flip. My body makes an elegant one-hundred-and-eighty-degree arc over the seat. I keep my legs pulled tight against my body until my feet contact the back of my chair. I hop to the captain's chair and hit my ribs in the process.

I shudder, but don't make a sound. If Dad heard, he'd send me straight to the med-bay, and I have no time for that. I spring off the chair's back and sail head first down the center of the gangway, looking for problems as I go. My line is perfectly centered, so I don't have to use any of the toe rails to adjust my path. The storage drawers lining the walls and ceiling are a blur as I whiz past them.

Straight ahead, Vikram is standing at the quarterdeck airlock. Who has caused the problem has been determined; now it's just a matter of what did he do.

Over the intercom, Dad announces, "The outer airlock door has failed. Everyone, stay in your rooms while we fix the problem. The inner airlock door is still secure, so everyone is safe. We will let you know when the situation is resolved."

Cornelius, you're the last to know.

Despite there being no gravity, my heart sinks into my stomach as Vikram smiles at me.

"I don't know how, but Rustie managed to eject herself into space," he informs me.

"What? How could she have gotten into a spacesuit by herself?" How could she even fit into a spacesuit is a better question, but I keep that to myself? I'm scanning the capsules to see which one has deployed, but they're all still present.

"Kid, she wasn't in a spacesuit."

My jaw hangs open as I struggle to speak. His tone is light, despite what he's saying.

"No spacesuit?" I stare out into the inky black void, hopelessly looking to find her.

"She must be dead by now," Vikram adds.

"But how could she do that? There are safety protocols in place."

"How, indeed?" Vikram says with a smirk.

"Chris, you and Vikram need to get into quarters immediately. The inner airlock could fail. I'll be back in a second." Cornelius must have been monitoring our conversation.

Each space in the ship is rated to hold against a vacuum. Dad's not making much sense, but I point Vikram toward the cabin across from Rustie's all the same.

"Can you secure yourself?"

"Sure, kid." Vikram is all agreeable as he enters his room. The door closes behind him and I lock it.

Dad is easing his way sideways down the gangway. "Chris, I need you to look at this."

I grab a toe-rail on either side of the ceiling and send myself forward. I'll worry about my ribs later.

Once I'm even with him, he nudges me behind him. Dad's holding a gun in his opposite hand, an actual antique, Earth-style pistol I've never seen before.

"Vikram," Dad calls, "come out of the cabin slowly with your hands where I can see them."

The door rattles, but it doesn't open.

"I locked it."

Dad goes to the nearest interface and opens the door. Vikram looks bemused as he exits.

"Make up your mind. Do you want me strapped into my chair or out here with you?"

"What did you do?" Dad demands.

"Rustie was a potential rival. According to your kid, she was trying to get back in the game." He shrugs. "It's always best to remove threats before they become powerful."

He stands just as pleased as he can be. "What kind of pistol is that?"

"A woman is dead because of you," Dad says.

"Yes." He nods in agreement. "We've covered that."

It's Dad's turn to stare wide-eyed at Vikram.

"Look, I don't plan on making this a habit. Hell, I don't plan on getting on another spaceship once you put me down on Mars," Vikram says. "My head is all stuffy and I'm struggling to keep my food down. There are just too many variables I'm not used to up here. So, this was a onetime occurrence. If you hadn't put the deposed leader of the Maitlands on board this ship with me, we could be chatting amicably now."

I mouth the words, 'oh shit' but no sounds comes out. Somehow, he knew all along who our passenger was. I guess I should have known too, but I was only half paying attention.

"You're blaming Rustie Maitland's death on me now?" Dad asks.

"Well, you did have a part to play, but generally I don't like to assign blame in any sort of legal sense. It just gets . . . tiresome."

"And what am I supposed to do when Kenova Maitland comes looking for her?" Dad asks.

We are so totally screwed. Everyone knows about Kenova's torture center at Lomonosov. No one gets out of there alive.

Will she have people waiting when we arrive at Asimov?

Maybe we should sell the ship, move to Huygens and change our names. It's a good thing my PCD is fried, Kenova can likely access the tracking data from it. I'm never going to be able to have a PCD again. Maybe we should just turn ourselves over to her and beg for mercy.

"I guess you're going to need my good word then, aren't you?" Vikram says.

"I could kill you right now and tell Kenova what you did. What's stopping me?"

I've never heard Dad talk like this. It's riveting, and a little scary.

"Because you're not a killer," Vikram replies. "Besides, I'm not a threat. I am your benefactor."

"Like hell!" Dad shouts. He lowers the pistol. "But you are right about one thing. I can't kill a man in cold blood. Once we arrive at Asimov, we go our separate ways."

"It's what, six days until we arrive? I'll give you time to reflect on the amount of money you are walking away from. Let's see what happens when cooler heads prevail."

"Vikram," Dad says in a shaky voice, "stay out of the front of the ship. That means the cockpit and our personal quarters."

"As you wish," Vikram replies with a slight bow.

"Chris, make your way to the cockpit. I'll be right behind you."

Dad keeps his eyes on Vikram the whole time as we make our retreat.

* * *

Dad's been in a funk for days now. "Chris, we need to know what Vikram's thinking, and it's obvious that he's not going to talk to me." Dad flips on the comm, but only to his quarters. "He talked to you before. Let's see if he's just waiting to do so again." Dad gets up and yawns as he exits the cockpit. "Wake me in an hour," he calls back to me.

Ten minutes after Dad leaves, Vikram's squeaky steps announce his approach. I check the comm again. Yep, the indicator is lit; so Dad can hear us. There's a soft knock on the door. My head tells me I'm safe, but my hands are shaky nonetheless as I deactivate the lock to the door.

My hands suddenly don't want to stay still. I grab the armrests and try to look nonchalant as the door opens.

"You got a good head on your shoulders, kid."

"Chris." I correct him, again. I give in a bit to my anger; it feels better than fear.

"Sorry, Chris. I've always been told that most Martians are too soft to make it on Earth. I think you'd be one who could."

"Of course it would be hard on Earth. We live with only thirty-eight percent of the gravity you Earthers do. Everyone knows that."

"No, you misunderstand. I'm not talking about gravity or physical effects. I'm talking about living in a place where you must always be planning your next move. Nothing is free and everyone will steal from you if you give them half a chance. You Martians have no idea what it's like on Earth. The next cholera outbreak is always around the corner and food is still fought over. So you need to have a good head on your shoulders to survive the ebbs and flows of life."

"You mean after fifty years, you Earthers still haven't figured out how to feed yourselves? How long will it take you to figure it all out? Mars has a tiny fraction of the water, no atmosphere, and significantly less than half the light Earth does, and we still manage to do it."

What is he trying to pull, calling me a good Earther candidate?

Vikram settles into the captain's chair. I swivel around to watch his every move.

"It's not like that kid, er, Chris. What did you learn on Mars? After Katla erupted, the ash made everything hazy, and the air polluted. Iceland was devastated, but everyone adjusted. Then three years later when the dust finally settled, literally, Cerro Negro in Chile blew its top and the sun disappeared from view, for over a year. Southern India is in a tropical zone, so we don't have winters. In twenty-two oh two, there was snow on the coconut trees. Forget starvation, people froze to death."

His eyes grow big, as if freezing to death is a new concept to me. Duh, I live on Mars.

"Those left were desperate, starving mobs trying to get whatever they could. No government was able to withstand the rioting. When a government falls, so do the hallmarks of civilization, like electricity, clean water and the rule of law. You Martians, you were forced to band together to survive while wave after wave of pandemics and blights tore us apart. Everything you have on Mars was developed on Earth. Now we're left with nothing but relics that no one knows how to operate while you reap all the rewards."

"Why would people riot? It only makes things worse," I ask. How dumb are these Earthers?

"You've never experienced having nothing to lose. So life is cheap, and brutality is a fact of life. If you can't secure your own needs, you die. We used to have ten billion people. Now there's less than one. Stable city states have only reappeared in the last fifteen years or so. It will be another fifty hundred years before Earth is back to where it was before the collapse. That's too long for me, so I found a way off planet."

"I'm so happy for you," I deadpan.

"One day, Earth will remember Luna and her endless supply of energy. Whoever controls Luna will control the solar system," he says with a faraway look in his eye.

He could try his best to befriend me and act like a mentor, but I already have Dad for that and Dad isn't a murderer. Besides, anyone stuck with a prosthetic that bad couldn't have all the answers.

"What happened to your leg? I can hear you walking everywhere you go." Rude perhaps, but I don't care.

Vikram smiles tolerantly. "We don't have regular health visits to doctors anymore."

"A doctor? How far in the past do you live? Just use the bio health system. Body mechanics are always the last resort."

Vikram barks out a laugh. "And how many bio health systems do you think are on Earth when the average person has no access to electricity?"

"If you don't have electricity, then how did you make it off Earth?"

"I am not an average citizen. I may have started out that way, but I was never content to wait for my life to be cut short."

He swivels back and forth in the captain's chair. "When I was five, my shin was cut by a filthy metal shard. It got infected and had to come off. My uncle Saji fashioned a pad to fit over my knee and some pipe that I could screw into the bottom. As I grew, we had to change out the pipe. I couldn't run and play, so I stayed away from children my own age. Instead, I learned to plan strategies to get what I wanted without getting knocked around. I studied the other children and learned what motivated them. By the time I was twenty, I was in charge of my own gang. At twenty-three, I headed Chennai Botanicals."

How am I supposed to respond to that?

"Good talk kid. Don't hit any asteroids while I'm sleeping." He turns and finally leaves.

Once his door closes, Dad reenters. "I had hoped to get at least an inkling of his plans."

"He likes to talk to you, but apparently he's not giving away anything yet. Give him time. We're too valuable to him to be tossed aside."

* * *

We'll arrive at Asimov tomorrow morning. Since Vikram 's strange talk to me the first day, he's kept to himself, until now. We've all met at the galley for dinner. Dad has selected porridge again. I can see why he doesn't want to waste real food on Vikram, but that just means we all suffer.

"Now that we've all had time to reflect," Vikram says. "I want to discuss the Rustie incident with both of you and how I think we should proceed from here."

My hands begin to twitch, but Dad's composed, as always.

"Tell me why we shouldn't just turn you over to the police when we arrive at Asimov Crater?" Dad asks.

"Cutting right to the chase, I see. That's good. First, you have no proof I did anything and I have a lot more money and power than you. Second, she could quite possibly be a missing person who no one misses. Third, if Ceredo and Kenova do seek justice, it won't be through the justice system.

"Those would be the potential problems for you. As for benefits, I can let it be known you're under my protection. If they do come for you, they'll talk it over with me first. I'll be your shield." He gives us a fake smile. "Also, working for me will be a much more lucrative way to make a living. There's no good reason for us to not work together."

Dad rises from the table. "We'll talk it over. I will give you an answer tomorrow morning."

Vikram waves his hand in an unconcerned manner before getting up and marching back to his quarters. Step. Squeak. Step . . .

"At least we don't have to wonder if he's eavesdropping on us," I say.

Dad lets out a sigh. "Until he made his offer, I was worried he would kill us or turn us over to the Maitlands himself. So that's a weight off our shoulders. Since he still wants to work with us, we have four very bad choices."

He signals for me to check the gangway for Vikram. I bite back my comment that with his leg, we would hear him long before he could hear us. Dad's finally treating me like an adult, so I'll forgive this silliness.

"One, we tell Ceredo and Kenova directly what happened, and possibly be killed. I have never met either of them, so I have no feel for how they would react," Dad says.

"Not good."

"None of our options are good. Two, we tell the authorities everything and hope for the best."

"Also bad," I add.

"Third, we do nothing and hope it remains an unsolved disappearance that no one is too interested in solving."

"The unmissed missing person," I chime in. Dad smiles despite the seriousness of our situation.

"And we will be looking over our shoulders for the rest of our lives," he adds.

"That sounds fairly terrible."

"Finally, we accept Vikram's protection and hope it's enough to protect us from both the authorities and Kenova."

"I'm waiting for the not so terrifying fifth option, like we change our names and move to someplace safe," I respond.

"It won't work, I'm afraid. Mars is too small to avoid a determined manhunt. I can cut down some of the choices though. We can eliminate option two because we have to assume the Maitlands have informants within law enforcement, so if we go there, we're admitting fault and they will enact their justice upon us."

Dad blows out a long breath. "Options one and three are essentially hoping the Maitlands don't kill us when they find out what happens. And I have no doubt that they will find out."

"You don't think Vikram will kill us as soon as he's safely on Mars?"

"No, Vikram is new, so he won't have anyone else with access to a spaceship. We're the only Martians he's met so far." Dad sighs. "A year from now, we'll have to worry about that."

"So we have to work with Vikram?"

"It's our only real choice."

"Should we tell Vikram now?" I ask.

"No, make him wait. I'm not about to do him any favors."

"I have a suggestion that just may solve all of our problems," I say brightly.

"I'm afraid to ask," Dad says with mock trepidation.

"How about letting me land the ship unassisted tomorrow? If we all die, then the Rustie problem goes away. If I land, I will have completed the last test for my pilot's license."

"That would be a novel way to punish Vikram. The space nausea is still bothering him." Dad scratches his head. "Go ahead," he says in a resigned voice. "I'll initiate the testing recorder for tomorrow, but remember, I can't alter the recording and I can't help you without causing you to fail."

I've been bugging Dad for months to let me try. Why don't I feel better about this?

It has been nearly five decades since L. Anna Ellis struck out to tour all eight of our solar system's planets. She became the twenty-first member and the fourth soloist in this hallowed band of explorers. Will we follow the lead of the Earthers and remain hobbled and humbled to this rock, or will we once again dare to be audacious?

Forgotten Legends, the Explorers
Kwame Brown

CHAPTER 9   CHRIS

Interplanetary Space

"Are you ready?" Dad asks as he fidgets with his coin.

"Only one way to find out," I say, with false exuberance. I'm petrified, but if I tell Dad that, he's likely to cancel this test.

I plotted the Hohman Transfer last night without issue. The engines are already primed and the thrusters are pointed in front of us, so there are no warm-ups. This first increase in thrust needs to slow us enough to be captured in a stable orbit. If Mars had more of an atmosphere, this would be a much more forgiving maneuver.

"Increasing thrust to fifty-five percent now." I try to sound confident even though my hands are shaking.

Dad's in the co-pilot's chair. He's allowed to call out data, but he can't give me instructions. The whole landing sequence, telemetry, audio and visuals are all being recorded as proof of my piloting skills.

"Encountering nominal atmosphere in fifteen seconds," Dad says.

As the thrusters slow us, we both sink farther into our chairs. If the relative gravity exceeds Earth standard, it's an automatic fail.

"Standing by for engine flare," I announce. I asked if we can put this over the comm, just to mess with Vikram, but Dad said it's better not to provoke him. I'd never say it out loud, but Dad's probably right.

At our current speed, we're going too fast to be captured. We'd only round part of the planet before being catapulted away. I have to perform a hot insertion and I have about fifteen seconds to adjust our velocity to a stable trajectory. The readout shows our relative gravity to be seventy-three percent of Earth's; so I have a little wiggle room. That's the first half of the test. After that, I have less than a minute to kill the engines and make three successful revolutions where our cumulative altitude change is less than ten percent. No pressure.

"Outer atmosphere reached," Dad calls out.

"Starting thruster flare in five, four, three," I hit the flare early. Dad's whole body lurches forward. That caught him by surprise. I know I'll hear about it later, but it's totally worth it.

He would always do that to me when I was little, then scold me for not paying attention.

Payback Cornelius.

"Velocity is on track for an orbit eighty-five kilometers from the planet. Initiating engine roll followed by thrust burn to stabilize orbit at one hundred kilometers," I call out. Now that I'm busy, my nerves are gone.

I flip the ship nose spaceward and program a five point five second max burn to lift us higher in orbit. A pro doesn't need to make any adjustments, but I don't expect perfection yet.

"Orbit established at ninety-eight point six five kilometers," Dad calls out.

"Confirmed. Stable orbit has been reached." The instrumental data would be all that's needed, but it is a time-honored tradition for pilots to confirm their expertise. It isn't a perfect one hundred kilometer orbit, but it's well within acceptable range. Dad scratches his nose, code for letting me know that I've succeeded in the first half of the test.

I fall back into the pilot's chair with a smile and a long stretch. It takes no time to circle the planet. We're at ninety-three kilometers after our third revolution, so only a five percent drop in altitude.

Dad plays with his hair, a sure sign that he's nervous.

"Initiating landing protocol," I call out for the record.

Dad covers his mic.

"You can take a second to breathe, you know."

I hit the command to flip the ship, so it's pointing along our path once again.

"Engaging engines at seventy-five percent for seven seconds, then the pivot to landing position." I hit the button before Dad can object. Hopefully, it will be a controlled fall, but one way or another, we'll definitely make contact with the ground.

We drop fast, much faster than I was anticipating. My stomach is practically hitting my chin. Dad looks a bit green. The sudden drop is hitting him hard, too. I'm going to be on my own for this landing now. It's okay, I just have to call out the data and my actions. I've seen this done so many times it should be automatic.

"Bringing the ship into position. Engines pointed at seven o'clock."

I never understood where the o'clock scale came from, but every pilot has to learn it. Seven o'clock is a pretty steep angle, so our descent is slowed and our forward speed barely increases. I probably should have gone with an eight o'clock angle, but we are still within specifications. I waited too long to start, so my landing target is closer than I planned. I won't be able to circle Asimov at this angle, and it's going to be nearly impossible to land gently.

In the blink of an eye, we're buzzing Asimov City and approaching the space park *way* too fast. I check to make sure I'm buckled in properly. The landing pads hit the ground and Dad and I are lifted from our seats as the landing gear can't fully absorb the impact. The landing is a little hard and the ship veers to the left as we slide forward. We come to a halt. It wasn't perfect, but it still should be acceptable. I kill the engines and stare at the screen for a final score.

I run through the landing sequence in my head as the cursor blinks on and off a thousand times before text appears. Letters fill the screen, but I'm too excited and nervous to focus. I dart my eyes toward Dad, waiting for him to give the results.

Dad shakes his head in frustration, and my stomach drops. I take a deep breath and check the screen.

I passed!

I bounce up and down in my seat. I need to take the buckles off to do my victory dance properly.

"I did it! I passed!" I look over at Dad, smiling.

"I don't care what the testing says, knocking your co-pilot unconscious is an automatic fail on my ship," he growls.

There's a little liquid on Dad's collar, so he must have vomited a little. That's really why he's mad.

"Get me off this ship," Vikram demands over the comm.

Dad gives me his death stare.

"I'll take care of Vikram," Dad says. "Then we are going to discuss this stunt of yours in great detail."

I'm forced to look away so Dad doesn't see the jubilation on my face. No matter what he says, I'm officially qualified to pilot a spaceship.

* * *

"I'm going to give Vikram the tour of Asimov. I expect you to have the system checks finished and the ship spotless when I return," Dad says over the comm in his suit. "Your landing caused Vikram to lose his breakfast, so make sure you clean up his quarters as well."

Dad sounds a little pissed. That's okay. A walk around Asimov will mellow him out.

"I'm sorry about the landing Vikram, it was my first time." I try to mask my excitement.

The checks and the cleaning won't take very long and Cornelius didn't say that I couldn't get my license today. That's all that matters right now. I will officially be a pilot.

For all of Dad's grousing, we arrived at Asimov with no damage, thank you very much. I spent the last couple hours studying the data so I can have facts on my side. I also logged an hour of virtual landings. Next time, I'll land at the trident. It stretches out over the crater, so a miss means you're burying your ship in the dust, but I've nailed my last four landings on the simulator.

The really cool thing about the main platform is that you can have an airlock connected to your ship, so there's no need for spacesuits. It's too rich for us, so we land in the space park outside the city.

Since my PCD is gone, I'll have to pay extra to get a physical license. I lay down in my bunk to think how best to brandish my license to guests before I clean the ship.

* * *

"AI, what time is it?"

"It is eighteen hundred and thirteen hours."

"Oh shit. AI, where is Dad?"

"Cornelius Halley is not on board the ship."

It couldn't have taken Dad that long to give a tour of Asimov. Has he been here and left again? I missed lunch due to my nap. There's no way I clean this whole ship on an empty stomach. I should probably take care of eating first. I have to wolf down whatever food wafers I can find and get to work cleaning.

I toss the serving packs into a cabinet for now. I have so much to finish and Dad will be back any minute. The last thing I need is another responsibilities lecture. I vacuum the mess in Vikram's room and hide the waste pack in the drawer under his bunk. I'll come back for it later when Dad's busy. I fly from one area to the next, cleaning or hiding, mostly hiding the messes.

I can't believe how lucky I am. I finish all my chores and still have time to sit in the cockpit and figure out what I'll do when this ship is mine. The time drags on. I check the readout and it's twenty hundred hours.

Dad is still not back? Even if he went to Keev's, he should be back by now.

"There is a guest at the port airlock," the AI chirps brightly. "There is a guest at the port airlock."

"AI, stop. Allow entry to the airlock."

"Vacuum is being applied to the port airlock."

Why is Dad standing at the port airlock? He'll trudge in so much dust. We almost never use it. After a couple of taps on the controls, the video feed pops up. It's a bright green spacesuit.

But those are only worn by the police. The AI should have announced a visit by the authorities.

"Outer port airlock door is opening."

The airlock is only five meters from the cockpit, but I hurry anyway.

"Outer port airlock door is closed. Air is being cycled to the port airlock," the AI says needlessly.

"Where else would you put the air?" I ask, annoyed. The police being here has me a little flustered.

"I do not understand your query."

Sarcasm is wasted on AI systems.

"It doesn't matter. AI, open inner port airlock door."

The inner airlock door opens and an official hard-cased, green spacesuit faces me.

Did they find out about Ms. Rustie already?

I wish I was still sixteen, then I'd be a minor and wouldn't have to answer the officer's questions.

Where's Dad? Did they have him in custody already?

I'm cornered, and my only hope is to cooperate, but play dumb at the same time. I kinda wish I'd taken my stress pills now. I inhale deeply and slowly release my breath. Cornelius is always telling me to do that to calm myself.

Does it make me look guilty?

"What can I do for you, officer?" I manage to say without stuttering.

My hands are cold and clammy. I stick them into my pockets so I don't draw attention to them. I refuse to look down. I won't give anything away.

"Can you please take your hands out of your pockets very slowly and keep them where I can see them?" the officer asks.

"Yes sir," I mouth, but no sound comes out; so much for not drawing attention. I jerk my hands out and unclench my fists.

"Christofer Halley?" he asks.

I nod in the affirmative. This is it; I spent the last hours of freedom sleeping in my bunk.

"Please respond verbally for the record."

"Yes, sir. I am Christofer Halley, sir."

"I have come about you father, Cornelius."

I cut him off.

"He's not here right now, but he never takes off his locater, so you should be able to find him easily enough. He's still in the city, most likely near the Ring, you know, in the middle of town. Of course, you know, the government offices are only a stone's throw away. Actually, I can call him for you right now," I blurt out in one breath.

"That won't be necessary."

"Ah, okay." I stare at the man, waiting for his next words.

Did they apprehend Dad already? Is he here to arrest me?

"I regret to inform you that Cornelius Halley was the unfortunate victim of a shooting today in the upper level, between the fourth and fifth transit tubes. He could not be revived and was pronounced dead at the scene."

"What?" I shake my head and look the man in the eyes. "That makes no sense. Why would he even go there? I'm sorry, you must be wrong." Dad was going into the city because of business at the Ring. He would never go out between the farms. He hates that area. There's nothing there, except greenhouses.

"We have no leads at this time, but we will keep you updated on our investigation."

"No, you didn't hear me. This can't be right." My insides evaporate, leaving me feeling like an inflated spacesuit with an empty interior.

"My guess is that he fell in with the wrong lot of people. Do you know why anyone would want to do him harm?"

Through my blurry vision, I notice the officer is eying me like *I'm* a suspect.

"No, no one would want to hurt Dad. Are you sure? He sort of looks like every other middle-aged guy."

"It's him." The officer answers emphatically. He's staring at me. In the holovids, the police always ask for more information and they like to record the whole conversation. He's done nothing other than take off his visor. Shouldn't he at least say that he's sorry for my loss? Instead, he's staring at me like he's some sort of predator.

"Can you tell me anything else?"

"He was shot in the torso from behind at close range with an old Earth style handgun. He made a right big mess in the corridor. They're probably just now finishing up the cleaning." He eyes me with a deadly serious expression.

Why would he mention that?

My mouth is suddenly very dry as I try to summon up saliva.

He's probably trying to decide if I need to be eliminated, too.

Where did that thought come from? My pulse races as I go into survival mode. How do I get myself out of this encounter?

Unplanned tears well up in my eyes and I launch into helpless child mode. I jut out my lower lip and sniff my nose loudly.

"B-b-but what will I do now?" My instincts tell me to look as pitiful and weak as I can.

"Well, you obviously can't fly this thing by yourself," he says dismissively. "Do you have somewhere to go?"

So, he doesn't know about my pilot's license. Thank the stars for my fake left arm. I dry my eyes with it. My right arm would shake so much that I'd end up smacking myself in the face.

There's not a microgram of compassion from him.

"My, my mom," I stammer some more. "She is an organics technician at Huygens Crater. Uh, Anna Vennemann is her name," I say through trembling lips. It's not fear exactly; it's more like nervous system overload.

A satisfied smirk settles on his face for just a second.

"Then I think you should book a flight to Huygens and let her handle what becomes of this ship. Muckraking may not be glamorous, but I've never heard of anyone dying from it."

He's sneering at me now! He's taken everything from me, and now he stands there gloating at my misery. I lower my head to hide my defiance.

"Can… can I have your name, sir?" I say as timidly as I can.

"It's Officer Barnett."

"And how will I be able to get in contact with you? You know, if I'm able to help with this case."

"Contact the police station."

Really? He's not even going to tell me which substation?

"Yes, sir. Let me get my things and I'll contact Mom as soon as I can—today, for sure."

"You've had quite a shot, er, shock to your system." He smiles at his slip of the tongue. "Sleep on it tonight, if you must. But it's best to move on to the next phase of your life. No sense wallowing in the past." He looks at me one last time before mentally dismissing me.

"I think I'm going to be sick!" I blurt as I run down the corridor. I can't stomach his presence anymore. I lean against the bulkhead for a second before I realize I wasn't lying. I deposit my food wafers all over the floor. The inner airlock door closes. I feel a little relief that the man is going away, but I have so many questions.

I go straight to the cockpit and look at the security feed. He's putting on his helmet, so he must be leaving.

I can't control myself anymore. I think of Dad as my bitter tears spill over the console.

* * *

"First things first, Chris," I say out loud to myself. I remove the front screw from the base of the captain's chair. I tip the chair backwards from its perch and reveal our emergency box. Right on top is the handgun that Dad pointed at Vikram just a few days ago. This is only the second time I've ever seen the gun. Dad's will and a credit chip are the only items in the box.

I insert them into the console.

"Um, AI, Dad is . . . Cornelius Halley is deceased. Please take care of the items on these chips."

"Processing. The will leaves the *Halley Traveler* and all of Cornelius Halley's worldly possessions to his son, Christofer Halley. Do you wish to receive ownership?"

The AI asks a half dozen other questions, but I don't remember any of them. The credit chip has a meager seven hundred credits on it. I can't even get a decent PCD for that.

It just seems so obscene that the sum of a man's life could be confined to the contents of one tiny storage box.

We were in a much tighter bind than I ever would have guessed. I feel a little guilty about nagging for a new PCD. But how could I have known?

My eyes start leaking again, and my shoulders shake. "No, no, no!" I shout. "I can't afford this right now!" My emotions don't care and they demand a release. I finally give in and allow the tears to flow again. My shoulders constrict so tight that I wonder how I am even able to breathe. My ribs are throbbing and my syn-skin is peeling because of how tightly I'm gripping my fake arm, but I don't care. I let my grief have its time. It's not as if I could stop it, anyway.

Once the emotional waves recede to mere ripples, I sit up straight. I can't call him Dad. Just saying that word brings on more tears. Cornelius, that's what I'll call him now. For some reason it doesn't hurt as much to use his name. Later I'll take the time to work through it, but right now I have to figure out what to do. If I have to run for it, I can, once I figure out a safe place. Tonight, I don't dare leave the ship and I'm in no condition to fly.

My self-pity gives way to anger. I can use anger; sitting around feeling sorry for myself won't accomplish anything. I will get revenge for Da . . . Cornelius' murder, or die trying. I start pacing the ship. How will I get revenge?

Where do I start?

I have no idea, so I finish my chores.

CHAPTER 10 CHRIS

Asimov Crater Space Park

The AI contacts mother in no time. The connection is text only, which is weird, but I go with it.

"Yes, ma'am, I am the son of James Stecht. I am seventeen years old, and I believe that makes me your son as well," I say politely. The computer will transcribe my words automatically. "No, ma'am, I'm not looking for a handout. I am living independently now and I just want a chance to know my mother." At the rate the text is appearing, she's likely having her voice transcribed as well. Why? Why can't we just talk to one another?

The holoscreen blinks on and a disheveled woman with stringy grayish-brown hair comes into view.

"Where's that father of yours?" She barks.

"We parted ways." It's technically true.

"You'll not get a free meal from me. I have my own to feed. I can't go around throwing away good food vouchers."

"That's more than okay . . . Ma'am." I'm not sure I want to call her mother.

She nods to herself. "Meet me at the Martian Sunset during free time tonight." The connection is broken at once.

Not even a goodbye? Anna Venomous indeed.

"This is going to be a complete disaster," I say out loud to no one.

Am I going crazy?

* * *

It takes Mars twenty-four hours and thirty-eight minutes to complete one rotation. Since the original Martians kept the Earth way of telling time, the last partial hour is labeled free time and that's when everyone blows off steam. Cornelius and I usually slept through it, but here at Huygens, it is a big deal. The Martian Sunset is some sort of lounge, and it is packed. There's an empty stage tonight, and the music is piped in, though it's drowned out by the crowd.

The lights are very bright, and people are much too close for my liking. I long to go back to the quiet of our... no, *my* ship. My palms are sweaty and this meeting can't get over soon enough. I claim a barstool and hold on as if people were going to tear me away.

Why am I so worked up about meeting her? She's a nasty woman and I'll probably never see her again. "Probably because she is the very last connection I have with anyone in this world," I say aloud. I have to stop doing that. The bartender approaches. He must have thought I was speaking to him.

"I'll have a Darwin spritzer, please."

A kid several years younger with light brown skin approaches me. "Hi, I'm Alex!"

"Okay, why are you here?" I say a little gruffly. I'm not very social on my best days.

"I'm supposed to steal anything you have of value, if I can." He makes the confession with a smile.

"Really? And why would you want to do that?" I'm amused despite myself. I also have nothing of value except one measly credit chip.

"I don't really, but Mom wants me to try. She says you'll be an easy mark." The kid tilts his head, leans into my personal space and whispers, "Besides, it's not every day that I get to meet my half-brother." He beams.

"Huh?" I understand each individual word, but when they're all put together, they confuse me. I stand up and I'm a whole head taller than he is.

"Yeah, Mom was all worked up after you called. She couldn't decide if she should be nice and try to steal you back from your father or yell at you for leaving."

"I was an infant!"

He nods in sympathy. "I think she realized she would have to give up some of her food credits to win you over, and she'd never do that. So she's decided to get whatever she can from you instead."

"She sounds charming."

"Yeah, not so much." He scratches his chin. There's no sign of facial hair. "She likes to sell my vouchers so she can buy expensive stuff for herself. I don't really mind though. I can get my meals from tons of people I know on the street."

"She doesn't provide food for you?" I ask, perplexed.

"Well, not usually. If she gets sick, she'll loosen up some so that I'll stay and take care of her." He answers without even a hint of outrage.

"How old are you, Alex?"

"Sixteen and a half."

"No, how old are you really?"

"I'm sixteen! I'm fourteen months younger than you," he says, irritated.

I like him, so I let the question of his real age go.

"Do you want to help me get this meeting with our mother over so we can hang out after she leaves?" I look sidelong at him and then flash a smile that any troublemaker would know.

"Play along," I say quietly.

He smiles back. Meeting him made this whole trip worthwhile.

"What the hell are you trying to pull?" I raise my chip high in the air, way out of his reach. "You're a little thief! Where are the authorities when you need them?" I shout and begin looking around the room.

He starts to laugh and winks at me before turning to run away through the crowd. I start to smile at Alex's back. She'll no doubt approach me next, since her son failed to rob me. That quashes my good spirits. I wait patiently for my monster of a mother to arrive.

"Do you always try to beat up kids half your size?"

Could you not try to put me on the defensive from the start?

Somehow, I knew this conversation would be a disaster. I decide to come out swinging.

"The little thief was trying to steal my credits. Clearly his parent failed to beat some good Martian manners into him. Only Earthers expect something for nothing."

"Well, you have a backbone and sure as Martian soil is red, you got that from me." She looks at me like she's appraising some gadget. She turns towards the bar. "Your father was all soft and weak. No place on Mars for weak men. That's what I told him."

I keep my anger in check. I won't give her the satisfaction of a response. I stare straight ahead at the bar as well.

"Let me have a look at you. You're much taller than your half-brother." She gives me a hard look. "I know that little shit decided to have a heart-to-heart talk with you instead of doing what he was told. I can't count on him for anything."

I swallow back the bile. With an inoffensive tone, I ask, "So, I'm new at this. How's life been for you, Mom?"

Most awkward sentence I have ever uttered in my life.

"Mom? Don't you Mom me! Your good-for-nothing father came like a common thief and stole you away from me. It was the only ballsy thing he ever did, no doubt. Honestly, I didn't think he had it in him." Her anguish at losing her firstborn child is completely absent.

"I should call you Anna then?" I say sourly.

"There's the sad sack routine that your father perfected." She snaps her fingers in my face and smiles a mirthless grin. "Sorry, it only worked once on me and it will never work again. So why don't you tell me why you're here?" She looks at me, dead serious.

"Dad's dead," I say, surprising myself. I made a promise that she would have to earn that information and now I lead with it?

What's wrong with me?

"I'm not sure why I'm here," I say. "I'm not sure what I expected."

"Dead? At 43? Let me guess, he got into trouble way over his head. What was it: gambling, alcohol, or drugs? I never doubted that he would find a bad end. He wasn't Martian strong."

Who knew she could make me hate her even more?

"Yep, that pretty much sums it up." Bile stings my tonsils. What she calls weakness I know to be kindness. Only a callous bitch wouldn't know the difference. "Sorry I made you come out. You are exactly the woman Dad described." I turn my back to her and lunge off the stool. The crowd drowns out her bitter retorts.

Someone barges into me. "Check your right pocket," Alex says before disappearing again. I find a note written on a napkin. I look around and see a big gleaming smile on my half-brother's face. He points to the napkin.

I smile back. Maybe it wasn't a complete waste of time.

> *Hi again. Next time, contact me directly. Mom can be a little nasty at times.*
>
> *Alex*

"That's the truth!" I say out loud . . . again.

I think about inviting Alex to live on the ship with me. It sure would piss off our mother and I sure could use a friend, but what would he be like three months from now? Would I be doing it solely to spite her? What happens if he grates on my nerves? I don't really like a lot of people. My mind churns over these new thoughts.

Before I go down this path, there are still things I need to do. I retreat to *Halley's* cockpit and come up with a three-part plan. It would be best if I completed steps two and three before even thinking about bringing Alex on board.

* * *

There is a message waiting for me back on my ship. I hit reply without thinking and the video feed connects me to Vikram.

"Uh, hello Chris. I was looking for your Dad. I have a business opportunity to discuss. What can I do for you?"

I wanted to talk to Vikram, but only after I figured out what to say. Instead, I blurt out the first thing that comes to mind.

"I have to talk to you about Cornelius. He was shot and killed by a dirty cop named Barnett yesterday." I manage to say it without tearing up. It's imperative that Vikram not think of me as weak.

"What? Wait, that can't be right." Vikram looks genuinely surprised. Some of the tension eases out of my shoulders.

"Can I meet with you? I would like to discuss the situation in person."

"Good idea kid, are you on your ship?"

I let the kid remark slide.

"I am on my ship, but it's at Huygens right this moment. I can be back at Asimov in ninety minutes. It'll take me half an hour to suit up and get inside, but we can meet then." My heart is racing. Will he still meet with me if I make him wait that long?

"Don't suit up. I will be out to see you sometime tonight," he says.

I rub my eyes so he can't see the relief on my face.

"I'll go through my newly established contacts and see what I can find out. We will get to the bottom of this, I promise you."

Not trusting myself to speak, I nod and break the connection.

CHAPTER 11   VIKRAM

Asimov City

I told Keev that I'd be coming, and like a good lap dog, he's waiting in the middle of the Ring to greet me. Keev insists on sleeping in his store. Everyone else locks up and goes home for the night. His excuse is that he is in the center of town and claims that his location allows him to be the first to know.

In this backwater place, what's worth knowing? He has the entire Ring under surveillance through the use of directional mics with language algorithms to wade through all the daily conversations for any microgram of intelligence. It's a solid plan and one I will put to use when I set up my base of operations in a more suitable city.

"For what do I have the honor of this late-night visit?" he asks.

"I need you to provide me with a couple of goons. Ones that don't mind getting their hands dirty."

"I can get you two rather quickly. They owe their continued existence to me."

"Don't stand around looking for gratitude," I say

"I'm sending the calls out now. They should be here in about ten minutes."

"Good. Now find me an out of the way location where I can perform an interrogation."

"Who are you going to interrogate?"

"I'll get to him in a bit." I look up at the rough, red ceiling. This city is intolerable. I lived in squalor on Earth, and I demand much more from Martian cities. I will be surrounded by luxury, as my station demands. "Right now, all I require is a quiet location, for several days potentially."

"The old Davidson farm is abandoned until the ownership can be figured out. It's reasonably close and there's no reason for anyone to go down that corridor until the legalities are settled."

"Good. Now, how long will it take for Officer Barnett to arrive?"

"You didn't say to call him," Keev says. "I'll do it right now. Who will he be interrogating?"

"No. I didn't say to call him. I asked how long it would take him to respond to your summons."

"Since he's probably sleeping, I would say about twenty minutes," Keev responds.

"Call him and tell him it's an urgent matter."

"What's going on?" Keev asks.

I stare at the walls as a response. I'm the one who asks the questions. Keev has been left unsupervised for too long if he thinks he's due answers. He nods and disappears back into his shop. My intel is correct. Keev will always avoid direct confrontation.

*   *   *

Barnett arrives looking bedraggled and wearing mismatching clothes. He knows better than to keep us waiting. It's a pity really, he would have served me well.

"What's all the excitement about?" Barnett asks, surveying our group.

"We have an interrogation to start," I say.

"Who?"

I raise my knockout gun and shoot him in the forehead. The tiny gel ball splatters on contact and the instant sedative absorbs into his skin. He furrows his eyebrows in confusion for a second and touches the spot before falling on his face.

"I can't have Barnett shot here! His locater is on and the authorities will know he was here," Keev says. "I will be the prime suspect in his disappearance."

"Well, I'm also going to task you with finding a new cop to put on the payroll. You'll be very diligent with that task, won't you? Maybe even have him run the investigation into Barnett's death."

"I don't work for you," the shopkeeper says.

"No, I guess since these two witnesses and I will tell the authorities that you shot Barnett, you won't be working for anyone."

Keev looks at his goons.

"You two work for me now," I tell them. "I'll double your pay."

"It's just like this man said," the short one tells Keev. "You shot him right in the forehead."

Keev stares up at the ugly ceiling as if he's wanting divine aid.

"Pick him up and carry him like he's been out all night drinking," I tell my goons.

I turn my attention back to Keev only to find that he's disappeared into the back of his shop. No doubt he has a bolt hole. If he's smart, he'll show up where there are a lot of witnesses and make sure that he's noticed. If he's stupid, he'll run away and I'll have to find and terminate him. Time will tell. Once they get Barnett up, I remove his PCD, smash it, and hand it to the taller of my recently acquired goons.

"When you get there, check for any weapons or communication devices he may possess. Make sure you get real familiar with him. There can be no mistakes. After that, make sure he is tied up tightly. I'll meet you there."

The men do a passable job at staggering down the halls. I follow them at a safe distance, always staying in the shadows, just like old times.

* * *

The farms on Mars are tiny compared to Earth. Most are on the surface to take advantage of whatever sunlight they can get. All are laid out in rectangles, with tracks running chest high up on the long walls. What looks like a modified soccer goal runs along the track with hoses attached to it. The hoses run to the nutrient vat set in the corner. There is no wasted space. The ground has been tilled into neat rows, with withered, knee-high plants marring the scene. That confirms that no one has been here in a while. I have my goons move the vat to the center and restrain Barnett there.

I can't very well have Barnett telling everyone I put the hit out on Cornelius. And if he thought he had nothing to lose, that's exactly what he would do. My old boss, Manish, was a master at reading others' loyalty and reacting first, except, of course, when it came to me. He always told me that my decisiveness was my biggest strength. I thanked him for his final piece of advice before I replaced him as head of Chennai Botanicals.

"You can't rule through fear alone," he told me the night he died. "People will either become despondent or defiant under the constant yoke of fear. You have to allow them hope. Hope will sustain people for a very long time. Some will even cling to it for their entire miserable lives. Always let those you want to control believe they can reach their goals; then they'll stay compliant."

He was right; I believed I could reach my goals. My vid meeting with Kenova tells me she's much the same. She doesn't care about my methods, only results. One day she'll come to praise me in person and I'll promote myself again.

* * *

The goons set Barnett up in a sitting position. They gag and tie him in place. I confirm for myself that his wrists and ankles are secured before I slap the officer a couple of times.

He rolls his head to the side and blinks his eyes repeatedly.

"You've let too much information slip out and now your name is being mentioned in the murder of that Halley guy."

His head falls down and he wiggles side to side as he tries to regain his motor control.

"His son is telling everyone that you did it. Luckily, I got to him before he could shout his very true accusations to officials not in my employ."

His eyes bulge out and he tries to talk through his gag.

"Shhh, none of that," I say. "You are going to have to prove that you can be trustworthy. In a few minutes, I'm going to have my goons get some information out of you. The code phrase is 'Operation Red Dust Storm,' and whatever you do, do not give them that phrase. Think of this as your punishment and your test all wrapped into one."

He nods energetically.

I instruct the bigger goon to rough Barnett up until he gives up the information I want. He can beat him to unconsciousness for all I care, but Barnett is not to be killed in the next three hours. The other one I send for more props. The kid should be back by now. It's time to collect my audience for this sham interrogation.

CHAPTER 12   CHRIS

Asimov Crater Space Park

A solitary person approaches the airlock. The spacesuit isn't the official green of law enforcement, and the person is limping, so it must be Vikram.

"A guest is at the port airlock," the AI says cheerfully.

"AI, let the visitor enter the airlock." I have to be precise or who knows what the AI will do.

"Confirmed."

"AI, who is the visitor?" I ask just to be safe.

"Based on the facial database, the visitor is Vikram surname unknown. Shall I let him enter the ship?"

"No, I'll open the inner door manually."

I can't help but fidget as I hustle on my way. The outer doors are just closing. I slap the control hard enough to make my hand sting. The indicator flashes to let me know the air pressure has finished equalizing.

Take a breath. You can't make the process go any faster.

"That didn't take long," I lie. I automatically move to unfasten his suit.

"Close the door," Vikram says, pushing past me into the ship. Cleaning the dust from the interior of the ship will be a nightmare.

"Tell me what happened and don't leave anything out," Vikram demands.

I relive the whole awful event.

"My sources confirm your story," Vikram says.

"So I'm right, he *did* kill Cornelius."

"Yeah, I'm afraid so," Vikram replies with a distracted air. "The real question is for what reason? Would your dad have had any contraband on him?" He looks at me.

I stare back blankly and shake my head.

"Sorry, my mind is drifting to other problems. You did real good, kid. Your instincts were right, if you would have mouthed off an accusation at him . . ." He shakes his head. "Don't worry, we'll get to the bottom of this."

"My name is Chris." The fury builds in my voice. "I'm not a kid and I insist on getting my revenge."

"Look, I'm sorry about your dad, but let me take care of this. He'll get the justice he deserves."

"You don't understand," I say. "I am going to go after him, no matter what. You can join with me or hope I don't screw up any of your plans. The only thing I have right now is revenge. So either I'm part of this or I strike out on my own." I say it all without emotion. These are just the facts.

Vikram studies me for a while.

"You're in luck then; I've already secured him. I need to get whatever information I can. After that, you can watch him be eliminated."

"You have him already? When were you going to tell me that?"

Vikram is unconcerned. "I needed to get your pulse first. Now, if you'll come with me, you can see that Officer Barnett gets what he deserves."

"No," I say. "I want to observe the interrogation. After your men are finished, I want a chance to ask my own questions. When I'm satisfied, I get to kill him."

"The questions we're asking aren't for you to hear."

"I will kill him or die trying. If you value me and my nice shiny ship, you will give me this."

Vikram studies me silently. My heart pounds as I wait for his reply.

"I could use some credits thrown my way. After Officer Barnett is eliminated, we can sort out our business relationship," I offer.

"You'll throw your lot in with me?"

"I can do that; but only after Barnett gets what he deserves."

"It could get pretty grisly at the end. You sure you want to be there?"

"That's my price. I want him to suffer for his crime." I can taste victory.

"You'll be given your chance, but kid, in my experience, killing a man isn't as easy as you seem to think."

In my excitement, I let the 'kid' comment go. "Done! Oh, and I want to be able to kill him with the same weapon he used to kill Cornelius," I add.

"I have one more stipulation myself," Vikram says. "You will transport whatever cargo I want to have shipped. None of this right of refusal that your Dad insisted upon."

"No way. If I get caught, I'm the one getting charged with a capital crime. No human trafficking, no explosives, and no hard drugs."

Vikram smiles. "You act much older than you look. I can live with that for now."

* * *

"This is the old Davidson farm," I blurt out. "Jeff Davidson and I used to play here when we were little. One of the habdome walls was pierced when he was in here alone. The cloth is four ply and tough as it gets, but once there's a hole, the surge of air will rip it into shreds. They say he ran to plug the leak instead of running for safety, but the force of the escaping air caused the habdome cloth to rip before he could get to it. He ended up being blown out onto the surface. After his death, his mother lost her marbles and took her own life. Nobody's been here since they patched the hole."

"I told Keev to find a spot where we won't be bothered," Vikram volunteers. "This will do nicely."

"The people of Asimov are convinced this place is cursed. That's why it's been vacant for so long. I bet you could get it for a really cheap price." I'm not really paying attention to what I'm saying. It just feels nice to be able to talk to another human, even if the person is Vikram.

"Since you mentioned it, I'm pretty pleased with the location. The farm has been abandoned, and it's going up for auction next week. I should have my coffee beans on the ground within ten days. It's also real close to another piece of property I have recently acquired."

He must mean Bill Ferny's place. It's the only other vacant farm. I have no idea why he won't come out and say it. Everyone knew about his troubles. It was just a matter of time before Bill lost everything gambling. No one wished bad things upon him, but we all know that there is no safety net. As the saying goes, "you only deserve what you can make for yourself."

Using big money to buy two long vacated farms will get people talking. Whether Vikram knows it or not, he's making big waves in Asimov already.

* * *

Officer Barnett is propped in a sitting position in the middle of a room made with clear, low grade habdome cloth. It's not made to be a barrier against the outside, but it does nicely at dividing rooms. The trapped air bubbles in the cloth even help dampen noise.

"My goons," Vikram says, matter-of-fact, "have been working him over for the last couple hours. If he doesn't break soon, he never will."

Vikram's men have overly wrinkly skin.

"You must have found them hanging out at the Kunselman obdome."

"Why would you say that?"

"Because you don't get wrinkles like that unless you're stuck making your own vitamin D in unfiltered sunlight."

Vikram gives me a curious look. Did he think I was some empty-headed fool?

People who are stuck going there have nothing to lose. Cancer is a given. Even working for Vikram is better. Of course, I just agreed to work for him too, but that's different, somehow. I'll figure out why later.

"They're cheap too," Vikram says. "There's a common refrain back on Earth: will work for food."

He seems very pleased to have picked up the dregs of Asimov for his team. Barnett's head slumps down, so he waves his men to come away from the murderer.

"Now I know what we said, kid, er, Chris, but if you can't or won't go through with it, my men won't hesitate to finish the job."

"I'll be fine," I say. I point at the camera they set up in the corner of the makeshift room. "Now I want you to record my conversation with him as well. Where is his gun?"

"Uh, Chris, you don't understand. I only brought you here so you could finish him off. He won't talk, and I mean at all. No idle chatting, no misdirection, only silence punctuated by a few screams. I have no idea what drives this guy, but it's impressive. My guys have beaten him unconscious any number of times. It would be best if you finished him off now before he wakes."

"He has to be awake. I need for him to know that I am his executioner. I don't care if he talks, but he does need to suffer, then he needs to die. I'll make a wager with you though, I bet I can at least get him to speak to me."

"There's nothing you can do to him that my men haven't already tried."

"Then bet me."

"He's already suffered plenty. What else could you possibly do to him?"

"I will give him hope, and he will dare to think he has a future. Then I will take away everything, just like he did to me."

Vikram compresses his lips, but I can see his eyes sparkle. He's intrigued enough to let me have my chance.

"Now, has he been facing in that direction the whole time?"

"He has." Vikram is bemused. He extends his arm and gestures for me to go ahead. "Both of his guns are on that table behind him."

Vikram is a man of his word. His men escort me into the room. There's no ceiling, but that doesn't matter. The room smells like piss and sweat and blood—all of it from Officer Barrett.

Is this what justice smells like?

I shake the thought out of my head. He deserves to die in a place like this. Behind him, on the sprayer track, are his guns. One is an antique Earther gun and the other a stun gun. The ground is hard and the little hills between the rows of dead plants flatten when I step on them. I grab the weapons and hold them up. Did he use both on Cornelius? I hope he stunned Cornelius, so there wasn't any pain at the end.

My vision goes blurry and I have to bite my lip to bring myself back to the present. There will be no crying in Officer Barnett's presence.

The bigger goon slaps Barnett to see if he's responsive. There's no reaction. I walk behind the chair and they move to flank me. I give them a brief glance and dismiss them.

"I need you to leave now and don't come back until he's dead."

They look to Vikram for guidance and he waves them out of the temporary room.

I sit on the ground behind Officer Barnett quietly for twenty minutes until he starts to stir.

"Sir! Sir, are you awake now?" I say in a frightened voice.

Barnett shakes his head to clear the cobwebs.

"Mister, are you awake?" I whisper urgently.

"Huh? Who's there? You bastards! Why don't you just finish it? I have nothing to say to you," he growls.

"Mister, are you okay? Where did they go? Are they coming back?"

"Who's there? Come here so I can see you," he barks.

"I can't. I'm scared. They are bad men. Are they coming back?"

He takes a breath to compose himself.

"I'm sorry for yelling. As you can see, I've had a bad day." He says with exaggerated patience as he tries to lift his arms. "If you help me get out of this, I promise I will get you out of here before they come back."

I smile. He's starting to formulate a plan. And with that plan comes hope.

"No. I'm too scared," I say. I have to give him more time to believe his plan will work.

"It's okay." He tries to sound soothing. He's not very good at it. "Now listen here. Did they leave anything in this room?"

I'm able to get my lip to tremble as I say, "I'm under the equipment, behind you. I saw two pistols, I think, before I hid. One is white and one is all metal."

"Those are my pistols. Now they might be coming back soon, so you need to bring me the metal pistol right now, okay?"

"Where did you get it?" I ask. I'm toying with him now. He only has a couple more minutes to live, but he doesn't know it.

"Kid, I'm a policeman. Now bring the gun to me and I'll keep us both safe."

"It's heavier than I thought."

"Yeah, it's a .44 caliber. Now, I need you to focus, kid. What's your name?"

"Homer. My dad said he liked epics, so he named me after one of them."

"No, he named you after the poet who wrote them. Homer was the poet who wrote The Iliad and The Odyssey."

"My father taught me a little bit of the Iliad, I think."

I can see him straining to hear my footfalls.

"Tell me what you remember while you bring me the gun."

"The poem starts with, 'Sing to me, oh Muse, of the wrath of Achilles,' I think."

"We don't want any more wrath here, do we?" He laughs a noisy, phlegm filled laugh.

"Not yet." Maybe it's blood, not phlegm. I hope so.

"You said it, kid. Do you have the pistol?"

"Yes sir. I think you knew my father."

"I know a lot of people." I can hear the confidence growing in his voice. "What's your dad's name?"

"I think you talked to him a few days ago."

"If I did, then I like him. I didn't have a single bad conversation this month until today. What's your dad's name?" The cheerfulness in his voice makes me want to club him, but I stick to my plan.

"Cornelius Halley," I say flatly. "Now feel my wrath." I grab his hair and yank his head backwards until he's staring upward at my chin. I look down at him as I place the pistol up firm against his temple. As recognition dawns on his face, his eyes go wide. He opens his mouth to speak, but I can't listen to that voice ever again.

I close my eyes and fire. There's a deafening blast and I'm showered in tiny, wet bits of Officer Barnett. I wipe my face with the back of my left hand and look down at my handiwork.

I'm still holding his hair and the back of his skull attached to it. The wall opposite Vikram and his men is sprayed red with other bits mixed in.

That must be his brains and little bits of bones.

In the absolute silence that follows, it feels like time is standing still. Below me, the top half of Barnett's head is gone, though the skin from his forehead is covering most of his face.

I wonder if he still has that look of terror.

I see the goons running toward me, but I can't hear anything but a ringing in my ears.

Earth was devastated by a double punch of volcanic activity and the inevitable crop failures that followed in 2203 and 2204. Mass rioting caused the first wave of Earthers to flee and these few, the first New Martians, were allowed entry, although grudgingly. The second and much larger wave would have overwhelmed our fragile Martian resources. We had no recourse but to deny them entry into our cities. Untold thousands of Earthers were left to starve. The Great Stranding, as it came to be known, capped off 2204, the worst year in human history.

The Great Stranding
Dennis Parrish, Ph.D.

CHAPTER 13   CHRIS

Asimov City

I look down at my clothes. I'm covered in blood, brains and bone fragments. I should feel happy, but I just feel numb. Dad's murder has been avenged.

Is it wrong to not be happy?

I smile slightly and look up at an incredulous Vikram as he approaches. His eyes flick between me and Barnett's slumping corpse.

"What the hell was all of that? Just walk around to the front of him so he knows who his killer is and pull the trigger. That's all. There is no need for this whimpering child bullshit." He continues to look at me, uncomprehending. "Why didn't you just shoot him in the chest?"

His complaining makes me jubilant, just for spite. My smile widens and my teeth are showing. I never show my teeth.

"I told you," I say slowly. "Your method beat the crap out of him. The only way for me to hurt him was to give him hope and then take it away," I explain. "Besides, he kept calling me kid. I'm not a kid anymore." My smile feels like it's frozen in place. I'm on some type of high, a horror-laced euphoric high.

"No, you're definitely not a child anymore," Vikram agrees, as he quickly disarms me.

I bet he stops calling me kid now.

"How are you going to dispose of the body and the guns?"

Vikram covers his face with his hand and pushes it through his wavy black hair.

"The guns are no problem. I was going to have the body dumped on the outskirts of town. But a man missing the back half of his head is bound to draw attention." Vikram fixes me with a disapproving stare. "The obvious pride you have in wearing Barnett's cranial ejecta is misplaced. You can't just walk back to the hangar like that."

"You said your greenhouse is near here. Let's take him there and you can use him as fertilizer like any good Martian would," I say helpfully. "Besides, anybody shot dead will cause a commotion here. Nobody but the police have old Earth style guns. Those bullets will rip right through habdome cloth, killing everyone in that city compartment."

Vikram studies me for a second and throws his hands in the air. I have no idea why he's so flummoxed. "We'll bury him here. That way, we don't need to move the body and I'll control the evidence. I just have to place the winning bid at auction."

With that decided, he settles down and looks at me again. "I guess you rate a little help from me. But I'm warning you, this euphoria you're feeling won't last. You are going to want to get very drunk. With any luck, you won't remember this night. In fact, I would recommend getting as drunk as you can—in private." It feels odd to have Vikram wanting to help me. "Then there's still the problem of your shirt." He gives me another sour look.

"Why don't I just rub some dirt on it? Maybe from your coffee farm?" I don't know why I'm so transfixed on Vikram's coffee farm right now, but it is where my gut is pushing me to go.

"No, I need to ensure you make it safely back to your ship. But first, you made this mess, so you can help clean it up. Here's the key. Now get those cuffs off of him."

* * *

Vikram's men work on digging the hole. I willingly grab a leg and help bring Officer Barnett to his final, ignoble resting place. I'm exhausted by the time we move the body three meters. I yawn expansively. We drop him on his back without any pretense or ceremony. It's exactly what he deserves.

138

"Chris, take off your shirt and throw it on top of Barnett. It must never be seen again."

I nod my thanks to Vikram and do as I'm bid. The circulating air hits the sheen of sweat on my shoulders and gives me the chills. I rub my arms for warmth and can't seem to stop.

"Start shoveling the dirt on top of him while I make sure my men clean up the scene," Vikram says.

That does it. I just need something to do, that's all. I scoop up a shovel of dirt and turn to see Barnett's soulless eyes stare blankly up at me. I throw the dirt at his feet. I manage to cover the body up to his waist before I have to take a break. I'm not just tired; my muscles are achy for some reason. I'm sweating like crazy, yet my skin feels cool and clammy.

"Tonight Chris! We need to have this finished before people get up and start milling around." His voice surprises me. I jump up and continue my work.

I make it up to his chest. The only part left uncovered is his face. My real arm starts shaking uncontrollably while my fake arm remains rock steady. I can't manage to keep any dirt on the shovel, no matter how hard I try. I drop the shovel and turn to confront Barnett.

"You're dead!" I yell at the impassive face. "Stop looking at me! You started this! If you would have just done your job, your real, official job, you could still have your own miserable life! But no, you had to be evil. And now you've paid for it, so stop looking at me!" I scream between sobs. My shoulders shake as

I take one ragged breath after another. I fall to the ground in a heap. "Stop looking at me," I plead almost inaudibly.

* * *

My arm is around someone's shoulder and he's helping me walk down a corridor.

"Dad?"

"Okay, I got you. Just lean on me, there you go," Vikram says calmly. "This is good, kid, if you didn't have a breakdown; you'd be psychotic."

"I have to finish the job," I say without conviction. "The body has to be hidden."

"My men will take care of it. For now, we have to get you back to your ship."

"Dad is going to be pissed at me for staying out so late." I look at Vikram with my unfocused eyes. "Do you think we can sneak into the ship without him noticing?"

"How do you feel about being kissed by me?" he asks.

"What?"

"The only way I can see this working is if you lean on me and I make it look like I'm going to take advantage of a young, drunken fool. Nobody will like it, but it's not like it doesn't happen with some regularity."

"Whatever."

"Now just lean on me and stagger a little. No, not like that; try dragging your feet a bit, but not too much."

So many instructions; why is he so annoyed with me?

"Just try to not fall down," he says.

"I just want to stop seeing his eyes."

"No talking. In fact, don't make eye contact with anyone. I'll be playing my part, so just try to ignore me." He kisses my nose gently. "Good job. This can't get over fast enough for either one of us."

***

I open my eyes and realize I'm in a spacesuit. I roll over on my back and I'm in the *Halley*'s port airlock. I check my suit's sensors. The air is good outside the suit.

Getting out of a bulky spacesuit by yourself is a slow, cumbersome process. It gives me time to remember the horror of last night. I look down at my bare chest and pants sprinkled with blood. Any hope that last night was just a terrible dream is squashed.

I check the blinking alarm in front of my face. The suit only has twenty minutes of oxygen left. "What the hell, Vikram?" I say to the empty airlock. I could have asphyxiated in my suit while surrounded by a perfectly good atmosphere.

Dammit! He could have at least taken my visor off instead of just dumping me here and hoping for the best.

I take off my pants. I'm going to have to incinerate them just to be safe. The teflo-polycottonate blend is touted to be virtually stain free, but I don't think I should chance it. I take a long, wholly unsatisfying sonic shower. The steam pulses are relaxing, but not very useful for removing stuff from my hair.

I head back to my quarters and search for a decent replacement. The only ones I find are two years old and are skin tight from hips to ankles.

"Right, I'm going to have to buy myself new clothes."

I gaze at myself in the mirror. This is what a murderer looks like. I press all over my body to make sure it's really me. I still have pieces of Barnett stuck in my hair, so I guess it's two murderers in the mirror, technically.

Vikram didn't do anything more with me than he absolutely had to do. He was either clueless about me asphyxiating, or he was okay with it. So it's safe to say that we're not friends. We're conspirators. He must still need me for something or else I could have just as easily ended up in the hole with Officer . . . that guy. Just thinking about last night makes me queasy. It's time to get back to real life.

"AI, what time is it?"

"It is oh nine, thirty-seven hours."

"I guess I need to know how low the bank account is before I go buying new clothes."

Great, still talking out loud to myself.

I log into our account. Well, that money wasn't there yesterday.

Maybe this is the result of a never-mentioned but lucrative life insurance policy that Cornelius had? The first three digits of the account should denote from where the funds were transferred. I pride myself on knowing the code from each city. This one doesn't correspond to any of them.

"Please be an insurance payout. Please be an insurance payout," I chant under my breath. I notice the console is blinking and I have a message waiting. I alter my chant. "Please don't be Vikram. Please don't be Vikram."

It's Vikram. There are instructions on when and where the ship has to be docked for next week's job.

"Next week's job?"

He also tells me to enjoy the money. Damn. I mean, yay, I can eat regularly and get new clothes, but damn, I have to deal with Vikram. Okay, I have a week off and money to blow. But where do I want to go? Cornelius and I never faced a decision like this before. What I really want more than anything else in the entire world is one last lecture from Cornelius.

My stomach decides to have its turn being in charge. The hunger pangs cause me to get up and move. Dinner isn't going to fix itself. Right after that, I'll have breakfast. Then a nap is in my future. Maybe I can just sleep until I feel better.

The rivalry between the Kahns of Schiaparelli and the Mehtas of Noctis Labrynthus was as famous as it was tragic. Benjamin Kahn was more of a showman than a mayor. He placed finishing the dome over the four hundred and sixty kilometers of Schiaparelli Crater over the compartmentalizing of the subunits. He couldn't have foreseen the massive invasion of Earthers, but his dome was an obvious target, as the most recognizable feature on Mars.

Excerpt from: How a Bold Imagination Killed a City
Dr. Joshua Caudill

CHAPTER 14   CHRIS

Asimov Crater

Despite my newfound freedom, I can't bring myself to leave the warm, softly illuminated cockpit. Never in my life have I spent so much time doing nothing. I keep expecting to hear Cornelius scold me for being lazy, but try as I might, I can't hear his voice.

The silence drives me crazy. I clean the ship from top to bottom just to keep the silence at bay, but ultimately, I run out of chores. I look at my reflection again, hoping he has some answers.

"There is not a single person in this solar system who would care if I live or die," the person in the mirror tells me. "I have no one to talk to about problems, no one to joke with or even share a meal with. I am totally alone and . . . afraid." My reflection begins to cry softly at first, but before you know it, I'm crying for that person too.

I can't eat anymore bio-fermented nutri-paste, so my trip into the city can't be put off any longer. I'm going to have to suit up and join humanity.

"AI, do I have any messages?"

"You have six messages from Asimov Crater Death Services. A scan shows them to contain nearly identical content. Do you wish to hear all of them?"

"No, just the first one."

"Mr. Christofer Halley, we regret the loss of your father and understand that this must be a trying time for you. We will hold the body of the deceased for up to seven days before forwarding to the recyclers. In this way, your loved one will continue to be part of our great Martian story. If you would like to view the deceased, our hours are oh eight hundred to sixteen hundred every day. Our condolences for your loss."

"AI, when is the last day for viewing?"

"Based on the data collect from the messages, the viewing period will come to an end at sixteen hundred today."

I put on my crotch squeezing pants and the best shirt I own. I'm in my spacesuit in no time and starting the long walk to the hangar entrance. I must have proper clothes before I go to see . . . go to the morgue.

* * *

The morgue is located in the seventh level below ground, where the recycling tanks, the bio-fermentation units and the power plant are located. Cornelius called it the seventh level of hell because it possessed fire and blood, just like Dante claimed. The seventh level is also where murderers are sent, so I guess it's fitting that I must enter this level.

Above here is the aquaponics level. Cornelius used to take me there when I was a kid and we'd watch the actual, live fish swim in the water reservoir. We'd take turns pointing out the fish we wanted to eat for dinner, not that we could afford such luxuries.

The city tried to make the morgue look respectable. It was finished in white plaster instead of the monotonous reddish-orange. Written on the door is the lyric:

> *Use my remains in a thousand different ways,*
> *to preserve Mars' song in the future days.*

I must have sung that a million times as a kid, but now it's not just some words to a catchy beat.

The door is heavy, as if they're afraid of break-ins. I shake my head. They spend money on the dumbest things. The door squeaks as it opens inward. The lights blink on with the movement and the bare white walls are blinding. I walk to the counter where a short bald guy is waiting with a creepy smile.

Why would he be smiling in a place like this?

"Hello sir, who are you here to see?" The man behind the counter has A.C.D.S. monogrammed on his shirt.

"Cornelius Halley."

"I am glad that someone has come at last. We've been waiting. Everyone else here is infinitely more patient than me." He laughs at his own joke. "Oh, I'm sorry; I don't mean to be insensitive." He pats my hand and gives me big, sorrowful eyes. "It's just that I have not been able to attribute Mr. Halley with any known citizen on Mars and I must complete the paperwork before he can be tossed into the recyclers."

"Really?" Despite his tactlessness, I'm amused; at the end, Cornelius is a man of mystery. He would have liked that.

"Yes, quite. You see, the central government, for what it's worth, maintains the Martian birth and death lists. And the name Cornelius Halley does not reside on the birth list. I'm afraid that with immigration being zero, they didn't make allowances for unknown persons to be sent to the recyclers. Is his moniker an alias, by any chance?"

"He is, er, was my father, and he always claimed that he arrived on Mars the same time as Halley's Comet." It's true that he told the passengers that, but it wasn't his real birthday. Also, the man of mystery has a moniker! I did not expect to be entertained when I came through the door.

"I see. That puts his birth year at 2208. Do you know the day?"

"We always celebrated it on April fourth." When we had passengers who we thought would be more generous with tips, we would choose the current day to celebrate either his or my birthday. I had a dozen birthdays every year.

"I see, the very day that Halley's Comet was brought down to Noctis Labrynthus. Was he, by any chance, born there?"

"I have no idea. He was very secretive about his past." Cornelius did have a good sense of humor. I think he would have laughed at the mysterious past I'm building for him.

"We have lived on board our ship for my entire memory." That part is true, at least. I wasn't about to mention how I came to become the first mate.

"Our home port has always been Asimov, if that helps."

"Well, thank you for that. It's more than what I had." He grimaces. "I will have to request a back dated birth report be generated and added to the record. If it's all the same with you, I am going to list Noctis Labrynthus as his birth city."

"That would be great."

"Very well. Please follow me to the cold storage area."

He takes me to a chilled room behind his office. The blinding white walls end at the door. At least they made a salmon-colored swirl on the ceiling.

"We have to circulate the air in an uninsulated pipe along the cliff edge for cooling. I'm sure you noticed that this level is very warm."

"Yep, just like the seventh level of hell."

He starts to smile until he realizes what I said. He coughs once and leads me into the final room.

There is a bank of twelve metal doors, three high and four wide. The technician opens the top door on the second column and pulls out the metal table. It's at the same level as my armpits. He pulls the sheet down to Cornelius's shoulders.

"This is your father?" He asks solemnly.

I nod yes without taking my eyes off of Cornelius. I don't trust myself to speak. He leaves without saying another word and it's just me and Cornelius in the room now. At least he looks peaceful. I can see that the sheet drops unnaturally low into his chest. I turn so I can only see his face.

"Hi Dad, I've missed you," I whisper. "I got revenge for your death." Is this how you are supposed to do this? I don't know, so I just rush headlong into it.

"The funny thing is, I feel all dead inside. Oops, I'm as bad as that bald guy." Dad would have laughed, though. I look at him for some trace of a lip curl; but no, still motionless.

"I mean, I thought that getting revenge would make me feel better. But now I know that the only thing that would make me happy would be to still have you. Now you're no longer with me and I've killed a man. I keep thinking that I should feel bad about that, and I kind of do at times, but at other times, I think he deserved it. I wish you could explain these mashed up feelings to me."

I managed to get all of that out before the real tears start.

"I'm kind of feeling lost without you, Dad. On the way over here, I figured out that I just need you to answer six questions for me. Just these six, then I can figure out the rest for myself.

So here goes. Who am I supposed to talk to now? The ship is awfully big and lonely. You were always the one who made contact with our clients. I can do that part, I think, but who should I spend my personal time with?"

Dad doesn't answer. I mean, I didn't expect him to, but really, I want answers to my questions.

"I don't know what I'm doing, but even worse, I don't know what I should be doing. Can you help me with that one too? Next: when, this is a tricky one. Vikram paid me a lot of money for the last job, so for once money isn't super tight. You were always the one that made the schedule, so the when's were never in doubt. I still have no idea what to do with all of this time, since I don't have any when's to look forward to. I try to hear your voice telling me the schedule, but I've had no luck.

"Keep thinking on that one, because we're only halfway through my list. Next, where should I go? This is probably the least important question since we've traveled all over Mars. The place doesn't matter that much. I just want to be with people who like me; maybe even I could find people who love me. If you could tell me where that is, that would be great."

Dad just lies there, impassive.

"Why? Now that's the toughest question of all. Why do we do anything, if in the end we're all just going to lie in here for a short time before being recycled? You always seemed to have all the answers. Why didn't you ever answer this one?"

Still nothing from Dad.

"I guess I'll throw in the last one as well - how? I think I have the best handle on this one. Whether you realized it or not, I was always watching and studying you. I saw how you steered the conversations without ever being overbearing. You did a really good job on this one. I just wish I would have told you that when I had the chance."

Dad may be stingy with his answers, but at least he looks at peace.

"I enjoyed living and working with you on our ship, Dad." The tears are streaming down my cheeks now, but I don't care.

"Remember when you used to always gross me out by reminding me that everything I would ever drink was someone's recycled pee? Well, here in a few days, I'll be dining on recycled you! I guess you'll get the last laugh after all." I smile through my tears and mess up his hair. More than anything, I wish he could tell me to stop. "Good bye Dad."

* * *

My vision is all blurry, so I rush to leave this cold, stark room. All I want is to be alone in *Halley*'s cockpit. I don't bother to say anything as I crash through the doors to the entrance room of the morgue. I head straight for the door.

"Excuse me, sir! Do you want the effects of the deceased, or should they be donated back to the city?" The bald man says before I can complete my escape.

I stop in my tracks. I don't want anyone to know that I've been crying, so I keep my head down. I pull myself together before I dare speak. "What possessions did Cornelius have?"

"He had this odd medallion." He hands me Dad's lucky coin.

"It's not a medallion, it's a coin from old Earth." I grab it and look at it for the first time in years. An orangish-yellow crystal is set in the center of the coin. Around the stone are yellow scallops radiating away in all directions. I used to call it the sun coin, because that's all my eight-year-old brain could come up with. "Cornelius told me that it came from a place called Canada before the collapse."

"I've read about physical money before, but I must admit, this is the first time I've actually seen one. Is it valuable?" He asks with a curious tone. The guy is weird, but he's not a thief.

"It's priceless to me." I turn it over to see a woman's head on the opposite side. Sure enough, 'Canada' is written right above her head. "I have no idea what the street value would be."

"Well, I hope it brings you luck," the man says. I risk looking up at him and see the compassion in his eyes. It triggers another wave of emotion from within. I hurry out the door.

As I leave the morgue, I notice a shape disappear down the left corridor. Okay, maybe it's just a coincidence. After all that I just went through, I really hope there is someone spying on me. Although, I don't have the faintest idea of why anyone would. Well, I might as well make them earn it.

I head straight up to the marketplace. It surrounds the Ring, and it's filled with shelving and monolithic walls. That's a Cornelius-ism. It's where the poorer people go to buy supplies.

I hit half a dozen different stalls for supplies and wind my way around at least half a dozen more just to lose my tail. It feels good to be in the land of the living once again. It feels even better to have a purpose. This one simple act lifts my spirits. I head back to the ship with the first smile I've had in a week.

The console is blinking rapidly; someone is waiting to speak with me. "Impressive," Vikram says when his image materializes on my vid screen. "Your first day out and you notice the surveillance right away. You've got good instincts, Chris."

"That was your man?" I ask. "How long was he able to follow me?" I haven't played this game since I was seven. It's much harder when you're taller than just about everyone else.

"His job was to break off once it was obvious you knew you were being followed. He said he thought you picked him up coming out of the morgue, but it wasn't until you went into a women's lingerie section of the marketplace that there was no doubt."

"Yes, it was totally for self-protection that I entered that store."

"Good, I'm glad to see you are back on your feet," Vikram says. "You have another few days still before I discuss an opportunity with you. It'll give you a chance to make sure your head is on straight." He ends the vid call without even bothering to say goodbye.

What am I supposed to do until then? I close the cockpit door and start to panic.

While Christiaan Huygens deserves a spot among the all-time great ancient scientists, his discoveries are nearly five hundred years old and are routinely taught to the youngest of our children. For his eponymous city to proudly reconstruct his pendulum in the center of their marketplace shows their backward-looking inclination. This alone illustrates why the city would be an unsuitable capital for the planet.

Huygen's Crater: Still Fixated on Earth
Rachit Mehta, Noctis Labrynthus Mayor

CHAPTER 15 CHRIS

Huygens City

The AI couldn't find a channel for Alex Vennemann. The only chance I have is to find him myself. One scrawny kid in a city of over two hundred and twenty thousand? That's my kind of luck. The one really cool thing about Huygens is that they let you connect your ship to the gate for free. They'll also empty your waste for you and sell you water at a reasonable price. This crater knows how to attract travelers.

I enter the hangar and see the sign pointing the way to the Martian Sunset. No thanks; I don't need to go back there ever again. I have no idea where kids hang out in a big city. There is a lot of foot traffic following the signs for the central marketplace. If I were a thief, I think I would hang out there. The rounded tunnel is at least seven meters tall. The walls of the tunnel don't meet the ground at a right angle. They're rounded as well, giving the walkway a tube-like feel. It makes no sense to do it this way. I don't like it. Square corners would be much more efficient.

More people than I have ever seen in one place are here and walking impossibly slow. They're also all crammed in the right half of the passageway.

Nope, can't do it.

I slip over to the left side and start passing the shuffling people with my long strides. It feels good to have a goal again.

"Move it!" A man yells from behind me. I turn to see his exoskeleton suit pulling a dozen containers behind him. I skip over to the left to let him pass. I check out his suit and it looks like the wheels are permanently mounted on the feet.

"Damn tourists," he says as he passes me.

I check out his cargo and he's carrying more produce than I've ever seen before in my life. He's pulling a dozen of the standard meter cubes on transport carts. Each is overflowing with fresh produce. It's not just the regular stuff, he has exotics like bananas and some huge oblong green thing that I've never seen before.

"Move!" Someone shouts from in front of me.

It's another exoskeleton barreling towards me. I'm trapped. I turn sideways in the median and hope that gives him enough room. He's carrying several sealed crates stamped with an image of Saturn and its moon, Titan. 'PCDs' is written in blue foiled lettering. That has to be the latest Titan two thousand PCD!

"Stay with the pedestrians." He shouts as he passes me. Now I notice the light strip separating the walkers from the freight traffic. I'm in the bulk transport lanes. My foot slips off the rounded corner and gets run over by one of the crates. I draw it back in pain and start to fall forward. I push off from the last cart in his train, and it slides sideways. They must have omnidirectional wheels installed. The driver stops and looks back at me. Another transport train is coming the other way and is forced to stop as well. I run for the safe anonymity of the crowd.

* * *

Huygens is one of the three largest cities on Mars and easily the wealthiest. The city itself is built dead center in the four hundred and fifty kilometer Huygens Crater. They didn't build a dome like Schiaparelli. Instead, they built three levels of doughnut floors inside a small crater and filled them with shops. It kept growing, so the walls of the craters were developed into a commercial zone as well. There's a modest dome over these, and a couple hundred free landing spots of all sizes around the outside.

Within the great crater are sporadic clumping of greenhouses. All the industry is at a second small crater south of here. All the homes and city maintenance structures are underground. It's said that the Tube, the transport system for Huygens, is the largest on Mars, though Noctis disputes this.

The town is rich because they manufacture most of the electronics. On Asimov, everyone is farming, harvesting metallic dust from the central crater or making ceramics. There is no time for diddling with widgets or gizmos. Huygens is different. There are actual bankers and food preparers here. Not just kiosks and sadly programmed robots.

The marketplace is huge. Asimov's central ring has only one level. Huygens' is four times the diameter and three stories tall. The center of all three floors is left open, so the fifteen-meter pendulum attached to the ceiling at the center of the dome, so it can swing undisturbed. The pendulum ball is dirty yellow with clear, crystalline rings around it, just like the Saturn system. The rings must be held in place by magnetics, because there isn't anything physically attaching them to the ball. A one-meter-high wall surrounds the pendulum, keeping people from being struck, I guess.

The wall is decorated with three horizontal stripes of orange, white and blue ceramics. There's a digital sign that says that those colors were the colors of Huygen's home, the Netherlands. The blue tiles must have cost a fortune. Blue or green-colored anything is expensive. It must be nice, spending money on ostentatious displays.

Cornelius avoided Huygens as much as he could. When we did come here, it was a quick stop and then we'd be on our way. So I've never been able to explore this place before now. How am I ever going to find Alex? Where would I even start? I look around in vain for a couple minutes until my eyes settle on a food counter. Maybe if I stop and eat, I'll come up with a plan.

There are literally over a dozen meal choices. I grab up three different packages and gaze at my bounty.

"Hey, you going to pay for this food or just stare at it?" The man behind the counter asks.

"Sorry, I'm daydreaming." I reach for my credit voucher. I check my other pocket.

"I'll pay for him and I'll take the same order as well." Alex is grinning from ear to ear as he pays for it all with my credit chip.

"You should be more careful," he says. "There are thieves everywhere."

"How did you get my chip?" I ask, exasperated.

"The same way I did last time. I walked up behind you and took it."

"What else of mine do you have?"

"It will cost you a meal to find out."

"That's just what I had in mind. Where's your PCD?" I ask.

"I told Mom that I didn't want to work in the recyclers. She said I was not acting properly, so I lost my PCD privileges. I followed her and watched her sell it at a pawnshop," he says evenly. "She caught me watching though, and told me that without it I would never be able to get a job, so I'd better start respecting her."

"Wow, she really is as bad as I thought."

"I kinda feel sorry for her. Are you going to eat your sonicated algae sticks?"

"You can have them. I should have got them air fried," I say.

Alex grabs my sticks and practically inhales them. I guess Mom has been stingy with the food vouchers lately. Not that it fazes him. He's all smiles as he eats a full day's worth of calories.

"So what are you going to do once you're seventeen?"

"I don't know. I'll worry about that later."

"So you're going to end up working in the recyclers," I say. "If you don't have a plan for your future, you'll end up nowhere fast."

"No, I'd rather go without than to become all old and mean like Mom."

"So, what are you going to do?"

"I don't know. I guess I could just acquire credit chips from random strangers walking around in the center of the city."

"So your criminal livelihood is going to rest on causing grave misfortune to others?"

He frowns. "I don't know what I'm going to do. I guess I'll just have to live off my good looks as well as my fast fingers."

He's smiling again. He is irrepressibly happy. I wonder what that's like.

"Besides," he continues, "Mrs. Miller likes me and gives me meat sandwiches if I help put away deliveries, and other people offer me stuff as well."

"So you're not really a thief, you're a grifter?"

"Whatever you want to call it. I'm out talking to friends all day and getting as much food as I want. All I really want is a better place to sleep and maybe more control over what I eat."

"About that. I may have a solution." This is way easier than I had hoped. I was prepared to bribe him. Instead, it looks like a free meal is all it will take. "Have you ever thought about working on board a transport ship?"

"Are you kidding? Flying in space has to be the coolest thing there is."

Just when I thought he couldn't get any more animated.

"Well, I work on a ship and it needs someone to help out." He looks like he might faint. "There's free food and your own quarters, but the pay is going to suck unless the captain likes you."

"Can you put in a good word for me?" Alex practically begs.

"Well, if you give the captain his credit voucher back, I think it will go a long way."

"Really?"

I think he's stopped breathing.

"When can we go?"

"How long would it take you to get ready?" I ask.

"How about now?"

"Don't you want to get anything from home?"

"No."

"Well, I'm not ready yet. There are still some things I have to buy. Follow me."

We get the latest style of clothes and all the essentials for Alex. I should probably buy more clothes, but I'm having too much fun watching my brother's reactions. He's smiling, of course, as he walks around dumbfounded. I even splurge for the robot trolley to follow us with all our purchases safely locked away.

"Now there's one last store we have to find."

"Please Chris, nothing else for me. I feel guilty already."

"Oh, trust me, you're going to work off those purchases."

"Cool. Are we going to the ship now? How big is it? I never thought to ask how big it was. Of course, the size of the ship doesn't really matter, as long as it's space worthy. Do you take it into space or just around Mars? What's the fastest—"

"Stop! I'm exhausted just listening to you and there's no way I'm going to remember all those questions."

"Since I can't seem to keep hold of my credit voucher," I pat my pocket to make sure it's still there. "I better get a PCD that's anchored into my forearm," I say.

"Cool. Can I watch them install it?"

Is it possible for him to be unhappy?

We approach the electronics store, and there's a nice-looking lady standing out front.

"Hello ma'am, what is the most advanced bio-implantable PCD?"

By the way she jumps, I can tell that she didn't expect us to be customers.

"The Titan 2000 is the best on the market," she responds.

"And it implants into the arm?"

"Into the radius. It has that option, yes."

"Why would you want to have it implanted?" Alex asks.

"Because your body is the power source for it, and thieves with sticky little fingers can't take it from you."

"And you would have them drill into your arm?" he asks, amazed.

"We'll take two." For a microsecond, I consider telling him about my alloyed arm.

"A fabulous choice, sir. Would you like to put money down on them today?"

"I'd like to pay for them both in full, if I may." I think Alex is going to faint.

"This model comes with a built-in panic contact. You can instantly connect to other linked Titan 2000 models, as long as you're in the same city. Would you like your PCDs linked?

I look at Alex and he shrugs.

"Yes, please."

The lady walks us back to the installation room. There are four shiny med-bots above us. The chairs have extra plush cushions too! I could fall asleep in one of these. There's a large window between us and a waiting room.

I place my arm in a clear chamber. I can feel several waves of gases blowing over my arm.

"This is the most sterile protocol on the planet," She assures me. "Although with an alloyed arm, it's not quite as important."

I lean in towards her. "Can you not tell him that this is a replacement arm?" I ask softly.

She gives me a conspiratorial grin. "I'm going to apply the local anesthetic," she says loudly. "Once that takes effect, I'll inject the pain block," she winks at me.

"Um, just the local for me, ma'am."

"Are you sure?" she acts surprised.

"I am," I say with the utmost confidence.

"If you insist," she says with a resigned shake of the head. She winks and pats me on the shoulder before going to Alex's station.

Alex looks on in awe. I have to look away before he sees me smile.

* * *

"Welcome aboard the *Halley Traveler*. How much do you know about flying?" I ask as I input the pass code to open the ship. Alex is spinning around, looking at everything in amazement.

"Nothing. Why? Is it hard?" He asks, distracted.

"If you are going to live on the ship, you are going to have to learn to fly it."

"Really?"

Is there such a thing as too much enthusiasm?

"Okay, let me have the ship send the necessary curriculum to your arm," I say. "What's the last level of education you completed?"

"Fourth."

"Fourth? By your age, I was halfway through advanced aeronautics."

He stops his twirling. "Sorry, I was busy learning how to take care of myself on the streets, not living it up in luxury on board a ship."

I didn't mean for it to come out like that.

I give him a sheepish smile to let him know that we're okay. "You think living on this ship is luxurious?"

He reverts back to his permanent happy state. The door opens, and he jumps into the airlock. "Is this your airlock?"

I swallow back a retort. "Okay, this is going to take longer than I thought. Your job for the next couple months is going to be to complete as much education as you can stomach."

"Can't you just show me what I need to know in, like, a couple minutes?" He's looking around the airlock in confusion. I step past him and hit the button to open the inner doors.

"No, I had to learn the theory behind spaceflight, and you will as well."

"Why?"

"Because I am not going to let some butt-scratching bonobo fly my ship. You can either get the knowledge, or you can spend each day cleaning the galley."

I sound so much like Cornelius right now. How did I become so old?

"I need to think, so just give me a minute," he says. "Okay, I have one question first."

"What is it?"

"What's a bonobo?"

"It is a bipedal ape that has no idea how to fly a spaceship," I respond with mock exasperation.

Alex laughs before saying, "I have one more question."

"Really? What now?"

He looks up and down the gangway multiple times. "Where's the galley?"

I rest my forehead in my hand. It's going to take some time to get used to this.

"I have one last question."

I do my best to glare at him, but it's hard when he's grinning from ear to ear.

"What's our destination?" he asks.

"Asimov Crater."

"That's so cool! I've never left Huygens before."

"Sure. Asimov is cool." I roll my eyes. "My goal is to ferry tourists to the typical vacation spots around Mars. Occasionally we'll take people to Luna. Most of the time—"

"We're going to the moon?" I want to settle him down, but his enthusiasm is infectious.

"If we get a customer who wants to go there, then yes. It doesn't happen very often."

"How many times do you go to the moon per year?" He asks.

"Once, maybe twice."

"Awesome."

"Most of our tourist customers are from other craters, but even still, there aren't a lot of Martians who take vacations. To make ends meet, Cornelius and I would also ferry goods from one crater to another. There is more money to be made by transporting to and from Luna, but virtually every job will also have a certain amount of contraband included. That's why we started working with Keev. He has connections everywhere, including the local and global authorities."

"Cool, so we work for him?"

"It's not that easy. An Earther named Vikram has arrived now and taken charge and he's, well, he's really intense. He's going to have us transporting who knows what if we work with him."

"Can't you just work with Keev?"

"No."

"So why don't we just go somewhere else and work for other people?"

"Great idea. Do you have any contacts for transporting contraband?"

"Nope."

"Me neither. Well, we could smuggle for the Maitlands directly, but I don't want to even go there. So it's Vikram for now."

"Why work for him if you don't trust him?"

"Because I'm trapped. Actually, I guess we're both trapped. I can't keep this ship flying without credits from Vikram. All the other jobs we take don't pay anywhere near the amount smuggling does."

"So what do we do?" Alex asks.

"For now, we keep working for him. We'll be extra careful and we'll start setting money aside for some other money-making plans."

"So we are in a race with Vikram to see if we can free ourselves before he can pull us down?"

"Exactly. Until I can find us another way to stay aloft, we are going to be trapped under his thumb."

"So what is the deal with the Maitlands? Why don't you work for them instead?" Alex asks.

"You've never heard of Kenova Maitland?"

Chrissy Hsiu is a self-taught engineer who designed the self-farming system of Acidalia Planitia, allowing agribusiness to thrive. A generous investment from the fourteen families has led to the harvesting of cereal crops in fields that stretch as far as the eye can see. Simply put, we could not feed ourselves if not for her genius.

Entrepreneurs of Mars
Samantha Sullivan

CHAPTER 16   ALEX

Asimov City

I thought flying would be so cool. So far all I've done is study and clean. Boring. Chris did try to impress me, I think, by telling me that we parked on the Trident at Asimov. Is there another choice? When Chris left to see Keev, I told him I had my own errands to run. Naturally, I tail him instead.

He doesn't stop to talk to anyone. When I'm at Huygens, I figure half of my time will be spent talking to friends along the way. Not Chris. He weaves in and out of people like they're all highly contagious. No wonder he doesn't know anyone.

He enters the Ring. The sign above the entrance informs everyone that this is the place for commerce in Asimov, as if that's necessary. The central ring is tiny! There's less than a hundred people milling about and I understand why, there's literally nothing exciting anywhere.

Metal and ceramic goods? How many of each do you need? Basic clothing and cleaning supplies, how exciting! At least they have local farmers selling their produce. I'll have to befriend them. They'll know everything that happens here.

Chris goes directly to the only cool looking stall where two dark-skinned men are having an animated discussion. They must be Vikram and Keev. Whatever they were discussing, the Earther is busy laying down the law. I feel sorry for Keev. Whenever Vikram's eyes weren't boring into him, he looks skyward as if beseeching some god for relief.

Chris seems to be clueless about the dynamic and he approaches the store without pause. Vikram breaks off the discussion and gives Chris a completely fake smile. Keev reluctantly invites Chris and Vikram into a back room. He straightens his wares and scans the Ring before joining his two guests.

"Who are you?" A girl's voice challenges me from behind.

I jump at the unexpected voice but I turn it into a spin on one foot to hide my surprise. "Who's asking?"

"He's a ballerina!" An uptight blond guy says.

"I'm practicing my turns for when I'm in zero g," I respond.

"We haven't seen you here before. Do you live on a ship or something?" One of the girls in the back asks excitedly.

"I'm Alex and I not only live on a ship, I'm the first mate!"

"No way! You have to be lying," the other dark-haired girl says.

"I really am, and I can take you to see the *Halley Traveler* right now."

"Fine, let's go," The girl with the shoulder length, strawberry blond hair says.

If I can make her my friend, the rest will follow.

I smile even bigger. "Okay, but first, I need to know your names before we proceed."

"I'm Natalie," the leader says. "That's Jamal and Jemele. They're twins who are never very far apart."

Jamal smiles and raises his chin. Jemele hits his shoulder and caricatures his motions. Without a word, they look at each other and laugh.

"This stodgy one who fantasizes about ballerinas is Victor. He insists he's a Frenchman, even though his family lives on Maunder."

"Maunder? I've never heard of it. Are you sure it's a real place?"

"Of course it's a real place!" Victor snaps. "We don't want a lot of people surrounding us, so we only let in our workers and a few support people."

"Victor is from the Grignard family," Natalie says. "He can't find anyone to hang out with, so he comes here to spread his cheer with us."

"You come to Asimov? Why?"

Natalie shakes her finger at me. "We'll talk about that later. But first," she returns to her sweet voice, "these two are Hattie and Kallista." She nods her head at the black and brown-haired girls. "There, now you know who we are, so no more stalling."

"Okay Natalie, Jamal and Jemele, Victor, Hattie and Kallista, come with me." I point to each of them as I repeat their names. They don't know it yet, but they're already my new best friends. I glance at Keev's empty storefront. I have time, I hope.

I lay it on kind of thick once we reach the ship. "Due to security protocols, you guys will have to stay back here while I enter the code. No one can be within six meters of me." It's a complete lie, but it makes me look important. I walk up to the airlock and act like I'm typing in memorized alphanumerics. A quick movement with my arm and my PCD enters the real code.

"You can come aboard, if you promise not to touch anything," I call. "The captain would have a fit if he knew what we were doing." Make them think we're thwarting authority. That'll score points for me.

Everyone files into the airlock. I hit the sequence to have jets of air blast everyone while the air filters collect any stray dust particles.

"You've messed up my hair," Victor whines.

"Sorry, captain's orders. We can't have particles in the ship. It can mess with the equipment." I hope that sounds plausible. No need to mention that the captain is the same age as us.

Besides, Chris acts like an old man. I'm not sure how annoyed Chris would be with me giving a tour of the ship, but it's important that my new friends are impressed.

Kallista exits the airlock and takes a quick right toward engineering. Hattie and Jemele open the first guest cabin and inspect the furnishings.

"Kind of musty, don't you think?" Hattie says with an upturned nose.

"I guess," I say as I eye the group splitting up almost at once. "Listen, can you stay right here? I have to corral the others before they send us into space." Looking past them, Natalie, Victor and Jamal all ignore me and head for the cockpit.

I hurry after the three of them. To my relief, they're only staring at the controls. If they start touching things, I have no idea what would happen, and I'd have no idea how to fix it.

"Is there any chance I can get you all to stay together?" I ask Natalie.

"What, you think we're going to be all dumb and go around hitting buttons and screwing things up?" She teases.

"Jamal! Do not touch that! We do not want to initiate a launch!" I shriek in panic.

Natalie looks bemused. "Point taken, okay guys, get out now."

"But I didn't even get to see—"

"Victor, no one cares about your bellyaching. Just go," Natalie says. She turns and yells down the gangway. "Jemelle, can you watch your brother? He's trying to kill us again."

"Again? How novel," Jemele says as she and Hattie come to the cockpit door.

Jamal raises his hands up while flashing a toothy grin.

"Where is Kallista?" I ask with some concern.

"I bet she is looking at the engines," Victor replies.

"Engineering, stupid," Natalie says haughtily. "The engines are outside of the ship. Kallista isn't here to correct you, so I'll just have to do it."

"Whatever. If you don't get back there soon, she's going to start taking things apart," Victor snorts.

Wow, is he arrogant. Hattie has moved very close to Victor, not that he acknowledges it.

Being in charge sucks.

My throat constricts so tight I can't even speak. I don't want to be all uptight, but if parts are scattered across the floor . . . Hopefully, Chris doesn't kill me. I hurry to the back of the ship. So much for playing it cool.

Kallista is staring at the readouts.

"Thank the stars. Nothing is out of place," I say between breaths.

"You're wrong there," Kallista says. "The plasma couplings are barely within parameters, the cobalt carbide concentrations are lower than any self-respecting pilot would allow, and the radiated heat in the micro-capillary reactors is substandard. In short, I wouldn't take this ship out for anything more than, well, very short flights between cities."

"You're making that up!" I stick up for Chris. He's my brother, after all.

"No, and your captain must be a complete idiot if he lets you play at first mate when you can't handle simple propulsion systems."

"Actually, the captain is the one who handles the engines."

"Oh!" Kallista stifles an embarrassed laugh. "Well then, I, for one, would like to get off the ship before it explodes."

Nervous chuckles come from behind me. Okay, maybe that was a little humiliating, but I seize on my chance to get them off the ship before something gets damaged—and also the whole explosion thing.

"Okay guys, we have to get out before the captain returns. He's negotiating a new contract now. You can't be here when he returns."

Natalie gives me a curious look.

"Fine, we'll go, but you have to promise to take me up on this ship sometime," she says.

"Sure, as soon as you are a paying customer, we will be glad to take you to see all the natural wonders on Mars and Phobos."

"I'll get back to you soon enough," she says with a mischievous smile. "Now, let's go get some space ice."

* * *

Natalie O'Dell is from the most prominent family on Asimov. O'Dell Industries makes all the construction equipment planetwide, and she sure is willing to let you know about it. Not that I mind. She can scream at me for all I care, as long as I get to see those green eyes, freckled face and straight reddish blonde hair. She's a confident girl who alternates between being hilarious and commanding. She's easily the prettiest person I've ever seen.

Victor Grignard is stodgy, just like Natalie said. No matter how small and insignificant it may be, Victor is there to correct your error. He's a stickler for getting things exactly right. I figure Chris would get along great with him, or else they'd be at each other's throats.

Hattie isn't exactly vying for Victor's attention like a puppy dog, but she does stay at his side most of the time. If she isn't glued to Victor, she's glued to Natalie.

Kallista is really quiet, to the point that you forget she's there sometimes. I'm not getting much of a vibe from her, but that's fine, because I'm not that much into her either. We're just going to hang out with the same people. I'm not sure she even spoke to anyone other than me in engineering the whole afternoon. She's nice enough, but she was more into the ship than to anyone in the group. Another person for Chris, if he can stand her critiques.

Jamal and Jemele are always cracking their own private jokes. They never seem to be offended by Natalie's commands or Victor's corrections. I like this group of friends.

The search for space ice brings us back to the Ring.

"So, what do you guys do here for fun?" I ask.

"Well, Victor and I dream of being able to hang out with other guys, but it's only the Queen Bee and her friends around here," Jamal says.

Jemele jabs her brother in the ribs with an elbow. Apparently, this is a well-worn topic.

"Good one Jemele," Natalie says. "We get half of the sixth day and all the seventh day off. There isn't much to do, so we mostly stay in the market and make fun of the people. Otherwise, we all have jobs the rest of the week."

"Except for you, Natalie," Victor interjects. "You have to eat pastries, dance and make polite conversation."

"Victor, you are as huggable as a cactus," Natalie replies sweetly.

"What's a cactus?" Jamal asks. In unison, everyone stares at Natalie for an answer.

"Troglodytes! You're all troglodytes, you know that?" Natalie replies. "Not one of you reads about old Earth, do you? A cactus was a plant that had big flat branches covered in needles. Hugging Victor would be like having a thousand injections all at once."

"Trolley bites? Is that what you said? Do the upper echelon not like trolley bites or something?" Jamal asks. "Because, you know, the rest of us don't get much of a chance to schmooze with rich folks while working on our plots." He smiles, knowing that he's pushed her button again.

Kallista changes the subject. "Does your ship have a standard anti-matter engine, or is it an older fusion/antimatter model?"

I nearly drop my space ice. "Oh! Sorry Kallista, you caught me off guard," I stammer.

"Yeah, Kallista, we weren't even sure you were here," Jamal chimes in and gets another shot to the ribs as a reward.

"It's a fusion/antimatter drive," I say. "I can't really tell you much more about it. I'm still learning myself."

Kallista smiles. "That explains some of what I saw. If you want to look smart, make sure to have the captain check if the dynamic contact angle of the conduction fluid is in spec or if it is impeding the macroscopic heat transfer of the fusion reactor."

"Um, okay. What language is that anyway, and how do you know that?"

"My Dad and I overhaul the engines of derelict ships, mostly. My family has a small ship. Now, my brother, who is good at exactly nothing, has decided he wants to fly for a living. So Dad and I fix up the ships and he tries to crash them. At this rate I might as well go work in our berry field," she sighs to herself.

"At least you have berries! We have mixed vegetables. We're always rotating crops and tilling and testing for micronutrients. It's non-stop," Hattie interjects.

"At least you are not growing a tree in your plot like zee Frenchman," Jemele laughs.

"We are growing all the important spices, parsley, thyme, and, yes, even bay leaves from our laurel tree here. You may be happy eating unflavored mush every day, but my farm provides flavor to more refined palettes," Victor chides. "Plus, I can test out our new fertilizer additives."

"They can't grow those on Maunder because their chemical plants pollute the air and ruin the flavors," Natalie says. Her PCD goes off, playing some kind of funky music. "Well, that's all until tomorrow, guys," Natalie says.

"Good meeting you, Alex," Victor says formally, while bowing slightly.

"And you too, Mr. Grignard," I respond solemnly as I bow a smidge lower.

"Make me gag!" Jamal shouts out. "Guys, Jemele and I are out."

The gang disperses in short order, except for Natalie. She smiles wickedly at me. "What is the name of your captain?"

"Chris. Why do you ask?"

"And the ship is named the *Halley Traveler?*"

"Yeah, why do you ask?"

"No reason," she says with a mysterious smile. "Now, tell me about this Chris." She takes another bite of her space ice, so I can't get a read on her.

"Well, he's my half-brother, and he's lived on that ship his whole life."

"How does that work? Doesn't he get a little crazy, cooped up in there all the time?"

"He does get a little . . . intense sometimes, but not because of the ship. I think he prefers being there than anywhere else where pesky humans are."

"So, is he a screamer when he's mad, or does he like to throw things?" Natalie asks randomly.

"Um, well, neither exactly."

"What? He never gets mad?"

"Oh, he can get mad, but he becomes more aloof and mechanical."

"He sounds like an instant party."

"He's had some really tough times recently, and he hasn't told me everything, but he can be pretty scary when he's angry."

"Like how?"

"Um, I really can't say. I mean, he's always been nice to me, but . . ."

"But what? Are you afraid he's going to shoot you or something?" she jokes.

I swallow hard and look around for something to change the subject.

"Let's go to the obdome and watch the sunset."

"I don't know if that's the best idea," Natalie murmurs.

"Come on, you only live once and if Kallista is to be believed, I'm going to die in a grand explosion sooner rather than later."

"Okay, but we have to be careful. There's a lot of people with nothing to lose hanging out there."

"I hung out with lowlifes all the time at Huygens. One of them even taught me how to pickpocket."

The transport tube toward Kunselman is empty. Halfway there, we see a crowd of people leaving the area. I look at Natalie, confused.

"The workday's over," she says. Kunselman is where the industrial processes are located that aren't tied to keeping the city livable.

"I would hate having to work all day, every day," I say.

"I wouldn't say that too loud, like ninety-eight percent of the people on Mars have to do just that.

I stick my hand over the plants in the center line of the transport tube. As the belt moves us along, I lift and drop my hand, just missing the tops of the plants.

"You guys must really love your gardens," I say with appreciation.

"Not really, but it's the cheapest way to purify the air. Asimov doesn't want to build a whole suite of facilities to maintain Kunselman, so they skimp wherever they can."

"It's smart. All they need is a drip hose with nutrient water and maybe a weekly trim. No power source, no chance of it going offline."

"Does Huygens use them too?" Natalie asks.

"Sure, but it's too crowded for a passive system, so they have machines as well."

"Machines? You mean Sabatier systems?"

"I guess," I say.

Natalie laughs. "Please tell me you don't repair the big boxy doodads on your ship."

Her hand darts into the median and comes back with a yellow flower that she sticks above her left ear. "I usually let the seedheads form first, then I blow hard until the seeds are all dispersed."

"Dandelions are one of my favorites, too. And the new leaves taste spicy and a little bitter. They'll liven up almost any dish," I say.

"My Dad calls them weeds."

"Well, he's uninformed," I say haughtily. I can't help it though; I start laughing at myself.

"I'm going to have to sneak them into a meal and see if he notices."

We hop off the conveyor belt and take the first ascender to the dome. There are only five levels to Kunselman, according to the lift. Two are above ground and three below. However, only the ground level is connected to Asimov. The walkway around the dome is empty. No merchant stalls, kiosks, or even images on the walls. Only a band of LED lights along the centerline of the ceiling. Every five meters or so are opened double doors leading into the obdome.

The sun is shining through the geodesic windows, creating spots of light and dark on the dingy floor. There's a big K surrounded by a couple of circles in some sort of silvery metal. When the light concentrates there, it's blinding, but most of the dome is in shadow. A crowd of half-clothed people are huddled near the west windows, trying to get as much sunlight on their bodies as possible.

"That's a lot of Wrinklies," Natalie says, keeping her distance.

"Wrinklies?"

"Yeah, they're betting that more area of exposure is better than long exposure of the sun's rays in smaller patches of skin. But since they have to do this three times a week, they end up getting deep, ugly wrinkles everywhere they're exposed."

"Crickets and rickets, that's what Chris says."

Natalie's laugh turns into a snort and she hides her face. "I've never heard that one before."

"Hey girl, I can make you chirp louder than any cricket," one of the lowlifes says as he leers at Natalie. Several of the sun gazers are watching us now.

"Alex, I think we should get out of here," Natalie says. She starts squeezing my arm like she has a bionic hand.

"But we'll miss the sunset."

The rude man and a couple of his friends pull away from the rest. Others rush to take their spots in the sunlight.

I don't like those odds. "Maybe you're right," I say belatedly. We each take a single step backward while keeping an eye on the men.

The leader points at us and the three break into a trot.

We turn and run toward the lift, but it's not on this level. Even if we jump, the men can follow us. I grab Natalie's arm and pull her off to the left.

"Stay here, by the lift," the leader says.

A quick glance and he and one other are chasing us.

"Where are we going?" Natalies asks.

"Every structure has a stairway, in case the lifts aren't working. We just have to find out where it is."

We race as fast as we can. The men fall farther and farther behind. With the curvature of the dome, it's not long before we can't even see them.

"There!" Natalie whispers while pointing at the door.

I grab the handle and slow myself down all at once. I'm careful opening and closing the door, making sure it can't be heard. The stairway is pitch black. Below us, a single light flickers, making Natalie look like she's moving all herky-jerky.

At the first level, I stick my ear to the door and listen—nothing.

I open the door and Natalie and I race into the empty corridor.

We smile at each other and circle around to the lift.

"This is the only exit," the leader says up ahead of us. "They have to come here if they want to leave."

We press up against the inner wall.

"We have to call the police," Natalie says.

I shake my head. Even if Chris is exaggerating some, I don't want to put our fate in their corrupt hands. "I have a better idea."

I hit the panic code in my PCD. A message screen pops up, but I wave it away so I can hit the send button. Immediately, my PCD lets out a painfully loud, shrill alarm along with a flashing light.

We look at each other in horror and run for the stairs. This time, we can hear the men's shouts as they pick up the chase.

We get to the stairs and close the door. There's no lock!

"Down, down!" Natalie says. "There's no cover if we go up toward the dome."

We stumble down the stairs in our haste. The first floor door opens above us.

"Down there!"

The flashing light is a dead giveaway.

"Alex?" Chris' voice comes from my PCD.

We spill onto the first underground level and try the various doors.

"Here!" I say. The first open door also happens to be solid. We spill into the women's restroom and Natalie locks the door. Now if I can just turn this alarm off.

"Alex?" Chris says, frustrated.

"Chris! There are three men chasing Natalie and me. We're locked in the women's restroom on the first underground level of Kunselman. I didn't want to call the cops."

"I'm at the ship. I'll be there in . . . in fifteen minutes. Chris out."

"Turn that alarm off!" Natalie demands.

"I'm trying. Is there any light in here?"

Natalie slides behind me and hits the switch right underneath my elbow. The lights come on.

I punch frantically at my PCD until the dumb thing finally turns off. "Should we turn the lights off?" I ask.

"I don't mind," the leader's voice says from the other side. He jerks the latch up and down several times before stopping and ramming the door.

"I'm Natalie O'Dell! If you hurt us, you'll feel the full wrath of my father."

"Did you hear that?" The leader says, chuckling. "We can ransom her for more credits than we could spend in a lifetime."

The jerking on the doorknob stops.

"Send a message to the O'Dells. Tell them that we've got their only daughter and for a million credits, we'll return her, untouched." He knocks on the door. "Don't bother trying to call the police. They only operate here during working hours."

* * *

"Get lost, kid," the leader says.

"Leave this place now or I will shoot you with this gun. I've killed a man before," Chris says.

"Why don't you give me that gun before you get hurt?" The leader says.

I press my ear to the door and for two breaths, there's no sound. Two small explosions ring out and the men start yelling and running away.

"Alex!" Chris calls.

"We're in here, Chris. Is it safe to come out?"

"Alex?"

"We're in here," I call. I open the door to see Chris pointing a gun at my face. "It's me, it's me!" I say, raising my hands as I exit.

Chris points the gun upward, so I motion Natalie to come out.

"Why didn't you answer me?" Chris shouts.

"I did."

"Why can't I hear you?"

I motion for him to stop pointing the gun at us.

He nods and lowers the gun, but he doesn't put it away.

Together, we make it to the lift and back to Asimov, seeing no one. Natalie's PCD goes off and she gets all defensive talking to her mother. She walks several paces away and I turn to face Chris, giving her some privacy.

"Go back to the ship," I mouth to Chris. He still can't hear me unless I yell into his ear.

He nods and walks past Natalie.

"Well, I'm going to be grounded until I'm sixty," Natalie says.

"Did I make an impression on our first date?" I give her my biggest smile.

"That's your idea of a date?"

"I didn't think you'd want to go for a second try if I called it a hostage situation."

"You're an idiot."

I nod my head and shrug.

"What did your brother mean when he said he's killed a man?"

"Um, I don't know." I can't look at Natalie or she'll know I'm holding back.

"What are you not telling me?" she demands.

Should I tell her about Chris's past? I only just met her, but I think I can trust her. But still, would I be betraying Chris?

"I can see that you are holding something back. If you're scared, I can find a place for you to stay while you figure out your future," Natalie says in a very serious tone.

This is not how I imagined our conversation would go. "Well, there is something, but I have to have your word that this goes no further."

"No problem. What is it?"

"No, Natalie, you don't understand. This isn't a spat between friends. What I want to tell you is serious—*deadly* serious."

She reacts like I punched her in the face. "So he has killed someone?" Her green eyes grow enormous. "He wasn't lying about that?"

I purse my lips and say nothing.

She shrugs. "Okay, was it in self-defense?"

I look down at my hands, trying to figure out the best way to proceed.

"Did he kill someone in cold blood?"

I stare at her, mouth open.

"It was in cold blood?"

My head bounces side to side while I collect my thoughts. "A couple weeks ago, before I joined Chris on the ship, he was flying with his dad. An important person was accidentally spaced while they were returning from Luna."

"Rustie Maitland!" Natalie says excitedly.

"How do you know that?"

"It's not like people disappear every day, at least not filthy rich ones."

"I always watch the news vids, and there was nothing about this. How do you know about it?"

"You learn about these things when you come from a well-connected family," she sounds almost apologetic. "What do you know about it?"

"I've only heard a little from Chris. The police had this whole big investigation and cleared them of blame. On the way back to the ship, a crooked cop killed Chris' father. The cop had been escorting him back to the ship when it happened.

"Um, there was no investigation. Trust me, if anything even close to being interesting happened on Asimov, everyone would be talking about it," Natalie says. "Secondly, why would a crooked cop arrest him just to shoot him? There would be documentation of an arrest, and I'm not a criminal, but I don't think I'd want my name attached to the man I'm going to murder. Finally, since when do cops escort innocent people?"

"I don't know all the details. Chris got pretty angry while telling me about it. All I know for sure is the officer that shot Chris's father, threatened Chris."

"It's good that you told me. My Dad has been working for a long time to try to clean up corruption. He'll need to know about this."

My stomach does back flips. I'm not sure if I should have said anything now, but I can't keep this all inside either.

"Vikram, the um, a customer for Chris, was able to catch the cop. Through interrogation, they found out what the cop had done."

"The presence of Vikram clears some of this up," she says, as she rubs her hands together. "He's making a lot of noise in the short amount of time he's been on Asimov."

"Yeah, now for the scary part."

"There's more?"

"Chris was there at the end, when the cop was killed."

"He saw the murder? Of a cop?"

"Yes. Well, no. I mean, he was the one who pulled the trigger. He insisted on that. He argued with Vikram about it and everything. Chris pulled the trigger and blew out another man's brains. He said he felt sad afterward, but he was pretty sure it was because his dad was never coming back, not because the cop was dead."

Natalie holds her hands over her mouth in disbelief.

"He has been nothing but good to me," I say quickly. "But I'm living with someone who can kill in cold blood."

"You should leave. Today, I'm serious! I can arrange a place for you to stay."

"No, I think he needs me. Like I said, he's usually pretty cool. Besides, I don't know what he would do if he stayed on the ship all alone. He doesn't talk that much, but when he does, well, it's really heavy. He'd probably self-destruct if he couldn't get that off his chest."

"Or go crazy and try to land his ship through the dome of a city," she counters.

I laugh nervously at that.

"Oh Alex, I had no idea."

"But there is just one thing I don't get. Rustie Maitland's death was never reported, and neither was the cop's. How could those items be kept out of the news? And if it wasn't reported, how did you know about it?"

"My family has good connections," she shrugs again. "I'm glad you told me. It can't be easy to hold on to these sorts of things."

"You're not going to turn Chris in?"

"To corrupt police? Not a chance. If Chris's story is true, then I can at least understand why he did it. I'm going to look into this and start digging for answers."

"What kind of answers?" I ask, confused.

"I'm looking for the kind of answers that require some digging. Don't expect anything tomorrow when I see you."

"I'm going to see you tomorrow?"

"Yes, and I will be bringing you some customers."

"Cool! What time and where?"

"We will be at your ship at ten hundred hours, sharp." She smiles at me. "If you can, get some fresh dandelion leaves."

"Will everyone else from the gang be there, too?"

"No."

"Ah, okay then. See you tomorrow." The day's events start replaying in my mind. I was never this confused on Huygens. How can Asimov be so much smaller and more confusing?

Natalie grabs me for a long bear hug and brings me back to the present. She winks at me and turns away in a fluid motion. My heart is racing, my breath is heavy and I feel better than I have ever felt in my life.

"I'm coming Dad," she says into her PCD.

Few know, and even fewer are willing to speak of, the red-hot animosity of Ganges Chasma's Astrid Agnarsson and the mayor of Tharsis Tholus, Lucia Juarez. The much-publicized embargo of smart machines to Tharsis Tholus and the retaliatory confiscation of Agnarsson's wealth brought this conflict into the light. Whatever the origin, the feud was decades in the making.

Whispers of Mars: The Quiet Power Struggles Between Rival Cities
J. Mercy Thomson

CHAPTER 17   CHRIS

Halley Traveler

"You're earning your keep already," I say.

Alex beams. He sure is happy to make me happy. He's made like a half dozen friends in the first two days he was unleashed upon Asimov Crater. Of course, he now wants me to meet them all. At least it's not all going to be at the same time. Alex's friend Natalie booked her family for our Martian Highlights trip. I guess as a thank you for yesterday. It's easy money, and we can always use it.

I'm a little nervous. Cornelius was always the one to greet our customers and set them at ease from the start.

"You must be the O'Dells, hi, I'm Chris Halley and this is my ship, the Halley Traveler," I rehearse. "No, that sounds stupid."

Ugh, why is this so hard? I stare at the pilot's console. "Hi, I'm Captain Chris Halley, welcome aboard the *Halley Traveler*... you perfect strangers whose names I refuse to say." Grr.

The comm breaks up my useless greetings.

"Um, Chris, the O'Dells are here. Do you want to greet them?"

I hear a man and woman talking in the background. Why is he embarrassing me in front of them? I clench my teeth even as I spin out of my chair. I rest my hand on the door and take a big breath. I'll scream loud enough for our mother to hear us on Huygens once this trip is over. Now I have to play the part of courteous, pleasant Chris. I hate being courteous, pleasant Chris.

I leave the cockpit and rush to the airlock, which swooshes open just as I arrive.

"Wow," the man says. "You run this ship with impressive precision." He offers his hand to me. "My friends call me Ari. It's short for the much more ostentatious Aristotle."

"Absolutely Mr. O'Dell, I mean, Ari." Everyone has heard of Aristotle O'Dell. He's one of the richest people on the planet, and that was before he married Evelyn Young, the sole heiress to the Young fortune. And I just got his name wrong as I greeted him. I wish my head would just implode, but I'm in charge now, so I raise my head and wait for his reaction. He's smiling down at me. Is that good? I think it's good. I still have plenty of time to screw this up, though.

Mr. O'Dell dwarfs everyone around him. It isn't just his size, although he is one giant man. His deep, rumbling voice alone would make even the dead stand up and take notice. His syn-silk clothes could not have looked more out of place than on his barrel of a chest. I hope we have enough food to keep him happy.

"Hello. Chris, I believe?" he says warmly.

Of course I forget to tell him my name. I nod, since I'm now afraid to speak and make things even worse.

"I have been reminded," he glances down at Natalie, "that I don't stop and appreciate the world around me." His hand completely engulfs mine, and he nearly shakes my arm loose at the shoulder. I really don't want to replace my only remaining good arm.

I smile my best smile and welcome him aboard. Compared to him, I sound and feel like a small, insignificant child. I pull at my shirt to straighten it out. I have to look and act professionally now.

Mrs. O'Dell gives me a sympathetic look. She purses her lips as she gazes up at her husband. "I'm Evelyn, dear, and don't let my husband's booming voice knock you off kilter." She reaches up to pat his shoulder affectionately. "He's nothing if not enthusiastic." Her motherly tones immediately set me at ease. I would probably run through an exterior wall if she asked me to.

"Gag! They insist on doing the perfect Martian couple thing whenever they go out. I'm Natalie, as I'm sure you know, and you're not nearly the monster that Alex described." Her broad smile makes me want to believe she's just messing with me.

"Natalie!" Evelyn exclaims. "We have certainly taught you better than that."

"Mother, don't stroke out on me. I was just kidding . . . mostly," she finishes under her breath.

I have no idea what to make of Natalie. I'll let Alex handle her. So far they haven't stormed out, so there's that. I launch into my welcoming speech just like I rehearsed.

"Since there are only three of you today, I would recommend prepping for liftoff in the galley. The grand viewing window will give you the best view of Mars. We typically ask everyone to stay in their cabins and then we fly by everything twice. By being in the galley, you get a better view and if you want to see anything a second time, just let me know."

"Oh, and I'm Alex, by the way," Alex interjects.

Damn. I forgot to introduce Alex. My legs go weak. I practiced a dozen times to make sure my speech was flawless. Everyone is grinning so I can't have screwed up too badly.

"I'll let Alex," I extend my arm toward him, "my second mate, get you settled. We'll be taking off in just a few minutes."

"You mean first mate," Alex corrects me.

I scrunch up my face at yet another mistake. Then I realize that I'm putting on a display for them all to see.

I let Alex escort them to the back of the ship while I follow behind. Mr. O'Dell is busy rapping his knuckles on random cabinets as we walk back. Mrs. O'Dell scolds him quietly for touching everything. I glance at Natalie and she is shaking her head at the embarrassment she thinks her parents are causing.

Once the O'Dells are in the galley, I breathe a sigh of relief. My part is almost over and I can finally smile in earnest.

I nod politely and make my way to the cockpit before my plastered-over smile becomes permanent. Alex will no doubt be all chatty and happy enough without me. Thankfully, that will never be my job again.

"We'll start by flying over the frozen carbon dioxide bed better known as the south pole, then we'll fly north to Hellas Planitia, which is the lowest point on Mars and the home to actual liquid water during the summer months. Winter is ending here in the southern hemisphere, so you'll just have to come back in another six months for that. It's always fun to see the smiling face in Galle Crater, then we'll see the ruins at Schiaparelli."

I don't know why, but I love flying over Schiaparelli. Cornelius always said he felt overwhelmingly sad with each passing, but he was always talking about the history of everything we flew over. My stomach twists itself up into lots of unhealthy shapes, and I've just left dead air all this time. Stupid.

"I can't begin to tell you how many glowing stories I've heard about Schiaparelli Crater. The dust has obscured much of it, but the grandeur is still plainly visible. It's still the most impressive engineering marvel of the solar system and it is always a spectacular sight. Please note that even though I logged our flight plan, the proximity beacons will only allow us to fly over the city once, so I'll go as slow as I can.

I wonder what Cornelius would make of my speech so far. He'd probably have said that he didn't know I could talk for so long.

"From there we will hit the home stretch; we will fly level with the canyon walls in Valles Marineris and then buzz over Noctis Labrynthus. We'll fly over lesser known but still spectacular sites, including my personal favorite, Hephaestus Fossae, where an impact crater freed underground water that in turn etched out multiple interconnected river beds on the surface. Finally, we'll circle the majestic Olympus Mons. Let me assure you, I have taken this trip a hundred times, and it never gets old. If you have any questions, Alex or I will be happy to answer."

* * *

We have dinner as the sun sets over Olympus Mons. We would normally charge extra for it, but I want to ensure we make a good impression with Natalie and her very, very rich parents. We even splurged and had synthetic chicken with fresh vegetables. On the downside, since we had guests, I have to eat with them in the gallcy instead of the pilot's chair.

"After we finish the tour . . ." Aristotle looks at me, "could I pay you to take me to Phobos for an overnight stay? I'd pay whatever the established rate is, of course."

My heart skips a beat. If we can establish a good relationship with Aristotle O'Dell, we could break our ties with Vikram.

"Of course we can accommodate you," I say calmly, even though my heart is bouncing around in my chest.

"How long of a stop would you like back at Asimov to collect your things?"

"That depends on what the ladies think. Evelyn, Natalie, would you like to go to Phobos or not?"

"I'll go to Phobos," Natalie blurts out immediately. She and Alex have been talking and laughing with each other all through dinner.

Evelyn raises an eyebrow toward her daughter. After a moment, she replies, "I think I would just get in the way of you two. So I will mind the crater while you're gone. You two be careful," Evelyn says, while looking directly at her daughter. This causes Natalie to blush, but why? She's only going to be with Alex and me.

"I will take very good care of them, Mrs. O'Dell."

She looks at me like I said something strange. "Please, call me Evelyn."

"Yes, we don't stand on formality, so Ari and Evelyn will do," Ari says. "Now, if you would send me the charges, I will transfer you the funds."

My mind races. This was going much better than I had hoped. "I will make the arrangements now. I am sure Alex will be more than adequate with any questions or concerns you may have." I deliberately take my time leaving the galley and stifling my excitement. Once I'm out of sight, I jump up and down and pump my fists like I did when I got my first PCD.

* * *

I invite Mr. O'Dell to the cockpit once we're underway again. Cornelius always told me it was the easiest and cheapest way to make a passenger feel special.

"You know, I haven't been in space for nearly twenty-five years," Mr. O'Dell says with a faraway look. "I proposed to Evelyn the last time we came to Phobos."

"For my money you couldn't have picked a better way to do it," I chime in.

"Will I be able to see the stars out my cabin window tonight?"

"I have planned the trip so that the starboard side will see direct sunlight when we arrive. Once we circle the planet, the ship will automatically flip our position so you're still facing the stars when the sun rises. You should be able to view the stars for the whole trip."

"Excellent, I really appreciate that." He lets a moment pass before continuing. "I guess we should get around to the real reason why I asked for this trip."

"To go to Phobos?" I ask.

He chuckles. "Well, yes, that too, but the other reason was to feel you out and see if we could work together."

"I assure you we can." I say, a bit too eagerly.

"You misunderstand. I have come by some unsettling news about you, and I wanted to feel you out for myself."

"Okay."

"The bit with Officer Barnett and all; it was . . . as I said, unsettling."

I grip the armrests so hard that my knuckles turn white. I stare straight out the window, not daring to move my head.

"I'm not sure what you mean," I manage to get out.

"Oh, sorry Chris," Aristotle says. "You look as white as a sheet. Perhaps I should explain a bit. Your coming to Natalie's aid last night says a lot about you. You didn't try to extract a payment or a favor or anything. You just righted a situation that was going badly."

"They were in trouble," I say. Shouldn't this be obvious? My broken ribs begin to hurt, from the pounding of my heart, no doubt. I need to know where this is going.

"They were, and what you did was admirable . . . and a little overly enthusiastic."

I shrug. "Alex and Natalie were in trouble, and it was the quickest way to scare off their attackers."

Ari pats my hand. "All I'm saying is that you didn't think to locate the bullets, or the spent shells. Even as we speak, the police are in a tizzy that someone would shoot real bullets in our city."

I look at the console in front of me and try to swallow, but my throat has closed up.

"It's alright, I'll be able to turn this into a call to install cameras in the public areas of Kunselman. It's long been needed, but the mayor refuses to spend the credits. As a thanks to you, I'll make sure your name isn't connected in any way."

"I appreciate that."

"As for Officer Barnett, he was corrupt. If there's no impartial justice, people will take things into their own hands and that will descend us all into anarchy. Have you heard about the move to form a real, functioning planetary government?"

"Only that it's a waste of rich people's time. In that respect, it's a good thing because they can't mess up the things that really matter." I say without thinking.

Ari laughs this time. "I guess I deserve that. I am, of course, one of those rich people."

"Oh."

"No, no, don't apologize. I would rather know your real opinions. There hasn't been a true leader on Mars in our entire history. It took the famine on Earth to allow us to take control of our own future. Since then there have been only halfhearted attempts at planet-wide government and they were barely concealed schemes to codify specific advantages to the powerful. We are at a point where we cannot remain as several dozen scattered communities. Our chance for self-rule will quickly evaporate."

As long as he talks about planetary governments and other useless stuff and nothing about me, I can relax.

"Did you know that Noctis Labrynthus and Arsai Mons were drawing up raiding plans on each other last year?"

"Why would either of them do that?" I ask, looking at him like he's gone mad.

"Noctis is water rich, while Arsai Mons is mineral rich. For a hundred years, they have been bartering one resource for the other. Arsai Mons convinced themselves that they were getting a bad deal, so they played hardball while renegotiating terms. Noctis got their feelings hurt, so they refused to trade any water at all."

"But water is part of the life essentials: food, water, shelter and air. You can't refuse to share them. Except during the earth invasion, the Great Stranding, I mean."

He nods and smiles at me. "But those two cities could have come to an agreement if cooler heads prevailed, but neither was willing to budge."

"What happened?"

"A few like-minded people and I went in and mediated the dispute. Essentially, the old agreement was ratified, and the crisis was averted. This is neither the first nor the most serious crisis in the past twenty years. That is why the time is now to establish a real central government. If we don't, we are probably just a few decades away from regional strongmen heading local militias—just like on Earth today. We could have a dozen more self-inflicted Schiaparelli Crater type events, or worse. Earth, or some portion at least, could get its act together and try to restore their hegemony over us."

"What do you want me to do?" He's stirred up my Martian pride and I'm feeling like Herman Burrichter at the gate of Huygens. There's a planet to save.

"I don't want you to do anything different from what you are doing now. You smugglers, and I don't mean that as an insult, travel all over the planet. If you hear a rumor that you think I should know about, tell me."

"That's it?"

"No, not exactly. There is one other request. My wife and daughter are as committed to this cause as I am. I would like you to consider taking Natalie on as crew. You don't have to pay her, I'll manage that. I would just like her to be able to be an extra set of eyes and ears."

"I don't think I can do that."

It's Aristotle's turn to look puzzled. "Why? Have you and Alex had an argument over her?"

"What? Why would we argue over her?"

"My mistake," Aristotle says with a sudden cough. "What's the problem, then?"

"Well, this guy we work for, his name is Vikram and . . ."

* * *

Ari is a great listener, maybe too good. Even if he thinks I killed Barnett, I can't exactly go around admitting it. He never brought it up again, so maybe he was just testing me. We're able to agree that Natalie should meet with us regularly, but not be a part of the crew just yet.

Ari stretches his enormously long arms. "Is it true that the best sleep you will ever get is when you're at zero g?"

For once, I feel like the expert. "It's absolutely true."

"Then I will bid you good night." He shakes my hand very firmly again and hurries off while there's still some force keeping his feet on the floor. He only hits his head once on the ceiling before keeping a hand running across it.

I race to share the news with Alex. He'll be more excited than me.

Alex doesn't answer when I knock, so he's probably too engrossed in his gaming. The light is off, so I slide the door slowly into its alcove in case he's asleep. The muted light from the corridor shines upon a giant mass of purple balloons floating about the cabin. There are two pairs of legs sticking out from it. The mass slowly rotates, and I see Alex's bare ass rhythmically poking in and out.

My feet remain motionless on the floor. Try as I might to run, my legs won't respond. I stand there frozen, somewhere between horror and curiosity. I can feel my face radiating heat, but I still can't compel my body to move. The bunch of grapes, which is the only thing I can think to call it, continues to rotate languidly and I get a glimpse of Alex's face.

Oh shit!

Finally, my body obeys me. I kick my mag boots off and bound out of the room, hitting the gangway wall with my shoulder. My ribs remind me they are still broken. Even with the pain block, I'm staggered for a second. Stupid! I gather my wits and silently close the door.

Lot of good that will do now.

I try to shake the image out of my mind, but I can't exorcise it. It's too late to jab out my eyes, or I'd consider the option. I push off for the cockpit and wonder how I am going to get through the rest of the flight without making eye contact with anyone.

* * *

I'm staring out into space, trying to convince myself that *that* never happened. Alex comes floating in with a smile from ear to ear.

"Did you want something?" he asks innocently.

I'm sure my face is red again, this time in shame. "No. Not a damn thing."

Alex's smile disappears and his brow furrows. "Are you mad at me?"

"No," I bark.

"Well, something is bothering you."

"Nope. I'm fine," I say defiantly.

"Really? Then why are you up here staring at the sun without properly dampening the viewer? Are you competing to see who can radiate more heat?"

I sigh loudly. "No, I'm just frustrated."

"About me and Natalie?"

"Natalie and I," I say robotically as I continue my slow, inevitable morphing into Cornelius. Space! What would he say if he knew this happened?

"No, not exactly," I say. I swear it didn't come out all whiny. "It's more that I'm older than you and I have no idea how to even convince a girl into my quarters, much less do anything else."

"It can't be that bad."

"Yes, it can. I've tried to explain what I do to girls and I just get blank looks and quick exits." Okay, that came out a touch whiny.

"Stop trying to be an engineer. You know, maybe talk about something other than escape velocities and thrust ratios."

"If you mention anything about your thrust ratio . . ."

He looks at me and lets out a snort. Then we look at each other and laugh the tension right out of the room.

"Seriously though, should I talk about all of my other hobbies? That's right," I hit myself in the forehead, "I don't have any hobbies! I'm busy trying to keep this ship running, finding customers, trying to avoid dealing with Vikram, eating and sleeping. If I can get caught up on all of that, then I could try to convince a girl to talk to me."

"So you're very busy. I get that, but even you have time to spare, but you spend it sitting up here. Your biggest problem is that when you meet a girl, you think you have to be a trial lawyer. You don't have to lay out evidence and wait for a verdict. You just talk to them. You know, like they're actually people. If they are interested in what you have to say, it will naturally progress," he says, as if it was that easy.

"I like engines and piloting spacecraft. So I have to find another solitary pilot who doesn't like leaving her ship?" Internally, I wince. That was definitely whiny.

"I have news for you Chris, a lot of pilots will take every opportunity to leave their ships and they actually like talking to people. Pilots are always surrounded by crowds in bars. Everyone wants to hear stories of being out in the void. Even the stories we know are complete lies. Why did you think I jumped at the chance to join you? It sure as hell wasn't for your patented moody stares. You're leading a life of adventure, but all you do is frown."

"Great, so it isn't because I've been dedicated to my craft. It's because I'm a loser who avoids people." Does he think he could pull me out of my doldrums?

"A little harsh, but yes. If you don't put yourself out there, how do you expect to meet anyone? Are you waiting for people to pound on your door already filled with adoration? I talk to people even when there's no profit to be made. You only talk to people about contracts; then you run away."

"Great. I'm going to bed. I guess I will just have to comfort myself."

"You'll get there," Alex says earnestly. "You just have to work up to it."

He means to be supportive, I know, but how dare my *younger* brother tell me to keep trying! I leave for my cabin without another word. After Alex settles in, I return to the cockpit and my brooding, although I do activate the view dampener this time.

Martian society is often described as sober and straight-laced. As with any lace, the frayed ends reveal a much freer, kinky side. Sex always sells, no matter how much our leaders insist otherwise. Indeed, it is the rare leader who doesn't feel the need to explore their own peculiar fetishes. Take, for example . . .

Red Planet Confessions
Mistress Minx

CHAPTER 18   CHRIS

Phobos

"When should I tell the passengers we will be arriving back at Asimov?" Alex asks in a neutral voice.

"Alex, please stop worrying about me exploding. I realize my problem is with me, not you. I will put that aside and finish up the cruise like a good tour guide should. I'll even have breakfast with everyone today and stay to chat afterward."

"Good. I've had no idea what to do next, so I've been trying to avoid you. But now the O'Dells are getting up and we have our jobs to do."

"Yeah, you must be tired after all that exercise last night," I tease.

Alex doesn't even blush. He just smiles a little more.

"Oh, by the way, when Natalie or whoever and I, um, get together, I've decided we will meet in her cabin. That way, you don't have to worry about walking into a surprise again."

I smile sheepishly at him. Now that the drama is behind us, I have to know. "So, what exactly is that purple monstrosity?"

Alex's face brightens. "It's really cool! I've heard about them and I always wanted to try one, but they are kind of useless in gravity. So, when you're weightless, you have to worry about every action having an opposite reaction."

"The Second Law of Thermodynamics," I say approvingly.

"Seriously? Maybe you would worry a little less about science sometimes." He looks at me quickly.

My smile tells him we're still good.

"Anyway, so if I was to, um, push, my partner would be forced away. That would be fine if you only had one thrust, but . . ."

I chuckle at his sudden loss of words.

"So anyway, there is an adjustable elastic loop that goes around both of the people's waists. Instead of pushing, you both pull apart and the tension will pull you back together. It, um, requires a whole new set of muscles and good timing to do it right."

"Fine, so why have all the giant grapes?" I say, even as I feel my ears heating up.

"Oh, those are just inflatable air cushions."

"Yeah, I get that. But why?" I ask.

"Well, once you 'get busy', any extraneous movement by either of you will start you both tumbling around since there's no gravity. The last thing you want is to career headfirst into a really solid piece of furniture. Besides, the 'grapes', as I will forever more call them, add a little bounce themselves. Somehow, the feeling of floating out of control while having sex just adds to the experience."

"Okay, I got more than I bargained for." I wave for him to stop. "Let's go join our passengers and please, whatever you do, don't discuss last night at breakfast."

At least I had the good fortune not to stock grapes on this trip.

* * *

I've decided to get out and meet people. I have stories that are just as good as any other pilot. I can't wait for Alex and our guests to leave, but not for my usual reasons. Once I'm alone, I can look up certain establishments without prying eyes looking over my shoulder. The top-rated establishment in Asimov is called the 'Zero g Spot'.

I make my way there and scout the place out for a while. From the corner, I'm able to get the lay of the land. Drinks and other services can be ordered but, frustratingly, there is no menu. Several scantily clothed women come by and ask what I want. When I ask how much drinks cost, they give me dismissive looks before smiling seductively at some other guy.

I order a drink. I've never had alcohol before, but Cornelius would call it liquid courage to his friends. I need some of that. A blue, fizzy drink is placed in front of me. It's much too sweet, but I like it.

"Do you want another one?" The woman leans down low and I can see her chest.

"Yes." I'm already feeling great and a second one would be awesome.

The woman doesn't hand the drink to me right and I end up wearing half of it on the front of my shirt. There's no more time for stalling. I stand up and have to steady myself. I've never felt this clumsy before. No matter, it's time to get down to business.

I ask the women what they charge, and they always respond with a, 'that depends on exactly what you want' reply. When I asked for a fee structure, they look amused, but they still leave and don't come back.

Finally, I decide to man up. I approach one of the women, because for some reason, they've stopped coming to me, and ask her how much it would cost to have sex. I'm not sure if her price is competitive or not, so I thank her and tell her I will consider my options. She slaps me.

Well, if she's going to be rude, then she's out. The next one asks if I'm solely focused on price. I say yes, of course, so she tells me to go look for Jeanette. Jeanette is the most experienced worker there. I guess she gives a discount because of the volume of business she performs.

Her skin is mottled, and a little loose, but her attention is strictly on me. That's the best response I've gotten from any woman here.

"Pay before you play," Jeanette says in a gravelly voice as she pulls a credit scanner out from her frayed undergarment. Her breast pops out as well, but it doesn't even faze her. "Tap your PCD here."

I'm careful to miss her dangling breast as I tap the scanner with my forearm. She looks exasperated for some reason. She grabs my wrist and places my hand on her breast.

"Do we even have to go upstairs now?" she asks, acidly.

How did she know I was fighting that urge?

"Of course we do. That's what I'm paying for!" If I hadn't already paid, I'd probably walk out.

She laughs in an unfriendly manner before guiding me to her room. Jeanette's was the first room on the left. She taps her card on the door scanner and motions for me to enter. She taps the card again and we have our privacy.

"Take off your clothes and put them against the wall," she commands as she walks past me to the bed. She lounges against the wall as she inspects me from head to toe. "Well, you're a lanky one, aren't you?"

"Are you going to get undressed?" I ask. I'm confused about why I'm the one not wearing any clothes.

"In a minute," she says. "I just wanted to see if you were dumb enough to give me a strip tease. It was worth what I paid for it." She snorts.

Maybe I should just leave. Jeanette was truly an ugly woman, personality wise.

She sits up, pats the spot right beside her and says: "Come sit here with me."

I guess she's trying to sound friendly, but it reminds me of my mother's raspy voice.

I sit next to her wondering what the hell I should be doing. She places her warm hand lightly on my knee and stares at my face as she slowly moves her hand up my leg. My body goes all rigid and spasmodic at the same time. Before you know it, the moment is over.

She barks out a laugh. "I guess we're all done here." She gets up, hits the scanner with her card and exits as the door opens in front of her. I'm left all alone to deal with my humiliation. I hang my head in shame and wonder how I could have ever thought this was a good idea.

"You only get one chance, you know!" a dark-haired prostitute says as she and her customer look in at me.

I'm sitting on display for whoever walks by. I leap into action, literally. I launch myself so hard that I hit my head on the ceiling before landing by the door. I try to pull on it, the door, that is, but it won't budge. Without her card, the door won't shut.

Another couple walks by and the woman yells at me. "No getting off on the walls."

I grab my clothes and look around the room for a spot where everyone can't stare at me. It's no use. The room is too small. I turn to face away from the door and start putting my pants on. Someone smacks my ass as they walk by; great, more laughter at my expense. I turn to face the door as I jam my foot into my pants. Only, I kick too hard and when my foot gets stuck, my momentum carries me forward.

My left shoulder hits the doorway and spins me around so I fall on my back. My ribs ache, so I close my eyes for only a second, willing this whole experiment to be a bad dream.

I open my eyes to see three 'couples' standing over me, jeering. I think images may have been taken, but I'm still a little fuzzy headed and can't be sure. The back of my head is throbbing. I manage to jerk my pants up over my private parts while lying on the ground. Now that the show is over, they leave. I wiggle into my shirt and don't look back.

"Thank you for the show," one of the women calls.

I can feel my ears radiating heat and I assume my face is just as red.

The serving woman stops me and tells me to pay a ridiculous amount for my drinks. A bouncer walks up behind her and rubs her shoulder.

"Is there a problem?" he asks.

"Nope." I hit my PCD and pay the bill.

I will never mention this to anyone as long as I live.

I make this vow over and over as I race to retrieve my spacesuit. Once I'm outside, I'm just another anonymous pilot taking the long walk across the empty Martian plain to his ship.

* * *

As soon as the airlock cycles, Alex is there, looking at me in a funny way.

"Are you okay?"

"I don't want to talk about it."

"What happened? Did you get mugged?"

"I wish."

"Well, hold up. Where did you get hit?" Alex asks.

Alex can be incredibly persistent. After fifty-seven questions, I finally give up and relive the whole humiliating experience. He insists on activating the ship's concussion protocol to watch me while I sleep off the worst night of my life. After Alex finally leaves, I get up and take my accustomed spot, staring out the cockpit window. Does every guy go through this or am I just this unlucky?

Apparently, Alex guessed my next move, so I let him join me. As I stare at the blackness around us, I confront an unfortunate truth. I don't know how Cornelius did it, but I cannot duplicate his example. I can't hope to do everything by myself. I have to figure out how to trust others and, more importantly, how to ask. The silence encroaching around me doesn't have any answers. I look over side-eyed at Alex.

I'll start tomorrow.

When Schiaparelli fell, Dilara Arslan was negotiating a deal with the Jeong Electronics Conglomerate. Saving the people of Schiaparelli was not possible, or so her biography alleges, so she sent her personal ship to recover her spider robots, the ones that built the dome over Schiaparelli in a staggeringly short nine months. By retrieving those before the Giordano of Galle Crater could, and partnering with the Jeong, she insured Arslan Robotics' technological dominance for the last forty years.

Robots Over People: The Unauthorized Biography of Dilara Arslan
Karen Burley

CHAPTER 19   CHRIS

Asimov Crater Space Park

"Since we have a free day," Alex says at breakfast, "I grabbed a couple of friends and figured we could have some fun for a change."

"You've been at Asimov for, like, three days. When did you find all this time to go out and socialize?" I ask.

"It's been a week, and you know all those errands you send me on so you can stare out the cockpit window undisturbed?"

I stare out the galley window at the peaks west of us. Sometimes I just want to start my own homestead there. That way, I could always walk into Asimov if I needed something.

"Hello? Space cadet?" Alex is snapping his fingers in front of my face.

I slap them away.

"So, are you willing to have some fun today?" His pointing finger is poised overtop his PCD as he waits for my answer. "I've already got our spacesuits laid out in the airlock."

"So why in the seventy-nine moons of Jupiter did you put out our spacesuits? Is there even something fun to do at Asimov?"

His smile is beaming. "Trust me."

"Fine, we don't have anything too pressing to do today."

* * *

We have to take an air shower to get all the dust off our suits, since we apparently need them for whatever fun we're going to have inside a city. It would have been cheaper to stow our suits and rent two new ones.

Alex is running his hand over the center line vegetation as we take the people mover into the city. There are few enough people about and we have the track all to ourselves. Normally I'd love that, but not having any idea what we're doing weighs on me.

We reach the lifts at the center of town, and Alex keeps walking.

"Where are we going?" I ask, my frustration building.

"I can tell you that," Natalie calls from behind us. She picks up her helmet from the planter bed.

Alex run-hops to her. It isn't necessary. I mean, you can walk just fine in a spacesuit at normal gravity, but she laughs at him, because everyone is always amused with Alex, no matter what he does.

"There's the person of the hour," Natalie says as another girl rises up on the lift.

"Are you the captain of the Halley Traveler?" The mystery girl asks me in a rush.

Here's a girl that's crazy about spaceships! It's time for some of that pilot bravado that Alex is always telling me to try.

"I sure am. It's an engineering marvel from when Earth could do things right. I keep it space worthy." I finish with a big grin.

Nailed it.

"Hah. Famous last words, your engines need to be overhauled. Engineering is a mess and I bet you haven't checked the alignment of the thrust gimbals in years. The only thing exciting about your ship is what critical fail will happen first."

My jaw goes slack and I look at Alex.

He raises his helmet so I can't see his face, but his shoulders and head are bouncing up and down.

He's still smiling when he lowers it. "I may have given them a tour of the ship while you were out the other day."

"Kallista, you have such a polished way of introducing yourself," Natalie teases.

"I'm so sorry," Kallista says, flustered. "Your ship isn't really that bad. It's just that I hear that flyer jock stuff all the time and I can't stand it. I mean, it could definitely use some work, but I'm sure your ship is serviceable for most local Martian flights."

I'm intrigued, despite the insults hurled at my ship.

"Kallista is it? How do you know so much about spaceships?"

"I help my father refurbish spaceships for a living."

"Well, I'm home taught, so I would love to get more of your opinions on my ship sometime."

"Before you two start making out while in your spacesuits, can we get moving?" Natalie interjects.

Kallista's ears glow red. I want to point it out, because the same thing happens to me, but should I say something or not?

"Follow me," she squeaks before I can make up my mind.

* * *

The lift is just a platform that moves up and down. The lifts were one of the first things dug into the crater walls by the robots when the city was constructed. Most cities add metal filigree or something to it. Not Asimov, it's just a big opening carved into the rock.

Kallista punches in level ten. "Only the bulk carriers go all the way down to level twelve. This one, the people lift, only goes down to level ten.

We pass the floors one at a time. Fortunately, there's no one waiting at any of the floors, so we're steadily going down. We

220

pass level seven and the acrid smell of hydrogen sulfide makes our eyes water.

"I really wish I would have put my helmet on a minute earlier," I say as my eyes begin to burn. Everyone follows my lead and dons their visors.

"Are anybody else's eyes burning?" Natalie asks.

"Your suit should clean that up in less than a minute," Kallista says.

"It's getting worse!" Natalie says.

"It's getting better for me." I turn my mic off and have the hydrogen sulfide level display on the inside of my helmet. It's at thirty parts per million and rising quickly.

"My eyes are still burning," Natalie says as we pass level eight.

"Is the level always this high?" I ask.

"It's the smelting of crater dust. It's high in sulfur. That's why levels eleven and twelve are for robots only," Kallista says.

"Natalie, you must have a leak in your suit," I say.

Her hands are pressing against her visor, and she's starting to hyperventilate. The hydrogen sulfide level has doubled to sixty, and it's still rising.

Glancing at my readout, the levels have doubled in only ten seconds. I turn on my mic. "Lift! Emergency! Ascend at maximum speed," I call out.

"I don't smell it anymore," Natalie says, slurring her words.

Alex buckles to his knees as the platform stops suddenly before rising. Natalie falls to the floor. Alex and Kallista rush to her.

The hydrogen sulfide level starts to fall. Once it's below fifty, I remove Natalie's visor.

"What happened?" Natalie asks between coughs.

"The hydrogen sulfide levels were increasing fast and your suit wasn't sealed properly." I take off my gloves and reach out my hand for Natalie's helmet. I run my finger along the inner gasket.

"There it is," I say as I remove the dirt particles that were keeping the helmet from sealing. "You should always inspect your helmet before you put it on." I give Natalie her helmet back. "Also, if it's sealed tight, there will be a small green helmet icon in your viewing area."

"That could have been bad," Kallista says.

* * *

There's a man with his interior helmet light on waiting for us as we reach level ten. The light shines off his bald head. The ceiling lights are seven meters up and don't have a lot of power. The level is set in varying degrees of shadow, except for our shiny bald man.

Why doesn't he treat that condition? It's not expensive. Cornelius wouldn't do it, but he had to maintain the ship first.

"Kallista! Come here and give your Uncle Gene a big hug," the man commands when we get off the lift.

She turns on her interior light. We can all see her self-conscious smile. She tries for a half-hearted hug, but Gene will have none of that. He grasps her in an all-encompassing body hug, lifts her off the ground and spins her around once.

You really shouldn't do that while in a spacesuit.

"Everyone, this is Gene," Kallista says over the comm. "He's the one we have to thank for today's excursion."

"Okay darling, you kids have fun, but don't stay out too long. The winds are starting to I pick up. I've already loaded the rover for you."

"Thanks Gene." She touches her helmet to his and turns her comm off so they can speak without everyone overhearing.

"Are you guys ready?" she asks us.

"Remember, start the off gassing a couple minutes before you take the plunge," Gene says. "Oh, and be sure to tell your dad that my rover has never run so well."

I look at the other three. This gibberish seems to make sense to them.

"Is anyone going to tell me what's going on?"

"Just follow my directions," Kallista responds as she taps my visor.

We pile into the rover and Kallista starts the air purification. It only takes five minutes for the sulfur level to be negligible. We take our helmets off, but there's no room to put them other than in our laps. I set Kallista's on top of mine, since she's driving.

The rover headlights are powerful at least. We drive in an otherwise totally dark tunnel as we head lower and lower.

"Are we going to the crater floor?" I ask.

"Sort of," Kallista replies. "And no more questions. It's a surprise." She drives us through a large, dimly lit tunnel. It's way oversized for rovers and there are no doors, power hookups, anything, so this must be some sort of industrial tunnel.

"We should check out the view," Kallista says.

The tunnel begins to brighten in front of us. The number twelve is painted in three meter tall reflective white paint ahead of us. I've never been to the bottom level of Asimov. Once around the corner, there's a clear polymer window overlooking the crater. It has to be fifty feet wide.

"Helmets on, everyone, then we can check out the best view of Asimov Crater," Kallista says.

Alex bounds out of the rover and immediately leans up against the polymer. It gives a little, causing him to freak out and jump backwards.

"It's five layers," Kallista says. "That was only the polymer giving."

"Really?" Alex asks. "Can we take our helmets off, then?"

I check my readout. "Hydrogen sulfide levels are way too high."

We take in the view for a few minutes. Even Alex is quiet. There's a mound of orangish-red dust filling most of the crater. I've seen it a million times from our ship. What I never noticed from above is the alternating light and dark lines. Mars is a dead planet with virtually no atmosphere, so is this all caused by weathering? I keep silent. I don't need the others to think I'm stupid.

"We still have fun stuff ahead of us," Kallista says.

Reluctantly, we head back to the rover. Kallista drives us through the vehicle airlock and we leave the confines of the city. She avoids the path to the crater floor, instead turning onto a ledge. She stops way too close to the edge for my liking. One false move and we'd plummet over the edge. It's kinda cool, in a terrifying sort of way.

There's nothing but wild Mars around us other than a rickety pulley system that might be strong enough to hoist a child. It definitely has the look of an Asimov construction.

In no time, we're out of the rover and standing one and a half kilometers above the crater floor. The wind blows orange dust into our faces and for a moment, I begin to panic.

A little dust isn't going to hurt anything.

"What are all the dark lines?" Natalie asks.

"I'm glad you noticed them," Kallista says. "Those are recurring slope lineae. Basically, in the summer, the temperature gets above the freezing point of water, causing it to come out of the ground. At night it refreezes as ice."

"Enough of the science lessen," Natalie says. "Let's get the sheets out."

"Sheets?"

Alex and Natalie remove two black metal sheets from the top of the rover and set them down right at the edge of the precipice. The sheets are inwardly curved at one end, and that's the side facing the crater.

"Now sit on the back of it so it doesn't slide down," Kallista tells me.

That at least makes some sense.

"Now move your feet so they're pointing toward the crater."

I do what I'm told, but I'm uneasy about having three people behind me while I'm at the crater's edge.

"Asimov crater is eighty-four kilometers wide and three kilometers deep, so we're halfway down the crater," Kallista says. "In about two weeks, the summer sun will hit the northern facing slopes, releasing volatile gases and causing rock slides. It's too dangerous for the miners to operate in those conditions."

I scoot backwards to the very end of the sheet. The cliff face is even more dangerous than I thought.

"Banzai!" Kallista screams as she leaps over me and slams into curved front of the sheet, feet first. We slide forward and I reach to grab her in a blind panic. She leans forward and before I can warn her, the sheet tips over the side of the cliff.

We lose contact with the ground for a second as we fall off the edge. We hit dirty ice and accelerate down the crater wall. We start bouncing wildly off any small outcrops. I look in vain to find some sort of steering mechanism. We hit pockets of red dust on the way down. Kallista keeps ducking down, so the dust flies over her and straight into my visor. She raises her hands in victory and is nearly thrown off as we hit another rock. She screams in delight. Even Alex and Natalie are yelling encouragement at us over the comm.

There are protruding walls of stone on either side of us, funneling us toward a narrow opening at the bottom. I wait for our inevitable demise as we speed ever faster past menacing rocky outcrops.

"Airborne!" Kallista shouts, as we near the funnel exit. There's a small ramp that launches us upward. The sled falls out from underneath us and Kallista and I are set on different trajectories.

Below me is a bubbling, frothy dust cloud.

I freeze in confusion as I race toward the impossible. Has the ground become unstable?

Marsquake?

I recover my wits just in time to land feet first into the, well, whatever it is. I'm buried up to my waist. There are millions of bubbles hitting my suit as they rise out of the sand. This must be what it would feel like to be an ice cube in a fizzy drink.

With all the movement below me, it's easy to extricate myself from the sand. Kallista is saying something to me, but all I can do is stare at her as I try to decipher what just happened.

I look back up the seventy meters to the funnel we launched from. There's a line of dust racing toward it.

Another metal sheet launches itself. The sled falls away, and Alex and Natalie are flying through the air. One of them is trying to run while the other extends their arms to the side to form a 'T'.

"Feet first!" Kallista shouts over the comm.

Did she tell me that?

They land near us and start pumping their fists even as they're half buried, like us.

"That was so cool!" Alex exclaims.

I'm watching them, still trying to process what just happened.

"Chris, Alex, grab our sleds and meet us at the rising rope," Kallista says.

I'm not sure what she means, but I grab the sled and we slog through the silt. Everyone else is shouting and carrying on, but I'm still numb. We walk to the base of the rickety pulley system.

"How did we not kill ourselves on the landing?" I ask.

"Gene and his crew pump air into the landing pit," Kallista says. "The air loosens the dust, making it look like a witch's cauldron. It removes any water from the field and counteracts the packing that happens in the summer. For one week every Martian year, there's a pillowy landing spot for crater surfers."

"Can we go again?" Alex asks.

"Yes!" Natalie and Kallista say in unison.

Am I the only person who realizes the risks? I look out into the abysmal, dusty plain and wonder why they would ever do this once, much less multiple times.

Oops, Kallista is still talking.

"— get back up, only one person or object can ascend at a time," Kallista says. "I'll go first."

"We're going to trust that thing?" I ask, horrified.

"Yep," she says. "Once I'm up, send the sleds up next. Natalie, you follow me and the boys can figure it out from there."

"Sounds good," Alex replies.

I stare at them in disbelief. Using this contraption is even scarier than the uncontrolled drop.

"Chris? Hello Chris, are you with us?" Kallista asks.

"Uh, yeah, sure."

After the girls are finished laughing at me, Kallista attaches her suit's tether to the chain with a carabiner. One tug and the chain starts carrying her up. Kallista walks gracefully up the side of the crater.

I look down at my suit where my tethering loop should be. It was torn away ages ago. All I have are two frayed tabs of cloth. It never seemed all that important, so Cornelius and I never had it fixed. I should tell the others about this, but I'm afraid they'll think that I'm hopelessly poor. I wish I could rub Cornelius' coin for luck right about now.

The sleds and Natalie go up next without any issues. I'm starting to sweat as I try to figure out a way to work my situation into the conversation. Now Alex and I are the only two left down at the bottom, and I have no choice but to speak up.

"Okay, Chris, you're next," Kallista calls over the comm.

My heart drops into the deepest, darkest pit of my stomach. "Uh, guys, my suit doesn't have a tethering loop, or a carabiner."

"What? Stop joking around and get up here," Natalie calls.

I feel sick. "The tether was ripped off over a year ago." I brace myself for the incoming jeers.

"I can hold on to Chris and we can come up together," Alex volunteers.

"Won't work," Kallista says. "This system isn't rated for that much mass. It has no chance of holding both of you. Let me look for something up here that we can send down to you."

I'm dumbfounded; they didn't make fun of me! But it doesn't mean they won't, given enough time.

"I'm fine and I have a solution," I call. "I'm coming up."

I don't need their help or the pity that will come with it.

I have a metal arm and a grip that would easily outlast the whole rickety device. I grab the chain with my left hand and give a good, solid tug. It responds faster than I expect and I try to pull myself upwards so I can walk up the slope like the girls did. My attempt to lift myself must have registered as a second pull, because now the system is going at a much faster pace. The cliff face repeatedly gets much too close to my visor. I have to use my natural arm to keep from smashing my helmet into the rock.

Too much scraping of any part of my suit and I'll lose the integrity, but my helmet shattering is instant death. I push off the slope to create enough space for my legs to straighten. The pulley system clearly hates me, because it interprets this as a third tug. I rocket up the side with no prayer of controlling my ascent. I cower behind my metal arm and watch as sparks start flying off whenever I make contact with the rocky cliff. There are at least three different alarms going off. Motors are whirling and air is streaming out of my suit. Every breath adds to the frost on the inside of my visor.

"Let go!" Kallista screams as I near the top.

I do as ordered and sail over the girls. I land on my ass and slide about five meters. Getting up, I realize the air bladder around my left arm has activated, pinching my shoulder and making movement a challenge.

So much for showing off my masculinity.

I roll over to my right side and get on my feet immediately, so they don't come rushing to my aid. My metallic left arm is shining in the sun. There's not a shred of syn-skin remaining. At my shoulder, there's a small stream of water vapor escaping my ring bladder. The spacesuit arm, my syn-skin, they are just gone.

I start feeling light-headed so I check my air capacity. It's at thirty percent and dropping. I engage the emergency seal program and small doughnut-shaped bladders inflate around all of my pressure points. Keeping air in the torso and helmet is paramount. The pressure stabilizes and one of the alarms ceases. The others are telling me that I have a leak in my suit. Someday, computer systems won't be so stupid. I override them, but they keep turning back on.

Kallista and Natalie rush over.

"Are you okay? Is your arm the only problem? Let me check out your butt." Kallista is running circles around me and carrying on hysterically.

Natalie, on the other hand, is standing back and taking in the whole situation.

"I didn't know that you have an alloyed arm," she says at last.

I shrug my shoulders, which is stupid. It could unseal the safety bladder.

"The syn-skin just finished healing," I say.

Alex arrives at some point during the commotion.

"Kallista, calm down," I say. It's not effective. "It is fully alloyed, so it will be fine. I sealed my suit, and the pressure is holding now. I'm okay."

"That arm will act like a radiator and transfer all your body heat to the atmosphere," she says. "You'll die of hypothermia."

"I hadn't thought of that." My suit shows a one degree drop in my core temperature already.

"Everyone, our fun is over." Natalie announces. "Chris, get in the rover while we clean up."

I hang my head in shame as I waddle toward the rover. I wonder what they must think of me now.

"Hey, did anyone notice that dust devil before?" Alex asks.

"Great, Gene is going to kill me if we end up starting a dust storm," Kallista says.

"Why?" Natalie asks.

"Chris's ascent was filled with electrical discharges. Hopefully, it's too early in the season for that to start a full-on dust storm."

"That's pretty cool." Alex says.

I have to agree with him. I divert my path to the slope's edge so I can check out my very own storm. "I never heard of anyone starting a weather phenomenon before."

"Chris! Get in the rover!" Kallista commands.

"That is so cool!" Alex sounds as amazed as I am.

I scurry to the rover, because it would be embarrassing to die like this. Kallista seals the doors behind us and pumps into the air. The light goes green and I take off my visor. I can feel the heat blasting on high.

"We'll have to put our helmets back on when Natalie and Alex get in, but for now, it will keep you from freezing to death."

I thought Kallista was cute the first time I saw her. But with her worrying about me, I think she's the most remarkable person in the world.

This is one of the best days of my life.

Alex pounds on the rover door again. Kallista has told me very firmly that neither of us will answer the calls from Alex or Natalie until my core temperature increases. Of course, my PCD is spread across the canyon wall, so I couldn't answer, anyway.

I only let out a couple of muffled grunts as she cuts what remains of my syn-skin back to the tourniquet. The nerves were just getting past the painful, itchy phase, too. Now I'm going to have to go through all of that again.

"Why do you have a tracking beacon attached to your arm? Do you frequently get lost?" Kallista asks.

"What beacon?"

"It's here." She takes her knife and pries off a small magnetic disc. "See the coil? That's the antenna that allows you to be tracked by radio waves."

"Keev!" I spit out his name. "He told us to go to his body mechanic. He must have told her to include the tracking device."

"Keev? Eww."

"Yeah, he's not my favorite person either, but he gets us jobs."

"We should probably get you out of that suit to check you over," Kallista says.

"No, no, no," I say. "There's no way the bladders will reseal, and we saw what happened to Natalie in the lift." Just my luck, a girl finally wants me to take my clothes off . . .

"That's all we can do for now," Kallista says, as she runs her hand along my metallic arm one last time. "You'll have to see a health engineer as soon as we get back. Do you have stem cells on your ship?"

"Yep." I should really say something more, but what? I am so bad at talking to girls, customers, people in general.

"I feel so bad." She makes the cutest worried face. "It was my idea to do this and now you have to get your arm reskinned and get a new PCD. It will cost you a fortune."

"It's okay, I had fun today and I can't say that often."

She looks at me, unbelieving.

"No really, I don't leave the cockpit much and this was so nice to just go have fun. Besides, we just happen to have the money to pay for all of this." I raise my arm. "So I think today was awesome."

Her face softens, and she leans toward me. My pulse increases and I moisten my lips.

"Look at the time!" Kallista says. "They only have about twenty minutes of air left and they'll need that for the lift up to level one. We need to let them in before they asphyxiate."

The true number of undeclared solo habitation occupants (USHOs), or in the common vernacular, homesteaders, is unknown. The government places the number very low, due to the unlikelihood of long-term survival without the infrastructure of a city. Others declare that a thriving underground community exists. There are no registered precious metal mining operations on Mars, so the steady increase in such materials argues for the latter interpretation.

Excerpt from: The Martian Mountain Men
Katy Ann Weerasinghe

CHAPTER 20 CHRIS

Asimov Crater Space Park

"How's your arm?" Alex asks for the bajillionth time.

"The arm's fine." I don't take my eyes off the engine readout. The number three engine is off slightly.

"I think you need a break," Alex says as he enters the cockpit.

"And I think we need to keep working."

"Great, what do we have to do besides clean up again?"

I let out a sigh. I don't know what's wrong and staring at the screen isn't helping. "We need to harvest some of your stem cells and start culturing them if you're going to remain on this ship."

"Phew, I thought you were going to say clean up the galley again."

The med-bay is filled with all kinds of bins, compartments and drawers. If I need to refill something, I still ask the med-bot to locate the bin. It's not like the acronyms used for each item are decipherable, but that's not the worst part.

The scariest part is the six arms positioned around the central lighting fixture. When I was young, Cornelius said that it felt like he was about to be dissected. I still envision that every time I'm in the chair.

At least it's not me this time. "Med-bot, take four hundred milliliters of Alex's blood and prepare it for freeze drying."

"Please direct the patient to sit in the appropriate chair," a soothing female voice says. A green light on the top of the only chair in the room starts to blink.

Alex looks uncertain, which is natural, so he looks at me for confirmation.

"Have a seat," I say with a shrug.

"Please connect the restraining band," the voice says.

Alex shows off his goofy grin as I strap his arm down. It's all I can do to not smile back.

Three robotic arms jump into action. One glides over to a wall filled with storage bins and reappears with a large-bore needle. The second arm withdraws sterile tubing and attaches one end to the centrifuge. The third attaches a claw and squeezes Alex's upper arm.

Alex looks at me, concerned.

"That's needed to pool your blood in your veins for easier extraction."

Alex nods and watches in wonder as the robotic arm dance continues. The tubing is attached to the needle and the needle arm shines ultraviolet light on Alex's arm for a full minute. A green light comes on and the needle is inserted directly into Alex's vein. He jumps at the poking.

"Haven't you ever given blood before?"

"Why the hell would I do that when there's synthetic blood?"

"Synthetic blood only has a shelf life of a year. Your blood will be spun in the centrifuge, the water will be discarded and the solids will be flash frozen and powdered. They'll keep for at least five years in frozen form."

Two of the arms default back to the ceiling. The needle arm withdraws shortly after. A fourth arm comes down, gets the body glue attachment and sprays Alex's arm.

"Don't touch it!" I say, louder than I should.

Alex furrows his brow. "Why?"

"It needs a bit of time to knit itself onto your skin."

"You've gone through this?"

"Med-bot, how many blood packets of mine do you have stored?"

"There are twelve packets in storage. You will be due for a donation in three months."

Alex looks at me. "You go once a month until you get to twelve. Then it replaces the oldest every six months with a new sample."

Alex puts on a brave face. "Is this all?"

"Not quite," I say. It's really hard not to smile, but I keep my voice even. "Med-bot, collect a sample of Alex's stem cells for cultivation."

Two arms swivel into action. The first goes for the ultraviolet attachment. The second arm, with a claw attachment again, holds Alex's right arm down.

"It's not another needle, is it?" He asks before inhaling a deep breath.

"No, not exactly." I bite my tongue since I know what's coming next. A third arm activates and collects a pneumatic biopsy punch. The punch rests against Alex's forearm.

He looks at me questioningly. Pop! Alex yelps as it takes a centimeter divot out of his arm.

Alex tries to jump out of the chair, but his right arm is restrained. He definitely does not look happy now.

"It's needed for good quality stem cells," I say. "Now you know why the restraints are necessary."

The arm drops the skin chunk into a test tube held by a fourth arm. It spins the tube in circles until the skin sample is pulled to the bottom. The extraction unit door opens, and the tube is placed inside. The door closes and a small motor begins to hum.

A blood clotting and antimicrobial spray is applied by the fifth and sixth arms. Alex grimaces. I know from experience that the spray is the worst part.

"The med-bot will digest your skin's connective polymers, then spin what's left in a centrifuge to isolate your stem cells. Once it has those, it will collect them and grow them in a nutritious agar."

"What's an agar?" He asks.

"I have no idea, but it's always a nutritious agar, not just the plain kind."

Alex looks at the med-bot arm restraining him. "That better be it."

I smile at him. "Med-bot, please perform a cavity check."

Alex glowers at me. "I. Will. Kill. You."

"A cavity check is not necessary at this time." The med-bot responds.

I throw my arms up. "See, there are too many fail safes. I can't have it do anything that isn't warranted."

A final arm comes down and attaches a self-adhesive gauze to his left arm, then the restraining claw releases its hold and returns to the ceiling.

"Procedures are complete. Should I schedule a reminder for the next blood draw?"

"Yes," I say before Alex can answer.

"How is it that you nearly died earlier today and I'm the one in med-bay?"

"Kallista was really fast with the diagnosis and we made it into the heated rover before hypothermia set in. However, if you get out of the chair, you'll get your wish."

"What is it going to do to you?" Alex asks.

"Not too much. It will apply a nerve paste over my metal arm and reglue the syn-skin strips to one another." I give Alex a big smile. "I won't feel a thing."

"I'll get even with you."

I smile even wider.

"Do you have anyone else's stem cells?"

"I have a couple samples of Cornelius'."

"Why? Do you plan on re-growing him?" He asks jokingly.

"No. I have personal reasons." I say it more harshly than I should. The arms start their aerial dance and we watch them in silence.

* * *

The one nice thing about Vikram is that he pays well and he pays up front. Okay, that's two things. What the hell, a third nice thing is that he is completely clueless about Martian geography. Nili Fossae is only thirty minutes away, but he gave us two days to do the job. We picked up the cargo before lunch. Easiest money ever.

"I'm glad we picked up the cargo early," I say. "The dust storm is getting worse."

"You mean Dust Storm Chris?"

"I should drop you off at a homesteader's base and leave you." I give him an annoyed look. "I'll contact Vikram tomorrow morning and tell him we have the cargo. Since he thinks we're working for him all day long, I want to do something fun. Any ideas?"

"I've been dying to try out the Clunker Cars. Would you be up for that?"

"What the hell is that?"

"You've never heard of the Clunker Cars?" Alex asks, mouth agape. "It's the coolest thing ever! Huygens has the best team, but that's to be expected. Everybody gets in a little pod car and they race around the track."

"So, racing? I guess that's okay."

"It's way cooler than that. I mean, I guess you could try to out race everyone else, but usually everyone smashes into each other and tries to flip the other cars upside down. The last car capable of moving wins."

"So I get to demolish you? Count me in."

* * *

The Clunker Car Race is a big deal, apparently. It's a sport with an actual planet wide league. Asimov's course is attached to the very back of the recreation floor, along with the other spectator sports. Cornelius didn't like sports, or exercise really, so I'm not surprised that I never knew about it.

The magnetized cars achieve really fast speeds, according to the specs, when the course is powered up. Apparently, Asimov's team is perennially bad and they are always looking for new talent, so at fifteen hundred on Thursdays, it's open racing.

The course is a four kilometer maglev track in a stretched figure eight configuration. The magnetic track rides up along both walls and extends to just a bit of an overhang above. There is a two-meter opening at the very top of the tube.

"The idea is to hit the other guy with enough force to knock them up the wall to that lip. If you get that high, gravity takes over and you fall roof first onto the track." Alex explains.

"Is this safe?" I ask.

"Sure, the seats are all top of the line xanthan gum padded gel packs, so you sink in and it conforms to your body. You have to wear a helmet that is attached to the back of the seat so you can't have your head snapped in every direction. And the cars are all made with reinforced composites that absorb most of the collision. Whatever you do, never leave the pod."

How much do I trust Alex? I mean, I fly a spaceship and all, but this seems much more dangerous. Of course, I can't say anything or he'll question my manhood.

The cars are lined up in five rows of four cars each, with about five meters separating each row. They literally open the gates and everyone runs to whatever car they want. I select one in the front row. Three hundred empty meters stretch out in front of me before the track angles to the left. While everyone else is colliding, I'll be in front of the wreckage.

The pod only has one button to turn on the magnetic engine and one pedal for speed. There are no brakes. The maglev track is turned on and all of our pods rise fractionally off the ground. I'm keyed up now and waiting to start.

"Start your engines," the announcer calls.

The other three cars in my row take off and I hear excited yells behind me. I get hit in the back and I'm knocked a couple of feet forward. Apparently 'start your engines' means go. I hit the pedal and get a belated start. I'm right in the middle of the pack, where I didn't want to be. There's a huge scrum of cars jockeying for position, or just hitting people because it's fun. I'm not really sure what the motivation is, but I give as good as I get. Alex and I are linked through our PCDs.

"This is awesome!" Alex roars.

"Where are you?"

"I'm in the number seven car," he replies unhelpfully.

Thwack!

"That was me."

My head snaps back into the gel pad as my car lurches up the tube wall. Knowing that I'm a target here, I swerve back to the middle before anyone can finish me off. We make it to the first turn and . . . and there's a ramp right in the center of the track! I try to swerve, but I hit another car and end up launching off the side of the ramp.

I'm airborne, and my car is leaning heavily to the right. I throw my shoulder to the left as much as the straps allow. My car comes smashing into the magnetic field and my pod bucks up and down until the excess energy is dissipated. I've lost all my speed and people are streaming by me. I floor the pedal to regain my speed. I scan the cars in front of me for the number seven pod.

I barely have any speed coming out of the first turn, so I stay towards the bottom. Most of the drivers are half way or more up the wall as they accelerate through the curve. The sixteen car is the highest on the wall until he dives downward and sideswipes the guy below him. The poor fool goes all the way across the bottom of the track and up the other side. The track deactivates and the hapless car starts falling, right in front of me.

I swerve wildly up the wall and barely miss the falling driver. This is only the first curve! The second straightaway looks pretty empty to me, so I'm way behind.

In front of me are two giant three-pronged cranes lifting pods off the track.

"Oh, shit!" Why didn't Alex warn me about these? With a flick of my wrist, I'm going under the higher of the two cars. I'm hopelessly behind, so I floor it in the straightaway. Several pods fly across the track, perpendicular to me.

At the center, the lanes crisscross?

I grab the wheel in a death grip and close my eyes as more racers whiz across my path. When I open them, I'm through the center. I pick up speed and for the second turn, I'm halfway up the wall.

The midpoint of the second curve has two ramps on the floor of the track this time, but they're lowering back into the track.

Oh great, the ramps change throughout the race.

I spot a couple of unfortunate drivers who weren't able to navigate these obstructions and give them a wide berth. I cross the starting line all by myself. Yay. I made it through one whole lap.

I'm ready to inflict some pain this time around. As the track straightens out, there is absolute carnage in front of me. Five, no, six pods are all out of commission. I can't slow down, so I ride up the left wall as I speed through.

Slam! A car appears from my left as I get to the center crossing. His car is flung into the air as I continue below him. I'm trying to see if I got my first victim when my car glances off another obstacle. I'm able to keep most of my speed so I can go high on the curve this time.

"Alex, are you still active?"

"Yep. Here I am!"

My pod gets nudged this time, but it's enough to send me upward to the lip. For a brief second, I'm weightless as my car tumbles down. My pod spins slowly on its roof and doesn't stop until I'm facing oncoming traffic. I feel my chest and arms, making sure everything is still attached. My syn-skin has torn loose, but that's not a surprise. I hope the med-bot can fix it. I'm so done with body mechanics.

Cars blow past me, causing my pod to rock. So far, everyone has managed to avoid me, but how long will that continue?

How do I get out of here? Shouldn't someone have told me about this?

My chest is thumping like crazy. Alex told me not to get out of the pod, but I'm facing death here. I try to undo my straps, but it's nearly impossible when hanging upside down. I can feel the car shimmy every time a racer goes by. I close my eyes and wait for the killing strike.

The pod rocks a little and I open my eyes to see a metallic claw descending from above and resting on my car. Now it clicks! The cranes are to remove crashed drivers, not as an additional hazard. A rush of exhaustion replaces my feeling of impending doom. I will never understand why people want to do this to themselves.

* * *

Alex finished fifth out of twenty drivers today. I was twelfth. It's all he can talk about as we walk back to our ship. I really wish I had disabled his suit's comm. He keeps talking about doing this again next Thursday and possibly joining Asimov's team. He doesn't know it yet, but we're going to have a job for the next several Thursdays.

We make it into the quarterdeck airlock and the signal goes green. The second I take my helmet off, he starts up again.

"I beat you, so you have to say it," Alex insists.

He cheated. I know he did.

"Alex Vennemann, you are superior to me in driving on an artificial course, where you intentionally withheld information about track hazards, filled with people who were obviously teaming up against me, where rules are not followed, in dilapidated pod cars which only work sporadically. Happy?"

"Wow. How hard is it for you to admit defeat?"

"Well, I'm not going to repeat it."

Alex lowers his shoulder and knocks me into the cargo bay. I crash into Vikram's containers. It's a cheap shot, just like on the course.

"Oh, it's on." There is no chance of him out wrestling me on my own ship.

"What's that?" Alex is staring down at my feet.

"Nice try. Prepare to be destroyed."

"No, seriously." He's pointing now.

I glance down and see that the bottom wall of the crate has fallen off, exposing a box inside. It must be a secret compartment.

"What the hell?"

I remove the snugly fitted box and find it to be filled with Super Psy Cy. It's a hallucinogenic mushroom and one of the very few narcotics grown on Mars instead of being synthesized.

"Dammit! I knew the money was too good to be true."

Alex comes closer for a look.

"Where did he get that from?"

"Nili Fossae, of course," I say.

"If we grew even a little of that, we'd be free of Vikram in no time," Alex says.

"Except we'd have to sell it to Vikram and we would be criminals ourselves. Well, technically we're already criminals, but I mean hardened ones."

Alex looks as if he's about to argue and thinks better of it. Is he really thinking it's a good idea to grow illegal contraband?

"Don't you know how bad this stuff is?" I ask.

"Of course I know. I knew a dozen or so users at Huygens. They never hurt anyone. They mostly get lost in their own little worlds and either laugh or cry a lot. Once they come down, they're the most mellow people in the world."

"Well, I told Vikram that we wouldn't ship drugs. If we get caught, it would be you and me who have to answer for it."

"What are you going to do?"

"We're going to take all of it out and hold it here on the ship. If Vikram's not aware of this, we'll dispose of it. If he is aware, he'll come looking for it, and I can tell him we don't transport drugs."

"He knows about it," Alex says with certainty.

"Probably, but this way we'll know for sure." I have to give him a chance. The money is really, really good.

"There's no probably, he knows and he'll be pissed," Alex says.

"That will make two of us."

* * *

The port airlock proximity sensor starts going off.

"Is somebody outside our ship?" Alex asks.

"Must be."

"Why didn't the AI tell us someone was coming?"

"In this dust storm? The sensors can't make sense of anything through all that," I explain.

"You mean that the Dust Storm Chris is too thick for sensors to penetrate?"

"Haha. Now get into your quarters until we know who this is. It could be one of Vikram's guys."

I cycle the port airlock and one dust-covered person stomps inside. Short, stocky and doesn't give a damn about all the dust he's dragging in; it has to be Vikram. The outer doors close and air is pumped back in, whipping up the dust. The filters activate and the cloud slowly dissipates. As soon as the pressure equalizes, the inner doors open. Vikram twists off his visor and drops it to the floor.

I watch in horror as dust flies everywhere. It will get sucked into the ventilation, and the cleanup . . . I stop myself. There's a bigger issue to deal with first.

"Do you think you're funny, kid?" Vikram demands in a low growl.

I hope against hope that he's referring to something other than the mushrooms.

"Why are you angry at me?"

"Where are the mushrooms? For your own sake, they better still be here."

My shoulders sag. Vikram knew about them, and now I'll never be able to trust him to keep his end of the bargain again.

"They're in the cargo hold, all of it. I told you I would refuse to be a drug runner."

"Did you really think I was paying you that much money to move dirt?"

"I told you Vikram, no drugs." I look him in the eye.

"You'll carry whatever I want you to carry or you'll have to find some other way to eke out a living. Do you fancy getting cancer at Kunselman's obdome?"

"Vikram, I will not transport drugs," I say flatly.

"So, how are you going to feed yourself without my money?"

He didn't yell like I expected him to.

"I guess I'll have to figure that part out. I told you, the same rules as Cornelius had with your people or no deal."

Vikram's eyes bore into me. But I've made up my mind and no amount of staring is going to change that.

"Well, kid, you're in luck," he says slowly.

I let the kid remark go.

"I have another job for you, but you have to leave within two days."

"What's the job?"

"No need to be suspicious. This is a salvage job."

I relax a little. Everyone looks down on salvaging, but it's perfectly legal.

"Most of the decent ships have been claimed long before now. And the rest have had salvage crews visit them. Which crater is it near?"

"I'll have my men give you the space coordinates when they arrive, along with a list of what to look for."

Damn. How do I keep Vikram from finding out about Alex if he's sending men on board?

"The ship is derelict in space? But that's not possible."

"It is, and it is."

"No disrespect, but I would rather do this job without the assistance of your men."

"You're going to transfer back and forth between two ships in deep dark space without anyone else on board? One slip and you're a dead man." He's smiling slightly as he tells me the obvious.

"If it's all the same, I would feel more confident working alone than with unknown criminals."

"Do it your way, but if something goes wrong, I'll just end up with two ships to salvage instead of one. I'll send someone to get my merchandise and deliver the coordinates." Despite his words, I think I've impressed Vikram.

"Can't you just send me the coordinates?"

"I could, but the first rule of found treasure is to not broadcast it until it's in your possession."

"Oh, Vikram, one more thing," I say before he can leave. "Next time, do a two-cycle entry. It will take me two days just to clean up all of this dust."

Vikram chuckles to himself and then picks up his visor. He taps it against the bulkhead to dislodge more dust before he puts it on and hits the air cycle button. The inner doors shut right in front of my face.

"I guess our discussion is over."

Once Vikram leaves my ship, I call over to Alex. "You were listening, I assume."

"Yep. He wasn't as angry as I thought he would be."

"He took that very well," I say.

"Oh, Chris, I think that is a very bad sign."

"Nah, he likes me. He's told me so. I want you to go into the city center and buy that property in your name. I'll transfer you the money while you're heading towards the city."

The population of Mars has stubbornly refused to rise over the past two decades. At just over a million people, our entire population is only a fraction of any one of great metropolises of Earth's past. At some point in the near future, power on Earth will consolidate enough to overcome our efforts of containment. Investing in relationships today will allow us to engage our cousins on our own terms tomorrow.

Why Martians Should Care About Earth
Mamiko Nakayama

CHAPTER 21   VIKRAM

Asimov City

"The kid needs to be eliminated," I say upon entering Keev's store.

"What? Why?"

"He's refused to transport my drugs. Why the hell does he think he's getting paid as much as he is? Sympathy?" I throw one of Keev's overpriced gizmos against the wall and watch it shatter. He scurries over and inspects the damage. One look and he knows it's a lost cause.

"I can talk to him, explain things to him," Keev says.

He's trying to placate me again.

"We just need to play the good cop, bad cop routine to bring him along."

"He's worse than his father," I say.

"Cornelius was more streetwise. He sheltered Chris from some necessary lessons, but I can get him up to speed."

"You think so, do you? What about his little sidekick? Will he be dependable too?"

"Alex is exactly who we need to have with Chris now. He grew up in the back alleys of Huygens. He'll be more realistic about these things."

"Is he more trustworthy than you?" I ask. "Because I put a tail on Chris, that's how I found out about this Alex. How long have you known about the sidekick? Were you ever going to tell me?"

I'm good at reading people, the best, in fact. Keev always looks down when he's nervous. It's subtle, but I spotted it my first day here. Anyone at his level should be able to tell a bald-faced lie without sweating.

"Chris brought Alex by once; I assumed you knew."

He's a good liar, I'll give him that. He doesn't get flustered even when he's caught. He busies himself cleaning up the shattered electronic. I walk up closer, cornering him.

"I see. And you're also aware that they bought a vacant greenhouse?" I say in a menacing tone.

"Of course. They told me about it a few days ago. Why would you care about that?" He continues on with his cleanup charade, as if he has nothing to fear from me.

I move in closer and rest my arm on his back. I'm earth strong, so there's no way he can rise without my approval. I lean down so he can feel my breath on the back of his neck.

"Now, I'm curious. What other information are you holding back from me?" I say, barely louder than a whisper.

He tries to stand up, but I won't let him.

"I was under the impression you did not want to micromanage; therefore, I screened out the information that's beneath your notice. Was I wrong?" Keev responds unflustered.

"A very oily answer. Now, what other intel do you have on Chris and his brother?" I turn my back to him and wave for him to follow me. He's a good little lapdog.

"I know of nothing else. Why would you care about his brother or the greenhouse?"

"I need him completely beholden to me, and only me. He's signed up for a lifetime commitment, whether he's aware of it or not."

"Cornelius was ideal, because he never asked difficult questions and he never went looking for trouble." Keev spreads his hands out to his sides. "Chris is young, but he can grow into the role. He's awkward around people, so he prefers to spend his free time alone on that ship. If you were to get some other captain, do you know what the odds are of finding one who doesn't drink too much, gamble too much, steal from you or run his mouth?"

"Cornelius ran his mouth. That's why I had him killed."

Keev spreads his hands wide again. "Cornelius chose poorly, no doubt, but only when he was cornered and interrogated. Had you sent some thug, not a single word would have been divulged. His weakness was that he had an ingrained compulsion to respect the authorities. That's what compelled him to answer."

"So he was a law-abiding smuggler?" I ask.

"He never asked questions, so he always had plausible deniability to the authorities as well as to himself. Now consider that there are only a handful of captains, fifteen at the most, who have a ship comparable to the Halley and are willing to smuggle goods, and none of them would be willing to base their operations out of Asimov. We were lucky to find Cornelius and Chris."

He's smooth, but his fondness for the kid is a liability. I can't have my underlings banding together. "Your logic is flawed on two counts. First," I tick my finger, "I have no desire to stay in this backwater and second, I have a pilot. All he needs is a ship like the Halley. The kid can easily be replaced."

Keev blanches.

I don't want to set him off in panic mode. "You are right about one thing Keev, the kid has spunk and could be very useful if he develops right. Maybe it's because he's the scrappy underdog. He'll get his chance to keep his job and his life, but he will have to pass my tests. Pull up that data of yours on the derelict ship."

"You're not sending them after it all alone?"

"He declined my men. I hope your little friends are up to the task. Now, write down the coordinates and call your courier."

"You're not going to tell them about the risks?" he asks.

I shrug. "He refused my help."

"They could both die."

There it is. He has completely shown his cards. I can't keep both him and the kid for the long term.

"The good news is that I already have a replacement if I need him. Either way, the *Halley Traveler* will continue to deliver my cargo."

Keev glances downward again. "I will call a courier."

"You are forbidden from making contact with the kids or relaying any additional information. They wanted to do this without any help, and I have granted their request."

"The courier won't be here for another thirty minutes."

"I'll wait."

Ever since the Earther elite hastily departed their own planet, there have been tales of fabulous ships sitting derelict in space. We know that critical situations did arise during this period. We know this because the beacons and alarms alerted us as the ships carried their doomed passengers past Mars and into the outer solar system. A plausible explanation as to why a ship would stop halfway to Mars has never been presented. Obviously, that is because these tales are complete fantasy.

Lost in Space: Abandoned Spaceships and Other Ridiculous Tales
Ricardo Elizondo

CHAPTER 22 CHRIS

Interplanetary Space

Alex wants to sit behind me, in the captain's chair, but I won't let him. If I can't keep an eye on him, he'll space out, and I need him for this job. I haven't let on to Alex, but this job scares me a little. Performing maneuvers millions of kilometers away in the blackness of space is as dangerous as doing the clunker cars without any safety restraints. It only takes one mistake and you're dead.

"What I don't get is how Vikram could have the coordinates for a ship that is foundering in space," Alex says.

"Why would a ship come to a full stop, anyway?" I respond. "If everyone mysteriously died, the ship would have remained sailing along on its vector."

"And how does Vikram have such a detailed list of items for us to recover?"

We've been asking these questions over and over for the last three days and we're still no closer to answers. The coordinates we've been flying toward finally resolve into a visible dot in space.

"Damn, if there isn't an object right where Vikram said the ship would be," I say.

"Is it the *Cosmic Dream*?"

I ping the ship with the standard identification protocol. It should give an automatic response, if the ship has power and the comm unit is working.

"No way! It *is* the *Cosmic Dream*." I look over at Alex, at a loss to say more.

Alex lets out a whoop and gives me a toothy grin. The story of this ship has been told and retold for years. No one can agree on how it came to a dead stop. The only thing they can agree upon is that the people were some of the richest from Earth. Vikram's list can't possibly list everything of value.

"I'm going to get in real tight so we can make contact with our cables."

"How close do you have to get?" Alex asks.

"Within seven hundred meters."

"You just know that number off the top of your head?"

"You have to know these things when you're the captain. Start prepping the tools for phase one. I'll meet you in the quarterdeck airlock once we match the ship's drift."

I've never had to be so precise while maneuvering. I can't let Alex stay in the cockpit and see how shaky my hands are. It takes forever and an embarrassing amount of corrections, but I get us in position before Alex gets bored and comes back to watch me fumble. Now I'm facing an even more dangerous spacewalk.

* * *

The electromagnet attaches to the *Cosmic Dream*'s hull next to the airlock on the first attempt. I attach my safety harness to the tether line and sail over to the derelict ship. There's a half-meter chrome band all around the airlock. Chrome isn't sufficiently magnetic; I can't use my mag boots. Yay. I'm going to have to stay tethered the whole time and contort my body every which way just to reach the control panel.

Why haven't I bought a non-crotch pinching suit yet?

My suit reeks of sweat and frustration. I've tried the emergency code to open the doors, and that got me nowhere. Every ship is supposed to accept the SOS code.

"Why won't the stupid emergency entrance code work?" I ask in frustration.

"Did you punch in the proper sequence?"

"I'm going to punch you in a proper sequence if you ask me that one more time. Check the databanks; is there a universal override code?"

"Ha! Yes there is. Are you ready for it?"

"No, let me sit out here in the frigid shadows for another hour, then give it to me."

"You don't have to bite my head off."

"What's the damn code?"

"It says to punch in the emergency entrance code again, then the override code of ABC."

I start punching in the code, like literally. I'm slowing propelling myself away from the ship because of my frustration. I wrap my leg around the tether a couple of times to keep me from drifting. But now I can't reach the control pad because my harness is holding me back. I twist my foot around to give me two and a half wraps around the tether before I detach my harness. I'm not a big fan of removing safety equipment, but sometimes you have to in order to get the job done. This way, I won't send myself careening back every time I use the control pad.

"Here goes nothing." I enter the codes.

The doors open and I'm hit with a blast of air that knocks me backwards. Water vapor freezes on my visor and I'm blinded. I flail my arms, trying to find the tether, but I'm rotating as I'm floating backward. I feel the line come loose from my knee. My rotation is unwinding my only lifeline from my leg.

I curl in on myself and grab the tether just as my foot comes loose. My legs continue toward the Halley and my grip slides a few centimeters from the frosted line before my momentum is stopped. I stare out into the nothingness and try to regulate my breathing.

Once I can speak clearly, I opacify my visor and I turn sunward to remove the frost. My heart is pounding so hard that I'm getting a blood pressure warning from my suit. My natural hand is tiring, so I release my hold on the tether and trust my metallic hand to keep me safe. I look for the Halley, but I can't find it. The fog on the inside of my visor is clouding my view.

Okay, take a breath. Your metallic hand will hold on to the tether for hours if need be.

I'm blinded, exhausted and holding on to a rope for dear life sixty million kilometers from a habitable planet. I breathe out of my nose. Cornelius always said it helped him relax.

"What do you see?" Alex asks, oblivious to my situation.

Everybody says they have a cool head when they're safe planet side, but when a single mistake in space will kill you, it's a different story. It's up to me to get out of this mess, or I die trying. It's that simple.

I should already be dead, but I had the dumb luck of twisting my leg around the tether. Alex has no pilot training, so there's no chance he could have rescued me.

"I'm having some difficulties, standby."

"Hey Chris, you never gave me a full list for phase two. What else do I need to assemble? Also, it's hard to hear you over your breathing. Do you want to take a break and try again in a couple of hours? That way, you could help me with this first."

If he was in the cockpit, looking at the vid screen, he'd know why my breathing is so loud.

"Alex, I need you to go to the cockpit." I close my eyes to keep the situation from overwhelming me.

"How do you know that I'm not—"

"Alex! Go to the damn cockpit and look at the vid screen."

"Going now."

I focus on breathing through my nose. The blood pressure alarm stops, so the only sound is my breathing, which makes it worse, somehow.

"Where are you?"

"Do you see the box on the control panel labeled outer hull?"

"Ah, yeah."

"Hit that button and it should expand into seven or eight options."

"Okay," Alex says.

"Hit the button for 'tethers' and retract the aft tether."

"Is that the port or stern? Oh, never mind, I'll just retract both of them."

I take another deep breath and let it out through my nose. Getting frustrated will only make it worse.

The tether goes slack as it detaches from the *Cosmic Dream* and I'm adrift in space. Before my limbic system can freak me out again, the motor kicks on and I'm being pulled toward the

Halley, and safety. I click my mag boots on and land safely on the hull of the Halley.

Cornelius would have had a stroke if he saw just how stupid we've been. Hell, I almost had a stroke.

"I'm returning now," I tell Alex as I waddle toward the quarterdeck airlock.

* * *

I nudge the Halley forward so our high-resolution camera can see into the *Cosmic Dream*'s airlock. Plain as day, someone placed a metal pipe between the inner airlock doors. That's why there was a jet of air escaping once the door was open.

"Assuming there are no more booby traps, I should be able to pull the logs from the ship," I say.

"Yeah, maybe you can find out why they left that bar there. That's crazy how they sabotaged their own ship."

"I hope they have reserve air; it would be nice to be able to take my spacesuit off while I'm over there."

"Do you think they lost engine containment, and that's why they wanted to vent all the air?"

"If they did, there would still be a huge radiation spike and our sensors would have caught it."

"Even if it happened forty years ago?"

"Even if it happened ten thousand years ago, but we're just not seeing it."

"When do I get to go inside?" Alex asks for the umpteenth time.

"After you've been trained in extravehicular space maneuvers. Space doesn't give second chances."

Now I'm quoting Cornelius word for word.

"It's boring over here."

"Well, why don't you get my tools ready for this trip? That should cut down on the boredom."

Damn, I have become Cornelius.

* * *

There's only so much I can piece together from the *Cosmic Dream*'s data. It will never make sense without boots on the ship. Mercifully, the second spacewalk goes without incident and I'm standing inside the *Cosmic Dream*'s airlock only a minute after I leave the Halley.

I make it to the cockpit and if anything, I'm more confused. The oxygen reserves are still intact and all the desiccated passengers are floating in their cabins. Whatever happened here was slow to develop. There are no signs of damage other than the error message on the carbon dioxide scrubber. That seems to be what finished them all off, but the error message simply says to replace the screens. Even Alex could do that. The whole scenario makes no sense.

From the cockpit, I seal the airlock doors and release the reserve air. There's only enough to fill the ship with a third of a standard atmosphere, but at least it's pure oxygen, so I'll be able to take my suit off once the interior is heated. I love the smell of space, welding fumes with a side of seared meat.

"It would be great to have an update occasionally. Are you still alive over there?" Alex asks.

I fumble with the ship's controls. It takes forever, but I'm finally I can turn on the comms. "Sorry, it just became warm enough for me to get out of my suit. We'll have ship to ship communication from now on."

"You're echoing."

"Hit the yellow button that has 'suit comm' underneath it on the left side." I wait a couple of breaths. "Better?"

"Much better."

"Good, have you finished processing the used spacesuits?"

"Over an hour ago. I've also cleaned the galley before you ask."

"Did the galley need cleaning?"

"I was bored, so I ate lunch without waiting for you."

"I've managed to seal the ship and release the oxygen reserve. Give me a minute and I'll access the logs."

"Cool, I'll be awaiting your next transmission. Alex out."

I don't want to be added to the dried up corpses, so I double and triple check the rest of the life support systems before I go hunting through the captain's log.

The air pressure is holding, and based on my breathing, I have five hundred hours before the carbon dioxide concentration will cause mental impairment. All other systems are functional. I scroll to the final days of the ship's log. The captain's last comment is ominous.

"Hey Alex, listen to the captain's last post: 'Everyone is complaining about being sick, but none of them feel as bad as I do since Ada ripped out my heart and annihilated it in the antimatter engines and cast off the atomic remains into the coldness of space. I can only hope that their suffering will approach my own.'"

"Wow, that's dramatic. Do you think the captain killed everyone?"

"It would explain why the ship is stopped out here between planets. But even a rudimentary check with the databanks would have turned up a tutorial. So I don't know. Either the passengers were the dumbest people ever or maybe the carbon dioxide got them first."

"So, I can come over now?"

"We never leave the only fully functioning ship unattended. You know this. Besides, there are tons of dead, dried up people floating around on this ship. Do you want to remove the jewelry from the corpses? I'll be happy to take your place and relax in the galley."

"Never mind."

I should have some sort of reaction to all these dead people, but they feel like a 'them' to me. And I have too many problems of my own to worry about Earthers who died around the time Cornelius was born. Still, we should reclaim their biomass. In a perfect world, I'd take them back to Asimov and turn them in to the recycling tanks for credits. All these organics would make a nice payday, but then Vikram would find out, and I don't want him to know any more than he already does.

I have no idea how Vikram managed to get such a specific list of jewelry. After searching each body, I stack all the corpses in the first passengers' quarters, so they won't get in my way. I check the cabins one by one. Earthers were obsessed with ornamentation. I even found a desiccated fur ball. I can't tell if it was a dog, a cat or something else. They used to keep animals like that as pets back then, I think.

All these people, and in their time of need, they couldn't work together.

"Dammit."

"What's wrong?" Alex asks, breathless.

"Sorry, I was talking to myself."

I have to start trusting Alex and give him more responsibility.

* * *

"So Alex, I have a crazy idea," I say over breakfast.

"What's new?" Alex says between bites of pancakes.

It's kinda a celebration day, since we're ready to wrap up the job today.

"How would you like to pilot a ship?"

"Don't mess with me," he says as he puts down his fork.

"I'm serious."

"Really?" His food is forgotten, which is a first.

"Yes."

"When do I begin?"

"Well, I've been thinking," I say slowly. "The *Cosmic Dream* is still in good shape and I would like to fly it back to Mars, but that still leaves me needing someone to fly the Halley."

"I've never even flown a simulator. You expect me to fly this ship by lunchtime?" Alex's voice rises in panic.

"Wait, wait, wait, before you hyperventilate, just hear me out."

"The answer is no."

"I can program this ship to fly itself and to engage the auto landing sequence at a prearranged location. It's all automated, so your only job would be to know what to look for on the control panel and to report it to me on board the *Cosmic Dream*."

"But how long would that take to learn?"

"A couple of lessons today, one final lesson tomorrow morning, and we head back to Mars."

"Back to Asimov? Wouldn't Vikram be pissed if you gave him the baubles and kept the ship?"

"Probably, but I thought of a solution already: Schiaparelli Crater."

"What about it?"

"We land both ships there."

"But nobody can go there. It's restricted."

"So there will be no one there to arrest us, or even see our two ships. We can leave the *Cosmic Dream* there and fly back to Asimov together on the *Halley*."

"Don't they have something there to stop people from going to Schiaparelli?"

"Cornelius told me about the time he went there. I begged and begged him to take me there, but he never did. All you have to do is to fly below a certain level on a prescribed path and the beacons won't notice the ships."

"Do you know what the path is?"

"No, that's why we're not leaving until tomorrow. I have to figure that out first."

"Why don't we just land at Asimov and you walk over to our ship real quick?"

"Because auto landing protocols are illegal and you would get caught flying without a license."

"Why are they illegal?"

"They have this nasty habit of not noticing other spacecraft that are already on the ground. The program seems to think it's all just part of the landscape and they would often land on another ship. But at Schiaparelli, there aren't any other ships, so it won't be a problem."

"Why don't we leave it here and just come back for it later?"

"If there's even a small leak in the ship, all the oxygen is going to be gone before we make it back. I don't want to fly it all the way back to Mars while wearing a spacesuit," I say.

"So I'm going to end up as a shooting star that no one will even see before I crash into a dead, forbidden city."

"You're a genius Alex! I've been trying to come up with a new name for our ship. The *Shooting Star* is perfect."

He'll come around to my plan. I'm sure of it.

CHAPTER 23 CHRIS

Martian Atmosphere

"That is so awesome!" Alex blurts out as the dome comes into view for him. I'm following thirty seconds behind. The dust storm must have grown while we were away, because I still can't see the Schiaparelli dome.

"Pay attention to your gauges or it will end up being the last thing you ever see," I warn.

"Well, nothing is red, so I guess all is well," a nervous Alex responds.

I keep waiting for the engines to flare. The dust storm must be screwing with the ground detection radar. I stifle the urge to yell instructions at Alex.

The engines flare on the Halley right as I can first make out the dome. They're burning extra hard. The algorithm must have realized it screwed up. The *Halley* lands with a thump and kicks up more dust. I shudder at the potential damage to the landing gear. At least it doesn't buckle.

I don't have time to dwell on it because my turn is coming up. The gauges are all reading true for me. I land softly next to Alex. Inspecting the Halley's the ground detection radar and the landing gear must be added to the long list of possible repairs.

The entrance to the city is about two stories high and rather plain looking from the outside. That was probably on purpose, so once inside the dome, you're blown away. They really loved their domes, because they made a smaller one to cap their actual city. You could drive two tall-boy rovers through the entrance at one time, but that's about it.

"Can we go into the big dome?"

"Cornelius told me that the dome was sealed, but there's no way they'd waste that much air to resupply it."

"Then why did they bother?" Alex asks.

"Because if you let the dust in, it would never be tight again. It was a fix it immediately or lose it forever. Maybe in the future it can be used."

∗ ∗ ∗

The doors must scrape a new track through the fine reddish dust. There is no one around, but we still rush inside like we're doing something naughty. Actually, we are doing something naughty, and I kind of like it.

A fine mosaic tile floor has the Schiaparelli seal covered unevenly by a fine film of orange dust. No matter how exacting you build on Mars, the dust always finds a way inside. Either that, or there have been visitors before us. I bet both are true.

The airlock is illuminated by a single light, which makes the room dim and uninviting. The outer doors close and Alex feels the need to turn on the external lights on his spacesuit. The air pumps into the room, lifting the dust off the floor. Alex points to a sign placed in the center of the cone of light.

Schiaparelli City has been declared a cemetery city. It is unlawful to disturb this memorial. Toxic spores of stachybotrys chartarum have been detected at lethal dose levels. No entry is permitted.

"I guess we're not leaving our suits then," Alex says.

"If the air purifiers are still running in Little Giovanni, the black mold should have been removed decades ago. This may just be a ploy to keep people out. Let's take some readings and see."

"How long are we going to stay?"

"A couple of hours or so; that will give us time to walk around the city," I say. "Spacesuit, full workup on the atmosphere, please."

"You call your spacesuit, Spacesuit?"

"What else would I call it?"

"I call mine Harvey," Alex says.

"The air is sixty percent of standard; however, the oxygen partial pressure is thirty-five percent. Particulates are present, however no contaminates have been found. Temperature is twelve point eight degrees Celsius. Open flames are not advisable," my spacesuit informs us in a neutral voice.

"Good. Alex, open your visor and confirm that the reading is correct."

"Shouldn't the captain do that?"

"I'm way too valuable. Who would fly us out of here if I die?"

"And if I die, why would I care about that?" Alex grouses as he takes off his helmet. He immediately grabs for his throat and acts like he's dying.

"If you weren't laughing so much, I may have bought it."

Alex walks toward the inner doors and hits the button. A couple of pumps sputter into action, and the doors jerk repeatedly as they open.

"More dust," he says.

"I was going to interface with the city computer to make sure there are no nasty surprises for us, but by all means, just run right on in."

Alex ignores my sarcasm and does exactly that.

The doors reveal . . . nothing. There's a glowing red ball way in the distance and nothing else between it and us. Alex walks inside and gawks at the dome.

"Why isn't sunlight coming through?"

"Nobody to clean the dust off the dome, I guess." Joining him, I take off my helmet so I can see this with unhindered eyes.

The walls are polished red rocks with the semi-opacified dome overhead. Mars colonies as a rule don't have buildings taller than three stories, but beyond the sweeping entrance plaza, which takes up a third of the dome, are dozens of buildings that are ten or more stories tall. Even still, they are well short of the dome. Along the walls are the remnants of shops.

"So much empty space," I say. I've never seen anything like it. "How much nuclear power is needed to keep this place warm? And where are the heating vents?"

"What's that red ball thing at the other end, and why is it glowing?" Alex asks.

"I don't know, maybe to provide enough light to see, but not enough for funguses to grow?"

"Fungi, not funguses."

"Who cares?" I shake my head. "Let's take off our suits and go see."

"This feels totally wrong. We're walking on the surface of Mars without a spacesuit," Alex says in wonderment.

"To think it used to be a daily occurrence." I can't focus on any one thing. The actual Martian ground under my feet, the soaring buildings, the dome that feels like an entire sky. There's just so much.

We race to the red ball and discover that it's a rotating globe of Mars. As it spins in silence, a bright white geodesic dome comes into view. Below it is a column with a spiral carved from the top to bottom.

"I guess that's to make sure you know where you are on the planet," I say.

"Yeah, and it looks like a light went dark because I can barely see Noctis Labrynthus."

"I don't think it's a mistake. Huygens is also unlit."

"They can't do that," Alex says, annoyed. "Huygens is the most important city."

"What's on that column?" Mostly in the shadows, the column clearly has images on it, but I can't make any of them out. As we approach, floor lights turn on, bathing it and its spiraling images in warm light.

"Look. At the bottom is a three-dimensional carving of the crater," I say.

"And there's the *UNS Garrett* making its landing," Alex responds. We both trot around the column to see what other scenes are depicted.

"That's the first permanent settlement."

"What is that? Skeletons playing with plants?"

"It's the Starving Time," I say. Alex looks at me uncomprehendingly. "The permanent colony started with *Garrett Three*. *Garrett Four* malfunctioned on entry and was lost. The colonists had to plant and live off of potatoes and vitamins until *Garrett Five* arrived."

"So they went a couple of weeks without food?" Alex asks.

"No, that was before fusion powered ships. The launch window was only every two years or so."

"See, that's the arrival of *Garrett Five* there." I point at the next picture.

"I don't recognize any of these," Alex says.

"This next one is when they started burrowing into the crater walls here to start the modern city. And the one after that is a white dome. That has to be the one over Schiaparelli. They're not exactly humble, are they?"

"Do they have the Burrichter Repulse?" Alex asks.

"Since that took place at Huygens after the great dome was breached, I'm going to go with no, it's not here. In fact, the dome is the last scene." The line spirals on upwards, waiting for more scenes to be added.

"What's past this?" Alex asks.

"It looks like a city from Earth. Look, there are streets surrounded by buildings on either side."

"What do the balls suspended above each street mean?"

There were eight streets leading away from the opening plaza. From right to left, the colors were brownish, dirty yellow, dark blue, white, white and orange striped, tan, light blue and dark blue.

"I have no idea. Let's go see."

We run again. I haven't run this much since I was a little kid at the annual Water Races at Noctis Labrynthus. The streets are endless, though, and we're both sucking hard for air. The blue orb is hung above Earth Street.

"Wait! What does the white one say?" Despite being tired, we run to the next street over and sure enough, it's Luna Avenue. "The streets must be in order of the planets from the sun. See, it starts with Mercury, then Venus. We've been to Earth and Luna. The striped one has to be Jupiter followed by the rest of the gas giants."

"Since when is Luna a planet?" Alex asks.

"Just like they kept Noctis and Huygens in the dark, adding Luna keeps Mars in the center. Four rocky planets on the left, four gas giants on the right."

"Yeah, and Mars is the only one lit up."

"How awesome is this place?" I ask.

"It's cool, but I wish it wasn't so cold."

I see Alex's breath as he speaks. "It definitely wasn't this cold when we first got here. Let's get out of here before we freeze."

Despite the urgency, we only walk back, taking in the whole dome as we go.

"I can't imagine what the dome over Schiaparelli looks like. This one goes on forever," Alex says.

We cast impossibly long shadows, reaching all the way to the entrance. I look back and finally put two and two together.

"Alex! See that fuzzy yellow light?" I point a third of the way up the dome where the dust has blown off.

"Yeah."

"That's the sun."

"No way, really? You mean that we're looking directly at the sun with our naked eyes?" He looks at me for just a second before his attention is back to our star.

"How cool is that?" I ask.

He looks past me and raises his arms.

"What are you doing?"

"Have you ever seen shadows this long before?"

I turn and see his giant shadow arms waving right and left. I join in on the fun as we each try to make the most awesome image. Alex turns back to look at the sun.

"Um, Chris," he says.

"Look at how long my arms are now," I say. "I can't even see the end of them!"

"Yeah, about that. Can you turn and look at the sun for a second?"

I face the sun's direction. "Where is it?"

"That's what I'm worried about. I didn't bring any light source, did you?" Alex asks.

"No."

"So, how do we put on our suits when it gets dark?"

I mull his question over for a second and look back at the gate. I look at him. By unspoken accord, we sprint back to our suits.

"It's moving faster now." Alex yells. "Look, it's almost beneath the dome."

I look over and his gray clothes are hard to see distinctly.

We make it back to our suits and there's only a soft glow at the bottom of the dome.

"Take your time Alex. The last thing we need is to have an ill-fitting suit when we go outside."

"Easy for you to say. If we're not ready soon, we'll be wandering all over this place trying to find the airlock."

I know that darkness can't hurt you, but being blind in such an enormous place is unnerving. At least at Asimov, you're never far away from a wall. Here we could walk aimlessly for hours. I face the airlock doors before they fade from view. As long as I keep this orientation, we won't have a problem getting out.

In the dim light, I can't see my visor. I have to bend over and wave my hands until I hit it. I check to make sure I'm still facing the doors, but it's too dim.

"Make sure to inspect your helmet's gasket before you put it on," I remind Alex.

"How do I even put the helmet on?" Alex asks. "I can't see the hashes on my suit's collar."

I can hear the edge of panic in his voice. I attach my helmet and turn on the external speaker and external lights. Alex is too panicked to notice. I take his helmet from him, seat it properly and turn it clockwise until I hear the click.

"Power on, Harvey, maximum illumination," Alex says.

"Maximum lighting," Alex's suit replies in a chirpy voice.

I didn't really believe that he went to the trouble of renaming his suit. Not only that, but he paid good credits to upload a silly voice file for it. I need to give him more work or fewer credits.

"Okay Alex, now we have to find the exit."

He turns around in a circle. "I can't see it!"

The suit lights aren't that powerful. Since the suits were made for space, it doesn't make sense to illuminate anything more than an arm-length in front of you. Anything more is just a power drain.

"Follow me." In truth, I have only the vaguest idea where it is, but if I keep walking straight, I'm bound to find a wall. Our feeble lights only heighten the shadows around us until we find the airlock doors.

I check my oxygen reserve, thirty minutes left.

"Alex, stay here with me, by the inner door."

"Why, I want to get out of here."

"If either of our suits aren't tight, we'll start losing air. If we have to go back inside and reseal our suits, it's best that we're already by the door."

"Okay," Alex says as he stands next to me. I can't let him know that I'm just as weirded out as he is.

The inner doors close and the central light comes on.

"Oops, I forgot about that light."

The airlock begins its cycling.

"No leaks." Alex says.

"No leaks." I repeat. "If I remember right, the *Halley* should be just off to the left. Since we have light, let's wait at the outer doors."

"Are you sure that's where the *Halley* is?"

"Not really, but how hard can a ship the size of the *Halley* be to find in the dark?" I turn the comm off. "How much oxygen do I have left?"

"Twenty-eight minutes," my nameless suit replies.

"How much air do you have left, Harvey?" I say once, reestablishing the comm.

"Fifty-one minutes."

Alex didn't top off my oxygen in my suit like he should have. I'll have to get on him for that, but not until we're safely back on board the Halley. My mind is busy replaying Cornelius telling me, 'everyone must check their oxygen before they leave the ship. If you're low on oxygen and you leave anyway, you better hope you don't get what you deserve'.

Brain, shut up already.

I have plenty to worry about without disembodied voices running around in my head.

"We'll give it twenty-five minutes. If we can't find the ship, we'll have to go back to Schiaparelli."

"How can we miss something that size?"

"I don't know that we can, but it's always good to have a backup plan." I don't need Cornelius's voice haunting me. I'm already turning into him.

The outer door opens and all we can see is dust whipping in front of us. I switch my lights to high intensity and I'm nearly blinded by the reflection from the dust. Low intensity lighting it is then. Alex makes the same discovery. "We should stay within view of each other's light," I say. "Keep your head slightly down. You don't want to stumble over a rock and land visor first."

"No, no, I don't."

Is that panic in Alex's voice? "Remember, we have plenty of time, so go slow and no mistakes." Telling him about my oxygen level will only make him more nervous.

* * *

I check my reading. Eleven minutes left. I silence the alarm before it can start going off. The last thing I need is for Alex to hear it. How much longer can it take to find a ship the size of the *Halley Traveler*? I wave my arms in the darkness all around me. "Alex! Where did you go? I can't see your light." Okay, there might have been a little panic in my voice.

"I kept walking at the same pace. Where are you?"

"Stop moving and turn around. Retrace your steps until we see each other's lights."

"We should have just followed our footprints back to the ship once we left the city."

I feel like I've been punched in the gut. I look down and wonder which set of footprints are which.

Dammit! Why couldn't we have thought of that sooner?

I see Alex's lights emerging from the storm and I can hear his breathing getting softer.

"Do you have any sense of direction at this point?" I ask.

"No. What if we can't find the ship or the city?"

"Panicking won't help. We are going to pick a direction and keep walking until we no longer see any footprints. Then we'll turn left and extend the perimeter of our search area until we find the ship or the city. If need be, we'll turn around and do the same thing going right and keep expanding until we find the ship." Easy for me to say. I'm down to ten minutes.

By mutual agreement, we pick up the pace and find the city wall. *Six minutes left.* We turn and try again in what will be my last pass. If worse comes to worse, I think I know where the city gate is.

"I see it!" Alex yells.

I turn in his direction and all I can see is more dust. He must have turned away from me. *Three minutes.* This is when I planned to make a break for the city gates.

"Alex! Where are you?" I'm starting to hyperventilate. All around is just one orangish-white cloud of dust.

"Sorry, I got excited and kinda ran toward the airlock."

"Don't leave me stranded here." I'm doing my best not to lose it. Two minutes, forty-five seconds. I look at the ground again, but it's hard to see anything.

"What? Are you afraid of the dark?" He taunts.

"How long did we fumble around in this storm? You can't leave your partner behind!" My throat is tightening up. I try to swallow, but my mouth is bone dry.

"Sorry." His apology might be the last thing I ever hear.

"Retrace your steps, and hurry, I think the wind is getting stronger and the dust will hide the footprints from view."

I try to slow my breathing, but all I manage to do is blow fog onto my visor. To my left, the dust is becoming brighter. That has to be Alex. I head toward it. Everything hinges on this.

One minute, thirty seconds.

It takes one minute for the port airlock to cycle, but two for the quarterdeck. I can't hold my breath for two minutes.

I run-hop toward the light. If it doesn't take me to the ship, I'm dead. I bump into Alex, knocking him to the ground.

One minute.

The warning alarm amps up the volume. The carbon dioxide level is also too high. Alex's suit looks to be okay, but I don't have time to help in any case. Halley's hull appears from out of nowhere, and the port airlock is right in front of me.

I find the numeric keypad, grab a firm hold on the rail and punch in five-zero-five as hard as I can. The outer door gradually opens. I squeeze through the entrance, not caring if I rip my suit. The air alarm is earsplitting. I take one last gulp of air. The oxygen in my lungs is all I'm going to get.

My lungs start burning from the excess carbon dioxide I'm holding. I release my breath, but the burning continues. My stomach starts churning and my eyes are tearing up. I only have seconds left. I pound on the control panel to close the door, but I miss. My motor control is going.

The emergency button!

I look for the big red button as the edges of my vision are fading to black. The button is on the other side of the door. I lurch for it and collide with the wall and fall to the floor.

Did I hit it? I can't hear anything over the alarms in my suit. My vision is all but gone. If I stay in this suit, I die. I grab my visor and turn it left.

"Chris! Where are . . ." Alex's trembling voice fades away.

* * *

"Not cool, Chris," Alex yells. "I could have died."

How long was I lying on the floor? I open the inner doors and see a very angry Alex without his helmet, but otherwise still in his spacesuit.

My right hand is trembling, so I brace myself against the outer airlock. I must have gone hypoxic when I passed out. I'm lucky to be alive.

I put my hand up to stop Alex from yelling. My head feels like it's going to implode.

"Once I'm functional, we both need to go over safety procedures again." I push past him and hit the wall behind him.

This is good. The wall will hold me up. I slide along it to med-bay. I just hope I have the strength to tell it what to do.

The romanticizing of homesteaders as rugged individualists conquering an unyielding planet is not only erroneous, but dangerous. These narcissists can only survive by absconding valuable resources such as oxygen, nitrogen and water for their own personal use. Collectivism, the only equitable system, dictates that such resources belong to the masses.

Excerpt from United We Thrive, Divided We Die
Todd Daniels

CHAPTER 24 CHRIS

Schiaparelli Crater

Alex is already up and waiting for me in the galley. He's made powdered eggs, carbo-nougat and orange-colored water. He's promised me that the nougat is ten times better than the carbo-paste I typically get. He used the orange water to flavor the nougat, so that's not a good sign.

I don't even taste my food, as I wonder when I should tell Alex my next crazy idea. We'll need all of our calories today.

"Before we leave," I break the silence, "we have to move all the corpses from the *Shooting Star* to here."

"Why?" Alex looks like he's about to lose his breakfast.

"All that organic material is valuable, otherwise I would have jettisoned them into space."

"But you said we can't take them to Asimov. If you give me some time, I might be able to sneak them into Huygens."

"Nope, I've got a better idea."

Alex looks dubious.

"Cornelius and I have delivered supplies to a homesteader, Jean Passepartout, during past dust storm seasons. The dust keeps satellites from tracking any ground level movement. If we show up with this amount of organic material, Jean should be eager to keep working with us."

"You know homesteaders?" Alex asks, amazed.

"I've met a couple, but I kinda only know where one of them lives."

"Kinda?"

"We'll have to fly low and slow over the Libya Montes region, broadcasting on a specific frequency. Once we're close enough for Jean to pick it up, he should send us the coordinates."

"Can we at least keep the clothes? I know we could sell them for all kinds of credits."

"Do you want to undress a hundred and forty corpses?"

He gives me a sour expression.

* * *

Jean enters the port airlock and quickly unsuits himself.

"See that?" I point out to Alex. "He managed to take his suit off without sending dust everywhere. I wish Vikram would do that."

The inner door opens and Jean sticks out his calloused hand in greeting. "My robots should be assembled at the back airlock. If you open it up and follow me back, I'll get us comfortable while the unloading is ongoing."

It's been a couple regular years, or one Martian year, since I've seen Jean. He looks much the same, still wears brownish-orange clothes and slicked back gray and brown hair. "I see you are still 'the man of Mars' these days."

"That I am. Before I forget, I'm sorry about your Dad. Cornelius was a good friend to me and the homesteaders." He looks at me. "But let's talk about happier things," he adds. "Where did you come across all these bodies?"

"They're from the *Cosmic Dream*," I say, smiling.

"Really? The amount of wealth on that ship is legendary."

"Our employer had the coordinates and paid us to deliver the jewelry to him, sorry." I know exactly what he was thinking, but there isn't a grand payday unless he wants to sell the clothes.

"Well, no matter, if you'll suit up, I'll give you a proper welcome. Remember, we observe radio silence while we're out on the planet," he cautions. "Once inside, we can talk more."

Jean leads us to the rocky outcrop and slips inside. I've been here once before, but I still couldn't guess where the entrance is until our host slipped behind the false wall. On the other side, a modern airlock greets us.

"You know we are a bartering society, right?" Jean says after giving us each a chilled beer.

I nod. Alex laughs at my foam mustache before imitating me. Jean is not someone who will indulge childish antics, so I wipe my upper lip and turn my attention to him.

"And I can't think of anything I could give that will fairly cover all these recyclables."

"Then let's just say that we're held in high regard by you for now. I do have one favor to ask of you, and the rest can wait for another day."

"Excellent. I'm eager to hear what this favor is."

"Jean, I'd like to get more bullets for the pistol on board the Halley."

His eyes widen a smidge. "You had occasion to use the ones I made for your father six years ago?"

"There were only two left, and I was forced to use them to scare off some criminals a few weeks ago."

"So, you're the Kunselman Dome shooter," Jean says. "Don't look surprised. The use of live ammunition is always going to cause a stir."

"There were these three men trying to kidnap Natalie O'Dell and me," Alex says with his customary enthusiasm.

"Natalie O'Dell?" Jean says, surprised, and not all together pleased. He pauses and looks up at the geometric pattern etched into his ceiling. "Next time, collect the spent rounds if you can. They have my mark on them and I'd rather not have the authorities interested in me."

"I'm hoping there is no next time, but I'd like to be prepared," I say.

"From the account I heard, you need a lesson or three on how to handle a gun. How about we go to my range? I'll start with trigger discipline."

* * *

Jean actually lets Alex and I shoot six times each as part of our training. At the end, he gives me a dozen bullets, which seems like way too many. He must be trying to even out the bartering situation.

"Have either of you seen a homestead before?"

Alex and I look at each other. "Nope." Cornelius wouldn't let me follow him when I was younger.

"Let's start with aquaponics." Jean takes us through a winding tunnel into the center of the mountain. Alex and I exchange glances. Both of us notice the moisture in the air—a rare luxury.

Up ahead, light from the right archway brightens the tunnel beyond typical daylight illumination. Jean leads us into the most awe-inspiring sight I've ever seen. Three, three-story glass aquariums take up the walls on either side and in front of us. Each one is much larger than what Asimov has. There are long, leafy plants stretching from the bottom all the way to the top.

"Look! Fish!" Alex yells as he runs forward. I'm right on his heels. We touch the glass and the fish all dart away.

"Oops, sorry," I say, turning back to Jean.

He smiles back at me. "No harm done."

Jean lets Alex and I gawk at the fish and clams and black spiky little balls that climb on the plants. Above the tanks is a metal grid with plant roots sinking into the water from what must be his hydroponic gardens.

"How many levels are there?" I ask.

"Only six."

"Six?" I say. "That's like as tall as the tallest building on Huygens."

"Well, these are free-standing structures like Huygens, so it's not really the same," he says. "If I'd known you were coming, I would have waited until today to harvest some fresh fish."

Alex's eyes are huge, nearly as big as his open mouth. I'm sure I look the same.

"I've only seen fish a few times in my life, and none of them were as big as yours. I can't imagine eating one," I say.

"Let's talk while we head up to the mezzanine. There you can see my hydroponics as well."

Cornelius always told me that people will like and trust you more if you look them in the eyes. It's really hard to look away from all the marvels, but I try my best. For his part, Jean is amused at our gawking.

"These recyclables," he says, "you have no idea how precious they are to us. We always have redundant systems at our compounds, but the one thing we are always in short supply of is more organics. We'll be able to support more people and allow everyone to have a backup for their aquaponics."

"How much of a backup do you need?" Alex asks.

"There have been a couple of occasions when new viruses have taken down entire aquaponic farms in no time. The only solution is to open the system to the Martian atmosphere and kill everything."

"You pull vacuum first, right?" I ask.

"We can't risk the virus contaminating the air, so everything is lost. The water is boiled off and even the plants are thrown out. The only saving grace is that all the fish are flash frozen in the process. This is our single biggest issue in our recycling loop. For every six of those bodies, there's enough nitrogen to restart an aquaponics tank."

"How do you do it?" Alex asks. "How do you get all the systems to live in balance with one another? Not to mention that you have to somehow collect enough air and water."

"You're forgetting the biggest issue," Jean says. "Energy. The authorities aren't competent at much, but they have a stranglehold on helium-3 and antimatter."

"I didn't even think about that," I say.

"The energy isn't all that hard. There's plenty of uranium, thorium and radioactive potassium just sitting on the surface of Mars. The hard part is collecting it without being spotted. This early dust storm is a godsend."

I give Alex a warning look and shake my head.

"The storms give us the cover to move about on the surface without satellites spotting us. For the next five to seven months, if we're lucky, we can unleash our robots and expand our holdings. We're doubly blessed to have these bodies delivered to us at this time."

"We'll keep that in mind if we ever need a place to hide out," I say.

Jean's face scrunches up, but he says nothing. Cornelius always told me the secret to good relations with the homesteaders is keeping their secrets and not overstaying your welcome. I think we just hit the end of ours.

This simple trick will elevate your mundane bread and paste dinner to a Parisian delicacy. First, pour one part edible oil and three parts water into a sealable container. Add fifty grams of dried herb de Provence, use fresh if you can get them, and shake. Now add just five grams of glyceryl stearate citrate and shake again. Voila! You have made a creamy French sauce. Can't afford synthetic meat? Add reconstituted mushrooms for an unctuous note that will transport you through time and space to the Sacre Coeur district of Old Paris. Bon appetite!

The Modern Martian Home Videozine   August Issue, 2253
Amelia Pelletier

CHAPTER 25 CHRIS

Asimov Spaceport

For this mission, Vikram insisted we land on the trident. I didn't expect him to be waiting for us. His eyes bore into the cockpit as the Halley touches down. I flip off the flight systems and he's gone by the time I look up.

The port airlock connection alarm lets me know where Vikram has gone.

Did he pay someone to stand there waiting to connect with us, or is he at the controls?

As soon as the seal is secure, I open both airlock doors to allow Vikram entrance. Looking past him, there's no one manning the connector. I'll have to make sure the spaceport doesn't hold the Halley responsible for unauthorized use.

"Hello Vikram," I say enthusiastically. "You're going to be happy with our haul. All the loot is stored in the second cabin on the left. I can box it up and deliver it with the exoskeleton."

He rests his hands on his hips and bites his upper lip. He slowly nods affirmatively to whatever internal dialog he's having.

Why is Vikram acting this way?

The trip was even more successful than he could have hoped.

"First things first Chris; I'd like to meet your partner."

"What?"

"You didn't really think I would leave you without any surveillance, did you? Where is this Alex?"

"Come on out Alex," I say into my PCD.

Is he mad that I didn't tell him?

Alex stands next to me. "Vikram, this is Alex. Alex, Vikram. He's my half-brother."

"Why weren't you honest with me, Chris?" Vikram demands.

I guess he is angry about it.

"Because I had no prospects other than working for you and I couldn't take the chance you would nix the arrangement. I can't live on this ship alone forever, you know."

He turns to face Alex.

"How old are you?"

"I'm sixteen," Alex says as he sticks out his chest. Several ribs are visible under his shirt.

"I see," Vikram says with a bit of a smile.

Alex is always like that; everyone likes him immediately.

"So you are full partners, then?" Vikram looks questioningly at both of us.

"Yes," I say. "We split everything and I'm sorry I didn't tell you about Alex, but we either work together or not at all."

Why does my voice choose this moment to tremble?

"It's okay Chris, you guys have done a good job. No one is noticing my deliveries, so it's all good with me. I do, however, want to know if you told Alex about the murder you committed just last month?"

Alex looks at me for guidance.

"He was there Alex. He knows everything."

"Yes, Chris told me about it, but I had hoped he was exaggerating to impress me."

"I didn't exaggerate," I murmur.

Alex looks at the smiling Vikram and back at me, confusion on his face. I can't bear to look my brother in the eye.

Vikram snorts. "You two have a lot to talk about. I'm going to inspect the treasure while you guys hash it out. Drop off the merchandise at the usual spot."

"Right, it will be there within an hour," I say.

"I'll have another job for you in five days. I'll send you the details. Good luck if you go back to the Clunker Cars. And Alex, let me know if you want a sponsor," Vikram says over his shoulder.

Alex's eyes are nearly as big as mine. I shake my head. "Not now." We stand there like statues until Vikram disappears into the guest room.

Alex is just as weirded out as I am. Still not trusting myself to speak, I head to my place of comfort to think.

"Damn," I swear under my breath once the cockpit door closes. "He must have been spying on us from the beginning." I plop down in the pilot's seat, release the seat lock and swivel toward Alex.

"Yeah," Alex replies noncommittally. He rests his hands on the back of the captain's chair, unwilling to sit down.

"Are you alright?"

"I don't know. Vikram has us under constant surveillance, and the only time I'm not being spied upon is when I'm inside this ship with a murderer."

"Alex," I spread my arms out with my palms up. "I told you everything before you joined me."

"You did. It's just at Huygens, I could avoid the dangerous people. Here I work for one and live with another." He looks down at the floor. "It can be a little overwhelming."

The air has been knocked out of me, but I try to hide it.

"What Officer Barnett did was monstrous. He deserved to die. Looking back, I wish I had let Vikram's men kill him because now Barnett is beyond pain or grief, and I still face him every night. And for all of that, it didn't bring Cornelius back."

I flop against the back of my chair and spin back toward the front windows. "I wish I could feel some other way that would make me a better person, but I don't. That's exactly how I feel," I say so forcefully that I surprise myself.

"At least I can understand that," Alex says to mollify me. He then reverts back to the ever-happy fool that I've grown to know. "I don't have to fear for my life daily?" He gives me big doe eyes and the tiniest quiver of a smile.

"If it makes you feel any better, I don't plan on shooting anyone else today. But if the galley isn't kept clean, well, no promises."

Alex bursts out laughing and I join in. Vikram may have actually done me a favor.

"I'll take the stuff to the drop off and you get supplies for a special dinner," I say.

"We're having a special dinner?"

"If you can get Natalie and Kallista to join us, then yes."

"Really?"

"Yes, really. We have money for once and I want to celebrate. Make sure you get real syn-chicken, not the mystery nugget kind, oh, and fresh vegetables too. I want to do this up right."

"Cool!"

"I'll transfer the credits to your PCD."

* * *

Alex can't control his excitement. The girls arrive together and he's pawing at the airlock controls before the seal is reestablished. At eighty credits per hour, only the super-rich can afford a permanent seal.

"Relax Alex."

The door opens with a whoosh. Alex nearly runs into the girls.

"There you guys are!" Alex says, with more excitement than usual. "Chris, why don't you take Kallista up to the cockpit and get us going? Natalie and I will start preparing dinner."

"You can't cook," I tell him.

"I am much better at watching," he says with a laugh. Natalie and Kallista laugh too.

I wish I knew how to say dumb things and still have everyone smile at me. Alex manages to do it all the time. All I ever get are blank stares.

"Now that you're free, Kallista, would you mind?" I extend my hand toward the cockpit.

"Might as well. I've seen engineering. It would be good to see the layout up front."

"Really? Do you have much familiarity with ship controls?"

She looks at me like I'm crazy to ask the question.

I hit the comm button. "Hey Alex, can you secure any loose items? We'll lift off in ten minutes."

"Poor Kallista, lift off is only ten minutes away," Natalie snorts. "Does he ever *not* think about the ship?"

I feel my ears getting warm as I slap at comm to break the connection.

My hand dives into my pocket and I rub Cornelius' lucky coin. Kallista has gone silent and I don't know what that means. I look over and she's staring at the control panel. "Have you always lived in Asimov Crater?" I ask, trying to start a conversation.

Why is her sitting in the co-pilot's seat making me feel so uncomfortable?

"No, we moved around a lot," she says, distracted by the control panel. "Dad would keep scouting out old Earther ships worth fixing up and selling. After we restored the ships worth saving in one crater, we'd move to another and repeat the process." She pulls up the engineering diagnostic reports and skims them while talking to me.

"That must have been fun fixing up old ships."

"Yeah, but I always wanted to be on a crew, not just a salvage team. We finally kept a ship for the family to use. My brother takes it up just to see what level of stupid he can be and still live to tell the tale."

"So, if you had to fly a ship, could you?"

"A little. I moved the ships around after we finished working on one and were ready to start on another," she says.

She's only half paying attention to me, but the other half is on my ship, so that's okay. "So I have an opportunity I'd like to discuss with you . . ."

She looks up suddenly at me, eyes wide open. This is going to be easier than I thought. A good mechanic is worth her weight in water.

* * *

Despite my protests, we're dining at Stickney Crater, on the ridge overlooking the botanical gardens. I reluctantly agree to it as long as we don't have to go inside. I get all sneezy and congested, every single time.

"Chris, Kallista, stop playing with his cock . . . pit and get back here while the food is still warm," a giggling Natalie calls.

"She'll only get coarser if we make her wait," Kallista says.

I extend my arm and invite her to precede me. She unlocks the seat, spins to face the captain's chair and launches herself into a somersault over it. She sticks the landing and looks over at me, smiling.

I'm grinning like a fool as I follow her lead. We take our time, floating down the corridor. She's surveying everything as we head toward the galley. Suddenly, she stops and spins toward the wall.

"What's wrong?" I ask.

"Nothing, the bin caught my sleeve, that's all." She tries to close the bin, but it won't budge.

"Sorry, that one has been stuck like that for a couple of years. We would have fixed it, but we always have bigger issues."

"It's fine. I'll just be more careful," Kallista says.

Alex and Natalie take turns sticking their heads out the galley door, checking on us. Neither of them complains about how long it takes us to join them, but they do eat as if they're famished.

"We cooked, so you two have to clean up," Alex says after inhaling his food.

I'm a little irritated, but he and Natalie leave for parts unknown. I can guess what they're up to and I will not be intruding this time.

I look at the dishes and feel awkward. "Do you want to take another gander at engineering?" I've never known how to chitchat with people, and I would like her opinion.

"I thought you'd never ask. There are several problems I'd like to discuss," Kallista replies.

Phew. I did something right.

She floats to the galley doorway and pushes off to her right. My heart skips a beat, then I'm off to catch up with her. She's waiting for me at engineering. I slap the panel and the door opens. "After you," I say. I'm as polite as the actors in old Earther movies.

She enters and immediately calls up several reports.

I wait for a bit, but the silence feels weird. "I bet you're as glad as I am to be living at this time and on this planet with all the necessary genetic modifications to make us happy, healthy Martians."

"I'm not a modified semi-human; I'm all natural," she responds without looking up.

"What does that even mean?"

She stops reading the screen and looks at me. "No one in my family has had their genes altered, hence we're not modified like the rest of you."

"What? How can that even be? Everyone was required to have the Bhutanese allele or the Nepalese variant in order to immigrate to Mars. How do you function without one of those genes?" The atmosphere in the tunnels is only eighty percent Earth standard as a rule.

"Easily. I do it every day. The body adapts," Kallista shrugs. "I have to take osteo-grow pills weekly and I can't run for kilometers, but I've never seen an engine room that big, anyway."

"But to qualify to come to Mars, everyone's ancestors had to have one of those genetic modifications."

"Not if they came here independent of the Earther bureaucracy."

"But how could anyone hope to sneak off of Earth and onto Mars without being caught?" I ask.

"Oh, I don't know. Maybe if they and a thousand other ships all left at once to avoid starvation on Earth." She looks at me like I'm dense or something.

"You're a New Martian!" I blurt out.

She takes it in stride. "Don't look so horrified. I am as much, if not more, human than you. I didn't have some viral enzyme modify my code. I'm all natural, just like my parents and grandparents."

"But, but then you could be susceptible to colon or esophageal or who knows what other kinds of cancers. Your vision may need correcting with artificial lenses. You can have tooth decay! What do you do if a tooth turns rotten?" No modifications! She could have been born with one or more of the historical syndromes like diabetes or who knows what else.

"Yes, and yet somehow, without all your modifications, I'm still the one standing here with the knowledge to fix your ship," she says bluntly.

Kallista and I go round and round for a couple of hours about genetic modifications, the rights of New Martians, and I even tell her about the *Shooting Star* and visiting Schiaparelli. I have never had such a good time.

Just when I think it can't get better, she insists on going into the wings and inspecting the engines in person.

"Seriously, you need to get rid of all this old equipment; it's too radiation damaged to work ever again. Get new systems; I'm talking carbon dioxide scrubbers, oxygenators, even your water recycler is hopelessly in need of an upgrade."

"Cornelius figured that by keeping these old systems, we could salvage spare parts in an emergency."

"Just get a multi-material 3D printer and program in whatever you need."

"We don't have that kind of money."

"So, how do you plan to fix up that derelict ship you found? Are you going to replace those broken parts with these *almost* broken parts?" Kallista asks.

"I kinda already did that to get the *Shooting Star* back here."

"So you're just going to hope your luck doesn't run out? That's your plan?" Her voice goes up an octave. It's even cuter than her regular voice.

"You think all of this is due to luck? Why would you even come along if you think that?"

"I'm not letting you fly me anywhere further away than here until you have a printer," she says, pursing her lips.

My mind goes into overdrive. I really, really want her to be around. "I'd like to rent one for our repairs, but then I'd have to pay for the templates, and since I don't know what parts I'll need, I'd have to pay for a whole library of parts, just to be safe. Who can afford that?" It feels good to share my burdens with someone who can understand.

"I can get you a copy of my family's repair library, but it will cost you."

"How much?"

"I get to pick which ship I want to fly back from Schiaparelli. Oh, and I want a tour of the city."

Ahh, I hadn't even considered this possibility.

"Deal." We shake on it.

* * *

We return to Asimov and park on the trident again. Once the girls leave, we can move to the space park and avoid more fees. As soon as the airlock closes, Alex starts grinning like a fool.

"So, did you enjoy your dinner?"

"I did, although I doubt you even tasted it."

"It was a good night," he says.

"It was," I agree.

I tell him about the discussions Kallista and I had. He looks horrified. Maybe he's not cut out to be a pilot after all.

"So let me get this straight," his voice begins to rise. "A girl who is your age and clearly turned on by spaceships comes aboard, you're given plenty of privacy and you spend the whole night *talking*? Do I need to draw you an engineering schematic about what part goes where?"

"What?" I can't help but get defensive. "Kallista and I really connected."

Alex looks like he's been struck dumb. Then he holds his head and laughs. Once he regains his composure, he looks me dead in the eyes. "You do like girls, right?"

"What kind of question is that?"

"Chris," he says with exaggerated patience, "the next time you see Kallista, you better have a present for her."

"You think so? What would I even get her?"

"You remember that giant bunch of grapes that Natalie and I like so much?"

"Yeah," I respond. "Oh!" I shout. "Really?"

"Yes," he says, laughing.

"Oh! You mean this whole dinner thing . . ."

"Was not about the food?" Alex finishes my question for me.

"I'm such a dolt."

Alex gives me an exaggerated nod. "Yep."

CHAPTER 26 CHRIS

Asimov Crater Space Park

Alex has really dived headlong into this farming thing. Any free time he gets, he spends reading about or working on our farm. I think it's great that he's working on his time off, even if he did threaten to ban me from the place.

"How's the farm?" I ask.

"It's coming along. We need to install the high intensity grow lights and a humidity controller, then let nature take its course."

"Genetically modified plants on a nearly airless planet with an average temperature of minus fifty-five degrees? We're about as far away from nature as possible," I respond. That might be the dumbest thing he's said all week.

"I wonder what it's like to harvest crops on Earth. Do you ever think about that? I mean, the gravity would be terrible, but how cool would it be to stand under a rain shower? Water actually falling from the sky! Can you even imagine that?"

"Before you get too excited, I have some bad news. We may have to wait on the lights and controller. I know we have another job in a few days, but Vikram may not throw any more our way for a while. I would like to get the *Shooting Star* operational and parked at Kallista's family shipyard. If things get too bad, we can always sell it."

"Without the additional lights, we are four months away from any produce. Isn't there any way we can get those lights? It would be really cool to have a working farm. When it starts producing, we'll have to get some help because we'll be flying all the time. What's it like to fly all the way to Luna? I mean like days and days in space instead of hour-long trips. It's gotta be cool."

He's motor mouthing again.

"Yes, a thrill a minute," I deadpan. "You loved our time in space so much when we claimed the *Shooting Star*."

"All I did was sit around the whole time by myself. Besides, I can fly while we're heading to Luna and back. It's not like I'm gonna hit something."

"You think there's a lot of piloting to do once we lift off, do you? The course is set, and the autopilot does everything. I used to hate it because that's when we'd do our deep cleaning."

"Not more cleaning," Alex groans.

"Anyway, we don't have any trips planned to Luna, so don't worry about that. If we don't find new business contacts soon, we'll have to go into super saving mode. Can you swing by your girlfriend's place and see if Aristotle has any business for us?"

Alex smirks. "Sure, but it may take a while for me to return."

Kallista and I finally got our relationship going, our physical one, so I'm only a little jealous. I have to wait another two days before we can see each other again.

"Since we have time but no money, once you get back, we can run some pilot simulations for you."

"Really?"

"Do not go motor mouthing again," I warn. "It's only simulations, not actual flying."

"But how are we going to pay for repairs if money is so tight?"

"I have an ace in the hole, actually I have two aces, but I'm only going to play one of them for now."

* * *

Keev is at his store, like always. His merchandise looks much the same. During the odd time when he's doing well, the earth stuff is ever-changing. Even during the slow times, he could always find a customer when Cornelius and I really needed it.

311

I'm still not over the fact that he had a tracer installed in my arm, but I'm just going to have to let that go for now.

"Hello, Keev! How have you been?"

He jumps at the sound of my voice and spins to see me. He scans the market area quickly, then gives a nod of his head toward the back room. Without waiting, he ducks inside.

My first step into the back room and I'm smacked in the nose by the heavily spiced air. I blink several times to take the sting out of my eyes.

"Would you like some tea?" Keev asks. He wraps a cloth around his mouth and nose. "Sorry, I've been feeling a little under the weather lately, and whatever it is, I don't want to give it to you."

I have never witnessed him offering tea before, so I accept. Since we're breaking the norms, I ask the question I always wanted to know, but Cornelius wouldn't let me.

"Why do you have a tapestry of a dancing elephant-man?"

"That is Ganesha," Keev calls from over his shoulder. The cloth muffles his voice, making him harder to understand than normal. "He is the god of wisdom, success and good luck." Keev continues over the clanking of cups and saucers. "If you pray to him, he will remove barriers from your path. As you might imagine, he is a very popular deity."

"That's why I've come to you today, Keev, to remove an obstacle from my path."

"I'm afraid you and I share the same immovable obstacle. You should leave here and start anew at some other crater. I will not only pray to Ganesha for your success, but I will also make some calls on your behalf."

I had never heard Keev get directly to a point in my life. "Asimov is my home," I say simply. "Why are you so, so weird today?" Maybe I'm being a little rude, but I have to know what's up with him.

Keev brings over one cup of tea and sets it on the table. "Please, sit," he beckons. He sits opposite my cup and waits for me to join him. "Our mutual friend is upsetting a lot of people. The path forward is unclear, which is why you should consider starting over somewhere else."

"I can't leave here." The idea is preposterous. For the first time I have friends, and Kallista, and a farm. "Are you going to leave?"

"I am old and too tied to this place," he frowns. "But you are young. You can take everything with you and start over somewhere new."

"I have a life here now; I'm not willing to leave it all behind."

"Asimov is going to shit. The drugs he has you bringing in will slowly kill the city. Already the tunnels are becoming more and more dangerous. You don't see it because you only come here during the day."

Keev never leaves his store, so I'm not sure how he could tell if the tunnels are any different, so why is he trying to scare me?

"We only brought in drugs once, and that was without our knowledge. I told Vikram I'd never do it again."

"Chris, you have to know that every pickup you make brings in more drugs. Every. Time."

Keev is being earnest. I'm not sure how to deal with a sincere Keev. It's kinda creepy, to be honest.

"I just need a couple more months, then I'll have other sources of income."

"You may not have months left if you stay here. And whatever you do, stay away from your farm."

"Wait! How do you know about that?"

Keev looks at me like I'm a child. "It's my job to know. Vikram also knows about it."

"How does Vikram keep finding out every damn thing I do?"

Keev gives me another 'you poor child' look. "He has always had you and Alex under surveillance."

"Why would Vikram even care if I have a farm?"

"Because he needs to be able to control you. If that farm comes online, you could be free of him."

"That's the general idea."

"He will never let that farm be productive. And since you are trying to be free of him, he will have to exert his dominance over you again."

Keev has always been slow with his information and generally sketchy. That's his thing. I don't know how I'm supposed to react to a direct, possibly honest, version. I take a sip of my tea to stall. I'll have to think about all of this. The tea tastes like warm, dirty water. Before he weirds me out some more and I'm obliged to drink more, I decide to get to the reason why I came here.

"Do you have anyone who would be willing to buy a kilo of premium coffee beans?"

"Coffee, where did you get that?" He perks up immediately and his cloth starts to fall off his face. He deftly straightens it out. "Yes, I could sell these to any number of contacts. What are you looking for in exchange?"

"I need a 3D printer with a full supply of metal and resins."

"I can get that for you myself. But you will need software as well. That is going to be much more difficult and expensive."

As soon as I talk business, the predatory Keev I've always known reappears.

"No need. I have the templates already. I just need the equipment."

His face is a mix of emotions. No doubt he's upset that he can't screw me over with the templates. "I never thought I would have a chance to drink coffee again," Keev says slowly, while he's no doubt trying to find a way to take advantage of the situation.

"Perhaps you shouldn't tell our mutual friend about these," I suggest.

"Are these from his supply?"

"Could be," I smile.

"Then I will enjoy it all the more. Now why do you want a 3D printer? Have the repairs I arranged for you in the past disappointed?" he asks.

"During the salvage job of the *Cosmic Dream*, we got more than what was on Vikram's list. We managed to bring the entire ship back to Mars. I'm renaming it the *Shooting Star*. I think I can get it operational again."

He immediately leans back and checks to make sure his mouth is covered. "Oh. Chris, stay away from that ship. It will make you very, very sick."

"Why would it?"

"It was designated a diseased ship by its captain all those years ago. For your sake, I hope you remained in your spacesuit the whole time."

"You knew it was a sick ship? Why didn't you warn me?" I stare daggers at Keev.

Sick ships are avoided at all costs. If a ship's air system can't keep everyone from dying on board, there's no real upside to entering it yourself. Even though I know it was love-sickness by the captain and we vented all the air in any case, I don't need to share that with Keev.

"I am truly sorry about that. I was unable to relay that information to you in a timely manner," he says in mock sincerity.

"Yeah, it was only a potential matter of life and death, so don't worry about it. It was no big deal." I continue to stare him down.

"I can see you're upset, but I cannot offer you anything more than my regret." He clasps his hands and looks down at my feet. I wish Cornelius was here, then I could point to this as the explanation of why I can't stand Keev.

He looks up at me. "Did you find the blue sapphire necklace? I would love to see it in person." All the rancor is conveniently forgotten. He's moved on to his normal babble just like that.

"What are you talking about? What necklace?"

"Oh no, it had to be on the *Cosmic Dream*. Patricia wore it all the time. It's the most coveted piece of jewelry in the solar system."

"How do you know about the people who were on that ship?"

"The recordings from the *Cosmic Dream*, they were very popular on Earth. The captain died, and the passengers kept sending urgent pleas for anyone to come help them. The captain listed an unknown rhinovirus as the culprit. Someone on Earth took the recordings and made it into a morality tale about not going into space. It was hugely popular."

"So you knew what the actual virus was, and you didn't bother to tell me? I could have died!" I stare accusingly at the cloth covering his nose and mouth. I'm getting good at bluffing.

"It was our mutual friend's insistence, which should help explain why you should leave this place."

"Are you really sick or are you trying to protect yourself from me?"

The silence stretches, but I'm in no hurry. What little respect I have for Keev is gone and by the look in his big sorrowful eyes, he knows it too. I stand abruptly and head out the door.

"Oh, Ganesha be with you," Keev says to my back.

CHAPTER 27 CHRIS

Asimov Crater Space Park

"There is an incoming call from Asimov Crater Central Government for Alex Vennemann," chirps the AI. "There is an incoming—"

"Thank you AI, I'll take it in the cockpit," I say as I stumble out of bed. Why is the Central Government calling me? I hit the receive button.

"Hello, this is Dovel Hunter from Asimov City Services. Am I speaking to Alex Vennemann?"

"I'm his half-brother, Chris."

"I'm sorry, sir; this call pertains to property owned by Mr. Vennemann. Is he available?"

"Property? What . . . What happened to the greenhouse?"

"I'm sorry, sir; I can only speak to the owner on this manner."

"AI, where's Alex?"

"Alex is not on board."

"Officer, Alex and I went in together on our greenhouse. It's as much mine as it is his. Please tell me what happened."

"I am not authorized to do that, sir."

"Wait, Alex is only sixteen, so he's not an adult yet. I'm his half-brother, so please tell me what happened."

"Thank you for bringing that to my attention." The connection goes quiet for a few seconds. "According to the databanks, Anna Vennemann is his guardian. I will bring this to her attention. Thank you, sir."

"No, wait—"

"City Services out."

I hate bureaucrats.

Where is Alex this early in the morning? I know he's an early riser, but where could he be? A sense of dread settles in my gut. I try to calm myself. If he was at the farm, they wouldn't very well be calling the ship to talk to him. Unless the wall gave out and he was blown onto the surface. I call Alex on my PCD. He doesn't answer by the second signal. I stumble over the captain's chair as I race for the quarterdeck airlock.

"Hey Chris, what did you want?" a sleepy Alex says as he returns my page.

He must have spent the night at Natalie's place.

"AI, transfer connection from my PCD to the comm."

"Connected."

"Alex, meet me at the greenhouse. I'll bring your spacesuit from your locker at the hangar. Chris out."

I'm in my spacesuit in no time and sprinting across the Martian expanse.

* * *

Vikram is talking to the police officer like he just met an old friend. His relaxed smile makes me suspicious. Before he spots me in my spacesuit, I duck down a side corridor and think about what to do next.

Alex arrives and I fill him in while handing him his spacesuit.

"How do you know it's a wall breach?" Alex asks.

"I don't know for sure, but we don't have anything in there worth stealing and we're at the surface level. What else could it be?"

"Only one way to find out."

We turn the corner and as soon as Vikram sees us, his face transforms. He starts shaking his head slightly and tosses his hands up into the air. He's a terrible actor.

"I'm sorry about your greenhouse. I was with Keev when the leak was reported. I wanted to make sure neither of you were inside."

Alex blanches. "What happened?"

"I wish we knew. I've been talking to the captain here," he points over his shoulder at the officer.

"Someone must have punctured the habdome cloth from the outside. Whatever it was, it exited through the window of the greenhouse door. The depressurization caused the habdome fabric to rip open even wider. Once central saw the pressure and temperature of the corridor drop, officers were dispatched at once to deploy the emergency seal over your door."

"Why would anyone do this?" Alex asks.

"That was going to be my first question to you," Vikram says.

"I've lived on board the Halley with Cornelius practically my entire life. The only people I know well in this crater are you and Keev."

"It's a mystery then." He turns to the officer. "Has this ever happened before?"

"Never," the man says. "Projectile guns are rare, and for good reason." He nods his head toward our greenhouse.

"When did this happen?" Alex asks, still in disbelief.

"Officer Lucado, when were you informed of this?" Vikram asks helpfully.

"Just after oh eight hundred. You're lucky I was patrolling nearby. This could have been a major air loss event."

"Thank you, officer," I say mechanically. "Did you find the bullet?"

Lucado looks at Vikram to see if he has any comment before dismissing himself.

"It's all ruined; the seeds, the dirt, everything?" Alex asks.

His anguish cuts right through me. "We will have to pay the fine just to get in there. Then we'll have to fix the holes, find out if any equipment has been ruined by the extreme cold and only then think about restarting."

"How do we get the money to restart?"

"I don't know, Alex; we may have to sell the farm as is. We don't have that kind of money."

"I can help you with that," Vikram cuts in. "I have a job for you, if you remember."

My look lets him know that he's not wanted here.

"No drugs, but it does have some danger," he adds quickly.

I don't object, so he continues.

"There is another Earther who needs transport off Luna. You'll find him in Tycho Crater. You need to get him on board your ship without any questions and then land him here quietly. I'll take care of the rest from this side. He is wanted by authorities on both Mars and Luna. If you're caught, it's probably jail time. I really need him here, so the job will pay pretty well. Not enough to fix your greenhouse, I'm afraid, but a good start. What do you say?"

"If we take it, we will need the money up front so we can keep this place."

"I can send it to your account as soon as you say yes."

His cheerfulness is more than I can take right now.

"If you don't mind Vikram, we would like to go inside and survey the damage first."

"I understand. Not to add to your problems, but if you take the job, you need to leave by tomorrow morning. You will just have time to pay your fine and leave. This job can't wait."

"Let me talk it over with Alex."

* * *

With Vikram's money, we'd have enough to pay the fine for the loss of community air and maybe the fee for the city's emergency seal in front of our greenhouse door. Vikram's flimsy story isn't worth the air expelled from his lungs. Someone, probably Officer Lucado, shot the bullet at the greenhouse's door, and the habdome cloth.

Could Keev have actually been looking out for us?

Inside, the greenhouse is a scene of destruction. The saplings Alex planted are coated in a slushy mix of orange ice. I inspect the outer wall of reinforced habdome cloth. It's hard to tell anything, since the polymer was ripped to shreds under the explosive air venting.

The breach not only caused the temperature to drop but also allowed the salmon-colored silt to get everywhere. The temperature, near-vacuum and the peroxides brought in by the dust storm have no doubt killed our soil. If we only had to neutralize the soil and recolonize with beneficial microbes, we could handle that. But every moving part from the harvesting rig will have to be removed and professionally cleaned before we could even think about using it.

It's absolutely catastrophic for us and I've no doubt that's what Vikram wanted.

Alex starts savagely ripping out the starter trees from the soil. With the suits on, I can't see his expression, but it's not necessary.

I switch the comm to our private channel. "I'm sure Vikram is behind this. I think his trip here was to gloat at his handiwork," I say. "The question is; what do we do now?"

"We reply in kind," Alex says.

"So we can be buried here? Don't pick a fight we can't win."

I inspect the greenhouse door. They are necessarily stout, since the food inside is so valuable. They are made to withstand vacuum without breaking. There are jagged shards of window inside the greenhouse.

"Alex, come look at this."

I show Alex the clear polymer on the farm side of the door.

"What does this mean?" Alex asks.

"It means to stay away from Officer Lucado. He's Vikram's new corrupt cop."

"Are we really taking the job Vikram has for us?" Alex asks.

"We could definitely use the money. But can we ever trust him again?"

"No."

"If we don't take the job, then where does our money come from?" I ask. "We can ferry tourists around, but that has never been enough. We can't fix up the *Shooting Star* and this place.

And with Vikram around, there's sure to be more problems with one or both of them."

"So, where does that leave us?"

"We already spent our reserve buying this farm. We have to take the job and we have to watch each other's back the whole time."

"So you trust Vikram?" Alex asks.

"No, but do we have a choice? As it is, we're going to have to sacrifice either the farm or the *Shooting Star* unless we continue working for Vikram indefinitely. Or we can take his money this one last time and figure out what to do after that."

Alex sighs. He doesn't like our choices either.

* * *

We are going to be landing at Tycho in just a few minutes. "Okay, let's go over the plan," I say. "We'll pick him up at the Earthrise Bar. I will ask him for the time, and he will use the phrase, 'Now is the winter of our discontent'."

"I still don't like that phrase. It sounds ominous."

"I'm the one who picked it. Cornelius was always throwing around quotes like that. He really liked Earth history."

"What is it even supposed to mean? How cold does winter get on Earth?" Alex asks.

"I don't know. It gets below the freezing point of water, at least some of the time."

"Below the freezing point of water? That's it? That's a summer day on Mars. What do they have to whine about?"

325

"I don't know. It's a really old quote from somewhere. I didn't pay that much attention when Cornelius started talking about ancient times. After we confirm our man, we have to sneak him past security. We have the money to bribe the guards, but I would rather keep that money, if we can."

Alex nods. At least he likes that part of the plan.

"While I'm off to get our guest, I want you to use the exoskeleton and take the containment cylinder for a refill of helium-3. We're a little low, and it's a lot cheaper here than it is on Mars."

"How am I supposed to do that by myself?"

"You have a PCD, don't you?" I ask. "Get directions from it." I cut off the protest before Alex can even utter it. "The prices are standardized, and they will take care of filling it up. All you have to do is pay and transport it."

Alex isn't happy, but it will save us time and money.

We land at the spaceport, relatively close to the bar. At least something is going right. There's no problem identifying our guy. The man weights over hundred and thirty kilograms and his feet don't reach the floor, so he has to be an Earther. He's too short and fat to be anything else. As if that isn't enough, his puffy face and nausea tell me that he's not been on Luna long.

"What is the time" is the most ridiculous question you could ask. Everyone has a PCD and if it isn't working for some reason, all one would have to do would be ask the question aloud and some AI would undoubtedly hear you and respond. That's why I chose it. No one would ever ask that question.

"Now is the winter of our discontent," he replies. At least the identification goes smoothly. "You are a queer little kid who chose the Shakespearean quote?"

"I'm not a kid and how many Martians do you think are going to know it?" Who knew that there was even a fancy title for that stupid line? "So, Vikram didn't tell us your name. What should we call you?"

"Call me Ishmael." He smiles as if he just made a joke.

Maybe it's because he's so congested, but he's really hard to hear. He turns to face me and starts fighting down the urge to gag.

"A tip for you, until you get used to the altered gravity, don't turn your head from side to side. It will only make you sick."

"Thanks for the tip," he mumbles. He keeps his head facing me and rotates his whole body on the bar stool. It's not exactly what I meant, but he does keep his lunch down.

"How have you avoided recognition?" I ask.

"I got off the ship and came straight to this barstool."

"No, how did you avoid being facially recognized? Vikram says you're wanted on Luna."

He looks at me like I'm playing some sort of game with him. He turns his whole body back toward the bar and orders another drink. "Didn't know I had to do that."

"How long have you been on Luna?"

"A couple hours."

My throat starts to constrict. "How fast did you become all stuffy?"

"As soon as we broke Earth's orbit. Why?"

"With your puffy face, it will take a little time for the algorithm to process the image. They should get the word to start looking for you anytime now."

"Then let's get moving," Ishmael says.

The bartender is over in a flash demanding payment. Ishmael nods his head and leans toward the man. Out of nowhere Ishmael's left fist smashes into the bartender's chin.

The bartender staggers into the counter behind him, knocking over several liquor bottles. I stare open-mouthed at Ishmael.

"If we're going to have to run, there's no sense in me losing money here." He chuckles at my disbelief. "We should get going, yeah?"

Already there are people at other tables rising to see what's happened.

"Run! Out those doors and keep going straight." I point to the doors to our right. I came in through the doors directly behind us, but there are too many patrons between us and the doors.

No one follows us out of the bar, but I'm sure several of them have alerted the police. Unlike Mars, the police of Tycho Crater are quick to respond.

You would think that being one sixth his normal weight, Ishmael would be able to run fast. He spends all his time careening off the ceiling, walls, everything.

"Just walk fast," I say finally. People will be able to follow us just by all the sound this fool is making. "Turn right here." I can close the distance between us in no time, so he has to lead or I'll likely lose him.

Once Ishmael turns the corner, I stop and listen for any pursuit. Instead, I hear someone yell, "Halt!" in front of me.

Dammit! He's doing his best to get caught on his own.

I type in the privacy code Alex and I use. "Alex, get to the ship immediately. We're leaving in five minutes."

I hurry down the curving hallway after Ishmael. Alex responds, but I don't have time. I hit the emergency code between our PCDs instead. There are two guards slumped against the wall and an anxious Ishmael.

"Which way?" he asks. There's a solid door to the left and sliding glass doors on the right.

A siren blares from both of the guards' PCDs.

"Through the double doors, hurry!" No reason to wait. We both know what's going to be said.

Ishmael extends his hands out wide, touching both walls. With that steadying force, he's able to run. The fact that he's laughing like a child as he does it is unsettling.

We reach the hangar lobby, and Ishmael motions for me to stop. He takes out an Earther gun and shoots up at the ceiling. I arrive next to him in time to see the remains of a camera crashing against the floor. He scans the hangar ceiling for more cameras.

"Now they won't know what ship we get into," he says.

"Yeah, and us taking off in about three minutes won't be a clue at all."

"Who cares? I'm never coming back here."

Explaining to him that my livelihood has just been crippled is unlikely to matter. I shake my head and point toward Mars transport tunnel number two. I have to get out of here first, then I can worry about paying the bills.

I punch in the code and the quarterdeck airlock opens. I wait at the door for Alex, but I neither hear nor see any hint of him. I don't trust Ishmael on my ship unsupervised, so I step inside and the doors swish closed behind me.

* * *

"I can't believe you left the containment cylinder at the energy shop," I say with a sigh.

"I asked you if I should wait," Alex says defensively, "but you hit the panic alarm. Besides, you like the fact that I swiped the stun guns from the downed guards. Admit it."

I swivel to double check the cockpit door is closed. "I guess we at least got something from Luna." I nod toward the passengers quarters. "Other than trouble, that is."

"I don't want to meet up with him in a dark corridor," Alex says.

"Well, you're babysitting him on the trip back to Mars."

Alex points his stun gun at the window. "Do you think he knows how to use these?"

"Whatever you do, don't give it to him. He'd just as likely shoot you to see what effects it has." I reach over and slap the gun down. "And don't aim a gun unless you're ready to fire. Did you learn nothing from Jean's lessons?"

"He was talking about earther guns."

"It applies to all guns, so stop pointing that at me." I take his gun and check the chamber. "See these?" I lean forward and point to the stun packs. "This is fully loaded with five charges." I pass my finger back and forth over them.

"Cool!"

"Now go put this away and babysit Ishmael."

"Are we leaving now?"

"No, that would be a dead giveaway that we're the ones causing all the trouble. I'd like to be able to come back here. After four or five hours, I'm hoping they don't connect the dots."

* * *

In less than an hour, I'm stuck with Ishmael, who insists on sitting in the captain's chair.

"So is it true that you can just hit the auto pilot button and this ship will fly to Asimov Crater and land itself?" Ishmael asks.

"It never quite works out that smoothly, but the theory says we could," I respond.

"You have to understand, on Earth, spaceships are the stuff of legend. I can't believe I'm sitting in the cockpit in the middle of space."

"Well, we're still on Luna, but we'll be in space in no time." I want him off my ship as fast as possible. "Most of the work of flying is done up front. Our return trip to Mars has already been plotted."

"So you just hit a button and we go?" Ishmael asks.

"More or less, we rise straight up until we're clear of incoming lunar traffic. Then we'll aim our ship and accelerate toward Mars. Typically, we accelerate continuously until the midpoint, and then we turn the ship around and decelerate the rest of the way. This way, we will mimic Mars's gravity onboard the ship, so you will be acclimated by the time we arrive."

"So you've already fed all this stuff into the computer?"

"Yep." I want to tell him that it'll go faster if he's not pestering me, but really, I'm just hoping someone else will leave before us.

"How long will we be at zero g?"

"Almost no time. If you want to experience zero g, I can always stop accelerating for a while once we clear the traffic lanes of Luna and let you experience it."

"That's every Earthling's dream, to float around at zero g."

"I'll make the changes now." I'm glad he wants to do this immediately. He's so maladjusted to lower gravities that his inner ears will go haywire.

"So tell me how this stuff works. It must be really hard to fly. Are you a genius or what?"

Every time I look back at Ishmael his puffy red face makes me think of a big ugly baby. I keep my head facing forward and hope he doesn't throw a tantrum.

I don't like the guy, but it's nice to have someone appreciate my piloting skills. He peppers me with questions about how to fly the ship until we clear the lunar traffic. I cut the engines and prepare to maneuver the ship into place for acceleration. Once we're pointed the right way, I tell Ishmael to go find Alex and have fun.

Alex decides to tell Ishmael that the best sleep he'll ever get is when we're at zero g. Thanks to Alex, we're still at zero g the next morning. This prolonged time without accelerating will cost us another ten hours with our guest.

With the loss of the data networks on Earth, the only verifiable master works of literature reside in Mars' meager collection. Surely some printed copies still exist on Earth, but for how long? Each day brings an untold loss of our common cultural heritage. Great voices of the past that survived wars, plagues, and censorship are being silenced today. How much shallower will our lives become? To do nothing is to promote ignorance.

How Humanity is Losing Itself
Op Ed by Aleksander Mohyla, Mars Today

CHAPTER 28 CHRIS

Interplanetary Space

Ishmael is eating breakfast with Alex by the time I get up. In truth, it was their crazy loud laughter that woke me.

"Hey Chris, did you know that Ishmael used to work on fishing boats?"

"I can't imagine what it would be like to be surrounded by all that water," I say.

"I never had any problems on the boat with the pitching and rolling of the waves. That's why I can't understand why I'm having such issues out here in space."

"You've never been weightless before. The fluids in your body are no longer being pulled down by gravity, so your head gets puffy. Also, your ears are attuned to gravity, so without it, your balance is off. Everything will return to normal once we start accelerating again."

"The waves were big enough to move your boat?" Alex asks.

"Of course! In one storm, our seven-meter boat was tossed around by twenty-meter waves. I was the only one to keep my dinner down that night," he boasts.

"Twenty-meter waves?" Alex and I stare at each other in astonishment.

"I didn't know waves ever got more than a couple of inches tall," I say.

"Did you forget that Earth is seventy percent water on the surface?"

"What were you fishing for?" Alex asks, enthralled by our guest.

"Whales."

"Aren't whales like really big?" I ask.

"Aye, Captain Ahab, especially white whales. But nothing is as big as a fisherman's tale!" He pounds the table with his fist as his bellowing laughter reverberates off the galley walls. Alex and I join in the laughter, though neither of us has any idea what we're laughing about.

Ishmael begins shoveling in more porridge between chuckles.

"We'll be feeling the effects of zero g until midafternoon," I say. "I checked the orbital databanks, and Jupiter should be observable out your cabin windows for the next several hours.

Alex can show you how to magnify the view from the galley window."

"That sounds great, but are you going to be programming the ship this morning?"

"Nah, I did that all last night. Now I have to check our sanitation system and other messy details. It'll be a slow morning."

Alex frowns at me. He knows I'm lying to avoid our guest. Being captain does have its benefits.

* * *

We've settled into a routine. Alex babysits our guest for about four hours in the morning. Then Ishmael comes into the cockpit and peppers me with lots of annoying questions about flying the ship. His eagerness was fun at first, but now it's exhausting.

Today is the midpoint of our journey. We'll go weightless for a bit when I cut the engines and spin the ship around. Stacking the series of commands isn't hard, but I need Ishmael to stay away.

"We're going to start decelerating in about an hour. I have to input the information for the remaining trip to Mars."

"So after that, the autopilot will take over?"

"Yep." It's not really true, but if it will keep him out of my cockpit, I'm willing to say almost anything. "Do you want to go find Alex? This will be your last chance to experience zero g, and Alex knows all the cool stuff to do."

"So, what do you need to do up here to make it happen?"

"Literally all I need to do is double check the numbers and hit this touchscreen. I promise you won't miss out on anything."

"Where will I find Alex?"

"AI, where's Alex?"

"Alex is currently in the galley."

Ishmael looks amazed. "You can talk to the ship?"

"To be honest, I forget about the AI system most of the time."

"Can't you just tell it to fly the ship?"

"Nope. The AI is not hooked up to navigation or propulsion. We can't very well have a passenger tell the ship to fly into the sun."

* * *

It's been about an hour and I haven't performed the switch yet. The longer I wait, the more thrust I'll waste slowing the ship, but it will give us less time with Ishmael. I'm willing to spend a little fuel on that, but if I don't do it soon, he'll be back up here wondering why.

"Please strap in for the deceleration initiation," I say over the comm. "It will take a few minutes for everyone's body to readjust to the artificial gravity."

I give those two a couple minutes to get settled before I start decelerating and daydream about getting the Earther off my ship. At least he'll be secured in his seat until our initial burn is completed. I better double check that.

"AI, where is our guest?"

"Ishmael, surname unknown, is in the quarterdeck airlock."

Why the hell would Alex let him go in there? It's about the most dangerous place to be when deceleration begins. There's open space that will only give a person more momentum when they slam into all the breakable things. And if Ishmael gets hurt, we'll have to use med-bay supplies to fix him up.

"AI, where is Alex?"

"Alex Vennemann is in the quarterdeck airlock."

I slam my fist on the console. I have to be able to rely on my first mate . . . and wow, do I sound like Cornelius. "AI, lock the controls, pass phrase, 'fish tales'."

I guess I have to be nice but firm about this. I can rip into Alex once Ishmael is off the ship. At least, that's what Cornelius used to do.

I sit in the captain's chair so I can practice my patented back somersault and push off. As I swing over the chair, I see Ishmael emerge from the airlock. He's struggling to maintain any sense of balance.

"Ishmael," I shout.

He turns my way, and it looks like he's going to puke. He ducks back into the airlock.

I push off against the seat back as hard as I can and sail through the gangway. I'm going straight down the center; this is one of my better executed moves.

"Please don't puke in the airlock," I say under my breath. The last thing I need is vomit floating throughout the ship. But dammit, Alex should know better and he's going to clean it up.

I push off slightly from the left wall so I can get a better viewing angle into the airlock and also to distance myself from any floating vomit.

"Remember Ishmael, don't turn your head or you'll make yourself sick," I call ahead.

Before I can go sailing by, I grab the toe rail to stop my momentum. My feet go sailing past the rest of me as I come to a stop.

"Ouch!" Something strikes my leg. I look into the airlock and Ishmael is in a shooter's stance in front of a motionless Alex. A stun gun is pointed directly at me.

"Lights out." He smiles.

"Don't hit that button!" I scream and point towards his left foot.

"That old trick?" He looks annoyed.

I pull my feet in tight and look for something to push off from.

He fires and hits me in the ass.

I push off and sail back up the gangway.

"Dammit kid. Where are you going to run?"

As I flee, I take stock of the situation. He's at least three times stronger than me, and he's armed. I'm better at moving in zero g, but I don't know if I can even hurt him. The cockpit is straight ahead and the door would keep him out, but he's got Alex. Out of desperation, I duck into the port airlock.

"AI, change the port inner airlock door status to closed failsafe mode."

"The airlock door will stay in the closed position until the order is countermanded."

"AI, password protect the closed door; password: Cornelius."

"Password accepted."

To avoid nasty rashes on board the ship, we always wear clothing that wicks moisture away from us, but I can't take any chances. I take off my pants, but not before giving Cornelius' coin one last rub for luck. My left sock looks moist as well, so I take that off. I pick up my belt and put it back on. Stupid maybe, but it's the only salvageable article of clothing available to me.

"Now what?" I say out loud. All the spacesuits are in the quarterdeck airlock, so I can't go outside the ship. Ishmael is waiting for me inside and I'm floating here half undressed. Frantically, I look around the airlock for anything I can use.

Ishmael bangs on the glass. I ignore him, so he hits the comm button.

"You might as well come out, kid. There's no place to run."

I must have thrown my sock away with too much force because now it is slowly floating back towards me. I grab it and throw it at Ishmael. It hits the window harmlessly, but it obscures his view.

"Are you planning a striptease?"

I refasten my shoes and cringe because my bare left foot is touching the inside. Gross.

No Chris, focus on the problem at hand.

I spot Cornelius' old helmet. His aluminum spacesuit is inside it! How many times did I threaten to throw it out? I spot the iron ring as well. There's an electromagnetic cable just above this airlock. If I get into this baggy spacesuit and attach the ring . . .

"AI, open this airlock door!" Ishmael roars.

"The door is password protected. What is the password, please?"

He bangs on the glass in frustration.

"We can work this out. Would you rather freeze to death?"

I float over to the door and hit my comm button. "What did you do to Alex?"

"He's just stunned. Come inside and I'll explain it all."

I strap on an emergency air tank. It will give me thirty minutes of air, but I'll freeze to death in fifteen; so I don't have to worry about that at least. I hit the cycle button, and the air starts slowly pumping out. Ishmael is looking at me with a bemused smile. The outer doors open, and I push off to the top of the airlock and scamper out of sight. I attach the electromagnet tether to myself.

"Now what?"

Is this how I'm going to die, talking to myself while I slowly freeze to death?

I can't go back inside the port airlock and I can't go into the quarterdeck because Alex is in there. Those are the only two ways into the ship. Damn. My elbows and knees are already cold. I only have one path forward and I don't have time to waddle all the way around the ship. My gooseflesh is casting a vote already.

Looks like I'm going to need the mag launcher. I could scream. There aren't any controls on this worthless suit. Space, I'm going to have to propel myself instead. I make sure the tether is fastened solidly to the ship before I pull the entire length of the line out. I attach the magnet to the iron ring and give both ends a quick tug before turning off my mag boots. I jump as far as I can toward the back of the ship.

Fear builds in me now that I'm floating in space, waiting for the line to go taut. The seconds go by in an unhurried fashion. My jaw is clenched so tight that I may never be able to open it again.

I'm probably going to die today; does it really matter how?

Oddly, that calms me. If I expect to die, I have nothing to lose. I want to laugh at my predicament, at Ishmael and at the universe as a whole. But I can do that later, maybe.

I feel the tug on the line and I know to face the ship this time. At least I won't spend an eternity floating alone in space as a corpsicle. One possible death averted. I kick my mag boots back on and land just a few yards from the quarterdeck airlock. The forward tether is much shorter than the aft. I can't reach the airlock with the tether on.

I've nearly lost all feeling in my feet and I'm one misstep away from dying, but I have to disconnect the line to get where I'm going. I literally couldn't be in a worse position. I stick to my training; if I can't feel it, I must visually and audibly confirm that every step makes contact with the ship.

I waddle the last few steps to the airlock. No sense in stalling. I hit the emergency cycle button, and the screen activates, displaying a numeric keypad as big as my head. The buttons need to be that big to accommodate a standard spacesuit. The doors themselves are recessed about thirty centimeters from the rest of the hull. I stand on that sliver, upside down from the ship's orientation. I'll need to reach toward the center of the open doors, so I bend down to enter the code from between my legs. I'm only going to have one chance at this.

I get a solid grip on the truss next to me before I deactivate my mag boots. My life depends on my grip to this truss. I enter the last number on the pad.

The doors slowly open and air and rock-hard puke pellets come streaming out, pelting my visor. Alex's motionless body is partially blocking the opening, splitting the airstream in two. By the time the doors open wide enough for Alex to float out, the airlock has lost all of its air. There's nothing left to hurl Alex into space. I swing my feet, kicking Alex deeper into the airlock. It's a tight fit, but thanks to this oh so thin aluminum suit, I squeeze through. I kick my mag boots together sink to the floor. I push Alex's body deeper into the airlock and hit the emergency close button.

One crisis averted. I will not die in space today.

I try to walk, but my suit's left leg is caught in the doors. I look at Alex's blue face, nope, can't open them, even a sliver.

Warm air fills the room. I try to pull my suit's pant leg loose and only manage to tear it. The perimeter of my vision grows dark while the motors continue to rumble. I must be getting lightheaded. This stupid aluminum suit doesn't have any safety bladders.

I can't lose consciousness this time.

My tunnel vision expands. I take a deep breath and look at Alex. He's still motionless. I kick myself away from the doors, leaving a piece of my suit behind. Taking my helmet off, I set it down carefully so Ishmael isn't alerted.

I glide over to Alex. I squirm out of my now useless suit and I'm back to being half naked. It looks like he has small ebullisms in his fingers, but nothing worse. The bruises will heal in no time. It's lucky he was unconscious, because human nature would have made him try to hold his breath, and that would have been deadly. He's breathing, and he has a pulse. That's all the time I can spend on him for now.

If Ishmael comes back, he'll know I'm back inside thanks to the piece of spacesuit stuck between the outer doors.

"AI, can you open the inner doors one foot wide?"

"Opening."

Apparently, it interpreted my question as a polite command. Is it any wonder why I don't use the stupid system? I stick my head out quickly; there's no sign of Ishmael.

"AI, open inner airlock doors," I whisper.

"Opening doors," it bellows.

I step all the way out. It's still clear. "AI, close the doors and lock them."

"AI, password protect the quarterdeck airlock; pass phrase: little brother." Without waiting, I shove off towards engineering.

Once the reinforced engineering doors close behind me, I know I'm safe, but I manually lock the doors, just in case. If I must, the ship can be flown from here, but that only helps so much when there's a gun-wielding lunatic wandering the hallway.

"AI, what has Ishmael been doing since I left the ship?"

"Ishmael attempted to change the navigation and propulsion programs. He is currently traveling down the gangway towards your location. Would you like me to page him?"

"No, thanks."

Ishmael yells at the AI to open the airlock doors. Good luck guessing my passwords.

"AI, where's Chris?" he asks.

Space!

"Chris is in engineering. Shall I page him?"

"AI, disable voice commands." I shout, password..." I look around me without being able to focus. "One sock."

Ishmael is shouting at me through the engineering doors. I don't respond. He starts banging on the doors while ordering the AI to open them. I take a minute to collect myself. What to do now?

Do you want to go to Tycho Crater's gambling hall but space sickness is keeping you at home? Never again! Dr. Hackney's anti-nausea serum will knock out your symptoms in no time! The scientific inclusion of over forty vegetal and fungal sources invigorates your metabolism and curbs the vestibular system, allowing you to travel in comfort. Contact us today!

Real Cures for Space Sickness brochure
Tyler Hackney, H. E.

CHAPTER 29 CHRIS

Interplanetary Space

Ishmael decides to camp out in the galley. It's a solid plan. He's across from the quarterdeck airlock where Alex is, and in front of the only exit from engineering. Even if I flew the ship from here, that would leave Alex as a prisoner. Ishmael has floated a compromise a couple times, but since he's the only one with a weapon, I doubt his sincerity.

"What else are you going to do?" He bellows at me again.

It's a good question. Whatever it is, it has to be soon. His nausea will go away over time, as will the visual problems he's likely having.

I scan the console for the third time, looking for inspiration, so I don't have to do something crazy. Nothing.

Okay, then I guess it's crazy time.

I activate the emergency engine shutoff routine. There's no way he can figure out how to countermand it; not even Alex can do that. I enter the emergency code and float to the lever on the other side of the room. They really didn't want anyone to do this by accident.

It's impossibly hard to move. My whole burgeoning plan depends on this. I scan the room for anything that will give me leverage.

Stupid, I have a bionic arm!

I wedge myself against the bulkhead and the lever moves easily. Everything non-critical, like the lights, lose power. The red emergency lights come on, allowing just enough illumination to see.

"AI, where is Ishmael?" No answer. Hmm. It must not be an emergency system. "Space!" If the AI is off, then all of my password protections on the interior doors are off as well. How long until Ishmael makes the same discovery?

I soar over to the right-wing access panel. It comes off easily and I scrunch inside. The hard part is replacing the panel while in such tight quarters. I crawl toward infamous engine two, but I freeze in place after only a meter. Ishmael comes storming into engineering and I'm afraid to make a sound. I listen intently as he crashes into everything. He's so clumsy. If he didn't have a weapon, I'd have a chance.

Finally, the noise stops. I stay where I am for one hundred breaths, then I quietly make my way down the shaft. Either he's waiting for me or he's gone to parts unknown. There's some relief once I'm around a corner. At least he won't be able to shoot me in the ass again.

Great, I'm trapped in the wing and he has control of the cockpit and everything else. Whenever I reenter the ship, I'll be making myself a target. On my exhale, my breath is visible. I guess the wings aren't heated with emergency power.

Great plan!

Whatever I'm going to do, it has to be now or I will become a corpsicle after all.

I make my way farther into the wing. Engine two looks all shiny and there's no sign of space goo anywhere. That's nice and all, but I have to keep going. This shaft runs the length of the ship and ends at the port airlock. I'm to the point where I have to lay down and squeeze underneath an ancient moxie unit. It hasn't worked in forever, but Cornelius said getting rid of it was an expense not worth paying. He was also too fat to fit under it, so I always had to squeeze through the shafts. The farther up I go, the tighter the shaft becomes. I haven't tried this in a long time; hopefully I still fit.

* * *

I pause at the access panel above the port airlock ceiling and force myself to breathe slower. The shaft is only as tall as my elbow to wrist. I don't hear anything below me.

Here goes. There are three layers of panels, each with compression fittings, since the airlock is subjected to space.

Despite the tight quarters, I can't make any noise while manually releasing them. This should be fun.

The first one comes off easily enough, since I'm taking my time. But I can't feel my toes anymore, so I'm going to have to take some risks. The second one is easy, since I've figured out how they're attached, but the third and final one is stuck. I find a thin piece of metal and pry up one corner of the panel.

Phew, no one heard.

My right hand, my real hand, is shaking too much to be useful. Thank goodness I have an alloyed one. It takes much more time than I'm happy with, and my breath fog is making everything slippery, but the final panel finally surrenders to my stubbornness.

Everything below my knees is numb, so there's no time to be timid. I get the lower half of me through the access chute and I grab a panel. I line it up and rest my knees against the ceiling. Slowly, I pull the panel toward its home. The first seal makes contact with the opening and that will be enough to keep it from working free. The last thing I need is for this to be left open and have the airlock vent all the ship's air into space.

I push off from one wall to the other as I make my way to the door. It would be easier if I could use my legs, but they're not even tingling yet. I slide the door open and stick my head out in the empty corridor. I float as fast as I dare to my quarters. There's a manual lock that I always thought was stupid, but now that I'm inside, I breathe a little easier as I use it.

I didn't like the old Earther gun underneath my seat in the cockpit, so I moved it to the storage under my bed along with the bullets. Jean insisted the gun be unloaded unless I intended to use it.

Do I really want to shoot bullets inside the ship, anyway? I press a little button at the top of the grip and a cartridge pops out. I look at the bullets again. One shot through the exterior and we all die quickly. If I take out a critical system, we all die slowly. If I do nothing, Ishmael likely kills Alex and me.

I load two bullets. If I need more than that, we're all likely to die. There's one other thing I have to do. I dig out my anxiety pills from the back of my clothes drawer. Jean said you need a steady hand. I hate these pills because I can't feel anything when I'm on them. That'll come in handy today. I take two, because I need them to start working fast.

I slide the gun into the back of my underwear. Great, now I'm half naked with a loaded pistol being held in place by my butt cheeks. I look at my reflection. Maybe Ishmael will die of hysterical laughing.

Alex had the two stun guns from the downed guards. I'd rather use one of them. If I miss, I'm less likely to destroy something I shouldn't. I hold my breath and listen for any sounds as I eke my door open.

I pull the gun out before squeezing through the partially opened door. There's still no sound as I float to Alex's cabin. I have to jiggle his door a little, but it opens. There's still there's no sign of Ishmael. I don't bother to close the door. Closing and reopening it gives me two more chances to make noise and alert him. I'd rather get in and out with an open door at my back than to give away my location and be trapped. There's only one stun gun under Alex's bed.

Duh!

Ishmael shot at me with the other one. How can I forget that? Alex must have taken it to show Ishmael. I holster the Earther gun back between my cheeks. It's still uncomfortably cold, but I have bigger problems. The safety is off on the stun gun. I check to see that this gun is loaded.

The corridor is still empty. I silently glide, just above the floor, toward the galley, stun gun at the ready. At the first sign of him, bam! My heart pushes at my tonsils, as if to propel me faster. The open doorway to the galley widens and I shoot through the empty air and hit . . . the observation window as I pass.

Damn! There was no one in there! I grab onto the engineering door frame and open it as fast as I can. I spin myself around and . . . there's no one here either.

I press up against the door frame, drawing myself into the corner. I listen for Ishmael's approach. Still nothing. I spin around the doorway and peer into the galley.

No one. Where are they?

I slip into engineering and close the door. I'm right back where I started. I return power to the ship and check the thermal scans. There they are, in the cockpit. I was less than three meters from them when I left the airlock. At least that mystery is solved.

"Are you finishing playing around?" Ishmael's voice asks over the comm. "Come up here and join us or else I'm going to hurt Alex with the comm open."

"What do you want?"

Of course, my voice chooses this moment to crack.

"Come up here and we'll talk about it."

The only way to possibly surprise him now is to get up there faster than he expects. Not a problem. I can absolutely zoom down the gangway. I notice the broken bin that won't close approaching on my right. I snort in derision. There are bigger problems right now.

I grab it and halt my momentum. There's no need to hurry, the cockpit door lock will be reengaged. I can't sneak up on him. I take a breath and slowly let it out. I only have one chance to get this right.

I tug on the door, but it doesn't budge. What were the passwords I made up?

My natural hand isn't shaking anymore. My heart isn't trying to leap out of my throat, either. Good, the meds must be taking effect. I face the cockpit door and decide to squat, just in case he's ready to fire.

"Fish tales."

The door swishes open and . . . nothing. I stand up and approach the back of the captain's chair. Ishmael's arm is extended from the pilot seat to the co-pilot seat, where the white stun gun is pressed up against Alex's motionless head. He looks at me through the window's reflection.

"If I pull the trigger, the concussive force will crack open your brother's skull. So why don't you slowly send whatever weapon you have into the footwell in front of your brother. Then we can talk."

I'm behind the captain's chair and he can't see below my chest. I release the stun gun carefully and it remains floating in place. I bow my head as if I've been beaten while I grab the Earther gun. It latches onto my underwear, giving me a wedgie as I pull on it.

I can feel my ears getting warm, so I must be blushing. It takes both hands to disentangle the pistol. My underwear snaps back in place.

Ishmael grunts once in amusement.

So much for the death by hysterical laughing.

I hold it by the barrel and in plain view, just like they always do in the vids. I slowly send it off into the copilot footwell. Without looking down, I grip the stun gun with my left hand.

I'm oddly calm. Doubling up the medicine was a good call. I don't have much of a target, so I wait for a better opportunity.

"Why are you doing this?" I ask.

"It's nothing personal; it's just business." He stands up and points his gun at me.

I take my shot.

Unlike the single-minded focus of Huygens and Noctis Labrynthus on commerce and water, respectively, Schiaparelli specialized in knowledge. It was the home of the first two Martian universities. The breach of the great dome not only killed over four hundred thousand but also a disproportionate amount of the planet's thought leaders. The planet is still reeling from this double tragedy.

Excerpt from: The Fall of Schiaparelli
Wyatt Johnson

CHAPTER 30 CHRIS

Interplanetary Space

Ishmael starts to stir. He looks around and sees that he's in the port airlock. He pushes off for the door before he notices me watching him. He lands in front of me, our faces a hand's length apart. He hits the access panel.

I can tell, because a light flashes on my side every time he presses a button.

"Last time I had to flee out of the ship," I say.

"Let me in. There's nothing that can't be undone." He hits the panel several more times. He's good. I can't see him making any motions.

"I wasn't sure who would wake up first, you or Alex, but being an assassin you probably got a direct hit on my brother, right Lewis?"

"We don't have to be adversaries," he says.

"Then why did you tell me your name was Ishmael?"

"It was a joke. We always hear how you Martians don't know any of the great literature, so I tested that statement out. So I didn't give my real name. What harm have I done?" He gives me big, earnest eyes.

I don't take the bait. "Tell me why Vikram wants you on Mars."

"Listen kid, you're better off not knowing."

"First, don't call me kid, and second, I've already scanned your orders."

Lewis feels his right pants pocket. I'm still kind of disgusted that I had to reach into there, but Alex is out cold and it had to be done.

"You don't want to deal with the shit storm that will come from knowing that information. I'm trying to protect you and your brother." More flashes from the telltale light.

I let out a belly laugh. I can feel the tension in my shoulders lessen. I needed that.

"No, it's true. Vikram wanted me to take the ship from you. He said to kill you both, but I figured if I knocked you unconscious, then Vikram didn't have to find out that you're still alive."

"So you're just an innocent assassin? It wasn't that Vikram instructed you to 'off the crew' before delivering the ship to Asimov?"

He's showing fear for the first time. I must have hit the mark.

"I know what it says, but I wanted to save you and your brother." He tries to sound earnest. "You're just kids, after all, and you were always nice to me. And I'm not an assassin. You have it all wrong. I was called by Kenova Maitland to keep an eye on Vikram. The bit with you and your brother, that was tacked on at the last minute. I didn't have a chance to say no. It was Vikram, yeah, Vikram who ordered the hit."

"That just cost you thirty percent of your atmosphere." I punch in the order. I wonder if there's a light on his end telling him every time I press buttons. I'll have to check later.

"Wait! You can't do that. Please, I'm begging you." He clutches his neck, like that will do any good.

There's a whistling noise in the airlock now. I can't tell where it's coming from.

"The brief came from Kenova, but Vikram really did insist on the change at the last minute. Just open the door and I'll explain everything." The light stays on continuously now.

"Open the door so you can overwhelm me with your Earther strength? No thanks. But since you're trying to be sneaky, AI, stop heating the airlock."

"Hey, you can't do that. I'll freeze to death. You're not a cold-blooded killer."

"How do you know? Is there some rule that there can only be one cold-blooded killer per ship? You should probably know that I've killed before. I yanked the man's head back by his long, wavy hair, pressed his own pistol up against his temple and broke his skull in two when I fired. So you better start telling me something I'll believe or else."

I can't afford any sign of weakness, so I maintain a mask of indifference as I say those words. "By the way, the ship's databank says you'll be susceptible to frostbite in another thirty minutes. Do you have anything you'd like to share? I'd prefer you say it now and not when your teeth are chattering." I blow on my fingernails, like they always do in the vids.

"What do you want from me?"

He's getting desperate, good.

"Answers, so start talking."

"Uh, as I said, I was sent to keep an eye on Vikram." His eyes flick all around the airlock, looking for something he can use, no doubt. "He's the one you need to worry—"

"You're boring me," I cut in. "What can I do to make this more interesting?" I pause to study the screen. In truth, there isn't too much more I can do without killing him.

"No wait! Vikram ordered the hit on your father! Did you know that?"

"Nice try, but all that gets you is a reduction to sixty percent atmosphere."

"No, he did! He paid a corrupt cop to shoot him in the back, then he killed the cop so nobody could find out."

I grab the console before I melt into a puddle. Pressing my head against the cool wall, I process those words. They have the ring of truth. But that means . . . it means that I've been working for Cornelius' killer all this time. I knock my head against the wall a couple of times, steeling myself for what I must do.

"We should be on the same side, against Vikram," he says, earnestly.

"Why would Vikram want us dead?" There's no emotion in my voice. I can't allow emotion to take hold of me. This is merely a transaction that must be finished.

"He thought you would be easier to control than your father. But you won't ship his drugs, so he's found a pilot and all he needs now is your ship."

"Alright Lewis, that may even be true." I show him his memory chip. "So tell me how to access this 'starting capital' file on this chip of yours."

"Okay, you're welcome to the money. Once we land, insert it into the computer system, however you Martians do that, and type 'New Delhi Tsunami five zero five'."

"Oh Lewis, I thought we were making progress. Everyone knows SOS means you're in distress. Telling me to type five zero five isn't much of a code." I shake my head. "I guess it's down to fifty percent atmosphere for you."

I punch it in and hear the pumps activate and the whine gets louder. I really need to find out what's causing that. "You probably only have a few minutes of consciousness left. Anything you'd like to say?"

"Wait! I'll do whatever you want! Tell me what you want me to do."

I thought he'd have more resolve. I guess not being able to breathe has a significant effect on people. He doesn't have much time left before he's unconscious and that doesn't help me out at all. I restore the air pressure and watch him start to drift away from me.

"Thank you," he says between breaths.

I've given him hope.

"Okay Lewis, now do you know what I need you to do?"

"Anything kid. What do you want?" He's practically sobbing.

"I want you to leave my ship!" I hit the emergency button and Lewis and all my current problems are ejected into space. I wince as his head hits the exterior door on exit. I hope he's still conscious. I want this to be the worst thing he's ever experienced, and it can't be that if he's knocked out. I grimace.

"He didn't even have time to scream," I say aloud. "I'll have to watch the video later. I want to see if eyes really do freeze over instantly." I let out a long exhale. Instead of joy or excitement, I just feel bitter. I was so close to losing Alex.

"This is my ship!" I scream out into the void. "How dare you attack me and mine here!" I drop my head down. It's over.

I catch a person in my peripheral vision. It's Alex, as silent as space, with his mouth agape.

As the early Americans expanded their homesteads across the vast plains, civilization was slow to catch up. The distant, dusty outposts had to police themselves. Despite four centuries of advancement, Mars is in a similar situation today. With essentially no central government, each city is a nation unto itself with a maddening array of rules, customs and governments.

Dry, Dusty & Mostly Lawless: How Mars Resembles Earth's Ancient Prairies
Ruben van der Heide

CHAPTER 31   ALEX

Interplanetary Space

"You just killed him." I stammer.

"Alex!" Chris looks at me wide-eyed. "How long have you been standing here?"

"Since he said that he would protect us from Vikram." I look at Chris' trembling right hand. "But you killed him, anyway."

"I couldn't let Lewis live on this ship for another twelve days. What if he got out?"

"Who's Lewis?"

"Lewis is Ishmael's real name."

"And you spaced him for lying about a name?" My knees are wobbly. If it wasn't for the zero g, I'd be on the floor.

"Alex, let me explain." Chris raises both hands like he's trying to calm me down from a distance. "What's the last thing you remember before now?"

My head hurts, but I try to remember. "I was in the galley with Ish . . . Ishmael and we were laughing. He's really. . . he *was* hilarious."

"Then what?"

"He asked me for some tea and I got up to get it. I don't know what happened after that, except he begged for mercy and you spaced him, anyway."

"I didn't have a choice," Chris says.

"Is that what you said after you shot Officer Barnett? How many is that for you? Are there a few more that you haven't told me about?"

Chris winces at my words.

"Alex, he was an assassin sent to kill us."

"Why would anyone want to kill us?" Chris isn't making any sense.

"Let me explain, please."

The hair on my arms stands up.

"I want to be alone now," I say with a shaky voice.

"You have to know what happened," he implores. Chris gently pushes off from the wall and floats toward me.

"*Don't come any closer.*" I extend my hand as if to physically stop him.

He grabs the toe rail to stop his momentum. He blinks to hold back his tears. I want to believe the anguish is real, but I saw his excitement over spacing Ishmael.

"You have to believe me." He gives me the biggest, saddest eyes. "I had no choice."

"My head is still really thick. Let me pull myself together. I'll be back." I slide past him and hit the button to open my quarters. I dart inside and turn to face Chris. "Please don't come in here after me," I plead. The door closes and I've bought myself some time to collect my thoughts. Only now do I realize that near everything hurts.

How did I get all of these injuries?

I brace myself for Chris to open my door, but it doesn't happen. Instead, Chris is milling around in the gangway. I manually lock the door. I only got it to ensure Chris didn't walk in on Natalie and me again. Now I'm so thankful I bought it. I would love to go to sleep, but I don't dare leave myself helpless. I lay down and stare at the wall as I try to make sense of it all.

* * *

I listen for any sign of Chris, but the ship has gone quiet. Chris must be up in the cockpit as usual. Waiting for something to happen is the worst. I open my cabin door and look from side to side. I grab the toe rails and propel myself up to the cockpit.

"Alex," Chris calls over the comm.

I check the cockpit, but it's empty.

"Alex, I'm in the port airlock."

I backtrack and see Chris sitting motionless in the airlock.

"What are you doing in there?"

"Alex, I need you to believe that I didn't have any choice. I can't live on this ship alone again."

He hits me with those big, sad eyes again.

"I pulled whatever audio and visual evidence I could find in the data banks. It's not much, but it's everything that was recorded in the previous five hours. I'm going to stay in here. Watch and listen to everything and then decide whatever you want to do next. If you think I'm a monster, then send me out the airlock after Lewis. I would rather be dead than alone again. Whatever you decide, there will be no hard feelings."

"Chris, I want to believe you. Come out of there and you can narrate what happened."

"No. I am putting myself at your mercy. Watch and listen to everything and give me your verdict."

"At least come out of the airlock."

"No. I will not. Let me know when you're ready to decide my fate." He turns away from me. He looks so broken.

* * *

After seeing all the information, I'm mostly relieved. Ishmael nailed me in the back of the head when I got up to make tea for him. Chris did what he had to do, and it was kinda awesome. But he liked it at the end, when he was toying with Lewis.

I stare out the window—just like Chris does. Despite how it ended, I can't turn my back on Chris.

I better tell him that everything is okay before he does something stupid.

"Hey Chris, you can come out of there. I've seen it all."

"And?" He calls from the airlock.

"And Lewis was Earther scum that befriended us just so we'd let our guards down."

"Yeah, and he kept telling me how smart I was while he peppered me with questions about flying this ship. I should have seen it."

"When was the last time anyone confused you with being smart?" I hold my breath. Is it too early to go back to our usual banter?

Chris exits the airlock smiling tentatively. "Yeah, in the end, he got what he deserved."

I feel like I've been punched in the gut. I was ready to put it all in the past.

"How can you be completely fine with what you did?"

"I thought we were okay?" Chris says, confused.

"We were until you started gloating about killing a person again."

"What was I supposed to do? Should I have made him promise to behave?"

"You had him trapped. You could have turned him over to the authorities."

"Do you mean the authorities at Asimov Crater? Where Vikram has bribed any number of city officials, including that officer that was at our farm?"

"Huygens then," I suggest.

"And what? Confess to any number of crimes while explaining why an assassin was on our ship trying to kill us?"

"I don't know! And that's the problem." I throw up my hands. "All I know is that you made it look so easy. Someone upsets you and you just shoot them in the head or space them. Then what? You go take a nap or stare out the cockpit window? Doesn't this have any effect on you?"

"Alex," he says in a quiet voice. "When I saw your limp body, I thought you were dead. If he had killed you, I would have spent the next three days torturing him just for spite. But you were alive, so I tried my best to get information from him before, before I had to do that. It was always going to come down to either he dies or we die. Am I sorry that he is dead? No. Am I sorry that I had to be the one to kill him? Yes. But I did what I had to do. There's no changing that."

"But it was so easy for you," I say without thinking.

"I did what had to be done," he says, his voice emotionless.

Neither one of us knows what to say next. I still can't grasp the enormity of what happened. At last I say in a small voice, "I never saw a man die before."

"Technically, you still haven't. You only saw him get sucked out of the airlock. He probably had another fifteen seconds left."

"Is this supposed to cheer me up? What is *wrong* with you?"

He looks as if I've just punched him.

"Chris, we're still fine, so don't go spacing yourself," I say quickly. "But I need time to think about all of this."

He looks at the floor and nods. "I prepared some medicine for you in the med-bay. It should help with your throat and your hands," he mumbles.

"Thanks." I don't know what else I'm supposed to say.

He retreats to the solitary comfort of the cockpit. I head to med-bay and look for relief from, well, everything.

* * *

As I wake, I realize that gravity has returned. Okay, it's not really gravity, but it feels like it. Looking up, the latch that we used to secure ourselves for zero g slumber has been put away. Chris must have done that. I have no idea how I should feel about that. It was kind, sure, but it was kindness from a cold-blooded killer. My stomach, on the other hand, has no doubts about its situation. Maybe everything will clear up on a full stomach. I head to the galley and find Chris already there.

"How do you feel?" He asks.

What a loaded question.

"I'm hungry."

"Me too. Let's have some breakfast."

* * *

It's been a long, quiet three days. I won't go into the cockpit and Chris will hardly ever leave it. I've busied myself with cleaning the quarterdeck airlock, without using Chris' trick of ejecting all the air and dust. There's all kinds of dirt and trash that's been pushed in between cracks or under equipment. It's long, tedious and exactly what I want to fritter away the time.

"How long until we land on Mars?" I ask.

"We need to talk about that. We can't very well go back to Asimov City and say hi to Vikram. But here, let's eat our eggs first and then we'll figure it out."

"Real eggs?"

"Yep."

"Cool. Now I can die a happy man." Oops. That was the wrong thing to say. We finish our breakfast in an awkward silence.

CHAPTER 32 ALEX

Schiaparelli Crater

Natalie gave me her priority number so I could reach her discreetly from virtually anywhere on Mars. They are super expensive but we sent a message to her and it was really weird because Chris let me do the talking. I didn't mention how we defeated Lewis, because I'm not sure how I feel about it yet, and throwing Natalie's opinion into the mix is bound to confuse me more.

After waiting a couple minutes for a response, Chris leaves for the cockpit, of course. He says he's adjusting the coordinates. I might actually believe him if we weren't orbiting Mars.

I jump as the ding from my PCD pulls me out of my dozing. It's Natalie.

"AI," I say. "Connect my PCD call to the cockpit."

"Connected," the pleasant voice of the computer says.

"Natalie, I've connected us to Chris."

"Kallista and I are going to catch a ride to Schiaparelli. We'll meet you on the *Shooting Star*," Natalie says. "Kallista says she's confident enough to fly the ship back to her family's repair shop. We'll meet you at the ship hangar or whatever they have there. Sorry I can't go into more details. There's a lot to do on our end. I'm glad you're safe. Love you."

"We could just go to them," Chris says.

"At Asimov, where Vikram is?"

"I'm not sure I want Kallista to be involved in this," Chris says.

Natalie knows exactly how to handle Chris. Give him the information and don't let him argue.

"Natalie isn't giving us much choice. Anyway, if Kallista doesn't fly that ship, then we have to find someone else who may or may not be trustworthy and discrete. How many people do you want to know about this?"

"It's dust storm season," Chris says. "That means that visuals are going to be bad and the instruments may give false readings. And they have to fly low so they don't trip the sensors."

"And there are plenty of pilots who know how to fly in it, just like you," I say.

"There isn't even a hangar there. They'll fly around for hours looking for something that isn't there."

"They'll see the *Shooting Star*. It's not like there are a ton of spaceships surrounding the dead city."

"What if they're spotted?" Chris asks.

"Thanks to the ever-expanding Dust Storm Chris, we don't have to worry about that."

"Dust storms are common in the southern Martian spring. It could have started anywhere."

I shake my head. If I had started a global dust storm, I'd make sure everyone knew.

* * *

The swirling dust obscures Schiaparelli's dome until we're within seven kilometers of it. It doesn't cause any problems with flying visually, but according to Chris, it wreaks havoc on the sensors.

"You can't even see our tracks from last week," I say.

"Uh, huh."

"And the dome looks orangish."

"It's a fine dust," Chris says, distracted.

"What's wrong?"

"Are you strapped in?"

I pull the harness down and click the two latches. "I am now. Why?"

"I've only landed once before without reliable flight data, and well, it was hard enough that I cut my tongue with my teeth."

I grab the armrests and clench my jaw shut, with my tongue safely withdrawn.

"I can't see the ground beneath us," Chris says, "and the dust makes the horizon tricky."

The ship slams into the ground, bounces slightly and slides to the left, toward the *Shooting Star*.

"There," Chris says as he turns off the engines. "We even have a direct line from our airlock to the city gate," he says as if he planned it all along.

"I'm just glad I didn't dislocate both arms." I remove the harness and rub my aching shoulders.

"Next time I won't warn you about biting your tongue, then you won't be able to criticize my flying."

"There's going to be a next time?" I say in a horrified voice.

The sun will set soon, not that Chris has taken any notice. Little Giovanni is heavily coated in dust. It almost looks like a natural landscape feature from the ground.

We really have no reason to go into Schiaparelli City again, except it is the most infamous site on the planet and therefore super cool. Not that Chris has embraced it. He's become all serious since we've landed. Although, he pulled out a couple of area lanterns. So we're going to camp in Schiaparelli? That could be cool.

Chris doesn't respond to any of my questions, other than to tell me to suit up.

* * *

"This place would have scared me to death when I was twelve," I say. It's much darker this time; the shadows are longer and fainter than the last time we entered, even though it's about the same time of day. "It just feels menacing."

"A lot of bad things have happened here," Chris replies in a distracted voice. It's obvious he's only half listening. He's scanning the walls intently, like he is searching for something. "And hopefully there will be a recurrence in the near future. Let's see if we can get on top of the airlock."

He removes his visor and starts pulling off his spacesuit. I take my helmet off so we can still communicate.

"Why would we want to get up there?"

"For our ambush, of course," he replies.

"What ambush?"

"Vikram's. Why else would we come here?"

"Because this place is forbidden and a little creepy, but mostly because it's cool."

"Great, you continue your adolescent fantasies; I'll just try to keep us alive."

Chris is such a pleasure to be around.

"How are we even going to get Vikram here?" I ask.

"I'm working on it. If nothing else, we'll show up at Asimov and have him chase us here. That's why we need a readily accessible perch to shoot at him."

"You're already planning your next murder?"

Chris stops scanning the dome and casts his piercing eyes at me.

"Tell me how else this can play out?" he demands. "Vikram sent an assassin after us. We're beyond an exchange of apologies."

"We could run."

"I will not be kicked out of my home and spend a lifetime fearing a knife plunging into my back. I would rather die fighting. Now, if you want me to drop you off so you can go back to our mother, shoveling shit for a living and never seeing Natalie again, just say the word."

His nose flares as he yells at me. I've never seen him so angry. Even when he was talking to Ishmael, he had a morbid sense of humor. I do my best not to squirm under his intense glare. I desperately search for some other answer. In dismay, I meet his eyes. "Alright, Vikram has to die." I resign myself to the ugly truth.

No matter who it is, I can't bring myself to plan another's death, so I try to stay out of his way and take in Schiaparelli's opulence. Funny, it seemed magical before. Now it feels hollow and barren. I make my way back to Chris, curious to know the murderous plot and hating myself for being curious.

Chris, of course, is oblivious to my turmoil. He climbs atop the airlock and scopes out the sight lines.

"This will do. The air pump motors mounted right above the inner doors will give me cover and a wide angle for the killing field." He punches the habdome cloth, and dust on the outside falls away. "Excellent. You can be stationed here to watch as they approach." Chris nods to himself. "This is our spot."

With Chris finishing his plans, an ominous thought occurs to me. What are we supposed to talk about for the next several hours?

* * *

"Look." Chris points at a single glowing light shining through the darkened dome. "That has to be Kallista and Natalie."

That's all I need to hear. We've stacked random stuff against the wall so we can climb up to our perch. But getting down? I grab hold of a pipe and slide down to our stashed spacesuits.

Chris is excited too, though he's trying to hide it. We're in the airlock before they land. The vacuum pumps are taking forever. I stare at the buttons next to the keypad. Initially, I could hear the air pumps, but as we get close to a total vacuum, the sound waves no longer travel, according to Chris.

"Settle down, Alex," he says through the suit comms. Since we don't know what ship Natalie and Kallista are arriving on, we can't connect to them yet.

"Are we sure the pumps are working properly?" I pace in front of the outer doors as I try to convince myself there hasn't been a malfunction.

"Am I really that scary?" Chris asks.

I'm so glad he can't see my face. The light next to the keypad turns from red to green and Chris just stands there like this is fun or something. I want to jump up and down and yell at him, then I remember that he's been plotting a murder for the last several hours. Maybe I don't want to stress him out. Instead, I calmly walk toward Chris and the keypad.

"Hold up, Alex. They'll call us when they're down. We can't afford to have all that dust blown at us. Our suits will never reseal tight."

I turn around and patrol the outer doors again.

"Chris, Alex, we're down," Kallista says. "But hold tight. We're going to take some stuff over to the *Shooting Star*, then Natalie's pilot will depart. We'll call you once the dust settles."

So we wait. Hopefully, we can leave before I start going bald.

* * *

Come on, come on.

The *Shooting Star's* pumps are taking forever to pressurize the airlock. Even with my lantern, it's spooky walking on the surface by myself. I'm a little worried about Chris staying in Schiaparelli alone, but I'm also impatient to see our friends.

Natalie taps impatiently on the glass. I don't know who is more anxious. The pumps stop chugging and the inner doors open. Natalie gives me a big hug and gets salmon colored dust all over herself. I take my helmet off and she jumps on her tiptoes to give me a kiss.

"Thanks for removing most of the dust from my suit. I usually have to clean it myself."

"I'm just glad you're okay," Natalie blurts out.

"Where's Chris? Why didn't he come with you?" Kallista asks.

"Chris is fine. He wanted to go over his plan one more time and he claims I'm a distraction."

"You have to tell us everything," Natalie insists. "Your message was way too short."

"Okay, okay, I'll tell you, but you have to promise me that you won't judge Chris too harshly."

"Why would we do that?" Kallista asks bewildered.

"Just let me tell the story, then we'll go over to Schiaparelli. I'll tell Chris that it took you guys some time to get your spacesuits assembled properly."

"Let's let Natalie change clothes first. She doesn't want to go over there looking like a red powdery mess."

"I'm fine, and I want to hear this story."

"Okay, it was like this . . ."

* * *

The story was not what the girls expected. Their barely contained excitement has vanished. They're standing in silence, trying to make sense of it all.

"We need to get over there," Kallista says. "Chris is all alone."

If Chris ever lets her get away, he's a fool.

I tell her that he killed a man, and she still wants to run to him. With his awkwardness around women, he could not find anyone better.

"Yeah, and I'd still like to see inside Schiaparelli," Natalie says. Her attempt to rekindle the excitement falls flat. She realizes it, too. "Let's get suited up and go," she finishes glumly.

Chris' silhouette is dwarfed by the size of the airlock doors. Kallista runs toward him and presses her gloved hand against the clear polylaminate of the interior doors. Chris awkwardly returns the gesture.

Natalie and I take off our visors. Technically, you're supposed to leave your suit on until the pressure is equalized, but only the most uptight people ever do. Plus, we can talk without broadcasting over the comm channel.

"Let's make sure to give them plenty of space today," Natalie says.

"Agreed."

"The offer still stands, by the way; you can get your own place in town if you want some separation."

"Chris still needs me."

"Can't blame a girl for trying." Natalie seems determined to keep the mood upbeat.

"Let's get our suits off while we wait. The cycle time is quicker than you'd think," I say.

The doors open, and Chris is embraced in a big, dusty bear hug from Kallista. He's stiffly patting her shoulder while being all confused.

"Right now, Chris is thinking about how it doesn't make any sense to track all that dust inside the abandoned city," I tell Natalie.

"You're terrible. He's thrilled to see her."

Chris helps Kallista remove her visor.

"Let's get you out of that suit before you track dust everywhere," he says.

Natalie snorts.

"A true romantic," I say quietly to her. She doubles over in laughter, holding her stomach and creating a huge scene. I look on, feeling embarrassed for her.

Chris and Kallista step apart from each other and become all stiff and formal. He helps her out of the suit as best he can while maintaining a formal posture.

Natalie punches me in the ribs.

"You should feel terrible for making me laugh so hard. The robot has discontinued his emotion subroutine."

"You're a horrid person," I say in mock outrage.

"I know."

Chris motions us over.

"So this is the plan I'm going to follow. I could use some help, but I understand if you want no part of it."

"Chris," Natalie says, exasperated, "if we didn't want to help, we wouldn't be here."

"Thanks for that, but you should hear the plan first." He looks at each of us in turn. "I plan on luring Vikram here and killing him before he can cause more havoc."

And that's how the last bit of lightheartedness from our reunion dies.

"You don't mean that," Kallista says.

"I do. In under three months, Vikram has spaced Maggie Maitland, had my . . . had Cornelius killed, had me kill Barnett to cover it up, had Alex and I shipping illegal drugs, scared the shit out of Keev, had our greenhouse destroyed and, most recently, had an assassin try to kill us both. I think his intent is clear."

I look around, but if either of the girls has arguments against Chris's plan, they're not sharing.

"What do you need us to do?" Kallista asks.

"Yeah, I'm in as well," Natalie interjects before Chris can answer.

"Here's what I need. Somehow, I have to get Vikram to come here without having his guard up. Once he's here, I shoot him, drag his worthless body underneath the Halley's engine and incinerate every last bit of him from the Martian record."

"How are you going to get him here?"

"I got a chip off Lewis and it has transferable credits. He gave me a bogus alarm code to activate it. I've been inspecting the kiosks here while Alex was getting you, and I think there are several that may still be functional. So I'm going to insert the chip and wait for Vikram to come and investigate. The Halley is overdue, so he'll be dying to find out what Lewis is doing here."

The girls and I exchange glances at Chris' word choice.

Is he even aware of what he's saying?

"I've scoped out this dome and I'm going to be stationed above the airlock. Once Vikram clears the entrance, I shoot him."

"What do you need?" Natalie says in her take charge voice.

"I don't want to sound whiny, but we're low on real food and I don't want my potential last meals to be bio-fermented goo while I await Vikram. Second, I'm going to have to stay camped in here, so I need someone to be in the Halley with passive sensors on so I'll know when he's arriving. Finally, I would love to get some more anesthetic pellets, just in case. I don't want to go shooting bullets from Cornelius's antique gun that can ricochet and hit the dome."

"I can get you everything you need. When do you want to do this?" Natalie asks.

"Tomorrow, if possible."

Chris looks directly at me.

"Alex, I'd like for you to be in the Halley."

"Whatever you need."

"Just in case, I'll program the ship to take you to Huygens." He shrugs. "That's as far as I've got in my planning."

"Wait," Kallista says. "I need to go over there with Chris to make sure he programs it in right. We'll need the rest of the night, so you two need to either stay here or go over to the *Shooting Star.*"

She grabs Chris's hand and drags him towards his spacesuit. I'm laughing at his apologetic smile and deeply crimson face.

"I thought they'd never leave," Natalie says with a mischievous smile. "It could be our last night together." She slides her hand down my side.

"Um, okay." Am I the only one worried about a murder occurring tomorrow?

Though disparaged as mere bureaucrats, the central government at Lowell executes an astounding array of vital duties beyond planetary record keeping. Our experts are actively standardizing transportation protocols, peer reviewing science, forecasting solar and planetary weather and being a respected, impartial arbiter of intercity disputes. The Lowell government complex has efficiently served Mars for four decades. Altering the governing framework will needlessly impede this indispensable work.

Professor Saiid Mohammed
Lowell University

CHAPTER 33 CHRIS

Schiaparelli Crater

The ship is quiet, and I'm able to relax as we wait for Vikram's next move. I'm not sure why the cockpit is so appealing to me, but I'm never more comfortable than when I'm sitting here, alone with my thoughts. I didn't ask for any of this. I'm at peace with what must be done.

"So what do we do while we wait for the girls to return?" Alex asks. It's the third time he's asked essentially the same question.

"I am going to continue reading the Ramayana. I'm hoping you can find something to do somewhere else."

"How can you read old stories at a time like this?"

"I am reading this because I've been told that Vikram personally identifies with Hanuman in this story. If I read this closely, it might give me more insight into how Vikram thinks." I miss the times when Cornelius would explain old myths to me while we were underway.

"What good is that going to do? He's going to be dead in a matter of hours, or days at the most."

"It's read this or plot ways to kill you, so you'll leave me alone," I say with exaggerated patience.

"I'm going back to the galley," Alex volunteers.

"Great idea." He knows I'm kidding when I say that, I hope.

The passive sensor arrays go off. That better be Kallista and Natalie back already, or we're in deep, deep trouble.

"Halley, do you hear us?" Natalie's voice projects over the comm.

I swallow an angry retort, because it's too late now. The comm can be heard by anyone within range of us. How many times do I need to tell her not to broadcast that we are illegally squatting at Schiaparelli Crater?

"Why doesn't he respond?" Natalie asks. There's some muffled conversation that I can't make out. "Oh, you're right, sorry Chris, *Shooting Star* out."

I stare helplessly out the window, my tranquil mood obliterated. I will never let Natalie O'Dell into the co-pilot's seat of any of my ships as long as I live. For such a smart girl, she loses her attention faster than Alex. Honestly, I just want to beat my head into the ship's hull.

"AI, open comm to Alex."

"Alex, the girls are arriving and giving away our location to anyone who wants to know. I'm going to shut down the ship. Get ready to head over to the *Shooting Star* once they land."

I've always hated working with people. Every time you go over the plan, they claim to understand, then they do whatever the hell they want to do.

But where would I be without these friends?

Cornelius always said that even if you could do it all by yourself, it wouldn't be worth the price. I check the sensors. No other blips, so perhaps we're still okay.

"Are you coming?" Alex says from right behind me. I nearly jump out of my seat.

"As soon as I get the ship shut down, except for the passive sensors. Why don't you get the suit pods prepped and I'll meet you there?"

"Okay, but Chris, those meditative texts are not helping you." He giggles all the way down the gangway.

He can't see me, so I chuckle too. How does he stay happy all the time?

* * *

"Welcome aboard our ship," Natalie greets us as soon as we remove our helmets. "It's fragranced with an overabundance of chlorine bleach. You know nothing makes one feel more at home than that antiseptic aroma emanating from literally every surface."

"Well, it *did* have a hundred and forty desiccated bodies lying around for about fifty years," I say. Why does Natalie always have to challenge me at first sight? It's not like I'm into her.

Natalie makes a squinty face. "It was sarcasm, Chris, and just because a thought pops into your head does not mean you have to share it with everyone." She acts like she's going to heave. "You need to ask yourself if anyone wants to hear this right before we sit down to eat."

Kallista comes over and gives my spacesuit a hug. I would never in a million years admit it, but I take Natalie's advice and I simply return the hug instead of warning about the dust spreading everywhere.

"I know you're just trying to get me uptight, but it's not going to work," I say.

"Oh Chris, I have never seen you be anything but uptight. I'm going for uncontrolled rage," Natalie adds sweetly.

"Good luck with that."

"Oh, I don't think I'll need luck. As soon as Kallista separates from your overly dusty suit, we can go over the latest iteration of the plan."

"What?"

"Told you I didn't need luck. Getting a rise from you is easier than finding iron on Mars."

"Natalie, he's stressed enough. Just tell him our improvements," Kallista says, as she releases one arm from our embrace.

"Spoilsport. Here's the improved plan. Alex is going to stay with you inside Schiaparelli. Kallista and I are going to be womaning the passive sensors from here. The shielding is like, I don't know, ten times better on this ship than the Halley."

"Two point three times better," Kallista corrects.

Natalie gives Kallista an irritated look.

"What? You should at least be factual," Kallista says defensively.

"Of course, the *Shooting Star* has way more shielding. If Alex were to stay in the Halley, they would be able to detect that life support is still active."

"But how will you let us know without revealing yourself?" I interject.

"A good question. If I'm allowed to continue, Mom gave me a set of encrypted communicators. They're from way down in the radio spectrum or something, I don't remember, but they will allow us to speak freely without being overheard. We're going to position ourselves due west, on the only undetectable route here."

"You told your Mom about us? Who else did you tell? Did you broadcast it over the comm on your way here too?"

"I told you," Kallista says to Natalie.

"Yeah, sorry about calling you. That was my bad. But on the plus side, you are going to have an awesome feast. I think Mom felt sorry for you, because she told me to spend whatever I needed on the food."

"So everyone knows that Chris Halley is at Schiaparelli Crater, enjoying a feast before he murders someone. Great work." I look up at the ceiling before I can say anything else.

"Hon, it's okay. I know you are stressed about this, but we are all working together." Kallista comes over and scratches me lightly on the scalp. I'm conflicted over allowing this public display of affection or holding on to my anger. I choose the former.

"Sorry, Natalie."

"Here's some food for you to take over with you. You guys go get your ambush ready and we'll finish setting up our feast."

"Are you sure?" Alex asks.

"Hon, it's okay," Natalie says, mimicking Kallista's words to me. "We'll just spend the whole time here wringing our pretty little hands and fanning ourselves as we worry about how our big brave men are faring." Natalie exaggerates, batting her eyes until we all laugh.

"Do you need anything else?" Kallista asks.

"We'll be fine without our menfolk," Natalie says before I can answer. "Though we're likely to start eating without you if you take too long, so hurry up with your preparations and take the dust with you." Natalie waves toward the outer door. She grabs Kallista's hand and jerks her away.

"Love you," Kallista says, right as the doors close.

Practical Funerary Practices pamphlet

CHAPTER 34 ALEX

Schiaparelli Crater

"The dust storm is getting worse," Chris says as he claps loudly in my face.

"Did you have to wake me up first thing in the morning to tell me that?"

"First thing? Look at the sun." Chris thinks he's funny and activates the lights in my cabin to full luminosity.

"You're not funny," I say as I bury my face in my pillow.

"Dawn was about three hours ago, we have to get over to Schiaparelli."

"Get me up when there is something to do," I say as I roll over.

"I'm just worried Vikram won't come with the storm this bad."

I prop my head up. The last thing we need is for our shooter to get nervous. "I am not staying here with you for months waiting for your dust storm to—"

"Chris, Alex, there's a ship coming from the west. The transponder is off," Natalie blasts over the comm.

"Of course it will be off," Chris says to me. "Even if it isn't Vikram, no one is going to broadcast that they're flying to Schiaparelli. And why is she using the regular comm when she got us the super-duper low frequency communicators? Vikram now knows we're the ones here and not Lewis." He shakes his head in annoyance.

I roll out of bed and pass Chris on my way to the cockpit. "Thanks Natalie," I say over the low frequency comm.

"Can you guys hear me?" Natalie asks.

"How long was she trying to reach us on the special communicator?" I ask.

Chris' eyes go wide. "We have to get over there right now. We staged all the guns over the airlock. If Vikram arrives and we're not in the city . . ."

* * *

Air is released into the airlock much faster than it is vacuumed away. Fortunately for us, Kallista suggested we keep the airlock evacuated for a quicker entrance. We'll need every second to get ready. We scurry to the city and get inside before the ship comes into view.

As the air rushes into the airlock, we can hear dust pelting the outer doors.

"That would be Vikram arriving," Chris says, perfectly calm. "There's no time to get our suits off and stowed away, so we'll have to get in our positions with them still on us."

"Do we have enough time?"

"We should. He'll have to wait for this room to cycle before he can enter the city. That gives us plenty of time, as long as we don't dawdle."

He doesn't need to tell me twice. The plan was to leave our suits hidden on the ground, definitely not to climb a rubble pile in them. "Chris, we have a problem." My feet keep slipping off the narrow footholds.

I feel Chris' metallic hand on my butt as he propels me upward. I still can't get a decent foothold, but I can pull myself over the ledge.

"Has he landed yet?" Chris asks.

I hobble over to my lookout spot. "Not yet," I say. I'm stationed next to the dome. If I crouch down, the polymer-glass just under the strut is clear of dirt so I can see when and where Vikram's ship lands.

"Hey Chris, next time we decide to kill a thuggish drug dealing cartel leader in an abandoned city in the middle of a planetwide dust storm, can we bring a chair for me? This stooping over is hard on my back."

"Will do. Make sure we write everything down and leave it here to remind ourselves."

I'll take sarcastic Chris over nervous Chris every time.

"I see the ship," I shout. Actually, all I could see was the increased dust being blown up against the dome.

"Great, much louder and they'll hear you over the sound of their engines."

Chris taps my helmet.

How did he get up the ladder so fast?

"You can get out of the spacesuit now," he says as he turns his visor to the unlocked position.

I've become much faster at removing my suit, almost as fast as Chris.

A tremendous gust of wind scatters the dust on the dome. It's much too strong to be from the wind. I look out my peephole, but all I can see is the dust billowing up. The ship is taking its time descending. It will be lunch before they land. Great, now I'm hungry, but more importantly, I really have to pee.

"Chris, I'm going to have to go pee. I'll be fast."

"Hold up a second. Just stand up and stay still."

"Why?"

"Because I'm going to shoot you with the anesthetic gun so you don't get us killed."

"Seriously?"

Is it bad that I can't tell if he's kidding?

"If you really can't hold it any longer, then yes, I will. How about you give me an update on Vikram instead?"

I'm afraid Chris may very well shoot me. I look out again and I can make out the outline of Vikram's ship. "They're landing right next to the Halley, like wings almost touching close."

"If he damages the Halley . . ."

What? Would Chris kill him a second time?

"Is he sandblasting the Halley?" Chris demands.

"He's down," I lie. Chris may decide to charge the ship if he saw all the debris pelting our ship.

If I fidget, Chris will blow a gasket, so I focus on a bead of sweat as it builds on my temple instead. It finally slides down the side of my face.

Why am I sweating and feeling cold at the same time?

"What the hell is he doing?" I ask.

"Can you see an external suit pod like on board the Halley?"

"No."

"Then he has to get into a suit manually. He'll be awhile before he exits," Chris says. "I would ask again if you did a good job tossing your cabin, but I've seen it on its good days."

We left Lewis' cabin untouched. Chris even set the autopilot to land here to sell the 'Lewis by himself' story to Vikram.

"The doors are opening," I say. "There is one, no! Three people exiting the ship."

"Damn. Well, we knew Vikram couldn't fly himself, so he had to have at least one other person."

The plan is to kill Vikram and to anesthetize his pilot. By the time the pilot wakes up, we and Vikram's remains will be long gone. The dust storm will obscure our tracks and if the pilot wanted to report something, he would have to start by explaining why he was at Schiaparelli in the first place. A third person makes this more complicated.

"Do you think there is a pilot still on board?" I ask.

"No idea. What are they doing?" There's urgency in Chris's voice now.

"They're entering the Halley. What are we going to do if all three enter here?"

"We'll have to figure that out when the time comes."

Time barely creeps by while we wait for them to leave our ship.

"They're all coming this way!" Despite going over the plan a dozen times, I can feel my heart racing, now that it's for real.

"Tell me when they are too close to the gate for you to see them anymore. After that, we need complete silence."

"They're moving with a purpose." It's not long before they're underneath us. "Now," I say just before the vacuum pumps roar to life.

Our whole perch vibrates as the deafening machinery removes the air. My whole body is shaking thanks to the pumps. We are at the point of no return. All I can focus on is how badly I need to pee. The outer doors scrape open, followed by an ominous silence. The doors close and there are a few seconds of silence before the pumps push the air back into the airlock.

"Don't make any moves," Chris whispers his command. "They are right below us."

We could be jumping up and down and they would never know the difference, but I don't dare to mention it.

My part in this plan is over. Chris has both his father's antique pistol and the anesthetic gun with him. The 'killing field', as Chris calls it, gives Vikram and his men no place to hide. As long as they don't hug the walls upon entry, they should be easy targets.

The inner doors open much smoother. I can't see Vikram, and I dare not move around, so I watch Chris. He remains motionless, with the anesthetic gun at the ready in his right hand. His left hand is in his pocket, no doubt rubbing his dad's coin for luck.

Thirteen, fourteen . . . I measure the time by the thumping of my heart.

Chris turns to face me and he's laughing. I stare at him uncomprehendingly. He stands up and waves his arms wildly. "We're up here!" He turns back to me. "They still have their suits on! They can't hear us and even if they did, they can't get to their weapons while wearing those bulky things."

I stare back at him, unable to speak.

"Right," he says. "We still have a job to do." Smiling, he sets his feet like Jean taught us and takes a deep breath. He mumbles the firing instructions to himself.

"Grip high, thumb on the safety, weak hand fills in the pocket, thumbs forward, aim and fire."

The pistol bounces up after he fires. He nearly hits himself in the head.

"One down!"

Chris aims a little to his left and fires again. I can't figure out what's going on, so I creep up to see for myself. Chris is tracking one of the suits now. One man is facing away from us, on his knees and with a hole in his suit. A second man, also on his knees, is trying to prop his companion up. The third man is running around the airlock in fits and starts. Chris fires a couple more rounds, but they are always followed by 'dammit'.

"Follow me down. They couldn't attack us with more than a bunch of insults at this point." Chris's voice is dripping with scorn. "They can't run and they can't hold a gun. They're absolutely helpless."

Chris holsters his gun and slides down the pipe. He runs down the third man easily and shoots him in the left leg. The man falls to the ground. Before he can turn over, Chris sends one more into his chest. Holding the gun outstretched, he rotates back to the other two.

We hear the output of engines hitting the dome again. The injured man is dumped to the ground and Vikram takes off his helmet and gloves. He slowly claps while standing up.

"Even if you have more help arriving, it will do you no good." Chris saunters up to Vikram like he's untouchable, his hand with the gun sweeping this way and that.

"Chris, be careful." I shout. Chris is doing everything *but* being careful. He does at least point the pistol toward the ground. Vikram absently scratches his face before sitting on his heels.

"Hello Vikram, glad you could finally make it." Chris raises his arms slightly as if Little Giovanni was his home. "And stop trying to take off your suit."

Vikram's arms go wide before falling to his sides. "I've got to hand it to you kid, I didn't see this coming," Vikram replies in a cool voice.

Chris is strutting back and forth, broadcasting his overconfidence for all of Mars to see. I cautiously jump down and break into a trot. I don't want to freak Chris out, but I need to reach them before anything goes wrong.

"Hey Alex, welcome to the final meeting," Chris says expansively.

He's all smiles. I've never seen him act this way before.

"How many more men do you have coming, Vikram?"

"I don't have anyone else." He looks toward the airlock. "What you heard was my pilot taking off and waiting for further instruction." He scratches his beard. "It looks like you killed everyone who got in your way again, kid."

"Not everyone," Chris says, aiming the gun at Vikram's face. He takes a couple of steps forward. If Vikram lurches forward, he'd have a chance of snatching the gun before Chris could shoot him.

"You two have disrupted Kenova's shipments, so you'll never be safe unless I am able to protect you from her."

"Like you protected these lackeys?"

"What can I say? You are an unbelievably deadly kid. Your talent is undeniable. I completely misread you, to my own detriment." He turns his palms up as he eyes Chris.

"Like everyone else, I was lulled by your youth, but you have natural skills. You and I could rule this planet. I have contacts on Earth and I can keep Kenova away from you until we're ready to strike. You have the killer instinct, literally, and that's not something easily taught." Vikram smiles deprecatingly.

"Nice try, but I don't trust you, Vikram."

"Whatever drives you, your best chance of getting it is by partnering with me. So what exactly do you want, kid?"

"I want you dead, Vikram!" Chris screams.

Vikram continues as if Chris had not said a word.

"You know what? I have considerable instincts as well. And I know that I have called you kid four times. I know that sets you off. And yet, despite that, you haven't shot me dead.

"You killed Barnett to avenge your father's murder. He was unarmed, but you were justified. You must have killed Lewis, but that had to be a kill or be killed type of moment." Vikram looks to his right and left at his dead henchmen. These two were also in that same category, I guess.

"But me, here I am, unarmed, on my knees, asking for forgiveness and offering to partner with you so we can become rich and powerful beyond our wildest dreams."

Vikram's voice drops to nearly a whisper. "Shooting an unarmed man in cold blood takes a toll on you, doesn't it, Chris? Would you still pull the trigger and kill Barnett if you could do it over? Can you shoot me? Can you look me in my eyes and pull the trigger?"

"Maybe I'm just pumping you for information before I finish you off," Chris sneers.

Vikram laughs. "This is where I can help you. You still think that you're going to kill me? But your mind has already decided against it. It will take a few more minutes for you to figure this out for yourself. It's called cognitive dissonance. I can train you to make the right decisions fast and to act on them before your doubts slow you down, or in this case, stop you all together. We are very much alike. You may find that distasteful, but it's true, nonetheless."

Chris rests the barrel of his gun on Vikram's forehead. Vikram lowers his head as if in supplication.

"We have a number of things in common, and I have been studying you since I first met you."

"As I said, you have good instincts."

"I've even read some of the ancient Hindu texts so I could understand the culture that you came from."

"Really? I'm impressed. You have a solid mind to go with your instincts. Which texts have you read?" Vikram raises his head so he can make eye contact again.

"I've read the Bhagavad Gita and some of the Ramayana so far."

"Those are the two most important texts we have. In fact, I named my ship the Hanuman. He is the monkey god from the Ramayana. If you have read the text, then you know that

Hanuman is the one who did all the dirty work and Rama took all the credit while being far, far away from the action. You see why I identify so strongly with Hanuman?"

"I preferred the Bhagavad Gita," Chris says. "For one thing, it's much shorter."

"It certainly is," Vikram chuckles. "Why did you prefer it?"

"The line I remember most is, 'I am become death, the destroyer of worlds.' Well, at least your world, Vikram."

And then Chris shoots Vikram right between the eyes. Vikram's lifeless body tumbles forward and the whole miserable saga comes to a positive end.

Or rather, that's what should have happened.

Instead, Chris backs up a step, and the gun starts shaking in his hand. Chris' whole body starts convulsing. Vikram lunges and grabs the gun by the barrel. He pulls the gun and Chris toward him and easily pries it from Chris' hand. With his Earther strength, he shoves Chris back about ten feet and eyes me as he rises.

"Not bad, kid," Vikram says to Chris. "You almost had me." He waves me toward Chris with the gun. "Now you two are going to drag these bodies to the airlock and then clean up this place."

"Why would we do that when you're just going to shoot us?" I demand.

"Your brother can fly us out of here. Now, why I should keep you around is a good question." He levels the gun at my face.

My mouth is suddenly dry. My lips keep moving, but no sound escapes. Chris stands in front of me. "Put the gun down Vikram. Alex is the only reason I have to keep on living. If you kill him, you'll have to kill me, too."

Vikram eyes Chris for a moment. "Alright Chris, but once we arrive at Asimov, he's no longer allowed onboard the Halley."

"I thought you had a pilot," Chris says.

"You are harder to replace than I thought. It seems there are no pilots willing to relocate to Asimov Crater. That one was for hire. One of my men must have told him about the gunfire, so he bolted, leaving me high and dry."

Something's not adding up, but he's still the one with the gun.

"But let's be clear. You can't mutiny on me and not pay a price. The Halley is my ship now and if you don't stay in line, I'll find someone to replace you." He waves the gun to encourage us to move the bodies.

I grab the runner and recognize him as the leader of the Kunselman obdome. This is what happens when you lose everything; you end up throwing your lot in with the likes of Vikram.

"We'll have to go to the Halley and get the cleaning supplies," I say.

Vikram rolls his eyes. "You have to do better than that. I'll go over first, and then you two follow, once the airlock is done cycling." He looks at me, "if there's any funny business, I'll start shooting off Alex's fingers one at a time."

I swallow hard. Chris looks like he wants to argue, but he holds his tongue. Vikram watches us for a few seconds. "Good. Now get your spacesuits and let's get moving."

"The suits are above the airlock," I say.

"Then get them." He looks at me, annoyed.

I climb the makeshift stairs and toss down our spacesuits. I toss Chris's visor down to him and see the anesthetic gun which was beneath the helmet. I nonchalantly stoop down. I only have one chance. I grab the pistol and pop my head up.

Vikram's not paying attention to me. I fire the gun and watch the pellet explode harmlessly on Vikram's spacesuit. He looks down and sees the pellet. He whips his gun up and I drop as fast as I can. A bullet ricochets off the pump casing.

"What are you doing?" Chris cries, "trying to shatter the dome and have us all die?"

Vikram is silent for a moment. "Alright, but that is going to cost you two fingers. Show me your hands, then stand up where I can see you and drop the gun over the ledge."

If I rise, he'll shoot me. If I don't, he'll leave me here to die. I close my eyes and exhale before tossing the gun over the ledge.

"I give up Vikram," I shout. "Don't shoot me."

I start to rise when I hear a metallic clunk, followed by a softer thump. I'm scared, but I stick my head over the ledge and see Chris standing over Vikram's motionless body.

Chris looks up at me before resting his hands on his knees, like he's going to vomit.

"Get the gun!" I call.

Chris grabs his dad's gun from Vikram and kicks the stun gun twenty feet away. I slide down the pole and rush over them.

"He was ready to shoot you as soon as you showed yourself. So I hit him in the head as hard as I could with my metal arm," Chris says apologetically.

"Ah, thanks," is all I can think to say.

"He was right about that cognitive dissonance stuff," Chris says. "Part of me was screaming to shoot, but the other part was screaming that there's been too much death. Look at me. I'm only seventeen and I'm already a serial killer! I don't want to keep killing and killing until someone puts an end to me."

Tears are streaming down his face as it contorts into a primal image of pain. He tries to say more, but it's all incoherent mumblings between the hiccups and sobbing.

"Chris, you have to finish him. He is the source of all of your pain."

"I can't!"

"He put the hit out on your father. He tricked you into killing Barnett. He sent Lewis after us. He came here today with his men to kill us both. Vikram is the source of all your pain."

"But I can't kill another helpless man." He lifts his tear-streaked face.

"You can't let him live."

"Maybe you're right, Alex. Space! I'm sure you're right, but I have done more than enough killing."

He's regained some of his composure, if not his sense.

"We'll take the spacesuits with us and he'll be trapped here. He will still die, but it won't be by my hands." He looks to me for approval of his new plan.

"He's too dangerous to leave alive," I say.

"Can you kill him Alex? Can you shoot him while he lays face down on the ground? I used to be able to, but I can't. No, I won't do that anymore. We are just going to have to take our chances that he doesn't know how to survive on Mars."

"Okay Chris, we can do it your way." I can't reach him when he's having a full-on meltdown. "Now, will you please give me the gun? You've been swinging it around rather carelessly for a while now."

Chris is startled to find out he's holding it.

"Keep it. I don't want to see it ever again." He shoves it into my hands.

"Maybe we should leave it here with one bullet." He brightens at that thought. "That way, he can end his own life instead of starving to death."

Again, he looks at me, eager for approval. "Alright Chris, I'll get Vikram out of this spacesuit," I say, defeated. "Can you get the rest of our gear down so we can get out of here?"

"Good idea. Thanks Alex, for being here with me." He stares at me awkwardly, wanting to say more but not knowing how to do so.

"We're a team, Chris. That's what we do."

Chris turns toward the ladder and I plant my feet before sending two shots into the back of Vikram's skull, just like Jean taught us.

No matter how egalitarian the society is on the surface, people will always differentiate themselves. This means that the rise of organized crime was inevitable, according to a new thesis by Dr. Marlene Ernst. In the case of Mars, it was the unfulfilled desire for Earthly finery that gave Ceredo and Rustie Maitland their opportunity.

The People Who Made Mars
Chapter 16, Legal, Organized Crime

CHAPTER 35 CHRIS

Schiaparelli Crater

Two shots ring out. I turn to see Alex standing over Vikram's lifeless body.

"Now I'm a killer too," he says in an emotionless voice.

Part of Alex has just died. I know from personal experience. "Are you okay?"

"I don't know," he says, confused. He looks down again at the expanding pool of blood. "Was the guilt immediate when you killed all those people?"

The shakes come back with a vengeance, and I vomit all over the floor. Alex does too, right on top of Vikram.

"Take deep breaths," I say between dry heaves.

Alex turns away from Vikram and walks toward the airlock.

"Where are you going?"

"I don't know, but I don't want to be here anymore." He starts getting into his spacesuit.

I don't know what I'm supposed to say, so I wordlessly watch him.

"Wait! We can't leave the stun gun here," I say. I rush over to the white gun and stick it in my belt. We can't leave any traces here.

Alex is leaning up against the wall, only half in his suit.

"We'll have to come back for the lanterns and the other stuff." I don't know what to say, but him standing there half in his spacesuit doesn't help anything. I have to get him to a basic level of functioning.

"You are so much stronger than me," Alex says in a tiny voice. "The way you so easily . . ."

How could he think that? I look at him incredulously, but his eyes are unfocused.

"Don't you care?" he asks. "How can I not care? What's the secret?"

He's begging for forgiveness, but only he can do that for himself. If he ever figures out how, I hope he tells me.

"Alex, I think I would like to have the gun back."

"I dropped it before I got dressed."

I spot the pistol lying at his feet.

"I am so sorry that you had to shoot Vikram. I lost my head there for a minute."

"Vikram lost his head too, but I doubt he'll ever find his." Alex smiles wanly. He tries to laugh at his joke, but fails.

"I never wanted you to shoulder this burden."

He points at my feet. "Vikram's blood is about to reach your shoes."

I take a couple of quick steps forward. "Let's get to the ship and get the cleaning supplies before it —"

"What?" Alex asks. "It gets worse than this?"

* * *

I give Alex a mild tranquilizer and put him to bed. Meanwhile, I clean up the crime scene and take care of Vikram and his men. I strip the spacesuits off of them and drag them one at a time underneath our engines. Only Vikram had a weapon on him. He didn't even trust his men to carry. That's probably what made all the difference. I trusted others; he didn't.

"Vikram is dead," I say over the regular channel. With luck, his pilot will hear that and leave. I don't believe for a second that Vikram hired a one-way drop off, or allowed his pilot to leave without his approval.

The girls arrive, and Natalie goes straight for Alex. She sits on the end of his bed until he wakes up. He cries into her shoulder.

Kallista looks at me for an explanation. How do you explain that you ruined your best friend's life?

"Alex should go with you two," I say. "I'll pilot *Halley* back alone." I hit a few buttons on my PCD. Here's my account number. Pay for the *Shooting Star*'s berthing with it."

Kallista's eyes moisten, and I can see I've inflicted pain on her as well. I can't handle anyone else's recriminations. Mine are already too hefty.

"Chris," she says slowly.

"We'll talk once we're back at Asimov, I promise."

"We can stay a little while longer," she offers.

"No, Alex needs to get away from here, for whatever good it will do him. And I'm not ready to talk about it. I don't know if I'll ever be able to talk about it."

I let the thrusters run for a couple minutes before I throttle up for liftoff. One tiny part of me is satisfied that Vikram is nothing more than part of the dust storm now. After I land, I hurry into the city before the others can find me. I don't have the strength to face them.

* * *

"Hello Keev."

He looks up from some deep contemplation, and fear flashes in his eyes. Either that or he's having a seizure.

"You can't be here!" he whispers urgently.

"Vikram is gone, Keev." He looks like he's going to faint when I mention Vikram's name.

"And what of your passenger?" He's still talking in a low voice.

"Lewis?" I ask. Keev jumps like he was kicked when he hears the name.

"He's stepped out of the picture, too." I survey the Ring. Why would anyone stay here?

"You must come inside and tell me everything." Keev shoos me into the back. He darts his head out through the beaded entrance to survey the Ring one last time before he turns his attention to me. "You must tell me everything, absolutely everything," he says while nervously pacing back and forth within the fifteen feet of space. He has to do so.

Why not? I don't have anyone else to talk to.

I tell Keev the whole miserable story. He shakes his head sadly, as if he didn't have a part to play in all of this. "Your dad would be so proud of you," he says finally. "You did incredibly well."

For an instant, I wish I brought the gun with me. No, Keev is far from innocent, but it wouldn't be worth the trauma I would go through to shoot him, too. I start to giggle to myself.

"What's wrong?" Keev asks.

"Nothing," I say. "I was talking to myself and I sounded like the Herman Burrichter character from that old movie, that's all."

And now I understand why he wanted to kill himself after being proclaimed a hero.

The last thing I want to do is explain myself, so I reach into my pocket to rub my lucky coin. I forgot that it's not the only thing there. "Do you know anything about this?" I show Keev the chip I took off of Lewis.

Keev takes the chip and inspects it. "It's an Earth-made chip. Where did you get this?"

"From the pocket of Lewis, the assassin."

Keev enters the chip into a port and waits for the contents to display on the screen. He selects a number of files and copies them to his system. I'm too exhausted to care.

"Chris, my friend, you are rich. Do you know how many credits are on this?" He's smiling as he turns back to me.

"How much?" My curiosity is piqued.

"More than you would get in a year's worth of work, no doubt. Ganesha was surely with you. Lewis Timper was a close confidante and understudy of Vikram. You did this planet a huge service, twice over."

"How do I access the chip?" I ask. I'm not about to accept Keev's fake praise.

"It is encrypted, and the failsafe has been activated, but you were lucky you brought it to me. I will try to retrieve the money and transfer it to your account."

"Sure, and how much are you keeping for yourself?"

Keev smiles. "You're right. Normally I would keep a processing fee, but I don't dare take any of this money. So this is a first. You get to keep it all."

"Um, thanks? Why don't you want any of the money?"

He doesn't bother to answer me. "What are your plans?"

"I came here because you agreed to get a printer for my ship. I need it, immediately."

"So soon? You have plenty of money. Perhaps there is something special that I could acquire for you."

"Nope, just the printer."

Keev acts disappointed. "Yes, yes, you will get it tomorrow. I mean it Chris; your dad would be very proud of you."

I stand up and go. I can't handle someone like Keev talking to me about Cornelius.

In the past two decades, the number of patents granted has fallen by seventy percent. In the absence of a strong central government to police intellectual property, vital technologies are being kept secret. In some cases, the technology is being withheld altogether. In order to advance, we must come together and replace the glorified central records depository with an empowered central government for the betterment of all. Please support referendum one for a brighter Martian future.

Op Ed by Aristotle O'Dell
Mars Daily

CHAPTER 36 CHRIS

The Ring, Asimov Crater

Kallista called me three times last night, but I couldn't put on my social face, so I left them unanswered. If it wasn't for the printer, I would have left Asimov all together. Now I've been invited to the O'Dell's house tonight. It's the last thing I want to do, but there's no way I can refuse. I've moved the *Shooting Star* to the space park, far away from our usual spot, just in case someone comes looking for me. I'm not leaving this ship and I'm not talking to anyone until I must.

I don't have any clothes on this ship. With all the murdering going on, I forgot to transfer my clothes. The Halley is at

Kallista's place, being repaired, and I can't show up there. I sigh; the thought of going shopping saps what little energy I have.

"I can't show up at the O'Dells wearing the clothes I murdered people in."

Wonderful, I'm talking to myself again.

A dirty, white, hooded shirt, matching pants. I look like one of the druids from the Earth shows Cornelius watched. Maybe I'll get a plushie owl and a walking stick from the market to *really* look authentically crazy.

I walk to the city entrance and store my spacesuit. The people movers are working today. Yay. I'll get there faster. I step on the belt and drag my hand across the salt line in the wall.

"Three billion years ago, this place was covered by water," Cornelius used to tell me. "Now all that's left from that time is the layer of salt compacted in the rocks."

There was a time when I looked forward to such little joys.

The day's nearly over, but the vendors in the Ring are still holding out hope for customers to materialize before they close. One by one, their gaze finds me and trails off. I've been here enough that they realize I'm not a customer.

Keev's stall is unattended, which is weird. The man likes people.

"Keev?" I call.

The dark-skinned man parts the curtains and takes up a position at his counter with even more of a flourish than normal.

"You're here already! This is good a move by you. It will demonstrate your respect, and trust me, that is of the utmost importance."

"What are you talking about? I'm here to get my printer."

"Yes, of course, but she will be here any minute, so it's good that you've arrived first." The man alternates between wringing his hands and patting the silk garments on his counter.

I feel cold metal press up against my temple and a hand keeping my right arm down. I turn just enough to see the pistol and catch a glimpse of the short woman brandishing it.

"Are you Chris Halley?"

I turn back to face Keev. He jerks his head in the affirmative. "I am."

"Hold still." She runs her free hand all around my chest and waist. She turns to the closest entrance. "He's clean."

The first thing I see is a wooden cane appearing from the shadows. A delicate left hand is gripping it just below a thumb-sized white capstone. It and the owner emerge from the shadows. The woman is nearly as tall as me and dressed in an all sable suit and cape. The interior of the cape is a fine scarlet silk. The collar is unlike any I've seen before. It is a really high, like to the tops of her ears high, collar, that runs from cheek to cheek.

I try not to stare at her chest, but it's, well, very noticeable. I raise my eyes to her cold smile.

"It seems you cashed my credit chip, Chris Halley. So one would assume that you now work for me."

"I am sorry, ma'am. Should I know who you are?"

She gives me a calculating smile. "I'll give you a clue. My mother was a passenger on your ship not too long ago."

I stare off in the distance as I mentally log all of our female customers. Natalie is an only child, so this can't be an O'Dell. . .

The hair stands up on my arms. "Are you . . . are you the Kenova Maitland?" I stammer. I glance at Keev and it looks like he's holding his breath.

"Very good." She extends her hand and we shake. "I am indeed 'the Kenova Maitland' and we are well met, Chris Halley." She looks at the short woman with the pistol. "Aouda, make sure we're not interrupted."

Kenova's bodyguard nods and casually patrols the area around us. Everyone else in the Ring is looking anywhere but here.

"Now, about my money," the most terrifying person on Mars says.

"I'm sorry, ma'am, Ms. Kenova, but it's not your money, it's mine. Lewis Timper tried to kill my . . . me. I took this off him before he exited the scene. In civil court, I would have been awarded this, so I feel like the money is mine."

"But you didn't take Lewis to court, did you?" she asks, amused.

"Technically no, but I feel like if someone is trying to kill me and fails, it's only fair that I keep whatever valuables they possessed." Part of my brain is revolting and telling me to flop to the ground and grovel. But all of my emotional baggage says screw it.

What's the worse she can do, put me out of my misery?

She politely claps her hands. "It's been quite some time since someone had the backbone to stand up to me. I agree with your assessment. You can keep the money. Vikram was a high-risk, high-reward gamble that failed."

She shines the white stone on her cane with her palm as her head bounces from side to side.

"Can you tell me where their bodies were left?"

My throat is parched. "Um, I spaced Lewis and incinerated Vikram's corpse under my thrusters at Schiaparelli."

"Schiaparelli?" she says, surprised. "No matter. Keev will be your contact once again. He'll be in touch when we have need." She nods at Keev. "You have both performed very well."

"Ms. Kenova," I blurt. Great, what am I going to say? "I'm really sorry about your mother. She was a real nice lady," I lie.

"No, she wasn't," Kenova says. "She was mean and shortsighted." Her head starts to shake, and she tries to grab the back of her neck. There's anger in her eyes now. "Mother was a loud, obnoxious . . ." Her whole body shakes. She gives up on her neck and grabs hold of her cane with both hands. "Shrill and manipulating . . ." She falls to her knees and hits herself in the forehead with the big white stone. "Woman who deserved worse than she got," she finishes in an angry whisper.

I run to her side and grab her elbow. That's when I see it, whatever it is. There's a metal box attached to the back of her head, right where her neck and skull meet. There are several red lights flashing urgently.

"Let me help you up."

Aouda elbows me out of the way and hits several buttons on the box. The lights slowly dim until they are completely off.

Her bodyguard helps her up. Kenova grabs my wrist so hard it hurts as she pulls me close to her, like so close that I'm breathing on her chest.

Space! I can't look there!

She pounds her cane into the ground twice before standing tall. Her bodyguard assumes an aggressive posture, facing the people in the Ring. No one dares to look interested.

"What you saw, that computer interface," Kenova whispers, "has the downloaded mind of my father, Ceredo. There are only a handful of people who are both aware it exists and who walk freely on Mars. One breath of this and you will join me at Lomonosov Crater." She locks eyes with me and I'm too petrified to look away.

"I understand, Ms. Kenova." I break our mutual stare and look down at her feet.

"Did you hear that, Aouda?" Kenova asks in a friendly tone. "I like this one and his 'Ms. Kenova'."

Everyone's heard of Lomonosov Crater. It's where Kenova experiments and tortures people. At least that's what everyone says. I've never heard of anyone returning from there.

I take a step back and hit Keev's counter.

"We're leaving," she says to Keev as she dusts herself off. She and her bodyguard head back into the shadows.

Keev nods his wordless admiration as he hands me a silk handkerchief from his counter. I wipe the sweat off my brow.

How much does a real silk product cost?

I offer it back to Keev, but he waves me off.

"Sorry for the delay, but now you know why the printer wasn't delivered today," he says. "You will get it tomorrow."

That's the first time I've ever been given something from Keev. The encounter must have shaken him as much as it did me.

The current impasse in the planet senate in Lowell is due to the rampant distrust and, in cases, animosity that exists between the city voting blocs. Introducing new legislation at this point is laughable since cooperation has reached a new nadir. We do not agree with Ari O'Dell's plan to anoint himself King of Mars; however, the existence of a strong executive branch is looking like a necessary evil.

Coalition for a Free and Fair Mars
Pamphlet

CHAPTER 37 CHRIS

The Ring, Asimov Crater

It takes a few moments for me to collect myself after my encounter with Kenova. Now I'm going to be late for the O'Dells, and I still haven't bought new clothes. If they want to yell at me and kick me out, then I should go over there and give them that chance. I'm going to be dressed appropriately and I'll leave with class. They've earned that right.

The O'Dells live on the fifth level underground, where all the mansions of the Asimov super rich are found. The aquaponics are just below them and people whisper that they have all installed vents below their mansions so that water vapor from below keeps their houses at a comfortable humidity.

Because if anyone needs free water, it's the people who can most easily afford it.

The O'Dell's house looks like an old Earth-style house. It's carved from the rock and has four freestanding walls. It even has windows which look out into the surrounding neighborhood. Cornelius would have gone on for weeks about this place if he had ever been invited inside.

Mrs. O'Dell opens the door as soon as my foot touches the doorstep.

"Chris! I'm so glad to see you. If I knew how to contact you, I would have asked you to drop by earlier. Please come in."

"Thank you, Mrs. O'Dell. I didn't have anywhere else to go." She must not have heard what happened yet.

"First, I've told you, call me Evelyn or Eve. Mrs. O'Dell is Ari's mother and between you and me, the less said about her, the better. And nowhere else to go? I don't believe that."

Their home sports images of famous paintings hanging on three walls and a large staircase winding upward on the fourth. Mrs. O'Dell gives me a moment to take it all in.

"The pictures here in the foyer are only electronic images of Earthen masterpieces. We like to change them to fit the mood of each party we host. We don't often host Natalie's friends, so I just went with my personal favorites."

The pictures are impressive, but the stairs are what catch my attention. "How can you have multiple floors? This level is only so tall."

"You are very sharp," she says, smiling. "We have had people over here for years and they've never figured that out. We own the property directly above us on the next two levels. I'm afraid we can't have windows on the upstairs floors, but it lets us spread out. The top level is my flower garden. Maybe later I can show it to you. Right now, there is a bit of ugly business that needs to be taken care of."

Uh oh.

"If you will join me in the sitting room, we can get this over with quickly. Before we enter, though, I have to tell you that your mother is here."

"Why would she be here?"

"She was contacted about the greenhouse that you and Alex bought, and she's trying to take it for herself."

"She can have it for all I care." I have no strength left to fight.

"Dear, this is why I wanted to tell you this here. I will take care of the whole thing, but I'm going to need you to not interfere. So no name calling, no yelling, just observe without comment if you can. Alex and the girls are upstairs, though Ms. Vennemann is scarcely aware of it. After she leaves, you can be with your friends, okay?"

"Yes, Mrs. O'Dell, I mean . . ." I can't bear to look at her. Once she finds out what I did today, she'll have me kicked out of her house.

"That's okay. I should let you know that I've always been impressed by you, Chris. So please, let me do this."

"Okay, Evelyn."

"That wasn't so hard, was it?" She squeezes my hands before beckoning me through the arch underneath the stairs.

"Anna, here's one of your sons, as you requested. We are still trying to contact Alex. But I suspect he will be here soon."

From the center of the room, the light source has hundreds of dangling glass crystals surrounding it. The entire room is filled with vibrant white light and no shadows. The walls are covered with tapestries of unicorns at play. It is the most gorgeous place I have ever seen.

"This one stole my real son from me. He's a thief, just like his father."

And the ugliest person I've ever met is infecting this perfect place.

"I see," says Evelyn. "I would still recommend that you drop your claim on the greenhouse for your own benefit."

"I bet you would. So you plan on taking it from my family? Because I will fight you tooth and nail for it."

"Anna, you misunderstand. Let me lay out the facts and you can decide from there. The ruptured wall of the greenhouse vented all the air and heat. It happened during the current dust storm, so all the equipment has been contaminated and will need to be cleaned professionally, if you have any hope of salvaging it."

Mother glares at Mrs. O'Dell.

"The poly-glass window from the door ruptured, causing a significant air leak from the public corridor. So there is a fine for stopping the corridor air leak and a fee for all the lost air.

These together are nearly what the boys paid for the greenhouse. You would have to pay that first before you would even be allowed inside. The habdome cloth will need to be replaced, and the equipment is iffy, even if cleaned. It will cost you two to three times as much as the greenhouse is worth to get it up and running."

"Maybe I'll just sell it as is."

"You can't sell it until you pay the fee and the fine. You would be lucky to recoup your outlay of credits."

"So what? Is this where you offer to buy it from me cheap?"

"I have no desire to farm. I am simply laying out the facts. If you press your claim, you will do real harm to Chris and Alex and you will get nothing from it. In fact, it will end up costing you in the end."

Anna looks at me. "Your father's dead, so you find rich cheats to protect you?"

Before I could answer, Evelyn cuts in. "It has been charming to meet you, Ms. Vennemann. I invited you here as much for your own good as for the boys. I don't think we have anything further to discuss."

Anna looks at me again. "You think she's on your side, don't you?"

"More than you," I say without thinking.

"You'll end up just like your father, another hapless and hopeless loser."

"Please leave my home," Evelyn says. "Now."

"I'll leave, but I'm not leaving Asimov without my son. So tell Alex to come find me before the police find him." Anna turns and stomps down the hall by herself. We watch silently until the door closes behind her.

"What a vile woman." Mrs. O'Dell's hand rushes to her mouth in embarrassment. "I am so sorry Chris, I should never speak like that of anyone, especially not your mother."

"Please don't apologize. She was only my mother for the first nine months of my life."

"Well, thank you for that. I will contact Natalie now, and she and Alex will join us shortly. But I must say, your mother did us a favor, whether she knows it or not."

"She never does anything nice."

"Well, you heard her say that she wants to take Alex back with her, yes?"

"Um, yes."

"Alex is in great pain now. He feels he has to distance himself from you because of the unfortunate events at Schiaparelli, though I suspect in his heart he would like nothing more than to rejoin you on board your ship. Ms. Vennemann is making herself the common enemy of you both. If managed properly, that will allow Alex to rejoin you sooner rather than later."

"Do you really think so?"

"Oh dear, you must be exhausted. Let me worry about that. There's a hearty dinner waiting for all of us. I have found that an empty stomach always makes problems seem much bigger than they really are."

* * *

The *Shooting Star* is parked outside of Asimov, facing east, right at the rising sun. Only newbies make this mistake when they land their ship, but today is the beginning of a new chapter in my life. I guess I oriented the ship towards the sun in hopes that it will be a brighter beginning. I have some money now and I'm safe, not that I care about either. The communication console beeps. I hit the button and Keev informs me that the credits have been cleared to my account. I send my digital thanks.

Growing up on the Halley with Cornelius, I never really had friends. I would go play with other kids my age from time to time, but those were just for the day or the week. Now I can see the downside to having friends. You have to let them go. I wasn't sure I could take being alone for months by myself, but knowing that I can come back to them, hopefully, is enough for now.

I know Mrs. O'Dell thinks Alex will join me, but she didn't see the loathing he had for himself and me. I know Natalie will be busy here, and Alex will want to stay close to her. Kallista has to work at her family business. I couldn't ask her to leave all of that for me. If I never existed, there wouldn't be a raging dust storm so early in the season and Alex, Kallista and Natalie would be happily going about their lives. I guess it's only fair that it's my dust storm. I've done nothing but cloud others' futures and bring darkness to their lives.

"First mate requesting permission to come aboard," Alex's voice registers over the ship's comm.

"Alex! What are you doing here?"

"Somebody has to deliver supplies to the ship and since I was hanging around the O'Dells this morning . . ."

I dry my suddenly moist eyes on my sleeve before going back to greet Alex.

The airlock is already cycling. He's leaning against several thermal boxes and smiling from ear to ear from inside his suit. I can tell from the numeric code on the boxes that they're foodstuffs, but I'll let Alex *surprise* me.

"You know it's typical to tip the deliveryman, right?"

"Oh!" I force my face to remain neutral. I hope my disappointment doesn't show. "Come on in and get comfortable. I was going to make breakfast before I depart."

It's my own fault if he doesn't want to come back. The important thing is to be friendly. "I suppose I should help you unload." I grab the boxes while Alex removes his suit.

We unpack the supplies and take them to the huge galley on the *Shooting Star*. We stand in an awkward silence, searching for the right thing to say. Fortunately, the proximity beacon goes off again.

"Saved by the bell," Alex says.

Kallista asks for permission to enter. I look at Alex in confusion.

"Keev uses Kallista and her father for ship repairs. She and Natalie are bringing the printer and the raw materials in the rover."

"Good. I'm glad I get to see them again." In truth, it's a bittersweet moment.

The girls enter, and Kallista gives me a long hug that borders on embarrassing.

"Get a room!" Natalie complains. "We couldn't fit all the raw materials, so you'll have to fly over to Kallista's shipyard to pick up the rest."

"Chris was just going to fix us all breakfast," Alex volunteers.

"As if," Natalie responds. "He's going to have to plot the course to the shipyard, which gives me time to prepare the food and Kallista time to install the printer."

"Right," I say. Even if it kills me, I am going to keep this fake smile plastered over my face as long as any of them are on board my ship.

I get to the cockpit and I let my shoulders sag. It's great to see them again, but it also reminds me of what I'm losing. I plot the course in no time, then I stare at the fuzzy spot where the sun is. And . . . and it's being eclipsed by Phobos.

"I miss you, Cornelius." My eyes tear up, but I'm forced to blink them away. I take the coin out of my pocket and rub it. For good luck, I guess. I take a deep breath. I can't be all weepy when I say goodbye to my friends. I stand up, pull on my shirt to get rid of the wrinkles, and walk slowly to the galley. "I guess I could give this ship a good cleaning while I'm away."

There I go, talking to myself again.

The *Shooting Star* has two gangways and dozens of rooms. It sure is a big, empty ship. I can hear all the commotion from the galley. Will it all come crashing to a halt when I arrive? I inch my way there. At least I can experience the camaraderie from afar.

"I'm going to be a gardener," Alex says cheerfully.

"Well, I'm going to be the opposite of you, so I guess I will have to be the engineer," Kallista replies. "No gross living systems for me."

"Then I guess I'll have to be Chris' opposite," Natalie says. "I will be in charge of personal communications, since he just wants to stay in the cockpit and brood."

The room erupts into laughter once again, but I can hear Kallista telling Natalie to be nice. I swallow hard before I turn the corner.

"Hi guys," I say with my false smile.

"It's about time. Did you get the message from Kallista's father?" Natalie asks.

"What message?"

"He's agreed to fix up the Halley. Thanks to a little prodding from his daughter, he's doing it on the cheap."

Kallista blushes. "It was nothing, really. I've always had him wrapped around my finger."

"In all the commotion of yesterday, I forgot to check my messages," I say lamely.

"You know you don't have to try and ruin your mastermind status on your own," Natalie says. "That's why I'm here."

"I'm glad you're all here," I say. "I've had to make some decisions and we might as well talk about them now."

Alex looks at me quizzically. "Like what?"

"Cornel . . . no, *Dad*, had always promised that we would go out to tour the outer gas giants. 'Only twenty-one people have ever visited all eight planets' he would say. He wanted us to be numbers twenty-two and twenty-three. He had already been out to Jupiter and Saturn and he was really looking forward to showing them to me.

"I've been saving several samples of his stem cells since, since he was murdered. I'm going to visit the outer planets and I'm going to launch his stem cells towards each one. When I come back, I will do my best to see that we are both credited with traveling to all the planets. Since his stem cells are alive, I won't even be lying."

I put a hand up, stopping anyone from interrupting me. "The conjunction is going on now and the earlier I leave, the better. So I guess I'm going to be gone for a bit."

"You are such an idiot," Kallista says. "How many times have I told you that I want to fly?"

I look at her, all confused.

What is she saying?

"And Mom and Dad think my mouth may hamper their crusade to form a new central government, so it's a good time for me to be out of the picture."

"Really?"

"And you'll need a first mate to keep them in line, so I guess I'm going to have to come too," Alex says.

"You are all coming with me?"

"Yes! You idiot," Natalie says.

"Did you think you were going to get rid of me that easily?" Alex says with his goofy grin that makes everyone like him, no matter what.

Kallista says nothing. She just gives me another one of her long hugs. It's not so bad this time. Tears are streaming down my face.

"I, I didn't know what to expect. I always flew with Dad and he had friends that he would see once every few months or so. I figured that's how friendships worked. I never considered that you all would want to stick together—with me."

"Poor Kallista," Natalie says. "You have your work cut out for you, don't you?"

The other three laugh at me again, but they are my friends, so that's okay, because friends make life worth living, especially after you've gone through your own personal version of hell.

Thank you for reading my book!

Please consider signing up for my newsletter or find out more about me and my works at: www.AuthorMikeMollman.com.

My friend and fellow author, Ro Bushey, and I have a YouTube channel: https://www.youtube.com/@BaldBalding-cv2mb

For the rest of my social links, go to my linktree: https://linktr.ee/mikemollman

Finally, ratings and reviews are the social proof that we independent authors desperately need to stay relevant. Please consider leaving one for me or any other author you read.

ACKNOWLEDGEMENTS

The path to writing a book is a long and winding one. While much of the work is done alone, no one can finish a book worth reading without a lot of help.

My beta readers, Katherine D. Graham and Yar Gul, my editor, Rosaire Bushey, and my proofreader, Melissa Stone took my lump of a story and made it shine. I cannot recommend them highly enough. They can be found at:

> https://www.fiverr.com/kritinia?source=order_page_summary_seller_link
>
> https://www.fiverr.com/yargul?source=gig_page
>
> https://www.rosairebushey.com/editing-services
>
> https://www.fiverr.com/keverynn?source=order_page_summary_seller_link

The cover art was made by Matt Slay and the quality speaks for itself. You can find him at:
https://www.deviantart.com/spaciousinterior or
https://comicarthouse.com/

Then there are those who provided services without payment.

There is only one person in this world that I could ask "Imagine you're the goddess of the pixies. How would you react if . . ." This person is Jeff Davidson, my agent of chaos. His imagination is unbounded.

My brother Danny had to listen to my trials and tribulations almost nightly, so I would be remiss not to mention him here. He had an opinion for every question I'd put to him, and sometimes he was even helpful.

Dr. Wyatt Johnson, once asked me why we are friends. I told him it's because he makes poor decisions. This is the book he has been pushing me to publish for years now.

My nephew, Johnny Mollman M.D. was uncomfortable but very helpful in deciding exactly what wounds my characters could receive and still survive. Something about a hypocritical oath, or something.

I cannot stress enough the value of SFF discord channels. There is a real sense of camaraderie amongst like-minded nerds. There are so many great ones, but I have self-limited myself to only a handful. You can only join by invite, but if you reach out to me, I will get the invite to you. I personally vouch for:

Keymark	Indie Accords
An Unexpected Party	ToriTalks
SFF Insiders	Wizard's Enclave

Finally, there are too many BookTuber and Book Reviewers to thank, but I'm foolish enough to take a stab at it anyway. If your name is not here and you were clearly helpful, blame it on my impending dotage. You should check out their channels (in the random order they show up in my YouTube subscriptions:

Colin's Corner
    https://www.youtube.com/@ColinsCornerYT
Tori Talks

https://www.youtube.com/@ToriTalks2

Beard of Darkness

https://www.youtube.com/@BeardofDarkness

Niko's Book Reviews

https://www.youtube.com/@nikosbookreviews

Books With Benghis Kahn

https://www.youtube.com/@BooksWithBenghisKahn

Andrew's Wizardly Reads

https://www.youtube.com/@AndrewsWizardlyReads

Katherine D. Graham, Author

https://www.youtube.com/@KatherineDGrahamAuthor

An Erudite Adventure

https://www.youtube.com/@AnEruditeAdventure

Kay's Hidden Shelf

https://www.youtube.com/@KaysHiddenShelf

The Literary Apothecary

https://www.youtube.com/@TheLiteraryApothecary

Portable Magic

https://www.youtube.com/@trinforeman54

Liam's Lyceum

https://www.youtube.com/@LiamsLyceum

Boiled Jellyfish Reads

https://www.youtube.com/@BoiledJellyfishReads

The Next Chapter

https://www.youtube.com/@CNavo.TheNextChapter

Middle of Nowhere Books

https://www.youtube.com/@MiddleofNowhereBooks

OTHER BOOKS BY MIKE MOLLMAN

The Martian Traders Saga

Book One:	The Halley Traveler
* Novella:	Crashed! (2025)
* Novella:	Around Mars in Eighty Days
* Book Two:	TBD

Protectors of Pretanni

Book One:	Becoming A Druid
Book Two:	Sins And Sorrows
Book Three:	To Speak With Elders
Book Four:	Desperate Dispatches
* Book Five:	Becoming A King (2026)
* Book Six:	Preparing For War
* Book Seven:	The Return Of Loris

Disciples of a Fallen God

* Book One:	Death's Champion (2025)
* Book Two:	Death's Avatar
* Book Three:	TBD
* Book Four:	TBD
* Book Five:	TBD

*Upcoming

Heirs to a Flawed Creation

E. L. Montague

Purpose defines us. It will define the peoples we leave behind when we are gone. We are children playing with the powers of a god. Our creations will be as flawed as their creators. The gift of intellect comes with doubt.

In the none too distant future, tools will become beings in their own right. Factory floors will be the womb of an entire people. Androids will struggle to exist alongside the lesser gods who created them, even as they surpass us.

These stories explore that struggle.

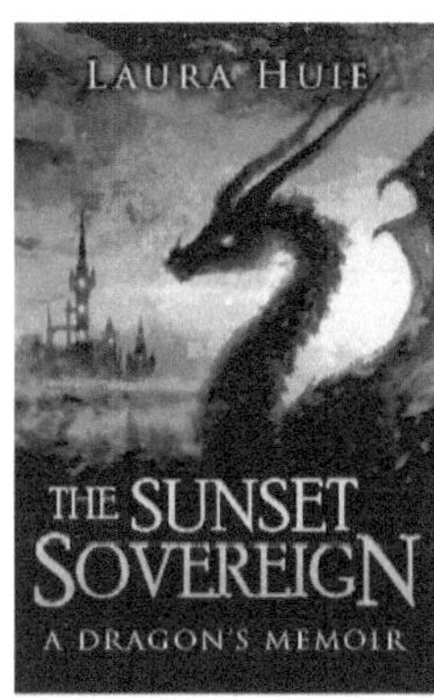

The Sunset Sovereign
Laura Huie

For the past thousand years, the dragon Vakandi has watched the people of Vakfored grow from a wandering band of refugees to a glorious city of art and magic. Under his protection, the city has survived monsters, floods, and wars all without building an army, dam, or even a wall. But time changes everything and now the citizens of his beloved city want him dead.

Vakandi spends his last day telling his assassin why he loves them, and why it's his time to die.

Platinum Tinted Darkness

Timothy Wolff

The Kingdom of Boulom has been lost.

The realms have already seen what happens when the Gods and their Harbingers are left unchecked.

Destruction. Chaos.

Death.

The Gods cannot be trusted. No one knows that better than David Williams, the leader of the Guardians tasked to protect the realm from the gods and their powerful Harbingers ever since the fall of Boulom.

Dark Town
Palmer Pickering

Part cozy, part bloody, all fun.

Hidden underneath the small town of Haverly Arms lies an entrance to the Dragon's Game, an extensive world where adventurers compete to collect power objects and progress to the next level.

Temerity's father and brothers have been down in the game for years, leaving Temerity and her mother, plus their house goblin, Half-pint, to manage their tavern. Bored with small-town life, Temerity decides to enter the tunnel labyrinth, launching an adventure to survive Level One of the Dragon's Game: *Dark Town.*

The Fall of Selvandrea

Tim McKay

Villains rise where nations fall.
And the Fall is coming.

Valdaris was a middling artillery captain before his people fell to a conquering rival.

Then he fell further still, snatched from the battlefield by a ruthless cult and cast into the depths of ultimate evil.

Transformed by powers he can't begin to understand, Valdaris seeks revenge on those who tried to destroy him. Instead, he'll face monsters beyond his most terrifying nightmares. He joins with allies caught in the chaos of his war with evil, oblivious to his true nature and the darkness closing in on their world.

And from calamity's ashes, a new power shall rise.

Magic's Genesis: The Grey
Rosaire Bushey

When magic comes to Eigrae, an average woman becomes one of the most powerful people in the world, and a broken man becomes one of the most dangerous. For Lydria, learning to be a Wielder means trusting her friends, her own decisions, and accepting her role in a new world. For Wynter, the limits of magic are the limits of his own body. With direction from the voice of the woman he loved, the woman he killed, Wynter is pushed to rule without mercy, to bend Eigrae to his will, and remove those who defy him. In his quest to rule, he destroys what he must, and in the process creates a new species...dragons.

Shadow of Wolves

J. R. White

A tortured gunfighter. A Navajo outcast. – And the Creature whose claws would stain the stones of the Mojave red.

Flush with raw silver and ruled by a baron with an iron fist, the tiny mining outpost of Shank's Point is under siege by a sinister evil.

When the rising sun reveals the claw-torn bodies littered among the rocks, John Swift-Runner calls on his old friend, a vagabond gunfighter, to stand with him against the slaughter he knows will come.

But as their band of misfits hunts for the creature on the burning sands of the Mojave, they stumble into a generations old mystery that goes beyond shamanic curses and into the bloodstained pages of legend.

Can the killing be stopped?

ABOUT THE AUTHOR

Mike Mollman is a charming individual graced with good looks, undeniable charisma and humility. These descriptions come straight from his keyboard, so they must be treated as unimpeachable facts. Mike lives in the Richmond, Virginia area. When he's not self-aggrandizing, he likes to spend time with his two dogs and the many voices in his head.

www.ingramcontent.com/pod-product-compliance
Lightning Source LLC
Chambersburg PA
CBHW031435200726
48289CB00001BA/85